2/16/13

**Praise for *New York Times* bestselling author
Susan Mallery**

"Mallery…excels at creating varied, well-developed
characters and an emotion-packed story gently
infused with her trademark wit and humor."
—*Booklist* on *Only Mine*

"Mallery's prose is luscious and provocative."
—*Publishers Weekly*

"When it comes to heartfelt contemporary
romance, Mallery is in a class by herself."
—*RT Book Reviews* on *Only Yours*

**Praise for bestselling author
Sarah Mayberry**

"This very talented writer touches your heart
with her characters."
—*RT Book Reviews* on *Her Secret Fling*

"Reading *[All They Need]* was like finding a twenty-
dollar bill in your coat pocket, then unfolding it
and finding a fifty wrapped inside.
It started out great and just kept getting better."
—*USATODAY.com*

SUSAN MALLERY

New York Times bestselling author Susan Mallery has entertained millions of readers with her witty and emotional stories about women and the relationships that move them. *Publishers Weekly* calls Susan's prose "luscious and provocative," and *Booklist* says, "Novels don't get much better than Mallery's expert blend of emotional nuance, humor and superb storytelling." While Susan appreciates the critical praise, she is most honored by the enthusiastic readers who write to tell her that her books made them laugh, made them cry and made the world a happier place to live. Susan lives in Seattle with her husband and her tiny but intrepid toy poodle. She's there for the coffee, not the weather. Visit Susan online at www.susanmallery.com.

SARAH MAYBERRY

Sarah Mayberry lives by the beach in Melbourne, Australia, with her partner (now husband!) of nearly twenty years. As well as writing romance novels, she writes scripts for TV, loves cooking and reading and shopping, and is learning how to be a good fur parent to her brand-new black Cavoodle, Max.

BESTSELLING AUTHOR COLLECTION

New York Times Bestselling Author

SUSAN MALLERY

Quinn's Woman

entertain, enrich, inspire™

Recycling programs
for this product may
not exist in your area.

ISBN-13: 978-0-373-18067-7

QUINN'S WOMAN
Copyright © 2013 by Harlequin Books S.A.

The publisher acknowledges the copyright holders of the individual works as follows:

QUINN'S WOMAN
Copyright © 2003 by Susan Macias Redmond

HOME FOR THE HOLIDAYS
Copyright © 2009 by Small Cow Productions Pty Ltd.

This edition published by arrangement with Harlequin Books S.A.

For questions and comments about the quality of this book please contact us at CustomerService@Harlequin.com.

www.Harlequin.com

Printed in U.S.A.

CONTENTS

Dear Reader,

There's something about a woman who takes charge and won't take prisoners. While most of my heroines fall into the "just like us" category—funny, caring and trying to make it through—a few of them have an extra dose of butt-kicking ability.

Quinn's Woman is one of those stories. D.J. teaches self-defense and is willing to use any means necessary to win. But she's also keeping secrets, and it's up to Quinn Reynolds to find out what they are.

If you've read me before and enjoyed Charlie in *All Summer Long* and Michelle in *Barefoot Season,* you'll adore D.J. If you haven't read me before, brace yourself for a fun, sexy and emotional ride. D.J.'s the best kind of heroine and Quinn is going to have you sighing in anticipation.

Don't you just love it when that happens?

Happy reading.

Susan Mallery

QUINN'S WOMAN

New York Times Bestselling Author

Susan Mallery

To that young girl who grew up with broken wings, and somehow learned to fly. You are, as always, an inspiration.

Chapter 1

"Try to bring this one back alive," Sheriff Travis Haynes said as he nodded at the slightly built private waiting by the edge of the makeshift podium.

"Alive I can promise," D. J. Monroe said as she grabbed a rifle from the stack on the table. "In one piece may be more complicated."

The men standing around chuckled, but the private in question blanched. D.J. tossed him the rifle, grabbed a second one for herself, then started walking. She figured her partner for the next fourteen hours would come trotting along as soon as he figured out she wasn't going to wait for him.

Sure enough, in about thirty seconds she heard rapid footsteps on the damp ground.

"What's your name, kid?" she asked when he'd caught up with her.

"Private Ronnie West, ma'am."

She gave him a quick once-over. He was tall—about six-three to her five-nine—skinny and barely shaving. His shock of red hair was bright enough to read by.

"Are you even eighteen, Ronnie?"

"Yes, ma'am. Nearly four months ago."

"You insulted about being paired with a woman?" she asked.

"No, ma'am." His pale-blue eyes widened as he glanced at her. "I'm honored. My sergeant said you were one of the best and that I was damned lucky to get a chance to watch you work." He ducked his head and blushed. "Excuse me for swearing, ma'am."

She stopped walking and turned toward him. The annual war games between the emergency services of Glenwood, California—sheriff's office, fire department and EMT units—and the local Army base were a chance for all concerned to practice, learn and have fun. The morning had been spent on obstacle courses, sharpshooting and tactical planning. D.J. didn't care about any of that. She looked forward to the search and capture phase of the games.

Between now and 6:00 a.m. tomorrow, she and her partner would be expected to bring in up to five enemy prisoners. For the past two years she'd won that section. It was a point of pride with her. The other players grumbled about her good fortune, not understanding it. Especially when she always took a relatively new recruit as her partner.

"Ronnie, let's get some ground rules set up," she said. "You can swear all you want. I doubt you can come up with anything I haven't heard. Or said." She smiled at him. "Fair enough?"

"Yes, ma'am."

"Good. On this mission, I'm in charge. You're here to listen, learn and follow orders. You get in my way, and I'll cut off your ear. Or something you'll miss even more. Understand?"

He swallowed hard, then nodded.

"Last, but most important, you've got a good six inches of height on me and weigh about forty pounds more. Is there any doubt in your mind that I could take you right here, right now?"

His gaze swept over her body from her Army-issue boots, past her camouflage pants and shirt, to her face.

He straightened and squared his shoulders. "No, ma'am."

"As long as we have that straight."

She ducked into the tent her team used for headquarters and picked up her backpack. Ronnie already had his gear with him. When she stepped back out into the misty afternoon, she pulled a knife from the pack and stuck it into her boot.

"Check your weapons," she said.

Ronnie frowned. "They're not loaded."

"Check them, anyway. You always check."

"Yes, ma'am."

He followed her lead and made sure both his side arm and rifle were unloaded. When he'd finished, she pulled her cap lower on her head and wished they could have had sun today. Telling herself the gray skies and low clouds would reduce the risk of shadows didn't make her appreciate the chilly dampness any more. It was nearly July. Shouldn't it be hot?

Northern California weather was frequently uncooperative, she thought as she set off into the forest. Ronnie trailed after her, making enough noise to pass for a musk ox. At least he wasn't a talker. The one from last year had chatted on and on until she'd been forced to grab him from behind and threaten to slit his throat.

Two hours later they were deep in "enemy" territory. She slowed their pace in an effort to keep her boy toy from giving away their position. Her oversize shirt was damp and clinging to her skin, which she hated. Water dripped from her hat. It was the kind of day better spent curled up reading, not combing the backwoods for swaggering men who thought they knew it all. Still, the war games helped keep her sharp. For her life was all about maintaining her edge; the book would have to wait.

Up ahead she sensed more than heard movement. She stopped, as did Ronnie. After silently handing him her backpack and ordering him to wait, she circled around a cluster of trees so that she could come out on the other side.

A man sat on a log, studying a map. She recognized him as a Fern Hill EMT guy. Midthirties, in decent shape, but not much of a challenge. Oh, well, she had to take what she could get.

After deliberately stepping on a fallen branch to make it snap, she retreated into the dripping shadow of a thick tree. The man sprang to his feet and turned toward the sound. His backpack lay on the ground, as did his rifle. He wore his sidearm, but she doubted he knew how to use it.

As the man stepped toward where she'd broken the branch, she circled behind him. When she was less than a foot away, she grabbed his arm, turned him, then swept out her leg to topple him to the ground. He landed hard, with an audible "oof" of air.

She was already on him. After tossing his sidearm into the brush, she turned him and neatly tied his hands behind his back. She was nearly finished with his feet before he'd even gasped breath back into his body.

"Okay, kid," she called. "You can come out now."

Ronnie appeared, carrying her backpack. He stared open-mouthed at the tied man.

"That was so great," he told her. "Really fast and smooth. He never heard you coming."

The EMT guy didn't look amused. "Now what?" he asked.

D.J. smiled. "Now you relax while we search out other prey. I'm not wasting Ronnie's time by having him head back to headquarters with just one guy."

"No way. You can't leave me. It's raining. The ground is wet."

D.J. shrugged. "It's war."

He was still yelling when they were nearly a quarter mile away. She would have liked to tape his mouth, but it violated the rules of the game.

Pity.

An hour later they came upon three men standing together, smoking. They were talking and laughing, obviously unconcerned about the potential for being captured.

D.J. studied the situation, then pulled Ronnie back far enough for them to have a whispered conversation.

"If you want to win, you have to be willing to do whatever it takes," she said as she slipped off her backpack. "Catch the enemy off guard with the unexpected. I'm going to wait while you get into position. You'll head east and circle around them. When I walk into the clearing, you'll be directly in front of me and behind them. When they're distracted, walk in with your rifle pointed at their backs."

Ronnie nodded, but she saw the doubt in his eyes. He wanted to know how she was going to manage to distract three men at the same time. She smiled. It was so easy.

First she shrugged out of her long-sleeved shirt. Underneath she wore an olive green tank and no bra. Ronnie's eyes widened.

She narrowed her gaze. He blushed, took a step back and stuttered an apology.

While he was busy wondering if she was going to cut off an ear…or something worse…she pulled the tank up to just below her breasts, twisted the fabric into a knot and tucked it against her skin. The stretchy fabric now pulled tight across her breasts and left her midsection bare. Next she loosened the drawstring waist of her pants and rolled them down to her hipbones. She stuck her sidearm into her pants at the small of her back. Last, she dropped her cap to the ground and unfastened the braid. When her long hair was free, she bent at the waist and finger combed the waves in a sexy disarray. She straightened and tossed her head back. Her brown hair went flying.

Ronnie's mouth dropped open. "You're gorgeous," he said, then gasped and quickly retreated. "Sorry, ma'am. I didn't mean to—"

She cut him off with a wave of her hands. "It's fine. Go get in position. I'll give you a two-minute head start."

She waited the promised amount of time, then headed

for the group of men. They were still standing around, talking and smoking. She stuck out her chest, then sauntered toward them, trying to look both easy and lost.

"I am *so* turned around," she said in a low voice. "Can any of your gentlemen help me?"

They were all regular Army, officers and seasoned professionals. But they didn't expect to see a half-dressed woman in the woods. It was damp and cold, so she wasn't the least bit surprised when their gazes all locked on her chest.

The oldest man took a step toward her. "What seems to be the problem, ma'am?"

They were all such idiots, she thought happily. They'd left their rifles leaning against a tree. Just one more step and the firearms would be out of reach.

D.J. stuck her hand into her hair and began to twirl a curl around her finger. "This is so not me," she said. "I mean what was I thinking? I don't even remember what team I'm on. I signed up for the games because my boyfriend asked me to, then the jerk dumped me three days ago." She blinked, as if fighting tears. "I'm cold and tired and lonely."

The men moved in for the kill.

"Hold it right there! Arms in the air."

She had to give Ronnie credit. He sounded positively powerful as he gave the order. The men turned toward him. When they looked back, she had her handgun pointed at them.

Two of the officers swore, one laughed. "Hell of a show," he said.

"Thank you."

In a matter of minutes, all three of them were tied up. The limit for captures was five. There was a bonus for up to four brought in before midnight. The earlier the "enemies" were brought back to camp, the bigger the bonus. D.J. had figured it would take her and Ronnie until at least nine or ten to get four, but they'd gotten lucky.

After the men were tied up, she unrolled her pants back to her waist and loosened her tank top. When she'd collected her gear, she shrugged back into her shirt.

"Don't get dressed on our account," one of the Army officers said with a grin. "Naked suits you."

"How flattering," she said, and turned her back on him. Why did men always assume women were interested in their attentions?

"You remember where the EMT guy is?" she asked Ronnie.

"Yes, ma'am."

"All right. Take these three with you and collect him. After you escort them back to headquarters, make sure they give us our bonus points, then meet me here. I'll be within a quarter mile of this position." She chuckled as she remembered his lack of stealth. "I'm sure I'll hear you coming."

"Yes, ma'am."

D.J. watched as her boy toy led away their prisoners. The officers were only loosely tied together. Rules of engagement required that they cooperate on the trip back in. They were allowed to do whatever it took to get away right up until that first step toward camp. But just in case they decided to give her private the slip, she'd taken down their names.

When she was alone, D.J. sank onto a log and drew her backpack close. The misting had finally stopped. It was nearing sunset, and the day wasn't going to get any warmer. She thought about starting a fire, but that would mean giving away her position. Something she didn't want to do. If no one got too close, she would stay right where she was until Ronnie returned. If she had to hide, she figured the odds of him finding her were close to zero. She would give him two hours to make his way to camp and come back. The return trip would be faster because he would flag down one of the jeeps circling the forest. If he didn't make it in the time she allowed, she would find one more potential prisoner herself and get back into camp by midnight.

Forty-five minutes into the first hour, D.J. heard something. It wasn't footsteps or brush moving. She couldn't actually place the sound, but it made the hairs on her arms stand up and her senses go on alert.

Someone was out there.

She silently slid off the log and into the shadowy protection of a tree trunk. After concealing her pack under some leaves, she confirmed she had her sidearm in place, then set out to find whoever was approaching.

She headed east first, then south to end up behind him. She worked on instinct, still not hearing anything specific, but knowing he was there. There were no bent twigs to give her direction, no footsteps, no startled birds or squirrels.

A couple of times she nearly convinced herself she'd been imagining the almost-noise and she started to return to her backpack. Then she would shiver, as if someone had raked nails on a chalkboard and she would know he was still out there.

It took her thirty minutes to make the circuit. When she ended up a few yards away from where she'd started, she was disgusted to find the guy pulling her backpack out from its hiding place. He'd gone right to it, as if he'd known it was there from the beginning. How had he done that?

D.J. dismissed the question. Once she verified the man had a purple arm band instead of an orange one like hers, she knew he was fair game. While he was bent over her supplies, obviously distracted, she moved in to attack.

She was less than a foot away when she pressed the barrel of the rifle against his back.

"Bang, you're dead," she said softly. "Now stand up slowly. Ghosts don't move fast."

The man calmly closed her backpack and put his hands in the air. "I heard you crashing around out there. What were you doing? Playing dodge ball with some rabbits?"

She didn't appreciate the question or the smirky tone of voice. For one thing, she knew she'd been quiet. For another, *she* was the one holding the gun.

"Keep your hands up," she said as she eased back far enough to keep him from grabbing the rifle.

When he was standing with his back to her, she considered her situation. The man was tall, a couple of inches over six feet, and well muscled. His stealth told her he wasn't an amateur like many of the participants. Nothing about him was familiar, which meant he was probably Army. Special Forces? Had they sent in a ringer?

She couldn't see his sidearm, which worried her. His rifle was on the ground next to his pack, but where was the handgun?

"How long are we going to stand like this?" he asked conversationally. "Or did you forget the next part?

You're supposed to have me turn around, then we eyeball each other. Once you've scared me with your rifle, you tie me up. Can you remember that or should we take it in stages?"

"You have some attitude, son."

"Son?" He chuckled. "Honey, you don't sound all that old yourself."

Arrogant bastard, she thought in annoyance. No doubt he thought because she was a woman, she would be easy to take. She was itching to kick his butt, but she wasn't going to start something before she knew she could finish it. She might be irritated, but she wasn't stupid.

"I have no interest in eyeballing you," she said. "Put your hands on top of your head, then get on your knees."

"But I just stood up," he protested, sounding like a spoiled child being asked to eat his vegetables. "Why don't you figure out what you want first, and then move me around."

She gritted her teeth. "Listen, mister, you—"

He moved with the speed of a cheetah racing in for the kill. One second he was standing with his back to her, and the next he spun in a graceful circle. His foot cracked against the rifle with enough force to send pain shooting up her arm. Involuntarily her fingers released the rifle and it crashed to the ground.

D.J. barely had time to notice. With her arm throbbing, she was at a serious disadvantage. Not that they were going to fight. Her opponent pulled his sidearm out of nowhere and pointed it directly at her head.

Her brain had started processing information the second the man had moved. She knew that he was as powerful as she'd thought, with lethally fast reflexes.

He was tall, had dark eyes and the faint smile curving up his lips contrasted with the cold metal in his hand. He was good. She gave him credit for that. But was he good enough? He'd kicked the rifle, not her. Had his mama taught him not to beat up on girls?

In keeping with her philosophy of using every weapon at hand, she decided to find out.

She ignored the gun and drew her throbbing arm up to her chest. With her free hand, she cupped her wrist and forced herself to whimper softly.

Whatever it took to win, she reminded herself even as she hated the thought of appearing weak.

The gun never wavered, but the man took a half step forward. "What? I kicked the rifle, not you."

She glared at him. "Maybe that's what you aimed at, but it's not what you hit." She sucked in a breath and bit her lower lip. "I think my wrist is broken."

He frowned. "I didn't hit your wrist."

She glared at him. "Right. Because in those boots you're wearing you could feel exactly what you connected with. My mistake."

Mentally she crossed her fingers, then nearly crowed with delight as he glanced down at his boots. One nanosecond of inattention was all she needed.

D.J. lashed out with her foot, connecting firmly with the man's midsection. Even as all the air rushed out of him, he grabbed for her leg. But she'd anticipated the move, and had already spun away.

The gun disappeared as quickly as it had appeared. He had to be weak from lack of air, but he still moved toward her. D.J. prepared for his attack, but when it came, she barely saw movement before she found herself tumbling onto the wet ground.

Part of her brain tried to figure out what exactly he'd done, while the rest of her recognized that the lack of pain anywhere meant he'd held back. He'd upended her with enough contact to send her tumbling but not enough to cause pain. How did he have that much control?

She wanted to summon up a little righteous indignation. How dare he treat her differently because she was female? But she was too busy scrambling to her feet and trying to figure out what he was going to do next.

D.J. crouched and cleared her mind. With a deep breath, she centered herself and knew she had to attack rather than wait to be bested.

As she moved toward him, she saw his arm push out. She ducked, spun and, instead of kicking at his knee as she'd planned, found herself slipping on the wet leaves. Something glinted and she instinctively reached out. Her fingers closed around his gun. He knocked her forearm with his hand so the gun went tumbling. She managed to kick it with a foot, sending it back into the air. With a graceful pirouette, she caught it and started to turn toward him. He ducked, her foot slipped again, and she began to fall. Her right hand shot out, and she accidentally brought the gun down hard on the back of his head. He fell like a stone.

Her first thought was that he was dead. Then she saw the steady rise and fall of his chest. Her second thought was that she had better get him tied up while he was unconscious, because it sure as hell wasn't going to happen when he came to.

Chapter 2

Quinn regained consciousness several seconds before he opened his eyes. He quickly registered the fact that he was lying on his back in the mud with his hands tied behind him. He silently swore in disgust. He'd been downed, not by superior training or force but by dumb luck. Wasn't that always the way?

Worse, the woman had tied him up while he'd been unconscious. Not that she would have been able to secure him any other way. He gave her points for gutsiness, but none for the lucky head shot.

Now what? He figured he would fake being out for a while, just long enough to make his captor sweat his condition. But before he could put his plan into action, he felt a hand settle on his ankle. His interest piqued— no way was he going to miss any part of a show—he opened his eyes.

The sun had gone down, but there was plenty of light from the small battery-operated lantern she'd set on the ground. He wasn't sure why she was willing to risk the light, but he appreciated being able to see what she was doing.

The woman crouched beside him. She felt along the inside of his left ankle and pulled out the knife he'd slipped into his boot. He turned his head and saw she'd already removed the one he'd tucked into his utility belt.

She ran her hand along the inside of his leg to the knee, then down the outside to his boot. After repeating the procedure on the other leg, she shifted and pressed her palm along the length of his thigh. When she'd nearly reached the good part, he grinned.

"A little to the left," he said.

She glanced up. Sometime in their scuffle, her hat had fallen off. He registered long dark hair pulled back in a braid, brown eyes, a well-shaped mouth and a sprinkling of freckles on slightly tanned skin. Pretty, he thought absently. No, more than pretty. She was both elegant and tough. An intriguing combination.

One of her well-shaped eyebrows rose slightly. "A little to the left?" she repeated, then slid her hand over his groin and patted him. "I know most men like to think of their equipment as a weapon, but it's not all that interesting to me."

He chuckled. "You say that now, with me tied up and at your mercy."

"Uh-huh. Just so we're clear, there are no circumstances that would change my mind."

She rose, stepped over to his other side and crouched again, this time running her hands over his other thigh. From there she felt her way up his stomach to his chest.

He liked the feel of her hands on his body. She moved quickly enough to show she really wasn't interested, but thoroughly enough to find any concealed weapons. Or so she thought.

When she'd finished going through his jacket pockets and checking the hem and lining, she sat back on her heels. "You seem to be disarmed."

"What about taking off my shirt?" he asked. "I might have something taped to my skin."

"If you do, you won't be getting to it anytime soon, will you?" She tapped his upper arm. "I tie a mean knot."

He'd already figured that out. Pulling against the ropes hadn't loosened them at all. He was going to have to find a different way to escape. Not that he wanted to go anywhere this second. His captor was the most entertainment he'd had in months.

He swept his gaze over her chest, lingering long enough on her breasts to make her shoulders stiffen. Then he returned his attention to her face. Her eyes narrowed and her mouth thinned, but she didn't complain. Somewhere along the way, she'd learned the rules—if she was going to play in a man's world, she would have to live by male rules. But that didn't mean she had to like them.

They stared at each other, a minor contest of wills. Quinn knew he could wear her down eventually, but decided on something more interesting. A challenge.

"You cheated," he said softly.

He waited for the blink, the blush, the guilt. Instead she only shrugged. "I won."

"You took advantage of an accident."

"Exactly." She shifted until she was seated next to him. "Would you have done things any differently?"

He wouldn't have needed an accident to win, but there was no point in saying that to her. She already knew.

"Besides," she continued, "that was my only chance to tie you up. You wouldn't have allowed it otherwise."

"Good point."

"So who are you?" she asked.

"Your prisoner of war. Do you plan to abuse me?"

One corner of her mouth twitched. "Stop sounding so hopeful. You're perfectly safe."

"Darn."

The twitch threatened to turn into a smile, but she managed to control it. When her expression was serious again, she said, "You never answered the question."

"I know."

She wanted to know who he was, and he would tell her…in time. Right now, despite the cool evening and the damp mud, he was enjoying himself. He had thought the war games would be boring and without any challenge. He was glad to be wrong.

She drew one knee up to her chest and leaned toward him. "If you won't tell me your name, at least tell me why you looked down. You're a good fighter. You had to know it was a mistake."

A good fighter? Now it was his turn to hold in a smile. He was a whole hell of a lot more than that. She'd never stood a chance, and he would guess she knew enough to figure that out.

Her chin jutted out at an angle that was pure pride. Who was she? Military?

"I knew you were setting me up and I wanted to see what you would do," he said.

She stiffened. "You were testing me?"

"More like playing with you."

Her breath caught in an audible hiss. Dark eyes narrowed again and he had a feeling she was itching to draw blood.

"Quinn Reynolds," he said to distract her. "Now that you've felt me up and all, we should probably be on a first-name basis with each other."

She ignored the bait. "So you won't tell me when I ask, but you'll share the information on your terms?"

"Something like that." He figured she wasn't going to offer her name, so he changed the subject. "Where's *your* partner?" he asked.

"He'll be back any minute, and then we'll take you to headquarters. He took in our first four prisoners. Where's your partner?"

"I got here too late to be matched up with anyone. Besides, I prefer to work alone."

"Of course you do." She sounded mildly amused. "You macho paramilitary types always do."

"That's more than a little judgmental."

"It's accurate."

Quinn couldn't argue with that. Instead he glanced up toward the damp, gray sky. "The rain's going to start up again. If you're not going to march me back to headquarters anytime soon, you could at least drag me under some cover."

She, too, glanced at the sky, but in the darkness, there wasn't much to see. He half expected her to leave him in the mud, but she surprised him by getting a tarp out of her backpack and spreading it under a nearby tree. Then she grabbed him under his arms and dragged him onto it.

Her strength impressed him, while her expression of annoyance amused him. What had her panties in a bunch? That her partner wasn't back yet? That they both knew he was better than she was and probably only her prisoner for as long as it suited him?

"So what are you?" he asked. "Not military."

She sat cross-legged on the edge of the tarp. "How can you be sure?"

"Am I wrong?"

She shook her head.

Just then the skies opened. Rain pounded the ground. In a matter of seconds the place where he'd been lying became a puddle. He pulled his knees toward his chest to get his feet out of the deluge.

His captor looked annoyed. He could hear her thoughts from here. How had he known it was about to rain? Who was this guy? Although he guessed she probably wasn't using the word *guy* in her mind. No doubt she'd chosen something more colorful.

"If you're not going to tell me your name," he said, "I can try to guess."

She adjusted the lantern and ignored him.

"Brenda," he said.

She didn't blink.

"Bambi? Heather? Chloe? Annie? Sarah? Destiny? Chastity?"

She sighed. "D.J."

He wanted to know what the initials stood for but didn't ask. She would be expecting that. Instead he said, "I'd offer to shake hands, but I'm all tied up at the moment."

She smiled. "I can see that."

Hey—a sense of humor. He liked that. A rough,

tough woman in a very feminine package. If he could just get her to give him another full body search, his evening would be complete.

D.J. glanced at her watch and knew that her boy toy wasn't going to make his way back to her anytime soon. It had been nearly four hours since Ronnie had left. He was either lost or captured. If he was close, she would hear him thrashing around in the bush. The silence told her she was very much alone with her prisoner.

She turned her attention back to Quinn. For a man who'd been left tied up on the ground for a couple of hours, he looked surprisingly relaxed. The rain had stopped, but it was still cool and damp. She shivered slightly. She would like nothing more than to head back to camp. There was only one thing stopping her…one very tall, very strong, very *male* thing.

"The rules of engagement state that a prisoner may do whatever he can to escape," she said. "However, once he and his captor start back to headquarters, he must go quietly."

Quinn nodded. "I heard that, too."

"And?"

He shrugged. "I was never one to follow the rules."

Just what she'd thought. With Ronnie helping her, she might have a shot at keeping possession of Quinn. But with only herself to guard him, he would get away. She hated to admit that, but it was true. He was too good.

She eyed his powerful body and wondered who and what he was. How much did he know that she didn't? Where had he learned it? She'd never met anyone like him, and being around him made her want to ask a million questions. Not that she would. Showing interest meant tipping her hand—something she'd learned never to do.

"If you won't cooperate, we're stuck here until morning," she said. "We'll be picked up by one of the patrols."

"Fair enough—I don't have to take a midnight hike, and you get credit for my capture."

She didn't trust his easy agreement. He was the kind of man who always had a plan. Still, he hadn't made any moves to get away…at least not yet.

He shifted so that he was more sitting than lying, leaning against the base of the tree. Then he jerked his chin toward her backpack.

"If we're stuck out here for the night, how about something to eat?"

At his words, her stomach growled. She hadn't eaten since breakfast. A flurry of phone calls had kept her from grabbing lunch before she'd headed out to the afternoon start of the war games.

She reached for her pack, then paused. "Where's your gear?" she asked.

"Hidden."

Hers had been hidden, too, right up until he'd found it. She wondered if she would be able to locate his pack, then decided it wasn't worth facing the cold, rainy night to find out. They could get by on what she had.

She dug out four granola bars, two chocolate bars, an apple and another water bottle.

"No fast food?" he asked. "I have a hankering for some fries."

"You'll have to wait until they show up on the prison menu," she said as she divided the wrapped snacks into two equal piles.

He eyed the food, then shrugged. "That beats an MRE."

Meals ready to eat. Prepackaged food soldiers could carry into combat. She'd tried a couple and, while they weren't as bad as everyone claimed, she would rather dine on what she had in her pack.

"So you're military?" she asked.

"Sort of."

"Special Forces?"

"Something like that."

She wasn't sure if he was being coy to annoy her or because he couldn't talk about what he did for a living.

She poured some water from the new bottle into the one she'd been using. When there was an equal amount in both, she propped one up next to Quinn. He half turned away from her, exposing his bound wrists.

"Want to cut me loose so I can eat?" he asked.

She chuckled. "Not even on a bet."

He rolled back into a seated position. "Then you're going to have to feed me yourself."

He didn't look very upset at the prospect. In fact, there was definite amusement in his dark eyes.

She ignored it, along with the teasing tone of his voice. If he thought hand feeding him was going to fluster her, he was in for a shock.

"I haven't seen you around town before," she said as she unwrapped the first granola bar in his pile. "You're not stationed at the base here, are you?"

"No. I flew into the country day before yesterday and got to Glenwood this morning. I'm here to meet up with my brother."

She broke the granola bar into small pieces and offered him the first one. He didn't bother leaning forward, which meant she had to stretch her arm out across his body. When her fingers were practically touching his mouth, he finally opened and bit down on the food.

He winked. "The ambiance needs a little work, but I can't complain about the service."

She ignored him. "Where did you fly in from?"

"The Middle East."

There was something about the way he answered the question that made her think she wasn't likely to get any more information from him. She waited until he'd finished chewing, then offered another piece of the bar.

"What about you?" he asked when he'd finished chewing. "You live in Glenwood?"

"Yes."

"What do you do?"

She hesitated because her natural inclination was to not reveal any personal information. Quinn waited, his expression interested, his body relaxed. Finally she shrugged and gave him the bare-bone facts.

"I'm a private consultant," she said. "I teach classes at local schools, telling kids how to stay safe. I teach women basic self-defense. I'm also on call with several state and federal organizations, along with some private firms. They bring me in to help in extracting children from dangerous situations."

"Domestic abductions?" he asked.

"Sometimes." Domestic abductions meant the kidnapping of a child by the noncustodial parent. "Sometimes it's a straight kidnapping for money or revenge."

She stopped talking the second she realized she wanted Quinn to be impressed. Don't be an idiot, she told herself. What did she care what this guy thought of her?

She fed him the last of the granola bar then unwrapped one for herself.

"Is there a Mr. D.J.?" he asked.

"No."

"Just no?" Quinn raised his eyebrows. "A former Mr. D.J., then?"

"Not even close."

"Why not? A pretty woman like you should be married."

She laughed. "You sound like an Italian grandma. I have no interest in getting married. It was an institution invented by men to get their needs met. They get full-time live-in help, including a maid and a nanny when they have kids. Not only don't they have to pay for it, but most wives will do all that *and* go get a job. Marriage is a great deal for men, but what do women get out of it?"

"Safety. Security."

"Right. Tell that to the women at the local shelter. The ones who have been beat up by their loving husbands."

"You've obviously thought this through," he said.

"It didn't take long."

She finished her granola bar and opened his second one.

"So you keep your men on a short leash?"

She leaned toward him. "I keep them in a cage."

She'd thought he might be offended by her opinions and bluntness, but instead he laughed. Her forearm brushed his chest, and she felt the rumble of his amusement.

His dark gaze locked with hers. "Do you have them

all running scared or are a few of them brave enough to stand up to you?"

"Most are too busy heading for the hills. They want soft, gentle, trusting women."

"You can be soft."

"Right. That's me. A delicate flower."

"You're still a woman, D.J. Combat boots and a few fancy moves don't change that."

She thought of herself as competent and independent. Not soft. Soft implied weak. "My moves aren't fancy and I have more than a few of them."

"Tough talk for a girl."

She held up the piece of the granola bar. "Do you want to eat this, or do you want to keep flapping your lips?"

He obligingly opened his mouth. She moved closer. This time, though, as he took the food, his lip came in contact with her fingertips.

There was a flash of heat where their skin touched, along with a flicker of tightness in her stomach. D.J. nearly jumped in surprise. What on earth was that? She didn't react to men. Not now, not ever. She liked some, disliked others and rarely trusted any of them.

Unsettled, but determined not to show it, she continued to feed him the granola bar but was careful to make sure there wasn't any more contact. As she finished her second bar, she tried to analyze what was going on. Okay, Quinn wasn't like most men she met. He was unfazed by her or by being tied up. He was an excellent fighter, probably in Special Forces and most likely stationed overseas. He was—

Tall, dark and good-looking. Of course.

Relief coursed through her as she realized what was

going on. Quinn Reynolds reminded her of the Haynes brothers. All four of them shared the same general physique, dark coloring and facial structure. She'd known Travis Haynes, the sheriff, and Kyle Haynes, one of the deputies, since she'd first moved to Glenwood. Over the past few years, she'd met the other brothers.

They were all good guys, and some of the very few men she trusted. Quinn looked enough like them to put her off balance.

Having solved the problem, D.J. relaxed. She fed Quinn his chocolate bar, ate her own, then used her penknife to cut the apple in two, then divide it into slices.

"I don't think your partner is coming back," he said conversationally.

D.J. glanced at her watch, then nodded in agreement. "Ronnie wasn't really good in the woods," she admitted. "I'm guessing he's lost. Or captured by an enemy."

"Are you sure you didn't leave him tied up somewhere?"

She grinned. "He and I were partners. I would never actually hurt him. I settled on threatening him."

"Was he scared?"

"Terrified. Barely eighteen and a new recruit. But he knew how to follow orders. We captured four prisoners in our first couple of hours. Three of them were army officers."

"How?"

She explained about distracting them while Ronnie sneaked up from behind. When she'd finished, Quinn shook his head.

"Do you always do whatever it takes to win?"

"I do whatever it takes to be in control. There's a difference."

He glanced down at her hand. "So I didn't kick you in the wrist before. You were faking it."

"Of course."

"I can respect that."

While they were discussing recent history... "How did you throw me without hurting me?" she asked. "I barely felt anything."

"I have great hands."

She rolled her eyes. "I'm serious."

"I am, too. Besides, I don't beat up on women."

With his abilities, he could beat up on anyone he wanted.

"Being female can give you an advantage," he said. "Men aren't always expecting women to be tough. Do you ever get into trouble using your femininity in a situation? Ever take on more than you bargained for?"

"I don't go in blind, so no. I'm prepared for every eventuality."

"Do you ever get personally involved?"

"Not even close."

He considered her answer. "You could do undercover work."

"Maybe." But it wasn't her style. "That would require a level of vulnerability I don't allow."

"Sometimes it comes with the territory. Aren't you the one willing to do whatever it takes to win?"

"No. To be in control." She studied him. "What about you? Do you ever go undercover?"

"Sometimes. Mostly I just creep around in the dark, waiting to pull people out of places they're not supposed to be."

Probably a simplistic version of his work, but one that made her want to ask a lot more questions. Doubt-

ful that he would answer them, she checked her watch.
It was after eleven.

"Are you going to get in trouble for staying out all
night?" he asked.

"Are you?"

"I hope so." He shifted so that he was stretched out
on the tarp. "If you're going to make me stay out in
the rain, the least you can do is cuddle close so we can
stay warm."

"I don't think so."

"That's the woman in you talking."

She started to protest, then realized he was right.
The temperature was cool enough to make her shiver.
Neither of them would get any sleep unless they could
warm up. But stretching out next to a strange man
wasn't her idea of a good time.

"Shy?" he asked cheerfully.

She ignored him and slid closer. While she'd "slept"
with a few men, she'd never been one for spending the
night. She certainly never allowed herself to fall asleep
after. Of course, in this case Quinn wasn't a lover—he
was her prisoner. That changed the dynamics.

He was big and tall and as she moved next to him,
she could feel his heat.

"I could use a pillow," he said.

"Fine."

She grabbed the pack and shoved it under his head.
He smiled at her.

"Thanks."

"You're welcome. Now go to sleep." She reached
to turn off the lantern, but before she could, he spoke
again.

"I can't. My arms hurt."

She glared at him. With them both lying down, his face was fairly close to hers. She could see the stubble on his jaw and the length of his dark lashes.

"I'm not untying you," she told him. "If you promise to behave, I'll take you into camp."

His mouth turned up at the corners. "I almost never behave."

"Why is that not a surprise?"

She reached behind her and clicked off the lantern, then shifted close to him. But somehow he'd managed to move just enough so that when she lowered her head, she found it resting on his shoulder.

Her first instinct was to bolt for safety. Because she didn't want him to know she was rattled, she forced herself to stay in place. A few minutes later, her apprehension faded. Quinn was tied up; she was safe.

She deliberately concentrated on slowing her breathing. After a few more minutes she became aware of the not-unpleasant masculine scent of his body. He generated plenty of heat, and she found herself relaxing.

"This is nice," he said into the darkness.

"Hmm."

"Don't I get a kiss good-night?"

Her eyes popped open and she stared into the darkness. A kiss? "No."

He made a low clucking sound. It took her a second to realize he was trying to imitate a chicken.

"Oh, yeah, that's going to work," she said.

"You're tempted," he said, "but nervous. That's okay. I understand. I'm a big, handsome hunky guy who turns you on. But you don't have to be nervous. I'll be gentle."

"You'll be sucking wind."

Obviously, the man didn't have any self-esteem issues. Although she wasn't the least bit concerned about her safety, what *did* make her jittery was the fact that the thought of kissing him was almost appealing.

"You're missing out," he said. "You know, you wouldn't even have to untie me. You could take advantage of me. I wouldn't mind."

"Shut up and go to sleep."

He sighed heavily. "Just one kiss."

"No."

"There doesn't have to be any tongue."

"Gee, thanks for letting me know."

"Come on. You want to. How long will it take? Then we can go to sleep."

Despite the craziness of what he was saying, D.J. found herself reaching for the lantern and clicking it on.

"You're getting on my nerves," she said.

Quinn puckered his lips like a man imitating a fish. She couldn't help chuckling.

He was big, dangerous, probably trained to kill and he made her laugh. What was wrong with this picture?

She sighed. "I want your word that you'll be quiet and go to sleep. No more conversation, no more requests."

"I'd cross my heart, but I'm a little tied up right now."

"Was that a yes?"

"Yes."

She leaned close. One kiss, she told herself. Just a quick peck good-night. It didn't mean anything. She wouldn't let it. She was just doing this to shut him up— not because she was the least bit…interested.

Her mouth barely touched his. There was the same flash of heat she'd experienced when her fingers had brushed his lips, and a tightening low in her belly. She braced herself for an aggressive response from him, but he didn't move. She wasn't even sure he was breathing.

Slowly she pressed a little harder. Not exactly deepening the kiss, but not ending it, either. Something warm and liquid poured through her. It made her thinking fuzzy and her body relax. It made her— Panic surged as she realized she was actually enjoying the close contact. Temptation, desire, need were all too risky. Too dangerous. She knew better. She'd spent her entire life knowing better.

But she wouldn't let him know she was rattled. Instead of jerking her head back, she broke the kiss slowly, then opened her eyes.

She braced herself for a verbal slam, but Quinn only smiled. Not a victorious smile, but one that said they'd shared something intimate.

No they hadn't, she thought as she turned off the lantern and settled onto the tarp. They'd kissed. So what? People kissed all the time. It didn't mean anything. It never had. She wouldn't let it.

Chapter 3

Quinn awakened sometime before dawn. He recognized the gray light outside the main flap of the large military-issue tent, then he stretched on the cot. The makeshift bed was a hell of a lot more comfortable than the tarp where he'd spent the first part of the night. Of course, then he'd had a sleeping companion. He'd traded the company of an intriguing and beautiful woman for comfort. Not much of a trade.

Memories of the previous evening made him smile. When D.J. woke up and saw he'd escaped, she was going to be spitting nails. Too bad he would miss the show. At least he knew she would come looking for him at camp, demanding to know how he'd done it. He'd made sure of that by leaving his cut ropes coiled up neatly beside her. The message was clear—he'd escaped *and* he'd had a knife that she'd missed. No way would she be able to resist a challenge like that.

Fifteen minutes later he was sipping coffee at one of the tables in the mess tent. He'd spread out the morning paper, but instead of reading, he was watching the main entrance, waiting for a tall, shapely brunette to burst inside and demand an explanation…not to mention retribution.

Instead he saw his brother stroll in. Gage looked around him, saw him and started across the dirt floor.

"You made it," Gage said, and grinned.

Quinn rose and they shook hands, then embraced briefly. After slapping each other on the back and reassuring themselves that each had survived and was well since their last meeting, Quinn glanced at the man who had accompanied Gage.

His brother stepped back. "This is Travis Haynes. He's the local sheriff here."

Quinn shook hands with the man, then frowned when he realized there was something familiar about him. He was sure he and Travis Haynes had never met; Quinn didn't forget faces. Yet there was something that teased at the back of his mind…almost a memory, but not quite.

Travis looked him over, then shook his head. "I'll be damned," he said, then motioned to the table. "We should probably sit down and talk this over."

Curious but not concerned, Quinn settled back in his chair. Gage took a seat across from him with Travis sitting to his right. Gage rested his forearms on the table.

"You're doing okay?" he asked Quinn.

Quinn sipped his coffee. "You have something to say, so say it."

Gage nodded. "I just—"

Travis leaned forward. "I should go. After you two talk we can all get together."

"No." Gage shook his head. "Stay. This concerns you. Besides, if Quinn has some questions, you're the best one to answer them." He returned his attention to Quinn. "Sorry to be so mysterious. I didn't want to tell you in a phone message or a letter. I appreciate you coming here."

Quinn shrugged. His work kept him out of touch with his family for months at a time. Their only way to communicate was to leave a message at a special number and wait for him to get back to them. Sometimes he was able to respond in a few days, but most of the time it was weeks or months. Gage had left his first message nearly two months ago. His second, requesting Quinn meet him in Glenwood, had been delivered just as Quinn had returned to the States.

"Have you talked to Mom?" Gage asked.

"A couple of days ago. She said everything was fine." He frowned. Had she been hiding something? Was she sick?

Not surprisingly his brother knew what he was thinking.

"She's okay," Gage told him. "I wondered if she'd mentioned anything..." He leaned back in his chair. "This is harder than I thought."

"Just spit it out."

"Fair enough." Gage stared at him. "Ralph Reynolds isn't our biological father. He and Mom couldn't have kids together. They both wanted them so she got pregnant by another guy. Someone she met in Dallas. His name is Earl Haynes. Travis here is one of his sons.

Which makes him our half brother." Gage grinned. "Actually, we have several. It seems there are a lot of Earl Haynes's sons running around the world."

Quinn heard the words, but at first they didn't have any meaning. Ralph Reynolds not their biological father?

A half-dozen memories flashed through his mind—none of them pleasant. Of his father walking away, of his father telling him he would never be good enough, of his father making it clear over and over that Quinn could never measure up to Gage. Of his father... Not his father? Was it possible?

"I had a hard time with it, too," Gage said quietly.

Quinn didn't doubt that. Gage and the old man had been tight. Always. While Quinn couldn't wait to get out of Possum Landing, Gage had stayed and made his life there. He'd been proud to be the fifth generation of Reynoldses in town. He'd become the damn sheriff.

"You're sure?" he asked.

Gage nodded. "Mom told me. Back thirty-plus years ago, it was more difficult for infertile couples to get help. Plus our folks didn't have money for expensive treatments. Dad was the one with the problem, not her. Dad—Ralph—came up with a plan for Mom to find someone who looked like him and get pregnant."

Quinn stiffened. "That sounds barbaric, even for the old man."

"She wasn't happy," Gage admitted. "Finally she agreed and headed up to Dallas. She met Earl Haynes. He was in town attending a convention."

"And nine months later you came along?"

"Yeah." Gage shook his head. "Ralph was happy

with his new son, everyone assumed he was the father and things were fine."

Until he'd come along, Quinn thought impassively. He'd long since become immune to dealing with the realities of not being wanted by the man he'd always thought of as his father.

"The following year she went back," Gage continued. "She got pregnant with you. So we're still brothers."

None of this was sinking in, Quinn thought. Nor did it have to. He would deal with it all later. For now, he relaxed in his seat and grinned at Gage.

"Damn, and here I thought I was finally getting rid of you."

His brother punched him in the arm. "No way. I'm still older, better looking and capable of kicking your butt anytime I want."

The latter made Quinn laugh. "Yeah, right." He turned his attention to Travis Haynes. "So you're a sheriff, too?"

"Law enforcement runs in the family. I'm a sheriff. My brother Kyle is a deputy. Craig, the oldest of us four, works for the Fern Hill Police Department, and my half sister, Hannah, is a dispatcher. Jordan is the black sheep—he's a firefighter."

Gage looked at Quinn. "I'm a sheriff and you do your own personal version of keeping the world in line. How much of that was because of the gene pool?"

Quinn had his doubts. "I'm not a fan of destiny."

"That's because there are a few things you still don't know." Gage pushed Quinn's coffee toward him. "Drink up. You're going to need it."

"Why?"

"It seems that Earl didn't just stop at sleeping with our mother. He also—"

Gage was interrupted by a commotion at the door. Quinn turned around and saw D.J. burst into the tent. She glanced around until she saw him. When she did, her brown eyes narrowed and she stalked toward the table.

She was walking, breathing outrage. With her olive-and-khaki clothes, her long dark hair, and a rifle in one hand, she was a female warrior at her most appealing.

A young officer started to cross her path, took one look at her set expression and carefully backed out of the way. Quinn doubted that D.J. even noticed. When she reached the table, she tossed the cut ropes in front of him.

"How the hell did you do it?" she demanded.

Fury spilled from her. Quinn didn't doubt that if she thought she could take him, she would be on him in a heartbeat.

Instead of reacting to her question or her temper, he casually sipped his coffee before pushing out a chair with his foot.

"Have a seat," he said calmly.

She ignored the offer. "I asked you a question."

"I know."

He met her gaze, prepared to wait her out. He wanted to smile but didn't let himself. He wanted to grab her by her hair, haul her close and kiss her until they were both panting. He didn't do that, either. Instead he waited.

He wasn't sure how long they would have played "you blink first." Travis stood and moved between them, ending the contest. He put his hands on D.J.'s shoulders and not too gently pushed her into the chair.

"Take a load off," he said. "I'll get you coffee."

She opened her mouth, then closed it. "Thanks," she said, not sounding all that gracious.

When Travis returned, he set the mug in front of her and sat back into his seat. "I see you've met Quinn, here. This is his brother, Gage."

D.J. glanced at Gage, nodded and returned her attention to Quinn. "I want answers."

He made a show of checking his watch. "I thought you'd be back sooner. You must have slept in. But after the night we had, I'm not surprised you were tired."

She half rose from her seat. Quinn expected the rifle to swing in his direction. But before she could get physical, Travis started to laugh.

"I don't think so," he said easily. "D.J. would have chewed you up and spit you out."

Quinn met her gaze and raised his eyebrows. "I'm not so sure."

If he smirked, she was going to kill him, D.J. decided. Right there in front of witnesses. Although she wasn't usually one for reckless behavior, Quinn had really pissed her off.

She watched him drink his coffee, as if he had all the time in the world. Which he probably did. He looked rested, showered and utterly relaxed. She was tired, dirty and had leaves in her hair. Worse—he'd escaped. She wanted to know how and she wanted payback.

She refused to acknowledge that some of her temper came from the memory of the brief kiss they'd shared. She still couldn't believe she'd given in and actually kissed him…and *liked* it. Not that she would ever let him know.

"How did you two meet?" Gage asked.

"D.J. got the drop on me during the war games," Quinn told his brother.

Gage, about the same age as Quinn, with the same dark coloring and strong, good-looking features, straightened in surprise. "You're kidding."

"Nope."

Gage's expression turned doubtful, and D.J. didn't blame him. As much as she'd wanted to be the one in charge, Quinn had been in control the entire evening. He'd only let her hold him prisoner for as long as it suited him. She wanted to know why. Even more, she wanted to find out all the things he knew that she didn't.

But how to ask?

As she considered the question, she picked up her coffee and turned to thank Travis for bringing her the mug. It was only then she noticed how much her friend looked like Quinn and Gage. The same general build, the same coloring. Even the shapes of their dark eyes were similar.

"What's going on?" she asked. "Is there some kind of Haynes family look-alike contest going on?"

Travis turned to her and smiled. "Funny you should say that."

Over breakfast in the mess tent, D.J. listened as Travis and Gage explained their surprising family connection. D.J. was more interested in Quinn's early years than in his being a half brother to the Haynes family. Somehow she couldn't picture a kid from Possum Landing, Texas, growing up to be a dangerous operative, but it had obviously happened.

She picked up a piece of bacon and took a bite just

as a tall, thin, very damp young man with flaming red hair walked over to the table.

D.J. looked Ronnie over and sighed. "Did you get lost or captured?" she asked.

He flushed. "Um, both, ma'am."

"I'm assuming you got lost first."

He hung his head. "Yes, ma'am. I apologize for not finding you again."

The men at the table had stopped talking to listen to her conversation. She eyed the eighteen-year-old. He already felt bad about what had happened. There was no point in chewing him out publicly. She'd never been into that sort of thing for sport.

"Mistakes happen," she said. "Go grab some food and coffee."

Ronnie stared at her with wide, uncomprehending eyes. "Ma'am?"

She allowed herself a slight smile. "I'm not cutting off your ears, Private. Go get some breakfast."

He beamed at her. "Yes, ma'am. Right away."

When he was gone, she looked at Travis who sat across from her, then at his brother Kyle. They were both grinning.

"Don't start with me," she warned.

"It's not like you to be a soft touch," Travis said.

"I'm not. The kid tried hard and he screwed up. It happens."

Kyle leaned toward her. "He thinks you're hot."

D.J. rolled her eyes. "Yeah, right. I'm sure I'm going to star in all his dreams for the next fifteen or twenty minutes."

Kyle chuckled.

D.J. ignored him. She scooped up some eggs. After

a few seconds, conversation resumed and she was once again listening rather than participating.

Quinn sat at the end of the table. She never directly looked at him, but she was aware of him. Of how he and all the other men seated here were physically so similar.

Craig and Jordan Haynes had arrived and pulled up chairs. Craig was the oldest of the Haynes brothers, Jordan the second youngest. Two fraternal twins, Kevin and Nash Harmon were also a part of their group. D.J. hadn't quite figured out their relationship to the other men. Apparently, when Earl had been in Dallas getting Quinn's mother pregnant, he'd also had his way with the twins' mother. Quinn and Gage had grown up with them as close friends, only recently learning they were in fact half brothers. Everyone at the table but her was part of the Haynes extended family.

She supposed there were some people who would have felt left out, under the circumstances. Not her. She'd been part of a family once, and now lived her life blissfully free of familial obligations.

Keeping her head turned toward Travis as he spoke, D.J. casually glanced to her left. Quinn had finished his breakfast. Now he sat listening, nodding occasionally and not saying much. While he'd been two parts annoying, one part charming and very talkative the previous evening and when she'd first arrived this morning, he'd gotten more quiet as the group had expanded. Didn't he do crowds?

She was about to turn away when Quinn moved slightly and met her gaze. His dark eyes didn't give away what he was thinking, nor did the neutral expression on his face. He could have been trying to decide if he wanted more coffee. Yet she *felt* something crackle between them. A tension. Awareness tightened her skin and made her shiver.

Unfamiliar and too powerful for comfort, the sensations unnerved her. Distraction came in the form of Ronnie returning with his breakfast.

By the time she'd introduced him to everyone and had slid her chair over to make more room, she had convinced herself that she'd only imagined the weird reaction to Quinn.

Travis waited until Ronnie had his mouth full, then grinned at D.J. "So, you didn't win this year."

The kid started to choke.

D.J. scowled at Travis, then pounded Ronnie on the back. When he'd swallowed, he gulped down half his glass of milk and shrank in his seat.

"About me not getting back," he began.

D.J. cut him off with a stern look. "Let it go, kid," she told him. "My streak was bound to run out sooner or later."

"Too bad she wasn't able to capture a prisoner all on her own," Quinn drawled. "No, wait. You *did* have someone, didn't you?"

D.J. ignored him.

Ronnie's eyes widened. "You lost a prisoner?"

Travis chuckled. "Don't go there, son. D.J.'ll take your head off."

Ronnie returned his attention to his breakfast.

D.J. couldn't help glancing at Quinn, who had the nerve to smile at her. Just smile. As if he was happy or something.

Nash Harmon, a six-foot, one-inch testament to Haynes family genes, rose. "I hate to break this up, but I have things to see to this morning."

Kevin, his twin, hooted. "Things? Don't you mean Stephanie?"

Nash smiled. "That's exactly what I mean." He looked over at Quinn. "You probably haven't heard. I recently got engaged. Of course, I'm not the only one. Kevin's planning a wedding for early October, and you already know about Gage."

D.J. noticed that Quinn's gaze settled on his brother. Gage shrugged. "We haven't had time to go into that. I'm getting married, too."

"Congratulations," Quinn said.

"All three of you just recently got engaged?" she asked before she could stop herself. "Is it something in the water?"

Travis rose. "Could be. That'll make you switch to bottled, huh?"

"In a heartbeat." D.J. shook her head. "Married."

She held back saying "yuck" even though it was what she was thinking. In her experience, marriage was all bad for the woman and all good for the man. Okay, the Haynes brothers seemed to have decent relationships. And her friend Rebecca had married a pretty okay guy, but they were exceptions.

It seemed that everyone had a place to be. In a matter of a couple of minutes, the table had cleared, except for D.J. and Quinn. She expected him to stand up, as well, but he didn't. Instead he sipped his coffee and looked at her.

She told herself this was great. Now she could get her questions answered. The only problem was his steady gaze made her want to shift in her seat. She wouldn't, of course. She would never let him know he could make her feel uncomfortable. Nor would she admit to wanting to know what he was thinking as he watched her.

She resisted the incredibly stupid impulse to touch her hair to make sure it was in place, as if *that* mattered, then turned toward him and decided to just go for it.

"How did you get away?" she asked. "The ropes were cut, but I'd checked you for knives. I'd put yours in the pack, which was out of reach. I checked it this morning and you hadn't opened it. So you had a knife on you somewhere. One that I missed."

She had the sudden thought that someone could have crept into camp and released him, but she dismissed the idea. She knew in her gut Quinn had gotten away all by himself. He'd managed to outsmart her and to do it all while she was sleeping.

Even more annoying, he'd left his jacket draped over her, as if she needed protection from the elements.

"How could you have missed a knife?" he asked, his eyes bright with humor. "You gave me a very thorough and very enjoyable search. If you'd like to check me again…" His voice trailed off.

She ignored the suggestion and the teasing tone of his voice. "Where's the knife?"

She half expected him to insist she come find it. Instead he flipped up the collar of his heavy military-issue shirt, and pulled out a short blade. Not a knife… just the blade.

Of course, she thought, impressed by the ingenuity. No one paid attention to stiff collars. The points were supposed to be that way. All Quinn would need to do was a little shift and shimmy to get his hands in front of his body, then the blade would be within easy reach.

The possibilities intrigued the hell out of her. "What else do you know that I don't?"

Instead of making a smart-ass response, Quinn stood. "This has been great," he said.

She rose and walked toward him. "Wait. I really want to know."

His gaze never left her face, yet everything changed. The teasing was gone, as was the humor. Instead, bone-deep weariness invaded his expression. He knew things, she thought as she involuntarily took a step back. He'd seen and done things no man should experience. His life was about a whole lot more than simply getting people out of places they shouldn't be.

"I'm not playing," she said. "I want to learn what you know. I'm a quick study."

"Why does it matter?"

"Your skills would help me with my work. I want to be better."

"Aren't you good enough to get the job done?"

"Yes, but I want to be better than good enough. I want to be the best."

"There is no best."

Of course there was, she thought. There always was. She worked her butt off to make sure it was her most of the time.

"I'll pay you," she said.

He smiled then. "Thanks, but I'm not interested. Take care, D.J."

And then he was gone. He simply walked out of the tent without looking back.

She watched him go and decided right then she was going to get him to change his mind. She didn't know how, but she would convince Quinn Reynolds to teach her what he knew. She would be stronger, faster, smarter, and finally the ghosts would be laid to rest.

Two days later D.J. still hadn't come up with a plan. What on earth would a man like Quinn want that she could give him? She'd paced most of the night, and when that hadn't cleared her mind, she'd awakened early for a three-mile run. Now she prowled her back room, pausing occasionally to jab at the punching bag in the corner.

"I can see you're in a temper this morning. Want to talk about it?"

D.J. turned toward the voice and saw Rebecca Lucas standing in the doorway of her workout room. She held a thermos in one hand and a pink bakery box in the other. D.J.'s spirits lightened immediately.

"Danish?" she asked, heading toward her friend.

"Of course. Don't I always bring Danish?"

"You're a good woman."

"I know."

Rebecca led the way to the main office, where she set the box on the front desk and opened the thermos.

"So what has you all crabby this morning?" she asked as she poured coffee into two mugs. "If you were anyone else, I would swear it was man trouble."

"It is, but not the romantic kind."

Rebecca handed her the coffee. "Too bad. You need a man in your life."

"Right. That would be as useful to me as inheriting a toxic waste dump."

Rebecca tisked softly as she poured more coffee for herself, opened the bakery box and pushed it toward D.J.

D.J. grabbed a napkin, then a cheese Danish. The

first bite was heaven. The second, even better. She slowly chewed the flaky, sticky, sweet pastry.

Rebecca took one for herself and nibbled daintily. As usual, all conversation ceased until they'd each downed at least one Danish and felt the kick-start, blood-sugar rush of refined carbohydrates and frosting.

D.J. finished first and licked her fingers. Rebecca dabbed at her mouth with a napkin.

They couldn't be more different, D.J. thought affectionately. Rebecca was all girl, from her long, curly hair to her wardrobe of soft, flowing, floral-print dresses. She wore foolish shoes, delicate jewelry and wouldn't be caught dead in town without makeup.

"You're looking at my dress," Rebecca said when she'd finished her Danish. "You hate it."

"No. It's great."

D.J. studied the light-blue flowers scattered on a white background, the scalloped neckline and the girlish capped sleeves, while trying desperately not to wince.

"I just don't understand why you have to dress so… girly."

Rebecca took another Danish. "We don't all need to look as if we'd just come from a sale at the army surplus store. Olive green isn't my color. Besides, Austin likes how I dress."

End of argument, D.J. told herself. If Austin mentioned he would like the rotation of the earth changed, Rebecca would set out to see what she could do to make that happen. She adored her husband past the point of reason. D.J. found the situation palatable only because Austin was a good man—weren't those few and far between?—and he loved his wife just as completely. D.J. believed down to her bones that if someone tried to hurt Rebecca, Austin would rip that person into stamp-size pieces.

Rebecca looked her over, making D.J. aware of her camouflage pants and heavy boots.

"You're expecting a war later?"

"Real funny." D.J. grabbed a second pastry. "So what's going on?"

Rebecca filled her in on the latest escapades of her four children, including David's increasing fascination with cars. "He's going to be a holy terror on the road," Rebecca said, her voice mixed with worry and pride. "He's already poring through Austin's car magazines and giving us suggestions for his sixteenth birthday."

The conversation continued. Rebecca made it a habit to drop in two or three mornings a week. D.J. enjoyed hearing about her family. As she didn't plan to get married, and doubted she would be a very good single mom, Rebecca's kids were as close to her own as she was going to get.

"I'm having a party next week," Rebecca announced as she poured them each more coffee.

D.J. held up her hands in protest. "No, thanks."

"How can you say that?"

"You have two kinds of parties. One is for couples, which means you're going to set me up with some guy I don't want to meet. The other is a girls-only deal where someone will be trying to sell something I'll find completely useless."

"Cosmetics," Rebecca confirmed. "And they're not useless. I know you're not a big fan of makeup, but you take good care of your skin. This line of skin care is really amazing. Besides, it would be good for you to get out."

"I get out."

"I'm talking about spending some time with normal women."

"I spend time with you."

Rebecca sighed. "Why can't you be more social?"

"It's not my thing."

"So what is your thing?"

D.J. thought of Quinn. He intrigued her. "There was this guy I met during the war games," she said.

Rebecca instantly brightened. "Did he ask you out?"

"It wasn't like that. I captured him, but only because I got lucky. I want him to teach me what he knows."

"Which is what?"

"I'm not sure. I've asked around a little and found out that he works for a secret branch of the military. I'll bet he knows more about killing people than anyone I've met."

Rebecca shuddered. "Not exactly someone you want to have over for dinner. What's the guy's appeal? You don't kill people. You keep them alive."

"The more I know, the better."

Her friend studied her. "You seem very determined. Are you sure this is only about the exchange of knowledge?"

D.J. didn't bother answering. It was a stupid question. Well, maybe not *stupid*. There had been that kiss.

She instantly shoved the memory away. The kiss had been nothing, she told herself. Any reaction she'd felt had been brought on by exhaustion or adrenaline or a spider bite.

"Why does your silence sound so guilty?" Rebecca asked.

D.J. did her best not to squirm. "I have no idea what you're talking about."

"Oh, I believe that." She flicked her long hair over her shoulder and shook her head. "If he's so special, can't you just date him? Does every encounter have to be a battle?"

"I asked him to teach me some things, but he wasn't interested. I even offered to pay him."

"Not exactly the best way to win him over."

"I don't want him to *like* me."

"Why not?"

It was an old conversation and one D.J. wasn't about to start up again. Rebecca had never understood her reluctance to get involved with a man. She didn't get that caring meant vulnerability. Danger lurked in most relationships. Men were bigger, stronger and, for the most part, meaner. Not all of them, of course, but D.J. wasn't taking any chances.

"I don't want a boyfriend, just an instructor," she said. "Don't try to change my mind. Just tell me how to convince him to help me out."

"I will, but under protest. You need a good man in your life."

D.J. rotated her wrist, motioning for Rebecca to get on with it. Her friend smiled impishly.

"There's only one way to get a man to do something he doesn't want to do."

Finally, D.J. thought. Information she could use. "What's that?"

"Give him the one thing he really wants and can't get any other way."

Chapter 4

D.J. hovered in front of the hotel room door. She hated to think of herself as someone who hovered, but there was no other way to describe her actions. She reached up to knock once, then took two steps back and shoved her hands into her jeans pockets.

This was crazy, she told herself. She shouldn't even bother. She wouldn't, either, except she really wanted Quinn to teach her a few tricks. But would he agree?

Rebecca had said to find something he wanted that he couldn't get any other way and offer it to him. Great advice, except she didn't know what would interest him. Except for something he'd mentioned while he'd been her prisoner.

He'd teased her about taking advantage of him, joked about her searching him more thoroughly and had wanted to kiss her. She might not have a date with a different guy every Friday night, but she knew something about the male of the species. The way into a man's frame of reference wasn't through great cooking, witty conversation or a sparkling personality. Nope, guys were more basic than that. Something she thought she could use to her advantage.

She stalked up to the door and raised her hand again. This time she knocked, then wished she hadn't. Planning to make a deal with Quinn was one thing, but going through with it was something else. She didn't usually offer to pay for things with sex. In fact it was something she'd never done. But desperate times called for—

The door opened.

D.J. had already come up with several opening lines. She didn't like to get caught unaware. But all her prep work hadn't prepared her for the impact of seeing Quinn again.

As a rule, a man was a man was a man. A few she liked, a few she wished were dead and the rest rarely made an impact on her life. She considered herself sensible, autonomous and rational. So why did the sight of Quinn standing in the doorway to his hotel room suddenly made her chest go tight?

Nerves, she told herself firmly. She didn't usually allow herself to feel them, but obviously they were bothering her. A few deep breaths and she would be fine. Really.

Quinn stared at her for several seconds, then smiled. As the corners of his mouth turned up, he leaned one forearm against the door frame and shifted his weight to one leg. The other was slightly bent at the knee. He looked relaxed…and predatory. Big, tall, powerful.

His physical resemblance to the Haynes brothers eased some of her tension, but not all of it. He might look like them, but could he be trusted like one of them? Did it matter?

"Afternoon, D.J.," he said. "This is a surprise."

"I'm sure it is."

He studied her, his dark eyes taking in every detail of her appearance. Once again she had the ridiculous urge to make sure no strands of hair had pulled loose from her braid.

She returned the appraisal, checking out his blue short-sleeved shirt tucked into jeans. His feet were bare and his hair tousled. It might be the middle of the afternoon, but he looked as if he'd just gotten out of bed.

He pushed off the door frame and stepped back. The invitation was clear. Come on in.

She stepped into the room, showing a confidence she didn't feel. Familiar statistics filled her mind—the number of women attacked in hotel rooms each year, the number of women date raped in hotel rooms, the number of—

She drew in a deep breath and consciously cleared her mind. Quinn wasn't going to attack her. She'd come here on her own. No one was drunk, no one was going to get hurt. Perspective, she told herself. If nothing else, she could stomp the hell out of him and make her escape. He might have fifty pounds of muscles on her but his bare feet were no match for her heavy boots.

"Have a seat," he said, motioning to a chair by the window.

She took in the plain room, the large bed, a desk with a straight back chair, the low dresser with the television. There weren't any personal effects lying around, with the exception of a hardback mystery propped open on the bed. No pictures, no wallet, no dirty socks.

Instead of taking the seat he offered, she grabbed the chair from the desk and turned it around. She was less than ten feet from the door. When Quinn sat on the edge of the bed, she had an unrestricted escape route to either the door or the window. Not that she planned to need either.

When he was settled, she tried to remember what she'd wanted to say. Somehow she'd forgotten all of her carefully constructed opening lines. So not like her. She would have to improvise.

"I'm impressed by what happened during the war games," she said.

Quinn grinned. "I'm an impressive guy."

She ignored the comment and the smile, not to mention the odd fluttering in her stomach. Had the sub sandwich she'd eaten for lunch not agreed with her?

"I haven't changed my mind," she told him. "I still want you to teach me what you know."

"I haven't change my mind, either. Thanks, but I'm not interested."

"I plan to convince you."

He arched his eyebrows. "How?"

"By any means necessary. I thought we could work out a trade. You give me what I want and I'll give you what you want."

Quinn had been hit on by a lot of women in his time. Some had actually meant it, while a few were just in it for the money. Still, not one of those invitations had surprised him as much as D.J.'s.

Sex for information? Why?

He studied her face, looking for clues. There weren't

any, except for a faint tension that told him she was more nervous than she wanted him to know. He lowered his gaze to her body. She wore a tank top and tight jeans. No bra. She looked good enough to start a war. He couldn't say he wasn't tempted, but he had long since learned that nothing in life was easy. People always did things for a reason. What was hers?

"What's so important that you'd offer yourself in trade?" he asked.

She flinched slightly at the question, then quickly brought herself under control. "I don't choose to look at it that way."

So how *did* she look at it? Her reaction told him she hadn't come up with the deal lightly. From their first encounter, he knew she was fearless, determined and always looking for an edge. Her seating choice made that clear. She hadn't taken the more comfortable chair across the room. That seat would have put her at a disadvantage. She wouldn't have had a clear line to the door and she would have lost precious seconds extricating herself from the soft cushions.

So what would make her want to subjugate herself to him just to learn a few moves?

"My work is important to me," she said. "I've told you that I'm often hired to help on cases where children have been kidnapped. I'm trained to go in with the rescue team, be they Federal agents or hired guns. Sometimes those situations get out of hand and I have to improvise. The more I know, the better I can react, the more kids get saved."

Uh-huh. Do it for the children, he thought, not impressed or convinced. He didn't doubt she was good, but that wasn't why she was here.

"And that's it?" he asked.

She shrugged. "I teach self-defense. My company offers seminars on everything from keeping your children safe to how to survive a mugging. The more I know, the more my students know."

"You're already well trained enough for what you do," he said.

When she started to protest, he cut her off.

"How many black belts do you have?" he asked.

Her full mouth twisted. "Three."

"You can handle guns?"

"Yes, but—"

He cut her off again, this time with a quick shake of his head. He stood and wasn't surprised when she rose as well.

He walked close, then motioned her to step forward. When she reluctantly did so, he circled around her. He studied the muscles in her arms and upper back, the leanness of her hips. He remembered how they'd fought together and what she'd tried on him.

"You've developed your upper body," he said, more to himself than to her. "Women are at a disadvantage there, but you've worked to mitigate that. You're strong, you have stamina, you're well trained. Like I said, you know enough."

"Not enough to beat you," she said.

"I'm unlikely to start kidnapping kids."

"I want the challenge. You should understand that."

He understood a lot of things. For one thing, the lady had secrets. But then, so did he.

"You'll never be strong enough," he told her. "There's always going to be someone faster, smarter, better."

"But what you know could give me an edge."

What he knew could haunt her and make her wish she was dead.

He turned away and crossed to the window. She wasn't asking about his world. She didn't want to know stories. She was only interested in his skills.

He glanced down at his hands. Sure, he could teach her dozens of things. Would they be enough? Would they make her feel safe? That depended on her secrets.

The irony of the situation was that he wanted to tell her yes. Not because he believed any of her reasons for why this was important but because there was something about her that intrigued him. She was a fascinating combination of tough and vulnerable. He long ago learned to focus only on work, to never allow himself to be touched by anything or anyone.

Could it be different with D.J.? She'd made him laugh, made him forget who and what he was. She'd made him remember a world that was normal. She was tough enough that he didn't have to watch himself all the time and vulnerable enough to—

He cut off himself in midthought. Wanting her was allowed. Finding her interesting was stupid but understandable. Anything else was a pipe dream and likely to mess with his brain in a way that would cause him to end up dead on his next assignment. No way would he go there.

Yeah, he wanted to help her. But he couldn't make it easy. She would never respect that.

He turned back to her. She kept her expression neutral, but he could see the effort she put into remaining impassive. She wanted to bully him into agreeing, or offer him another tempting deal.

"You're not in good enough shape," he said. "You'd never be able to keep up with me."

D.J. was nothing if not predictable. She immediately bristled and glared at him. "I can handle anything you can."

"Sure." He deliberately sounded unconvinced.

"I'll prove it to you."

Exactly what he wanted.

He pretended to consider her suggestion long past when he'd already decided, then shrugged. "You get one chance. You blow it and it's over."

"Fine."

"We'll start in the morning. Go for a run, then work out. If you can keep up, we'll talk about me teaching you a few things. You fall behind or start complaining, it's over."

Her gaze narrowed. "I don't complain."

"We'll see."

He returned to the bed and took a seat. D.J. settled into her chair and tried not to look pleased. Most people wouldn't notice the slight tug on the corner of her mouth or the flash of determination in her eyes, but he'd been trained to see past the obvious to the nuances hidden below. She'd already decided she was going to blow him away in the morning. She was determined to be good enough to make him eat his words. He couldn't wait.

But first there was the small matter of payment.

"Not sex," he said.

"What?"

"You won't be paying me with sex."

D.J.'s gaze turned suspicious. "Why not?"

He allowed himself to smile. "That would make it too easy."

"So how do you want to get paid?"

"I haven't decided yet, but when I do, you'll be the first to know."

That evening Quinn drove across town to meet his brother at the local bed and breakfast where Gage was staying. He'd offered to reserve a room for Quinn, as well, but Quinn preferred the anonymity of hotels. B and B's required interaction, something he wasn't always good at.

He'd spent most of the previous day with his brother. The two of them had talked about the discovery of new relations. There weren't just new half brothers to consider. There was also a half sister, spouses and children. Each of the Haynes seemed to believe in large families.

The large, extended Haynes clan was a far cry from the world he and Gage had known back in Possum Landing. While the Reynolds family boasted aunts, uncles and cousins, the actual numbers didn't come close to those of the Haynes.

He parked his rental car and walked up the front stairs of the large, restored Victorian house. Gage was waiting for him inside the front parlor. Travis Haynes was with him.

"Hey, Quinn." Gage shook his hand, then slapped him on the back. "You're still in town. I thought you might have to bug out."

"Not this time." Quinn's work required him to be ready to leave at a moment's notice. More than one visit home had been cut short.

He greeted Travis. "If you're here, then who's running Glenwood?"

Travis laughed. "My youngest brother."

The three men settled into the overstuffed sofas in the parlor.

"Quinn, I have to warn you that my wife is already talking about a big family get-together," Travis said. "We've had quite a few since Gage, Nash and Kevin showed up. I figured Elizabeth had it out of her system. But now that you're here, she's worried you're going to feel left out. So brace yourself. We're talking picnics, bowling nights, barbecues, that sort of thing. Wives, kids, dogs and babies."

Quinn figured his brother must have hinted that he wasn't much for socializing. "I can probably muddle through a barbecue or two."

"Good. I'll do my best to keep the plans simple, but honestly, Elizabeth doesn't listen to me. She's always been independent."

He spoke with the confident affection of a man secure in his relationship. Quinn knew Travis had several kids and ties to the community. Gage would be able to relate to a life like that, but for Quinn it was as foreign as life on Mars. He'd turned his back on normal the day he'd accepted his current assignment. At the time, he'd been warned that he was unlikely to ever be able to go back. The job wouldn't stop him, but what he'd seen, what he'd become, would.

At first Quinn hadn't believed them, but now he knew they were right. He lived in a shadowy world that didn't have room for relationships, caring or commitments. For a long time he hadn't minded, but lately he'd started wondering if there was something else out there. Something beyond staying alive and getting the job done.

"We're all talking about how you got the drop on

D.J.," Travis said with a grin. "Last time I saw her, she was still furious about you cutting your ropes and getting away while she was sleeping."

Quinn shrugged. "She was good."

"Not good enough," Travis said. "I don't know what it is you do, but you're well trained."

Trained didn't begin to describe it.

"Who is she?" he asked. "I know she's into teaching women self-defense and keeping kids safe, but where did she get her education?"

Travis raised his eyebrows. "Interesting. The lady was asking about you, too."

The information pleased Quinn. He liked knowing that D.J. had been thinking about him. Had it been as more than just a potential instructor? He remembered her temper, her competence and the soft pressure of her light kiss.

Trouble, he thought. But the best kind.

"Are you interested in her?" Gage asked. "She's nothing like your usual women."

Quinn laughed. "True enough."

Gage looked at Travis. "My brother tends to seek out beautiful women who have nothing to say."

"Maybe I'm not into conversation."

"I know you're not."

"I like to keep things simple."

"D.J. is a lot of things, but not simple and not easy," Travis warned.

"I already figured that out," Quinn told him.

D.J. was a challenge. In the past he hadn't been able to risk that. He couldn't get involved in anything that would last more than a few days. Ties weren't part of the job. After living on the edge of humanity for months at a time, ties became an impossibility.

Were they possible now? Could he remember what it was like to want a woman for more than sex? This was the first time in years he'd sensed possibilities. D.J. might be the only woman he'd ever met he couldn't scare off with the truth. Was that a good thing for either of them?

"She's been in town about four years," Travis told him. "Before that she was in southern California. If you want to know any more background, you're going to have to ask her yourself."

"Fair enough."

Travis leaned forward. "Quinn, you're family. My brothers, Hannah and I are glad you and Gage found us. We want to get to know you better. Our father wasn't one for giving a damn about his kids, so we've learned to look out for each other."

He hesitated, then shrugged. "But I have to be honest. D.J. isn't like other women. She's tough and determined. A hell of a fighter. But inside—I can't explain it. I'm not going to be an idiot and tell you to back off. But I care about her. We all do."

"I understand."

Quinn did. Torn between newly discovered family, and the loyalty that went with that, and his relationship with D.J., Travis didn't want Quinn to use D.J. and dump her.

Gage shook his head. "Travis, she seems more than capable of taking care of herself."

"She is."

But he didn't sound completely convinced. Quinn got that, too. Despite the attitude and the muscles, there was still something vulnerable about D.J. Maybe it was the weight of the chip on her shoulder. Lugging something that large around was bound to slow her down.

Quinn thought about reassuring Travis, but his half brother didn't know him from a rock. Words were meaningless until there were actions to back them up. In time Travis would see that Quinn had no interest in using anyone. He saw D.J. as unique and appealing.

What on earth would Travis say if he knew D.J. had offered sex in exchange for Quinn teaching her what she wanted to know? He had a bad feeling Travis wouldn't believe him, and might even want to take things outside. Not exactly a good way to start a brotherly bond.

No, that information was better left private. Quinn wasn't going to say anything, and he doubted D.J. would be telling the world what she'd done. It would be their little secret…and it reminded him he still had to come up with what he wanted from her in payment. The possibilities were endless.

Travis headed home about an hour later. Quinn glanced at his watch. "Don't you have a blonde waiting for you upstairs?"

"No. Kari's in San Francisco for a couple of days visiting a friend of hers. We could grab a bottle of scotch and get drunk."

Quinn held up his hands. "Thanks, but I'm not in the mood for a hangover."

Gage laughed. "I'm not, either. I guess we're getting old."

"It was bound to happen."

His brother stretched out his legs in front of him and rested his hands on his stomach. "I talked to Mom today. She and John are working out the final details of the wedding. Are you going to be able to get time off?"

"I don't know. I'll do my best."

"Mom would really like you there."

"I want to come."

Quinn figured in the past ten years he'd missed enough holidays and special occasions for three lifetimes. While his father—make that Ralph Reynolds—had been alive, he hadn't minded staying away. But in the past few years, he'd felt a tug to be home.

He studied Gage. They looked enough alike that no would mistake them for anything but brothers. Older by a year, Gage had been the favorite son. A gifted athlete, smart, popular. For a long time Quinn had been right behind him, inching close to his sports records, sometimes beating them. He'd gotten as good grades in most subjects, better in a few, but it hadn't mattered. Not to the man who raised them. In his eyes, Gage could do no wrong and Quinn could do no right.

"You still miss him?" he asked.

Gage looked at him. "Dad?"

Quinn nodded.

"Sometimes. Yeah, I guess. I can't think of him as anything but my father." He grimaced. "I did at first. When I found out the truth, I figured I'd lost my whole world. I didn't know who I was or where I belonged."

"Five generations of Reynoldses in Possum Landing," Quinn said.

"Right. I wasn't one of them anymore."

Quinn would consider that a good thing, but he knew his brother wouldn't agree.

"What changed your mind?" he asked.

Gage smiled. "Kari. She pretty much slapped me upside the head and told me to get over it. It didn't take me long to see that she was right. Dad might not have gotten Mom pregnant, but he was still my father in every way that matters." His expression darkened. "Not comforting to you, I know."

Quinn lifted a shoulder. "He was who he was."

"There was a reason he hated you."

Quinn looked at him. "I already figured that out."

"What do you mean?"

"You said they couldn't have kids and that Mom got pregnant by Earl Haynes. That was the deal. But something happened, and she went back the following year. I don't know if she went just to talk to him or if she had something else on her mind. Whatever the reason, she came back pregnant. I'm guessing Ralph didn't appreciate that. You were the son he always wanted. I was the living, breathing reminder of his wife's infidelity."

Gage sat up straight and swore. His reaction, not to mention his stricken expression, told Quinn he'd nailed it in one.

Once he knew the logistics of his mother's pregnancy, the rest hadn't been hard to figure out. Funny how years ago he would have sold his soul to understand how the man he'd thought of as his father could love Gage so much and hate him with equal intensity. He remember being ten and crying himself to sleep. He remembered his mother holding him, trying to convince him that his father *didn't* hate him. He'd begged her to tell him why his father acted the way he did and she never had. How could she?

After all this time, he finally understood, only to realize that knowing the truth didn't change anything. It hadn't mattered then and it still didn't matter.

"I'm sorry," Gage said.

"I wasn't your fault. I'm not sure it was anyone's."

The old man was dead. The past was over. Quinn was more than ready to move on.

"You and Kari set a date yet?" he asked.

Gage hesitated, as if not sure he would accept the change in topic, then he grinned. "New Year's Eve. She says it's because it's romantic, but I think she wants to be sure I never forget."

Quinn had seen his brother with the tall, pretty blonde, and he was surprised they were willing to wait so long to tie the knot. "Why the delay?"

"Mom's wedding. If Kari and I had picked an earlier date, Mom would have cut back on her own plans. She and John want to take a long honeymoon in Australia and neither of us wanted them to cancel. Kari and I have our whole lives together. Waiting a few months won't matter."

Gage sounded like a man sure of his place in the world. But then, he'd always been like that. He was the one who fit in. Now he'd found the one woman who could make his world complete.

Quinn was pleased. He still remembered his brother's hang-dog expression when Kari had run off eight years ago. Gage had been planning happily-ever-after with a young woman who had a different idea of her future. Yet somehow they'd managed to find each other again.

"You ever think about what would have happened if Kari hadn't left town the first time you two were together?" he asked.

Gage nodded. "I used to think about it all the time. After she came back to Possum Landing, I realized we'd both been too young. I'm not sure we would have made it. This time I know we'll have a long future together."

"Good for you."

His brother looked at him. "I want to ask if there's anyone in your life."

Quinn laughed. "I don't stick around long enough for that to happen."

"Will you ever?"

Stick around? "I've been giving it some thought," he admitted.

"I'm not going to ask you about your job," Gage told him. "If you want to talk, I'm more than willing to listen."

"I appreciate that."

"If you want to talk about Dad, I'll listen to that, too."

Quinn knew the offer was genuine and he appreciated it. But after all these years there wasn't a whole lot left to say.

Chapter 5

D.J. arrived at the park where they'd agreed to meet five minutes before her appointment with Quinn. She'd walked the three blocks from her office, using the time to try to clear her head and focus. She hadn't been all that successful.

Lack of sleep, she told herself as she stretched her legs. Under other circumstances she would say she was on edge. Not this time, though. There was no reason to be. Quinn was just some guy who knew things she wanted to know. Nothing more.

As she bent over to stretch her hamstrings, she pressed her lips together. Okay, maybe, just maybe Quinn got to her in a way that most men didn't. Maybe there was something more to her reaction than simple admiration for his abilities. She pushed her palms to the grass and felt the pull in the backs of her legs. Maybe she found him attractive.

D.J. wasn't entirely comfortable with *that* concept. While she was willing to acknowledge some men were better looking than others, she didn't usually care one way or the other. Any interest she had in their physical nature was more in the lines of their potential threat value. Of course, it didn't matter if she thought Quinn was handsome, right?

She wrapped her arms around her calves and pressed face into her knees, then straightened. And nearly screamed.

Quinn stood less than ten feet away. Somehow he'd approached with such stealth that she'd never heard him. Her heart jumped into overdrive, and sweat broke out on her back. Proof of her vulnerability made her want to back up fifteen feet, but she forced herself to stand her ground.

"Morning," he said with an easy smile. "Ready to kick butt?"

Faking a confidence she didn't feel, she planted her hands on her hips. "As long as it's yours."

"We'll see. You warmed up?"

She nodded.

"Then let's go."

He headed for the jogging trail. She fell into step beside him.

They'd both dressed in shorts and a T-shirt. The morning had started with a light fog, but it would break up quickly, then the temperature would warm. She wasn't sure what he thought of her attire, but she found his slightly distracting. His gym shorts exposed the muscled firmness of his thighs, while the worn T-shirt pulled at his broad shoulders. Once again he reminded her of a predator.

She told herself that the slight tightening in her stomach was a natural reaction to being around a dangerous animal. It didn't have anything to do with his chiseled body or loose-hipped grace.

D.J. matched Quinn's long-legged stride. As he picked up the pace, she kept her breathing slow and deep. Their feet pounded out a steady rhythm.

"We're going to need to find a gym at the end of the run," he said. "I planned a route that will have us finish up at your office. I figured you'd know the closest place to work out."

How did he know where she worked? Travis or Kyle, she told herself. They knew where her office was located, and they were Quinn's new family.

"I have a weight room in the back of the office," she said as they jogged under several trees. "We can finish up there."

"Great." He shot her a grin and picked up the pace. "Six miles okay by you?"

Six miles? At nearly a run? "Not a problem."

They arrived back at her office in less time than she would have thought possible. D.J. considered herself fit and athletic, but Quinn had continued increasing the speed of their run until she'd been gasping for breath. But she'd kept up and she hadn't complained.

After unlocking the front door, she walked into the empty front office. Her part-time help didn't start until after lunch.

She'd left a six-pack of bottled water on the reception desk. After tossing a bottle to Quinn, she took one for herself and downed about a third of it. She wanted more, but knew she had to wait and let her body cool down a little.

Sweat dripped off her. She'd pulled her hair back into a French braid that morning and the long end was plastered against her T-shirt. She felt hot, flushed and in desperate need of a shower. But there was still part two of the tryout.

"The weight room is back this way," she said, careful to speak slowly so she didn't gasp the words.

By contrast Quinn was breathing evenly, as if the run hadn't winded him at all. He was sweating, but not in any distress. He sipped his water.

She led the way down the short hallway to the big open back room. When she'd rented the office, she'd specifically looked for a location that had space for a workout room. There were mirrors along the rear wall. Weight equipment lined the right side of the room, while thick floor mats defined a sparring area on the left.

D.J. finished her water and tossed the empty plastic bottle into a green bin marked Recycling then faced Quinn.

"Let's do it," she said.

His eyebrows rose. "Why don't you take me through your regular routine?"

She preferred to work out alone, but this wasn't about what she liked. She had to make a point.

She grabbed twenty-pound free weights and started with walking lunges. From there she headed to the machines. Quinn didn't say anything as she went through several exercises, although she could feel him watching her. His silent attention started to get irritating, but it was his physical strength that made her uneasy as he started to work out with her. He could leg press seventy pounds more than she could. After she used a set of weights, he picked them up in one hand as if they weighed nothing. When she went to the barbell for chest presses, adding on enough weight to make her shake through the last set, he stood by her head and spotted her. After she finished, he casually picked up the equipment and slipped it back into place without breathing hard.

Pausing to wipe sweat from her face and neck, she studied him in the mirror. On the run, she'd been too busy trying to keep up to really catalogue the powerful muscles ripping through his body. Now she could see the definition and thickness of his chest and the strength in his legs. He wasn't cut like a gym jockey. Instead his muscles had a purpose. He was the kind of man who knew how to make his living the hard way.

He scared the hell out of her.

D.J. swallowed the fear and kept herself focused through her tricep presses, then leaned back on the bench and exhaled.

"That's it," she said, wondering if she had the strength to stand. Her bones felt as if they'd turned to putty. Her muscles were as resistant as cooked pasta.

"Not bad," he said, holding out his hand.

She glanced from it to his face, then back. She understood the gesture. He was offering to help her to her feet. The logical, rational part of her brain said to save her own strength and accept the assistance. The less-in-control side of her psyche warned her that once he had her hand in his, he could easily flip her and get her in a lock that she could never break.

Deliberately D.J. grabbed his hand and pulled herself up.

Nothing bad happened, unless she counted ending up standing too near to Quinn. They were only inches apart—so close that she could see the various shades of brown and gold that made up the deep color of his irises.

"You work hard," he said. "You're strong and disciplined."

His words pleased her. "Great. So now—"

He cut her off with a smile. "Now let's see what you can do on the mats."

She wanted to groan in protest. She wanted to flop down on the floor and sleep for a week. She wanted a full body massage followed by some time in a sauna. Her legs quivered at the thought of supporting her weight for even one more second.

"Why not?" she said instead and led the way to the sparring mats.

Quinn stood across from her. He was relaxed, his legs slightly bent, his arms at his sides.

"Attack me," he said.

D.J. wished she was big enough so that just sitting on him would squish out all his air. Unfortunately she wasn't, so she was left with no option but to do what he said.

She considered several tactics. Her only chance at something close to a decent showing was to surprise him. She feigned a jab with her right hand, shifted right, made a quarter turn toward him and punched a kick right at his—

Thunk. The floor came sailing up from nowhere as she found herself flat on her back. Now she was not only tired, but sore all over. She scrambled to her feet.

"Again," he said.

She attacked, with no better luck at times two, three

and four. On the last tumble to the ground she was too close to the edge of the mat and her elbow connected with the wood floor. Pain exploded with such intensity that she thought she might throw up.

Quinn knelt down next to her. "You okay?"

Speech was impossible, so she nodded. He reached for her arm and probed her elbow. Even the light brush of his fingers made her grit her teeth to keep from gasping.

"Nothing's broken," he told her.

Great. If "not broken" hurt this much she would hate to encounter actual bone shards. She'd had a broken arm as a kid and didn't remember it hurting so badly. She forced herself back to her feet, expecting him to tell her to attack again. Instead he moved in front of her.

"We'll do this one in slow motion," he said. "You start your moves and I'll show you how I counter them."

He took her through the movement step by step until she saw how he had managed to stop her each time.

"Now that you know what I'll be doing, you can respond differently," he said.

"Okay."

"Ready?"

She nodded and moved in. This time when he spun and grabbed for her, she stepped out of reach. Nanoseconds later his leg shot out and connected, an arm moved and she was flipped and sailing onto the mat again. But instead of stepping back as he had before, he moved forward, bending toward her.

D.J. hadn't expected him to get so close. As the air rushed out of her body, her mind blurred at the edges. Quinn disappeared and in his place she saw her father looming over her. She could smell the liquor. People always said that vodka had no odor, but they were wrong. The scent seeped from her father's skin and made her stomach get all tight and sore.

She could see the man's bloodshot eyes, and the angry twist of his mouth. The baseball bat in his hands rose and then slowly sank toward her. She braced herself for the crunch of hard wood against bone and tried not to imagine the pain that would explode when he broke not just her body but her soul.

She blinked and he was gone. There was only Quinn staring down at her, his brown eyes crinkling slightly as he smiled.

"You got the wind knocked out of you," he said. "Can you breathe?"

Could she? She tried an experimental breath and felt air fill her lungs. She felt both hot and cold, as if she'd just broken a fever. She could taste the terror—it was metallic, just like blood.

"You've got potential," Quinn said, as he held out his hand again.

She wanted to run, to scream, to disappear. But she'd long ago learned that the only way to conquer her fear was to face it head-on. She took the hand he offered and let him pull her to her feet.

When she was standing, she resisted the blinding need to bolt. Instead she crossed to the small refrigerator in the corner and pulled out a bottle of water.

"Want one?" she asked.

"Sure."

She tossed him one, then took hers in her hand. After gulping down half of it, she placed the cool plastic on the back of her neck. Then she walked the length of the exercise room and tried to get calm.

Irrational fear caused a chemical reaction in the body, she reminded herself. The fight-or-flight response was triggered, and her mind was no longer in control.

She was fine. Or if she couldn't believe that, she *would* be fine in just a minute or so.

She walked back and forth three times, then risked glancing at Quinn. He was watching her. While she knew there was no way he could figure out what had just happened, she couldn't help feeling vulnerable and afraid.

Fear. She hated it. Fear was weakness, and the only antidote was to be strong.

She stopped in front of him. "So?"

She made the word a challenge.

"I'll take you on," he said.

She felt both relief and apprehension. She wanted to learn, but why did he have to be the one teaching her?

"Great." She drank the rest of her water. "How long are you going to be in town?"

"A few weeks."

That surprised her. "Don't you have to get back to your assignment, or whatever it is you call it?"

He shrugged. "I'm on leave. Voluntarily. I'll be around long enough to teach you a few new moves."

Leave? Why? But she didn't ask. There was a more important question.

"What do you want?"

He twisted the cap off the water bottle and downed the liquid in several long, slow gulps. A single drop escaped from the corner of his mouth. She watched it trail down his jaw to his throat where it blended in with the sweat glistening there. When he'd finished, he turned his dark gaze on her.

"Let's see," he said. "You've offered me money and sex. What else you got?"

The blunt question stunned her. "You're the one who has to define the price. I decide if I want to pay it."

"Good point." He looked her up and down. "Okay. Here's the deal. I'll give you the lessons you want. In return, you'll keep me company while I'm in town."

She relaxed immediately. "You mean sex."

"I mean dinner."

She blinked. "What?"

"Dinner. It's the meal that comes after lunch. I want you to have dinner with me tonight."

She took a step back. "Hell, no" hovered on her lips, but she sucked in the words.

"One dinner in exchange for teaching me while you're in town?" she asked.

"We're starting with one dinner. There might be more. I might even want you to join me for lunch."

She really wanted to say no. Nothing about this appealed to her. For one thing, it didn't make sense. For another, she hated anything to be open-ended. She wanted the rules defined up front.

"You can pick the restaurant," he said. "This is your town, after all. But nothing cheap. No fast food, no burger places. Somewhere nice. And you have to wear a dress. I want to see cleavage and legs."

She nearly decked him for the last crack. "I don't date."

"This isn't a date. It's business."

He moved close. She braced herself to ward off an attack, but instead he simply tucked a loose strand of hair behind her ear. She found herself wanting to lean into the tender gesture. So, of course, she didn't.

"I've been out of the country a long time," he said. "Is it so hard to believe I want to have dinner with a beautiful woman?"

She nearly spit in surprise. "Somewhat attractive" she would have bought, but beautiful?

"I don't play boy-girl games," she said. "They're all designed to make sure the boys win."

"I'm not a boy."

There was a news flash. She narrowed her gaze.

He grinned. "Dinner in exchange for lessons. What's not to like?"

She wanted to throw his offer back in his face but couldn't say why. What was the big deal about having dinner? Logically it was easier than having sex with him. Except sex was little more than a bodily function. She could disconnect and it wouldn't matter. Dinner… dinner was complicated.

"Fine," she ground out as she clenched her teeth. "Dinner."

"I'll pick you up at seven."

"No, I'll come get you at your hotel."

"Works for me."

She glanced at the wall clock. "You probably have to be somewhere, huh?"

He laughed. "Subtle, D.J., real subtle."

He made no move to leave.

"I have to get to work," she said. "I have a business to run."

"Fair enough. Just answer one question."

She braced herself, knowing she wasn't going to like it. "What?"

"Why did going out to dinner with me throw you more than what you'd offered before?"

She might have known he would see her discomfort. She searched for a good lie, but couldn't find one. Which left the truth.

"Sex is easy because it doesn't matter."

His expression didn't change. "It can."

"Has it ever for you? Even once?"

He hesitated. "Maybe a few times."

"Sure. It's that way for guys. Why does it have to be different for me?"

He studied her face. "I guess it doesn't. See you tonight."

He walked out of the room and headed for the office. When the front door closed behind him, D.J. breathed out a sigh of relief. That was over.

Except it wasn't. Even though Quinn had physically left the office, she couldn't stop thinking about him. When she thought about their dinner that night, she felt an odd combination of apprehension and anticipation.

Crazy, she told herself. She barely knew the man. He didn't matter in any significant way. Nor was he ever going to. Letting a man get close was a recipe for disaster.

With a shiver, she remembered the flashback she'd had of her father. Cold seeped into her, but she ignored it. He was long since dead and she'd never spent a single day mourning the loss. She refused to waste another minute thinking about him now.

D.J. felt like an idiot…probably because she looked like one.

She sat in front of the mirror and fingered the curlers in her hair. Rebecca lightly slapped away her hand.

"You'll mess up my hard work. Now try the darker lipstick."

D.J. dutifully picked up the tube Rebecca gave her and applied the color over the medium pink she'd already put on. When she was finished, she waited for her friend's pronouncement.

Rebecca tilted her head and wrinkled her nose. "Better, but not perfect."

"It's lipstick. It doesn't *have* to be perfect."

Rebecca muttered something under her breath and reached for another tube from the bag she'd dragged over. While she searched for the right shade, D.J. studied her reflection in the mirror and wondered—for the seven hundred and fifty-second time—why she'd agreed to the date.

Not a date, she reminded herself. Payment. Unfortunately the definition clarification didn't make her feel any better about what she was doing. The smoky eye shadow and dark mascara didn't help, either. Makeup, jewelry and high heels were typical female trappings she generally avoided for an assortment of reasons. Tonight she was hampered by all three.

Simple diamond studs—a loan from Rebecca—glittered at her ears. Per Quinn's instructions, she would wear a dress. Per Rebecca's insistence, she would wear high heels. With her hair up in big, fat curlers, she felt like a contestant in a low-end beauty pageant.

"Try this," Rebecca said, handing over another tube.

D.J. cleaned the brush and carefully applied the color. This time her lips looked full and lush. Surprised, she leaned back to judge the effect.

"See?" Rebecca sounded triumphant. "It *can* be perfect. Now dab a little gloss in the center of your bottom lip. It will make you look pouty."

D.J. rolled her eyes. "I'm not the pouty type."

"You are tonight. You're going to knock his socks off."

"I hate to disappoint you but everyone will be keeping his or her clothes on."

Her friend grinned. "So you say now. But that could change. Things happen."

Not likely. Quinn had already turned down sex as payment, and there was no way he would get it any other way. Her interest in the man was strictly business.

"You're too damn cheerful," D.J. muttered as Rebecca began tugging the curlers from her hair.

"I can't help it. You're going on a date with a gorgeous single guy. You're even wearing a dress. I have high hopes that he's the one."

D.J. felt badly for not explaining that the dress had nothing to do with her desire to impress her date, but she wasn't comfortable telling Rebecca about her deal.

"I'm not looking for 'the one,'" she said instead.

"You always say that, but I refuse to believe you. You need the love of a good man."

"Not even on a bet. I'm strong and independent. This two-by-two crap is simply social conditioning."

Rebecca unrolled the last curler, then reached for her brush. "You've missed the point completely," she said as she fluffed curls. "While having someone love you would be nice, the more important lesson is for you to love a man. Cover your eyes."

D.J. didn't want to be having this conversation in the first place, so she dutifully covered her face with her hands and held her breath as her friend doused her in half a can of hair spray. She felt a few picks and tugs, then was completely covered in a second fine, sticky mist.

"Open," Rebecca said.

D.J. peeked through her fingers, then dropped her hands to her lap and groaned. "I look like a porn star."

Rebecca's lips pressed together in disapproval. "We'll get some clothes on you."

D.J. tugged at her robe. "I meant my hair."

"What's wrong with it?"

D.J. gestured with her fingers, but couldn't begin to explain how she felt about the cascading curls tumbling down her back and over her shoulders. Fluffy bangs fell to her eyebrows. She felt all girly and inept.

"You look fabulous," Rebecca said. "Now for the dress."

She disappeared into the closet where D.J. knew the pickings in there were fairly slim. While she would put on a suit for business presentations, that didn't exactly fit the outfit Quinn had described. Most of her dresses were pretty conservative and—

Rebecca reappeared with a box in each hand. The shoe box she'd been expecting, but the other one got her to her feet and glaring.

"No way," she said.

Rebecca dropped the shoe box onto the bed and pulled the top off the other one. "You have to."

"I don't."

Her friend pulled out a black lace dress that D.J. had bought on impulse from a catalog and had never worn.

"It's beautiful."

D.J. shook her head. "It's practically nonexistent."

Rebecca shook out the dress. It was black lace, with

a low neckline and a hem that barely covered her thighs. The long sleeves weren't lined, and the back dipped nearly to her fanny. The only thing that kept the shoulders in place was a small section of elastic and prayer.

"Not on a bet," she growled.

"You want to look good for your date, don't you?"

"It's not a date."

"You have to."

"I don't."

"For me?" Rebecca looked beseeching. "Please?"

The knock came right on time. Quinn crossed to the door and pulled it open. He had a smile prepared, along with a few inconsequential comments. But the sight of D.J. sucked the smart right from his brain.

He opened his mouth, closed it and nearly reached up to rub his eyes. He had to be seeing things. Yeah, he'd demanded a dress, cleavage and leg, but he'd never thought she would listen. He'd expected to be challenged; he hadn't considered he could be blown away.

From the top of her thick, curly hair down to black pumps with a narrow heel sharp enough to be classified as a weapon, she was living, breathing, erotic temptation.

Makeup highlighted her perfect features. The dress—a barely legal scrap of black lace—dipped low enough to expose the space between her breasts and more than hinted at the concealed curves. Long, long, toned legs stretched endlessly, making him wonder what it would be like to have them wrapped around him and pulling him close.

Wanting slammed into him. Wanting and need and more than a little surprise. Damn. She got him good.

But he couldn't risk a compliment. Not when that's what she would be expecting.

"You're on time," he said.

"Whatever. Just so we're all clear. This isn't a date."

"Of course not."

His sports coat hung over the chair by the door. He grabbed it, along with his room key and stepped out into the hall.

"Are we still allowed to have a good time?" he asked as they walked toward the stairs.

"Sure."

He chuckled at the tension in her voice.

When they stepped into the parking lot, she turned toward a black SUV. So the lady wanted them to take her car. Quinn glanced from the high step up to her short dress and couldn't wait to see her climb in.

"Want me to drive?" he asked.

She hesitated, then handed over the keys. "Okay."

He hit the unlock button, then opened her door. She ignored the hand he offered and climbed up into the seat. Her skirt rode up to the top of her thigh, giving him a clear view of female perfection. On cue, heat exploded in his groin, nearly searing him with the intensity.

It was going to be a hell of an evening, he thought as he closed her door and walked around to the driver's side. D.J. taking him prisoner was the best thing to have happened to him in years.

Chapter 6

They were immediately shown to a table in a quiet corner. D.J. was grateful to be out of the line of sight of the front door for a couple of reasons. First, she didn't want to see anyone she knew walking into the restaurant. Second, if she couldn't see the exit, she would be less tempted to bolt for it.

She slid onto the smooth leather of the booth bench and set her small purse next to her. The steak house was dark and elegant, and midweek it was half-empty.

Quinn glanced around. "Nice place," he said. "Come here often?"

D.J. thought about her nonexistent social life. A big night out for her was joining Rebecca and her family at a pizza place. "I've been a couple of times. The food is good."

The waiter appeared and handed them menus, along

with a wine list. As he detailed the specials, Quinn flipped through the wine list.

"May I bring you something to drink?" the waiter asked.

Quinn looked at her. "Do you drink wine?"

"Sure."

He ordered a bottle of cabernet sauvignon.

She'd been thinking more along the lines of half a glass. Not that she would let him know she was concerned, because she wasn't. She would drink as much or as little as she wanted.

When the waiter left, she opened her menu and tried to read the selections. But she was too nervous. Her attention kept snapping back to the man sitting across from her.

He'd been appealing in military garb and tempting in jeans and a shirt. In a suit, he looked like a successful CEO attending a board meeting. The dark fabric of his jacket make his eyes look black. The crisp, white shirt emphasized the firm line of his jaw. His tie looked like silk and was the color of brushed silver.

She shifted slightly and glanced at his face. He was watching her. Thinking what? Did he know he made her nervous? Had he figured out how much she hated that he made her nervous?

Before she could decide, the waiter appeared with the bottle of wine. He opened it expertly, then poured a small amount into Quinn's glass. Quinn rotated the liquid slightly, inhaled the fragrance of the wine, then tasted it.

"Fine," he said with a nod.

After the waiter had poured for both of them and disappeared, Quinn raised his glass toward her. "To what each of us is about to learn," he said.

She wasn't sure she liked the toast, but she couldn't come up with one on her own. So she touched her glass to his and took a sip of the wine.

It was surprisingly smooth, with lots of flavor, but no bitterness. She was more of a white wine kind of gal, but this wasn't bad.

"Very nice," she said, and set her glass on the table.

"I'm glad you approve." He glanced at her menu. "Do you know what you want?"

She closed her menu and went with what was easy. "Salad, steak, baked potato."

He nodded, then motioned for their waiter. After ordering for her—what was it about the phrase "the lady will have" that sounded so elegant—and himself, he waited until the waiter left, then turned his attention back to her.

"You said you didn't grow up in Glenwood," he told her. "What part of the country are you from?"

D.J. couldn't remember mentioning anything about her past, but maybe she had. They'd chatted during their six-mile run. At least, he'd chatted and she'd panted her way through labored conversation. It was possible she'd gasped out a few insignificant facts while her lungs were screaming for more air.

"I grew up in southern California," she said. "Los Angeles."

"Glenwood must have been an adjustment."

"An easy one."

He raised his dark eyebrows. "Small-town America at its best?"

"Something like that."

She reached for her wine. She didn't want to be talking about herself, she wanted to know about him. What did he do for the government? How long had he trained and where? Was the knife concealed in his collar the only weapon she'd missed in her search of him or had there been others?

All important questions, but she wasn't sure how to make the transition from idle chitchat to real talk. She didn't date much and had never been very good at it. Probably because it had never been important to her.

"I told you that I grew up in a small town in Texas," he said. "Sort of like Glenwood. Everyone knew everyone else. You met my brother, Gage."

She nodded. "Nash and Kevin Harmon, too. All Texas boys."

"More than that." Quinn rested his fingertips on the base of his wineglass. "It's all gotten complicated." He looked up at her and smiled. "Family stuff."

She did her best to ignore the smile and the way her stomach muscles clenched in response. "Complicated how?"

"Nash and Kevin grew up without a father. The guy who got their mom pregnant never wanted anything to do with her or them."

D.J. thought about pointing out that might have been the best for all concerned, but didn't want to distract him from what he was telling her.

"It turns out that their father is the same guy who fathered Gage and me. We're all half brothers to the Hayneses."

D.J. stared in surprise. "I'd heard that old Earl Haynes was something of a ladies' man, but I had no idea his exploits crossed state lines. When did you find this all out?"

"Gage was the first to learn the truth a few months ago. Kevin and Nash found out next. They put a call in to me to meet them here."

She wasn't a fan of having a lot of family, but not everyone was like her. "So you've gone from one brother to more than half a dozen, plus a half sister. That's going to mean sending out a lot more Christmas cards."

He grinned. "I hadn't thought of that."

The waiter appeared with their salads. After he left, Quinn continued.

"You know the Haynes brothers, right?"

"I know Travis and Kyle the best. A lot of my work is coordinated through the sheriff's office. Jordan lives here in town, but he's a fire chief, so we don't have as much contact. I've meet Craig a few times, and Hannah's great."

"They're all in law enforcement," Quinn pointed out. "Except Jordan, and he's close enough."

She picked up her fork and smiled. "They wouldn't agree with you. Everyone gives Jordan a hard time about being a firefighter."

"My brother's a sheriff. Kevin is a U.S. Marshal, Nash works for the FBI and I..." His voice trailed off and he shrugged. "It's strange."

"Not necessarily. A lot of time brothers go into the same line of work. Besides, if you're going to join a ready-made family, this is a good one."

"They're big on wives and kids."

"Actually I think just one wife apiece, but plenty of kids." She took a bite of her salad. "Are you married?"

She thought he might tease her or make a joke, but instead he shook his head. "Not my style."

"Work?"

"That's part of it."

What were the other parts?

"So what does D.J. stand for?" he asked.

"Nothing interesting."

"I don't believe that." He ate some of his salad. When he'd chewed and swallowed he said, "Debbi Jo."

She shook her head.

"Darling Jenny?"

She took another sip of her wine.

"Dashing Joyce?"

"I'm ignoring you."

"Darlene Joy?"

She broke off a piece of bread and bit into it.

"It can't be that bad," he said. "Give me a hint."

D.J. knew it *was* that bad. "I don't hint."

He sighed theatrically. "I'll have to ask around town."

"Ask away. No one knows the truth."

"Really?"

She shrugged. "I keep my secrets."

"What other secrets do you have?"

"If I tell you they won't be secrets."

"Good point." He studied her. "You look beautiful tonight."

The quick shift in topic left her mentally stumbling. Worse, the compliment actually made her toes curl in her too-high and very uncomfortable pumps.

"I, ah, thank you."

"You're welcome. I appreciate that you got into the spirit of my request for your clothing this evening."

"I pay my bills in full."

"Is that what this is?"

"We have a deal. I honored my end, I expect you to do the same."

He raised his glass as if toasting her again, but he didn't say anything. She watched him drink. There was something about the way he looked at her. He wasn't just watching, he was learning. Studying. The attention should have made her uncomfortable, and in a way it did. But it also left her very aware of his maleness. She'd done the boy-girl thing when it suited her purpose, but never without a reason. Never just because she wanted to.

"You're a hell of a woman, D.J."

While the quiet praise didn't make her toes curl the same way his telling her she was beautiful had, the sincerity in his voice eased through a tiny crack in her usual solid protective wall. She felt herself relaxing in his presence. Accepting him. Liking him.

The latter should have put her on alert, but she didn't want to think about safety and staying distant. Not for a few more minutes. It felt good to simply *be* in the presence of a man whose company she enjoyed.

"So tell me about growing up in L.A.," he said.

Her good mood shattered like a glass dropped on tile. Wariness returned, along with the need to bolt.

"There's not much to tell. I lost my parents when I was eleven. There wasn't any extended family, so I was put into foster care." She held up a hand before he could say anything. "The people I was with were fine. Genuinely nice. They worried, they gave a whole lot more than the state paid them to give."

All true, she thought. In just under seven years she'd been with two different families, and each experience had been textbook perfect. She'd been well fed, clothed, even fussed over on occasion. What no one had figured out was that by the time she was eleven, the damage had already been done.

"I finished high school and went on to college. I had a partial scholarship, some grants and a couple of part-time jobs," she continued. "I graduated and ended up here."

D.J.'s brief outline of her past was like looking at a black-and-white sketch and being asked to guess the colors that would be used later. There was a broad picture but no detail. Not an accident, Quinn thought. She didn't want anyone to know about her life. He wasn't special in that—he knew she kept the truth from everyone.

He found himself wanting to discover all the nuances that had created the woman sitting across from him. Interesting, as he usually wanted to know only enough to maintain a very temporary relationship. Long weekends were generally the length of his emotional commitment. The less he knew about his women, the less chance he had to find something he didn't like. He leaned toward affairs that touched his body and nothing more.

With D.J. he was willing to risk knowing more. Was it because he sensed she would surprise him only in good ways? He didn't doubt that she would be a hell of a lover—just thinking about all that physical energy and determination channeled into sex was enough to make his breath hitch—but there was another layer that intrigued him. The person underneath the facade. Who was she?

"What about you?" she asked. "How did you get from Possum Landing to Glenwood?"

He pushed away his salad. "After high school, I did the college thing, too."

"Let me guess. You were a football star."

He leaned back in his seat and grinned. "I was very popular."

"I'll bet. A cheerleader on each arm."

"On a good day." He narrowed his gaze. "You would have looked hot in the outfit, but I can't see you being a cheerleader."

"I was too busy winning at my own sports. So did you play in college?"

"Some. After graduation I went into the military. Officer training."

"Of course."

A smile tugged at the corner of her mouth. He responded in kind.

"You're impressed," he said. "It's not the uniform, it's the power."

"Uh-huh. Keep talking."

"Once I had my commission, I was tapped for Special Forces. From there I was moved around."

"Doing things you probably can't talk about."

"Right." He wasn't surprised she understood.

"You said you rescue Americans from places they're not supposed to be. How do they get there?" she asked.

He grimaced. "With enough money, people can persuade a pilot to drop them off just about anywhere. Sometimes what starts out as a safe trip turns bad when there's an unexpected regime change. Things get hot, and my team and I go in. Most of what I do doesn't get covered in the local press."

"Of course not." She played with her salad fork. "It must be nice to be away from all that for a few weeks.

You don't have to spend all your time looking over your shoulder."

He nodded.

In the subtle lighting there were hints of red in her dark-brown hair. The loose curls brushed across her shoulders and down her chest, drawing his gaze to the cleavage exposed by her low-cut dress. Despite the lace covering her arms, he could still see the definition of her muscles.

She wasn't like anyone he'd ever met.

"Don't you want to ask if I've ever killed anyone?" he asked, because it was a question his dates eventually got around to.

He should have known better.

D.J. picked up her wine. "It wouldn't occur to me that you haven't. You wouldn't get your kind of experience any other way. You are who and what you are for a reason."

The quiet acceptance in her voice tempted him. There had been a time when he'd thought normal might be possible. That he could find the one woman who would understand. Who could accept what he did and know why. He'd long ago given up on the hope of finding her. There was no way she existed...or did she? Was D.J. a possibility or was he fantasizing, based on a tough talk and perfect thighs?

"You did promise that you'd be in town for a few weeks," she said as the waiter cleared their plates. "I expect a return on my investment." She plucked at her long sleeve as she spoke.

"I'm on indefinite leave."

She waited until the waiter left before leaning forward. "Why? Were you injured?"

Not in the way she meant. "I want to consider my options. My work requires a level of disconnection I need to be willing to continue. Maybe it's time for a change."

This was the first time he'd verbalized what he'd been thinking about for the past few weeks. He waited to see if the words felt right or not. When there was no definitive answer, he finished his wine and reached for the bottle.

"I was supposed to kill someone and couldn't." He poured himself another glass and topped up hers. "I'd never refused an assignment before. Never had reason. But this time…" Everything had been different, he thought grimly.

Her dark gaze never left his face. There was no recoil, no disgust, no foolish questions.

"You had a good reason for refusing," she said. She wasn't asking, she was announcing.

"Yeah."

There was no way she could know, but he liked her assumption. She was right.

He'd been sent to kill a double agent. It had happened before and he didn't mind killing one of his own if the operative had crossed to the other side. But the double agent had turned out to be someone Quinn had known for years. His former commanding officer and mentor. He'd felt as if he'd been trapped in a bad spy movie, only the players and the bullets were real. When the time came, he couldn't do it. He'd had the man in his sights and he'd been unable to pull the trigger.

Someone else had been sent in to take care of the problem, and he'd been brought out for evaluation. When he'd asked for leave, it had been granted. Until then he hadn't minded what he did for a living, but he

knew he couldn't keep cleaning up messes like that—
not without paying with the price of his soul.

Silence surrounded them. Quinn searched for a casual topic, some distraction. He didn't usually talk about
his work in any detail. He certainly never told the truth.
So why had he with D.J.?

She tilted her head. "So when you sneak into foreign
countries, you probably don't get the exotic stamps on
your passport, huh?"

"No. Under those circumstances we tend to avoid
immigration."

"Bummer. The stamps are the best part of traveling."

Her easy acceptance relaxed him as much as it made
him curious. "Why aren't you involved with someone?"

"I'm not an idiot. I don't need a testosterone-filled
male dominating my life. What's in it for me? More
work? More financial obligations? I don't think so."

Her answer made him chuckle. "What about kids?"

She smiled. "I would like children." She made a show
of glancing around the restaurant, then she leaned close.
"What with you being out of the country and all, you
may not have heard. Marriage isn't required for children anymore."

"You're kidding?"

"Nope. Isn't modern science amazing?"

The waiter arrived with their entrees. As they were
served, Quinn watched D.J. There was a reason she
was so against marriage in general and men in particular. Someone, somewhere had hurt her. Who had done
it and how? He knew there was no way she would tell
him, but that didn't stop him from wanting to know.

When they arrived in the parking lot of his hotel, D.J.
gave Quinn a pointed look. He knew she expected him

to say good-night and climb right out of her car, but he didn't plan to make things that easy for her.

"Why don't you pull into a parking space for a few minutes?" he asked.

She sighed heavily, as if this was a major inconvenience, then steered the SUV into a parking place and turned off the engine.

He was amused by her insistence at driving back from the restaurant. She'd said it would be so much easier to just drop him off. The implication being that she wasn't about to go up to his room. Just as well, he hadn't planned on asking her. Not yet.

"What time do you want to start tomorrow?" he asked.

"Mornings are best for me."

"That's fine. Your place had all the equipment we'll need. You did a good job outfitting it."

"Thanks. It's part of my work. I hold weekly classes there for women."

"Not men?"

She shrugged. "They're welcome to attend, but they never do. Guys don't have the same issues. While there are some unprovoked attacks in the animal world, humans are the only species where the females instinctively fear unfamiliar males. No man walking down a dark street at night thinks anything about seeing a lone woman, but that same woman is aware of every man around her."

He'd never thought of it in those terms. "I guess you're right," he said.

The lights in the parking lot illuminated her face enough for him to see her roll her eyes.

"Gee, thanks."

He held in a grin. "You don't strike me as the type of woman who is often afraid."

"I'm not, but I take care of myself. I know how to fight and when to get out of the way. I don't put myself into dangerous situations."

He leaned toward her. "I'm dangerous."

"You're a known danger, and I'm prepared."

"Not possible."

"Want to bet?"

She was bluffing. They both knew that he could take her easily. Yet she faced him fearlessly.

"Tough as nails," he murmured. "It's one of the things I like best about you."

Her eyes widened and her mouth parted. She looked stunned by his statement. Stunned and maybe a little pleased? He couldn't tell.

Tension flared between them, and he took it as a good sign. Awareness was only one step removed from arousal, and he sure wanted her plenty aroused.

He braced one hand on the dashboard and leaned toward her. But before he'd moved more than a couple of inches, she stiffened. The reaction was subtle, something he felt rather than saw. He stilled instantly, then relaxed back into his seat.

Another man might have been discouraged or figured she wasn't worth the effort. Quinn knew better. There was something to be said for a woman who was— to quote Shakespeare—"not so quickly won."

He rubbed his eyes. Shakespeare? He was quoting Shakespeare? Damn, but he had it bad.

"We're going to have to figure out how many lessons dinner was worth," he said casually.

She turned her head to glare at him. "A dinner I paid for," she snapped.

He stared out the front window and faked a yawn. "I offered. You insisted." He'd backed off because an instinct had told him that was the better strategy. "The dress was great. And those shoes—pure fantasy material."

"Five lessons," she told him.

"Two."

"Three."

"Deal."

He put his right arm on the door by the window and rested his left on the console between their seats. "Okay. You can kiss me now, but I want you to really put some effort into it. It needs to be better than that last kiss."

If D.J. had had a weapon at her disposal, she would have killed him. Right there in her vehicle, knowing it was going to mess up her leather seats. Fury roared through her. She wanted to scream, to kick, to grind his bones into dust, then bake them into bread and leave it out for the crows.

How dare he? *She* could kiss *him?* The nerve. The absolute, unadulterated nerve of his pompous, egotistical, self-centered—

"I can hear you sputtering," Quinn said mildly, his eyes half-closed. He turned toward her. "Afraid?"

He nailed her with that one word. Damn him, he'd probably known it would work. She found it amazingly difficult not to rise to a challenge.

She clamped down on the knee-jerk response and forced herself to smile casually. "Not interested."

"Of course you are. Just come get what you want, D.J. I'm all yours."

She wanted to slap him. Worse, she wanted to do what he said and kiss him. She *hated* that he was right— that she *was* interested. Why did he get to her? She didn't want to be interested. Not in him. She hated that her stomach got all tight and her toes curled and, yes, that more than once during dinner she'd thought about them kissing and, well, maybe doing more.

It was crazy. She knew the danger of getting involved. Of caring and being vulnerable. She simply didn't let it happen. Not ever.

There was only one solution, she told herself. She had to bring Quinn to his knees and not get involved herself. That would teach him to mess with her.

She drew in a deep breath, then slid closer. The console was between them, so she had to lean over to reach his mouth. She braced herself for the embrace that was sure to follow. His arms would close around her and she would want to bolt. But he didn't try to hold her at all. Instead his hands stayed where they were and she was free to stretch until her mouth touched his.

The second they kissed she was assaulted on several levels. The heat of him. The firm softness of his lips. The scent of his body and how the male fragrance teased at her. Awareness melted through her, making her muscles relax and her thighs clench. Wanting, she thought, both aroused and dismayed. She wanted him.

Fear battled with the need to prove herself, and his challenge won. She brushed her lips against his, discovering the shape, the edges, before tilting her head slightly and parting her mouth.

He accepted her invitation with a quick stroke of his tongue against her bottom lip. Tiny jolts of need zapped through her body. She had to shift her weight so she could get closer, all the while ignoring the sudden sensitivity of her breasts.

When his tongue slipped inside her mouth, she touched it with her own. The heat surprised her, as did the sweet taste and growing need. She was melting. Disappearing into the passion. Against her will, one of her hands crept up to settle on his chest. She could feel the warmth of him, even through his suit jacket. She wanted him to take it off, that and his shirt. She wanted to feel bare skin. To feel *him*.

Even as her body surrendered, her mind went on alert. She told herself this was not a good idea. That men were inherently dangerous, and none more so than Quinn. The hunger had to be controlled. Sex was a weapon, not something she could risk enjoying. Not ever.

Her throat felt tight. She swallowed against sudden dryness. Funny that her throat was so dry when other parts of her were so very wet.

One of Quinn's hands settled lightly on her back. She braced herself against the need to escape, only it never came. She didn't want to run away; she wasn't afraid. She was hungry. Starving. She wanted him to touch her more. Everywhere. She wanted to be naked, with him inside of her. She wanted his hands on her body. She wanted to hear the screams of her own surrender.

The image of them making love filled her brain. It was so real, so vivid, that she half expected to feel the thrust of his penetration. It was so immediate that fear swamped her. She straightened in her seat and tried to keep him from seeing that she was shaking.

"It's late," she said abruptly. She stared straight

ahead, not wanting to look at his face and know what
he was thinking.

There were several heartbeats of silence. "I'll see
you about nine in the morning," he said.

She was afraid if she spoke anymore her voice would
crack, so she only nodded. He opened the car door and
climbed out.

After changing into sweats, D.J. paced the length
of her cottage house. Usually the small rooms were a
sanctuary, but tonight the space was cramped and confining. She felt restless and knew the cause.

Quinn.

Hunger burned in her. Hunger and wanting and need
and all those dark emotions she avoided. Now she knew
why. They kept her body from being a tool. They made
her edgy, vulnerable.

Why had she kissed him? She shook her head. Silly
question. She'd kissed him because she'd wanted to,
and now she paid the price. He'd aroused her, but more
than that, he'd touched something inside. He made her
weak, and she knew what that meant. Weakness meant
danger was close. Very close. The strong crushed the
weak. Broke them into pieces and left them for dead.

Chapter 7

Quinn stepped into the small diner at seven the next morning. Travis had left a message at his hotel, inviting Quinn to join him for breakfast.

He saw the other man at a booth by the front window and nodded at the hostess as he made his way back.

"Morning," he said as he approached.

Travis set down the paper he'd been reading and poured coffee from a carafe left on the table. "How's it going? I wasn't sure you'd want to get up this early."

Quinn shrugged. "I don't sleep much."

A job hazard, he thought. Years of not being able to relax meant that sleep was hard to come by. Last night he'd added sexual frustration to his list of reasons he couldn't doze off. Kissing D.J. had left him hard and more than ready to have his way with her. Talk about a hell of a kiss. Still, it had been worth every sleepless toss and turn.

Travis glanced at his watch. "My brothers and Hannah have an open invitation to join me, but they know if they're not here by five after seven, I go ahead and order without them. I guess it's just you and me this morning."

Quinn drank some of the black, steamy coffee and leaned back in the booth. "Not a problem. How's the sheriff business?"

"We're having a quiet summer, which is good. In another month the high school kids will start to get restless. They'll get involved in petty stuff." His dark gaze settled on Quinn. "Nothing like what you're used to."

Quinn shrugged. He knew that Gage would have mentioned what he did, but only in the most general terms. "Small towns have their advantages. You don't have to watch your back so much."

"Good point." Travis smiled. "So how was dinner?"

Quinn wasn't surprised that news traveled fast, although he doubted D.J. would be amused to know they'd been the subject of gossip.

"Good. The company was better."

"I was surprised to hear you and D.J. were going out."

"Because she doesn't date much?"

Travis hesitated. "She's a private person."

Nice save, Quinn thought. He appreciated that Travis was trying to protect someone he cared about, and he liked that D.J. wasn't as alone as she pretended.

"She's a complex woman," Quinn said.

"Aren't they all?"

"I don't claim to understand them," Quinn admitted. D.J. less than most. There was something in her past that had her on the run. Not physically, but emotionally. While she'd easily offered him sex in exchange for him teaching her what he knew, last night she'd completely panicked in the middle of a kiss. He had enough ego to want to believe she'd been blown away by his great technique, but he had to admit there was more on the line than that. Something had scared her, and he wanted to know what.

"What's going on between the two of you?" Travis asked bluntly.

"She's hired me to teach her a few moves."

"I have an idea about what you do, more from what your brother didn't say than what he did," Travis told him. "You beat D.J. at the games, which no one has done before, so I understand why she would want to learn from you. But that doesn't explain dinner."

Quinn wasn't sure he was willing to admit that D.J. having dinner with him had been his payment for three lessons.

"She's a beautiful woman," Quinn said by way of stalling.

"Most guys can't get past how tough she is to notice."

"*I* noticed."

Travis smiled. "I want to ask what you plan to do about it and I don't have the right."

"Don't sweat it. I like knowing D.J. has someone looking out for her."

"Yeah? Don't tell her about it. She'll bite my head off."

"After she breaks your legs," Quinn agreed with a grin.

"Am I too late?"

Quinn turned toward the speaker, a tall man with long, dark hair and an earring. Travis moved over to make room.

"Austin. You're up early."

The other man nodded and slid into the booth. When he was settled, he stretched his hand across the table.

"Austin Lucas."

"Quinn Reynolds."

They shook hands.

Quinn took in the too-long hair, the cool, gray eyes and the sharp, intelligent gaze. He recognized the signs of another loner.

"Austin is an honorary Haynes," Travis said, handing his friend his menu. "We've been hanging out since we were kids."

"I've met your brother, Gage," Austin said. "He's a good man."

"I agree."

The waitress appeared then and took their orders. She replaced the empty carafe with a full one, brought another mug for Austin, then left them alone.

"We were talking about D.J.," Travis said. "Quinn had dinner with her last night."

"I'm surprised," Austin said. "Normally she likes to chew men up and spit them out before breakfast."

His knowledge implied a level of intimacy that made Quinn uneasy. He tried to define the tightness he felt inside. Annoyance? Jealousy?

He studied the man across from him, and Austin met his gaze. Apparently Austin read the concern there because he said, "D.J. is good friends with my wife. They couldn't be more different, but Rebecca says that's what makes the relationship interesting."

"D.J.'s an interesting woman," Quinn said.

Austin glanced at Travis. "Should we be worried?"

"Not about me. I'm one of the good guys," Quinn said.

"Are you?" Austin sounded surprised.

Quinn supposed it was a fair question. There were almost no circumstances under which he would describe himself that way. Except for this one. He had agreed to give D.J. what she wanted, and he would. In the process he was unlikely to damage her heart.

Travis leaned forward. "Quinn, you're family now, and we all look out for each other. The thing is, we look out for D.J., too. I guess we're going to have to trust you to respect that. Fair enough?"

"Sure."

Quinn agreed easily, but he had a bad feeling that life had just taken a turn for the complicated.

By morning D.J. had herself under control. She'd put the kiss and her reaction to it in perspective and decided she would forget it ever happened. Yes, she'd reacted to the man, but so what? Her life had very specific priorities, and being the best was the primary one. Quinn had information she wanted and she was going to get it. End of story.

As for payment for future lessons, they would have to negotiate that when the time came. She was opposed to any more dates. They were—

The front door to her office opened, and the man in question strolled in. Whatever she'd been thinking flew from her mind, like a flock of sparrows frightened by a stalking cat.

But the mental hiccup wasn't nearly as annoying as

her visceral reaction to his large, male presence. The second he walked in, her mouth went dry, her palms went wet and her thighs caught fire. It was damned annoying.

"Morning," he said cheerfully, as he shut the door behind him. "You know what they say—'When the student is ready, the teacher will appear.' Here I am. You'd better be ready."

She tried to smile at his humor, but she was too caught up in how tall and broad he looked. The shorts he wore emphasized his long, powerful legs. His T-shirt stretched over muscles that could probably bench-press the weight of half a cheerleading squad.

"Did you sleep well?" he asked.

"Of course," she said, lying through her teeth.

He looked calm and rested, as if he hadn't been bothered by their kiss. Fine. If he could play that game, so could she. Better than him in fact.

He crossed to stand next to her, then put his hand on her shoulder. "Let's go."

"Fine by me."

As she turned toward the back, she casually shrugged off his touch and raced into the workout room. She hated the heat that lingered on her skin and the heaviness she felt low in her belly. The irony of the situation was that she was far more worried about her sexual reaction to him than by his potential to physically hurt her. Most women, if they knew the truth about what he did, would have been terrified to simply be in the same room with him. D.J. could trust his professionalism while they worked out. It was his guyness and sensual appeal that made her sweat.

Once in the back, they went through a series of

warm-up exercises and stretches. Like Quinn, D.J. wore shorts and a T-shirt. She'd pulled her hair back in a French braid. She wanted to be free to move, but she didn't look forward to a lot of skin-on-skin contact. Telling herself she wouldn't react was one thing. Remembering what had happened the previous night and knowing the potential for sexual disaster was another.

Before they walked to the mats, they both tugged off their shoes and socks.

"We'll take this slow," Quinn said as he moved into the center of the mat. "You remember what we did last time?"

She nodded. They'd been working on a frontal assault.

"I showed you how to counteract it," he said.

"You showed me, but it didn't work."

He grinned. "I'm really good."

"Quit bragging. This session isn't about you."

"Fair enough. So let's go."

He faced her and waited for the attack. She moved in and mentally braced herself for his response. Seconds later she landed flat on her back.

"I remember this part," she grumbled as she scrambled to her feet.

"We'll take it slow," he told her. "Watch me."

Forty minutes later she was making progress. She could count on a draw about 20 percent of the time and victory about 30 percent of the time. Which meant the other 50 percent of the attacks could leave her dead.

"This is why you get the big bucks," she said as she once again sailed through the air and landed on the mats, staring at the ceiling.

"You know it."

He stuck out his hand to pull her to her feet. The movement was familiar enough that she barely hesitated before taking the offered help. When she was standing, she wiped the sweat from her forehead. Quinn, of course, still looked morning-shower fresh.

"I'm going to come at you from behind," he said, moving in close. "There are several traditional attack positions."

His body pressed against hers and his arm came around her throat. Her attention split neatly down the middle. One half reveled in his heat and the large hand resting on her waist. Even as her bones began to turn to liquid, the rest of her fought against a powerful fight-or-flight response.

"You can easily get away from this hold," Quinn said. "Keep your chin down and go for leverage. A more controlled and deadly attack will put pressure here."

He shifted until his hand cupped her throat. Instantly her fear escalated until she desperately wanted to break free and run. The second he pressed in with his thumb, her stomach rolled and adrenaline flooded her system.

"The difference between stopping blood to the brain long enough to knock someone out or kill them is all a matter of degree," he said, sounding amazingly conversational.

She drew back her arm to elbow him in the midsection. From there she would grab his arm and pull him over her—

He released her and stepped away. "Now you try it on me."

The panic faded as quickly as it had appeared. There was only the chemical aftermath that left her feeling shaky and slightly light-headed.

Ignoring the sensations, she stepped behind him and raised herself on tiptoe so she could wrap an arm around his throat.

"We have a height problem," she muttered as her breasts flattened against his back. "This would be easier if you were shorter."

"Hey, nothing worth having is easy."

"Thanks for the bumper-sticker-level psychobabble."

She tried to squeeze his neck with her hand, but she couldn't get a good grip. The warmth of his skin and the scent of his body didn't help her concentration, nor did the fact that her hands were small. She felt inconsequential and feminine. Neither reality thrilled her.

"Can't I just shoot you?" she asked.

"It would shorten our lesson time," he said, and bent his knees. "Is this better?"

She was able to grip more firmly. "It helps."

"Don't get used to it. Once you've mastered the technique, you'll have to deal with me at my full height. You can't always be sure your assailants will be shorter than you."

She was about to agree with his point when she heard a familiar voice calling out her name. A quick glance at the clock showed her it was nearly ten-thirty. Time had flown.

"Back here," she called, and stepped away from Quinn. "I guess we'll take our break now."

He turned toward the doorway and raised his eyebrows when Rebecca entered. D.J. followed his gaze and nearly groaned.

Just perfect, she thought, heading for the small refrigerator and pulling out a bottle of water. She was hot, sweaty and badly dressed. Rebecca was feminine perfection in a white summer dress, perfect makeup and tasteful pearl earrings. Tiny flat sandals exposed the pink polish on her toes. D.J. had never been jealous of her friend before and refused to start now. What did she care if Quinn thought Rebecca was the perfect woman? Not only *wasn't* she interested in him, her friend was happily married and hadn't looked at another man since meeting Austin nearly ten years ago.

So why did D.J. suddenly feel like a "before" picture in a magazine makeover?

"You have company," Rebecca said. She had a carafe in one hand and a box of doughnuts in the other. "Am I interrupting?"

"Not at all." D.J. jerked her head at Quinn without actually looking at him. She didn't want to see him drooling. "Rebecca, this is Quinn. He's teaching me to be a better fighter."

"That statement begs a thousand questions," Rebecca said as she set the doughnuts on a table and put the coffee next to them. Then she crossed to the mats and held out her hand. "Nice to meet you, Quinn."

"Likewise."

Despite her best intention, D.J. glanced at the two of them. They seemed to be caught up in a staring contest…and still clasping hands, she thought glumly. Not that she cared. Men like him didn't interest her. No men interested her. She didn't do the romantic, boy-girl thing. Remember?

"I met your husband this morning when I joined Travis Haynes for breakfast."

Rebecca pulled her hand free and sighed. "Isn't he wonderful?"

D.J. took comfort in the fact that if Quinn had been

blown away by Rebecca's feminine charms, he'd just received a dose of reality. She might be pretty enough to have her portrait in the National Gallery, but she was a one-man woman. And Austin was her man.

"'Wonderful' isn't how guys describe each other," Quinn told her.

Rebecca smiled. "Good point. Would you be willing to describe D.J. that way?"

He turned his gaze on her. D.J. drank from her water bottle and tried not to care. "Maybe."

"I think that's secretly a yes." Rebecca linked arms with him. "I stop by in the morning a couple of times a week. I bring fattening food and coffee. D.J. and I do girl talk and get a sugar high. Harmless fun, but we like it."

They walked out of the workout room, leaving D.J. to grab the doughnuts and coffee and trail after them.

"What do you do?" Quinn asked.

"Mostly I'm a wife and mother, but I work part-time at the Glenwood Orphanage. I used to run it, but after I married Austin and started having babies, there wasn't time."

"You're very traditional."

"I suppose so."

When D.J. reached her office, Rebecca and Quinn had already pulled up chairs around her desk. She sank into her seat and slapped the doughnut box in front of them, not sure why she was irritated. So Rebecca was talking to Quinn. What did that matter? Wasn't it easier than D.J. having to talk to him?

Rebecca winked at her, then turned her attention back to Quinn. "Don't let the modest offices fool you. Our D.J. is very successful. She flies all over the country, sometimes all over the world, rescuing children. She gives lectures and demonstrations."

D.J. grabbed a doughnut. "I'm still in the room you know."

Rebecca smiled. "Of course you're here, but I doubt you've been talking about all your accomplishments." She glanced back at Quinn. "D.J. can be very modest."

D.J. bit into the doughnut and rolled her eyes.

Quinn reached into the box. "She mentioned that she helps when kids are abducted."

"Yes. There's a lot of danger, but she goes right in. She looks tough, but the kids are never scared of her. I guess they sense she only wants to help."

This was as painful as dental surgery, D.J. thought. She didn't like being talked about.

"Let's change the subject," she said brightly. "Let's talk about Quinn. Guys like to be the center of attention."

Rebecca looked surprised. "I didn't know you knew that." She turned to Quinn. "Where are you from?"

"A small town in Texas."

"I know you have a brother. Well, I suppose now you have several. What about your mom? Are you close to her?"

D.J. frowned. Talk about a strange question. Rebecca turned to her. "Don't give me that look. How a man treats his mother can be an indication of character. Well, unless she's a horrible woman, like Austin's mother was."

Quinn grinned. "My mom is terrific and I get along with her extremely well."

D.J. wanted to crawl under the table. Great. So Rebecca wasn't even going to be subtle about the matchmaking.

"Are you seeing anyone?" her friend asked.

The second the question was out, D.J. wanted to smack her head into the desk. Was Quinn seeing anyone? Had she even thought to ask that herself? The man could be married, and she'd been offering him sex.

She held her breath until he said he wasn't involved at this time.

"Have you ever been married?" Rebecca asked.

Quinn glanced at D.J. "You could rescue me here."

"Why?"

He laughed. "No," he told Rebecca. "No ex-wives."

"What about significant relationships?"

"My work keeps me on the move."

"Uh-huh." Rebecca delicately bit into a doughnut, chewed and swallowed. "That's a better excuse than some people have." She stared intently at D.J., then smiled at Quinn. "D.J. doesn't get out much, which you may have noticed. Not that she doesn't need to."

D.J. glared at her. "I'm still right here in the room."

"We all know that. I'm just stating the obvious."

"So what exactly is her dating history?" Quinn asked.

"It's very sad," Rebecca told him. "It's not that men aren't interested. A lot of them are. Some of the problem is her surly attitude."

D.J. had just bitten into a doughnut and found herself choking. Rebecca pounded her on the back until she waved the other woman off.

"My surly attitude?" she asked, outraged.

Rebecca merely smiled. "Am I wrong? Do you in any way encourage men to be a part of your life? Don't you make a habit of scaring off anyone even faintly interested?"

"Okay, then," D.J. said as she stood. "You probably need to get going."

Quinn leaned back in his chair and grinned. "Don't make her rush off on my account."

"Of course not," D.J. said, trying to ignore him and her rising embarrassment. "You would love to sit here and listen to wild stories about my past."

"It's more interesting than cable TV."

Rebecca rose. "I'm trying to help," she said as she collected her purse. "Quinn seems very nice."

D.J. wanted to die. She couldn't believe that her friend—make that her *ex*-friend—was acting this way.

"I'm not going to be speaking to you later," D.J. told her.

Rebecca patted her arm. "Of course you are." She walked to the front door, then turned back. "It was nice to meet you, Quinn. Don't let her scare you off."

"Likewise," Quinn said. "Your husband's a lucky man."

Rebecca sighed. "He knows. Oh! There's going to be a big dinner at my house tomorrow night. Just another Haynes get-together for the new members of the family to commingle with the rest. I hope you'll be there."

"I wouldn't miss it."

Rebecca turned her attention to D.J. "I'm really going to need your help setting up things."

"Not even on a bet."

"D.J., you have to."

Rebecca wasn't being subtle, but D.J. figured arguing

in front of Quinn would only increase his entertainment factor. She gritted her teeth and nodded.

"Fine. I'll be there."

"Good."

Rebecca wiggled her fingers at them both and ducked out of the room. D.J. stared after her and thought briefly about throwing a chair across the room, but wasn't sure it would do anything for her frustration level. At least she had plenty of energy to continue sparring with Quinn.

"Let's get back to work," she told him as she rose and headed for the back of the office.

He didn't budge. "Not so fast. I have a question."

D.J. could only imagine. "How did Rebecca and I get to be friends?"

"Nope. What do the initials stand for?"

She blinked at him. He wanted to know her real name? "Not even on a bet."

"I'm not going to help you until you tell me."

She narrowed her gaze. "I've already paid for my lessons. You owe me."

"Maybe, but I'm not moving until you cough up the truth."

She stared at him. He looked comfortable and more than prepared to sit there well into the afternoon. She considered her options: there weren't any. She couldn't force him to move and she couldn't continue the lessons without him.

She sucked in a breath and braced herself for the laughter. "Daisy Jane."

Quinn's mouth twitched, but that was his only reaction. "It suits you," he said.

She took a step toward him. "Don't make me kill you."

His twitch turned into a grin. "You couldn't even bruise me, little girl. Let's go."

Chapter 8

Quinn arrived at the party shortly after seven. Judging by the number of cars in the driveway, there was a houseful of guests. After parking his rental car, he sat in the driver's seat for a few seconds and told himself this was just a family event. No danger, no threats.

The reminder wasn't to make himself feel better, but to keep himself from going into work mode. Crowds usually put him on alert. He'd had to rescue more than one hostage from an overflowing temporary prison or a bustling outdoor marketplace. He knew how to move without being seen, how to slip in and out with no one realizing he'd ever been there at all. Not exactly qualities that would make him a favorite guest.

He climbed out of the car and pocketed the keys, then headed for the front door. It opened before he could knock.

Rebecca Lucas stood in the foyer and smiled at him. "Right on time."

He jerked his head toward the crowd behind her. "Was everyone else early?"

She laughed. "The women and kids started arriving around four. The husbands are just starting to follow. As for this being 'everyone else,' you haven't seen all your extended family in one place yet, have you?"

He shook his head.

She smiled. "Then brace yourself."

She took his arm and drew him inside her large, welcoming home. He had a brief impression of warm colors, oversize furniture and lots of people.

"Most of the kids are out back playing," Rebecca said. "But a few of them are running around. I won't even try to match them with parents just now. You'll be doing well if you can remember who is married to whom."

She paused by three women and introduced them as Elizabeth, Travis's wife, Jill, Craig's wife and Holly, Jordan's wife.

Quinn nodded and shook hands. He had a good memory for faces and names, but keeping this group straight was going to be a challenge.

"Hannah's around here somewhere," Rebecca told him. "She's an actual Haynes. Her mother is over there. Louise knew Earl back when she was in high school. There's still Sandy, who isn't here yet. You know all the Texas clan, as we're calling them. Oh, there's Gage."

Quinn turned and saw his brother walking toward him. Gage smiled at Rebecca. "Quinn's getting that trapped look, so I'm going to rescue him before he bolts."

Rebecca nodded. "We are overwhelming all at once. I had the advantage of meeting the brothers individually. When I married Austin, only Travis had a wife. So I've been able to get to know everyone slowly. You're being thrown into the deep end. Let me know if you need a life preserver."

"Will do."

She patted his arm and walked off.

Gage led him to the kitchen where a cooler filled with beer and sodas sat on the counter.

"How you doing?" his brother asked.

"Fine."

"Too much family?"

Quinn considered the question. He'd never been much of a joiner, and he rarely hung out with friends. But that was more about circumstance than temperament.

"I'm okay as long as there's not a quiz on names."

Gage chuckled. "We've all been through that one. You'll figure it out."

While Gage pulled out two beers and opened them, Quinn glanced around at the kitchen and family room. Several kids gathered around the coffee table and played a board game. Nash and Kevin sat on the sofa. Stephanie stood next to Nash, her hand on his shoulder, his arm around her waist.

He turned in the opposite direction, back the way he'd come. There were the wives he'd met, a few kids and…

Damn, he thought silently and shook his head. He wasn't just checking out the surroundings; he was looking for D.J.

She was prickly, difficult and spent most of their

time together wanting to bash his head in. So why was he so hot to see her again? He accepted the beer his brother offered, and grinned. Because she was never boring.

He spotted movement by the back door and glanced toward it. D.J. stepped into the house. She wore a short-sleeved shirt and jeans. Instead of her usual boots, she had on open-toed sandals. Her hair was loose, her expression happy. She had a little girl by the hand and bent down to hear what she said. After listening intently, D.J. nodded, then pointed toward the front of the house. The little girl—tiny, with pigtails and a bright-pink shorts set—released D.J. and ran in the direction she'd pointed. D.J. straightened.

He knew the exact second she caught sight of him. Not only did their gazes lock, but the temperature in the room climbed about forty degrees.

Gage handed him a beer. "Isn't that the woman from the war games?" he asked when he saw her.

"Yeah. D.J."

"Short for?"

Quinn shrugged. No way was he going tell the world her secret. Calling her Daisy Jane would be something he did in private.

Kari walked into the kitchen, and Quinn greeted his brother's fiancée.

"How was San Francisco?" he asked.

Kari leaned against Gage and smiled. "Good. How are you, Quinn? I haven't seen you in forever."

"I'm well. Congratulations on your engagement." He waved his beer bottle toward his brother. "You know Gage is getting the good end of the deal, don't you?"

Tall and pretty, with big blue eyes and an easy smile,

Kari had always been a small-town beauty. Gage had been crazy about her from the second they'd met. But once she'd left Possum Landing, Quinn had figured they were through for good. Funny how they'd finally hooked up again.

Kari rested her head on Gage's shoulder. "I think we're both getting a good deal."

"All that and a diplomat," Quinn said. "How'd you get so lucky?"

Gage shrugged. "The results of living right."

"Dumb luck if you ask me."

Kari eyed him. "You could find someone, Quinn."

"Not likely," he told her, then took a long drink of his beer.

"My brother's lifestyle doesn't allow for anything longer than a fifteen-minute relationship," Gage said.

"Lifestyles change."

Kari had a point. Quinn excused himself and turned. D.J. wasn't by the back door any longer, but he knew she hadn't left the house. He headed for the living room and found her talking with Rebecca.

"Ladies," he said as he approached.

Rebecca winked at D.J. "It's your young man."

D.J. groaned. "He's not my anything."

"He's something, because I can feel the heat between you two from here."

"What you're feeling is a premature hot flash."

Rebecca laughed. "Not even close." She looked at Quinn. "Maybe you should consider getting her drunk."

D.J.'s eyes widened. "Rebecca, you can't be serious. That's a horrible thing to say."

"Quinn isn't going to hurt you, and you need to lighten up. And I need to take care of my other guests."

She smiled at them both, then sauntered away. D.J. narrowed her eyes and watched her go.

"I can't believe she would sell me out like that. Statistically women who get drunk while—"

"Shut up, Daisy Jane."

Her mouth dropped open. "What did you say?"

"You heard me. Whatever the statistics may be, they don't apply to this situation and you know it. Quit acting like I'm some college kid out to take whatever he can regardless of the consequences."

Several emotions flashed across her face. If they had been alone, he was pretty sure she would have exploded into some kind of fit, but the presence of the extended Haynes family would keep her quiet.

"Don't call me that name," she whispered through gritted teeth.

"Why not?"

"I hate it."

"It's charming."

She looked mad enough to spit. Instead she crossed her arms and contented herself with glaring. "I can't believe I'm stuck here," she grumbled. "Rebecca lied about needing help. When I arrived, there wasn't one thing for me to do, so this was all a ploy."

"Sure. She's trying to get us together."

"Doesn't that bother you?"

"Nope. It shouldn't bother you, either. Rebecca cares about you."

D.J. grunted in response. "She needs a hobby."

"I think you're it."

Three kids about ten or eleven burst into the house and ran toward the kitchen. D.J. stepped out of the way.

"There's a pool table in back," she said. "Want to see if it's available?"

"Sure."

As she turned to lead the way, he put his hand on the small of her back. She froze and looked at him.

"What do you think you're doing?"

"Being polite," he said.

She'd gotten all stiff. He could feel her muscles practically locking in place. Despite her obvious displeasure, tension crackled between them.

"I can get from point A to point B without assistance," she said and pushed his hand away.

"Why are you so afraid?" he asked, his voice low.

"I'm not. Just because I don't like to be mauled, doesn't mean there's anything wrong with me."

"A good story but I'm not buying."

"Fine. Because I wasn't selling."

They wove through the crowd. Quinn couldn't keep from grinning. D.J. sure as hell wouldn't make it easy, but when he finally won her, it was going to be worth all the effort. He had a feeling he'd never met anyone like her before and was unlikely to do so in the future.

He supposed there were men who would see D.J. as a woman to be tamed, but not him. He liked her feisty and difficult. He wanted her strong enough to stand up for herself and comfortable telling him to go to hell if that was where she thought he should be.

The game room was huge, with a pool table in the center, and three full-size video games set up along the far wall. A big fireplace stood in a corner. They had the space to themselves.

D.J. pulled the cover off the table and folded it. Quinn pulled balls out of pockets and set them on the table.

"I haven't played in a while," he said. "I'd like to take some practice shots."

"No problem." She leaned against the table and smiled. "What are we playing for?"

"Is everything a competition with you?"

"Pretty much."

"What if two people happen to have a mutual goal?" he asked.

She shrugged. "How often does that happen in life?"

"What about at work?"

"Okay. There, but almost nowhere else."

"I can think of a couple of places."

She sighed heavily. "Is everything about sex with you?"

He grinned. "Pretty much."

The corner of her mouth twitched and he knew she'd recognized her own words tossed back at her.

"We could play for money," she said.

"Not interesting enough. What about articles of clothing?"

D.J. shook her head. "There are children in the house."

"I'll take my winnings on account. Time and place for collection to be detailed later."

"What makes you so sure you'll win?"

He waited until she was looking at him before answering. "I always win."

"So do I."

"Then that will make the game more challenging for both of us."

He thought she might protest or call him names. Instead she shrugged. He wondered if that was because she was so confident of her abilities or because she didn't mind losing.

He wanted it to be the latter. He wanted to know that she felt the tension between them as much as he did. He wanted her to want him. Something—some secret from her past—made her wary. He could accept that. He was willing to wait until she trusted him, and he would do what was necessary to earn that trust.

He took a few practice shots. His work might be intense, but there were also long hours of waiting. He'd spent a large percentage of them playing pool with his men. The rhythm of the game came back to him, and when they tossed for the break, he was confident he was going to kick butt.

D.J. won the toss and went first. As she bent over the table, he admired the lines of her strong, lean body. Just looking at her legs, at the curve of her hips and rear made him ache. He wanted to go up behind her and press himself into her. He wanted to run his hands down her back to her waist, then circle around front until he cupped her breasts. He wanted to turn her, kiss her, touch her, taste her. Take her.

He wanted her wet, willing and screaming his name. And if he acted on any of his fantasies, he was likely to get a black eye.

She called the ball and pocket, then took her shot. The ball dropped neatly into place. She lined up her second shot. With her head down, her long hair flowed over her arm. He watched the play of light on the wavy strands.

"Why do you wear it long?" he asked when she'd sunk the second ball and straightened.

"What?"

He moved close and touched her hair. "It's beautiful, but why haven't you cut it?"

D.J. told herself to move out of reach. She hated people pawing her. The thing was, having Quinn twist a strand of her hair around his finger didn't really feel all that bad. Sure he was close, but not in an aggressive, macho way.

"My mother had long hair," she said before she realized she actually intended to tell him the truth. Or at least a part of it. "When I was little, she used to brush my hair for hours, and then I would brush hers. We used to try different kinds of braids and ribbons and promise each other we'd never cut our hair short."

Quinn listened intently. His dark gaze never left her face.

"So it's worth the risk?" he asked quietly.

She nodded, knowing exactly what he meant. Long hair *was* a risk. It could be grabbed, pulled, used against her.

"I wear it braided and pinned up to my head on assignments," she told him. It wasn't enough, but it was as much as she could do.

"Did you ever cut it?"

She nodded. "Once. I felt like I'd lost her."

The confession surprised her. She'd never told anyone that before. The realization made her nervous, but not nearly as much as the low-grade wanting she felt deep inside. She'd been waiting to see Quinn from the second she'd awakened that morning. Anticipation had slowed time to a crawl and when she'd tried to distract herself, nothing had worked.

She'd imagined what he would look like and how he would smile at her. She'd changed her clothes three times before heading over to Rebecca's. She felt giddy and foolish and tingly. Things she never allowed herself to feel.

He laced his fingers through her hair, then twisted the long strands around his hand. The action pulled slightly. Not enough to cause her pain. Another woman might not have even noticed, but D.J. did. Her senses went on alert, even as her muscles tensed.

The world blurred slightly in warning, then she was no longer in the spacious, well-lit, rec room. Instead she was a child of nine or ten. She could feel the close confines of the small space she'd squeezed into in an effort to escape. But her mother wasn't so lucky. Even as D.J. closed her eyes she could hear the screams, the pleading.

Her father had grabbed her mother by the hair. D.J. didn't remember what her mother had done that was so wrong. She could only feel her father's drunken rage. The sounds were so sharp. Her mother's voice, her father's breathing. The slick slide of the metal knife against the edge of the counter.

They'd been out of sight then, and D.J. had only been able to listen to the thunks of the blade against the cutting board. She'd heard her mother's gasps, her father's admonition to stop misbehaving. His claims that this was all *her* fault.

He'd gone back to drinking then, and had eventually passed out. D.J. remembered crawling out of her hiding space and finding her mother sitting at the kitchen table. Long, dark hair covered the cheap flooring. Her mother's hair had been hacked off unevenly. There were a few streaks of blood on her neck where the knife had cut through skin.

Her mother had never said anything about that night,

nor had she tried to grow her hair back. But she'd continued to brush her daughter's hair, to braid it and tie it up in ribbons.

"D.J.?"

The light touch on her arm brought her back to the present with a stomach-clenching jolt of fear. She swung, prepared to take on her attacker, only to find herself staring at Quinn.

"Want to talk about it?" he asked quietly.

Talk about it? No. Not even a little.

"I'm fine," she told him. "Just lost in thought."

She thought he might call her on the lie, but he didn't. Still shaking a little from the flashback, she lined up her next shot and missed.

Quinn took over the table. She stayed back, watching his smooth, easy movements. When he sent the third straight ball tumbling neatly into the pocket, she got the feeling she'd been had.

"Let me guess," she said. "You've been hustling since you were a kid?"

"No. I learned in the military."

"You're good."

"Thanks."

He flashed her a grin that made her toes curl. The reaction was so unexpected, she nearly tumbled over in surprise. More to distract herself than because she wanted information, she started asking questions.

"So what was life like back in those football-star days?"

"Pretty typical small-town stuff. In Texas, high school football is practically a religion. I couldn't wait to be old enough to play. I did okay in school, drove too fast, chased girls. The usual."

His growing up hadn't been anything like her world. "You close to your folks?"

"To my mom. I never got along with the old man." He straightened. "Whatever I did wasn't good enough. I spent the first fourteen years of my life trying to figure out why he didn't love me and the next fourteen trying not to care."

"I don't understand."

Quinn shook his head. "Neither did I, until a couple of weeks ago. Apparently he and my mom couldn't have kids and he was the problem. There weren't much in the way of infertility treatments in Possum Landing thirty-plus years ago. So he convinced her to find a guy who looked like him and get pregnant. She did and he accepted Gage as the son he never had."

D.J. hadn't thought much about how the Reynolds brothers had come to be related to the Haynes brothers. "Earl Haynes just happened to be in town?"

"Up in Dallas at a convention. My mom went back the following year to see him. She not only found out Earl wasn't the man she thought, she ended up pregnant a second time. Her husband wasn't willing to overlook the infidelity. Eventually he forgave her, but he never forgave me."

"Because you were a constant reminder."

"Something like that." He shrugged. "We never talked about it. He just made my life hell."

"Does knowing the reason make a difference?"

"I thought it would, but no."

D.J. could understand that. Knowing why something happened didn't always make the situation any easier to deal with. She understood everything about her past, and the knowledge was less than useless.

She couldn't see Quinn's pain, but she felt it. Oddly enough, it was something they had in common.

"My dad was a bastard, too," she told him. "Big, mean. Scary. He's the main reason I like to be in control all the time."

Confessions weren't her style and this one made her more uneasy than most. She braced herself for questions, or for him to tell her that she wasn't in control. Instead, he nodded.

"Makes sense."

He turned back to the game and continued to play perfectly. When he dropped the eight ball in the center pocket, he winked at her.

"That's gonna cost you a shirt, Daisy Jane."

"I was thinking of something more like a sock."

"It's my victory. I get to pick the item. Quit arguing or I'll make it your panties."

She reached for the rack, determined to win the second game. He broke, then promptly missed the first shot. She had a feeling he was giving her a break, but she wasn't about to complain. Not when she wanted to kick his butt and make claims on his underwear.

"When did you start learning martial arts?" he asked as she nailed her first shot.

"In high school. I worked all summer to pay for the lessons."

"I still say you would have been a terrific cheerleader."

"Oh, please. I wasn't interested in prancing around and showing off for boys."

"Some of the squads are very athletic."

She lined up the next shot. "That's true. If it had been something like that, I would have. But at my high school the girls were into looking good, not competing. I ran track."

"No archery or fencing?"

She glanced at him, but his expression was innocent enough. "It wasn't offered."

"How old were you when you earned your first black belt?"

"Seventeen."

She still remembered her pride. How she'd felt strong and safe for the first time in years.

"Did you have a boyfriend?"

She straightened. "Think about it, Quinn," she said. "I ran track, I had a black belt. What do you think?"

He walked toward her. "That you scared the boys away."

"Most of them."

He stopped next to her. "When they got too close, did you beat them up?"

She knew he was teasing and wanted to smile, but the memory of those days only made her sad. She'd never fit in. No one could understand what drove her to always want to be stronger, faster, better. She'd started to learn how to protect herself, but she'd never been able to escape being lonely.

"I didn't have to," she told him. "They never got that close."

He set his cue on the table and rested his hands on her waist. "Too bad. They should have called your bluff. Look at all they missed out on."

She didn't know what to respond to first. His closeness? She told herself to step away, but she couldn't seem to move. His comments about the past? She *hadn't* been bluffing. Her toughness had been as real as she could make it. As for missing out…did Quinn really think that? Somehow she'd always assumed the boys were never all that interested. If she wasn't girly and instantly willing, she wasn't worth the trouble.

"Quinn, I don't think this is a good idea," she told him.

"Daisy Jane, if we waited until you figured it was time, we'd both be long dead and mummified. It's up to me to move things on."

He lowered his head slightly. She could feel his breath on her cheek. "Stop calling me that."

"Sure thing, Daisy Jane."

Before she could protest or attack, he kissed her.

She'd known he was going to. How could she not? So why hadn't she bolted?

The answer became clear the second his mouth brushed against hers, sending heat flaring through her entire body.

She wanted this. She who had always prided herself on never trusting a man enough to let him get close wanted to give in. Not to any man. Just to Quinn. Just this once.

She must have dropped her cue because her hands were suddenly empty when she raised her arms and locked them around his neck. His lips were warm, firm and searching. She liked how he moved back and forth, teasing her, arousing her. Impatient for more, she parted her mouth, inviting him inside.

He responded with an eagerness that made her press against him. They touched from shoulders to knees, with her breasts flattening against his chest and her stomach nestling his rapidly growing arousal.

His tongue slipped into her mouth. She greeted him

with a soft caress, then circled him. He responded in kind. The sensual contact made her breasts ache. When his hands slipped from her hips to her rear, she arched harder against him. He dug into her curves, squeezing.

His long fingers brushed against the backs of her thighs. Liquid need melted her from the inside out. He was hard to her soft—so male and powerful. The length and breadth of his erection made her wonder what he would look like naked. Every part of his body would be strong and unyielding. From there it was a short, erotic step to imagining herself on the pool table, legs spread, him filling her as they—

The image was so real, she felt a jolt deep inside. As if he'd really entered her. Passion grew, as did a steady, throbbing ache. She *wanted* him to be inside of her. She *wanted* him to touch her. If he put his fingers between her legs and rubbed against her slick, wet flesh she could…

Terror swept through her as she completed the thought. If he touched her, she would give in. She would surrender control.

"No!" she gasped as she pulled free. "Stop."

Prepared to push him away, she was surprised when he instantly stepped back.

"D.J.? What's wrong?"

"I—" She was shaking. Her chest hurt and she couldn't breathe. "I can't," she gasped, then turned and ran.

By the time she got home, she'd managed to catch her breath, but the trembling lasted for hours. She felt both frightened and embarrassed.

So Quinn had kissed her. It didn't mean anything.

People kissed all the time. She'd made a big deal out of nothing.

Only it wasn't nothing to her. Quinn had asked if she'd beaten up the guys who got too close. That had never been a problem because she managed to scare them all off. Even when she hadn't meant to.

How many times had she been left alone, lonely, wondering what she'd done wrong? How many times had she wished she could trust enough to be honest, to explain why being involved was so scary for her? But no one had ever stuck around long enough for her to gather her courage. After a time, she'd stopped missing them. She'd moved on. Just as she would do when Quinn left.

She wouldn't remember him for long. He wouldn't matter. He *didn't* matter.

D.J. sat in the dark and tried to avoid the one thing she refused to admit. That she was lying about all of it. Especially about Quinn.

Chapter 9

Quinn's cell phone rang early the next morning. As there was only one person with the number, he knew who was on the other end.

"Reynolds," he said when he'd pushed the talk button.

"Hey, Quinn."

"Major."

"How's it going?"

Quinn wasn't sure why his commanding officer was calling. Major Ron Banner didn't do social. Either he'd received the report or he'd made a decision. Quinn wasn't sure which he wanted it to be. If his boss was looking for an answer...Quinn didn't have one yet.

"I'm doing great," Quinn told him.

"Good. You're visiting family, right?"

"Yeah. Big reunion kind of thing."

"Sounds fun."

Quinn picked up his coffee. "But it's not the reason you called."

"Fair enough. The report's back."

"And?"

"The shrinks think it's a good thing you refused to take out the target. He was your former mentor, you had an emotional connection with him, and the situation wasn't life-and-death. They feel that if circumstances had been different, had he been threatening innocents, you would have taken care of him. They called it controlled resistance. It seems you have a moral code."

"Who knew," Quinn said dryly, more than able to read between the lines. Yeah, the psychologists had given him a gold star. That didn't matter squat to his CO. "You're still pissed I didn't follow orders."

"It makes my life complicated," his boss admitted. "But you know it happens."

"Because your team of assassins is a temperamental bunch?"

"Something like that. You passed on a kill. What I want to know is if it's going to happen again. The shrinks say you're ready and willing to return to the job. I'm not so sure. You still want to be a killer, Quinn?"

Those in charge, those who wrote the handbooks, passed out assignments and made sure the men were debriefed, psychoanalyzed and kept happy used words like *targets* and *operatives*. Quinn, his boss and those on the team called it like it was.

When he wasn't busy rescuing Americans from sticky situations and honing his skills, he was moving around the world, taking out those who had been deemed undesirable. He was an assassin on the government payroll. As Ron said—a killer.

Quinn considered the question and realized he didn't have an answer. Not yet. "I don't know. I need more time."

"Take as much as you'd like. I only want you on-board if you're a hundred percent. No second-guessing, no conscience."

"Fair enough."

"You'll stay in touch?"

"Sure thing."

He heard Banner making notes in a file.

"Say another three weeks?" his boss asked.

"Fine."

Quinn disconnected the call and dropped his cell phone on the bed. In three weeks his CO would call again and ask the same question. "You still want to be a killer?" That time Quinn planned to have an answer.

Did he? Sometimes he told himself it was just a job. He was given an assignment and he carried it out. At the end of the month, he got paid. No big deal.

But lately things weren't so simple. He knew he could go back to work tomorrow and do a hell of a job. But what did that say about him? What did that make him? And did he want to be that man?

Restlessness filled him. He stood and paced the length of the room, then glanced at the clock. He was supposed to have a lesson with D.J. in an hour or so, but there was no way he could do that. Not today.

He grabbed his keys and headed out to tell her.

Fifteen minutes later he walked into her office and found her on the phone. She smiled at him, then flushed and turned away.

He remembered the pool game, the kiss and how she'd run out on him. Thinking about what went wrong had kept him up half the night. Had it just been the previous day? It felt like a lifetime ago.

He dropped his keys onto her desk and headed back to the workout room. There was a punching bag in the corner. He walked toward it, grabbing tape as he went.

After he'd shrugged out of his shirt, taped his hands and pulled on gloves, he faced the bag. He warmed up with a few easy swings. He jogged in place and stretched out muscles. As heat loosened him up, he focused on the bag and went to work.

He punched methodically, treating the bag like a person, breaking down the midsection, then going for the head. When his mind's eye told him that enemy was bloodied and broken, he mentally replaced him with someone new and fresh, then started in on him.

Energy filled him. His ability to focus allowed him to laser in on the bag. Blow after blow sent it spinning, wobbling. Sweat dripped down his face and chest. He cleared his mind of everything but the way his body moved, the power of his hits and the rhythm of his feet.

Sometime later he sensed D.J.'s presence. She hovered just at the edge of his peripheral vision. He finished the sequence, then stopped and faced her.

"I had some things to work out," he said.

She nodded.

"There won't be a lesson today."

"I understand," she said.

He wondered if she did. He wondered what she saw when she looked at him. He was normally so controlled. So careful. "Are you afraid?" he asked.

She raised her chin slightly. "Of course not."

He had the feeling that she was almost telling the truth.

He knew if he moved toward her now, while the pain and confusion was still with him, that she would back away. He would see more than fear in her eyes—he would see terror.

Who had done that to her? A parent? A boyfriend? Had she been attacked? Raped? What? There was something in her past. Something dark and ugly. It had left her scarred and broken. It had shaped who and what she was.

He supposed there were those who would be put off by the imperfection. Disgusted maybe. Not him. He wanted to know what had happened so he wouldn't make any wrong moves. He didn't want her to be afraid of him. He wanted her to feel safe.

Dumb-ass, he told himself. Like that was ever going to happen. As if he could ever be good enough for her. As if they could have something together.

He turned back to the bag and pounded it until it swung like a flag in a gale-force wind. He hit the bag over and over, until his muscles ached and he couldn't see with all the sweat burning his eyes. Until he was too tired to ask questions or care about answers.

When he stopped, she was still there. Still watching. He pulled off the gloves, then worked the tape from his hands. He sensed that she wanted to speak, and prayed she would stay silent. What was there to say?

He'd been wrong to want her, to kiss her. To like her. He'd allowed himself to forget who and what he was. A killer. A man without a soul.

His CO wanted answers, and Quinn didn't want to deal with the questions. How did he know what he wanted from life? How was he to find the best way to go? If he walked away from his job, from all of it, then what? Could he find his way back to normal? Did he even remember what that was?

All those people last night at Rebecca's house. They'd been family, yet they were strangers. Even Gage. None of them knew what he did, who he was. If he walked away, could he be a part of them? Did he want to be?

He grabbed his shirt and brushed his damp hair off his forehead.

"I'll see you around," he told her.

D.J. nodded without speaking.

He wanted to explain, but what was there to say? He was going to find high ground, hole up and lick his wounds. He was a solitary creature and no matter what else he wanted, that wasn't going to change.

That afternoon D.J. tried to focus on paperwork, but she was having trouble concentrating. She kept thinking about Quinn, about what had happened that morning.

She'd dreaded their session together because of the kiss at Rebecca's and her reaction to it. She'd wanted to be cool and sophisticated. She'd wanted to impress him. Passion had threatened to overwhelm her and she'd bolted like a scared schoolgirl.

She'd tried to think of a reason to cancel their session. Before she could come up with one, he'd stalked into the office, looking exactly like what he was—a dangerous man. Something in his eyes had made her want to get out of his way. Suddenly the kiss didn't matter. Not when she had to face down a warrior.

He hadn't worked out on her punching bag, he'd attacked it, as if it possessed demons. She could still hear the sound of his gloves hitting the bag. The steady thumps, the low grunts of effort, the shuffle of his feet on the floor.

Something had happened, but she didn't know what. Something had set him off. At first she'd thought they could spar together and he would deal with whatever was bothering him. But after she'd seen him at the punching bag, she'd known that wasn't possible. He'd become too deadly.

D.J. stood and walked out of the office. After locking the front door, she crossed the small parking lot to her SUV and climbed inside. When Quinn had walked out that morning, she'd thought he looked…alone. Crazy, she told herself. If Quinn was a solitary person, it was by choice. But she couldn't shake the notion that he'd been feeling isolated and separate—sensations she was intimately familiar with.

She drove through town but not toward her place. She wasn't ready to go home—not yet. She cruised past the shopping mall, a park, several restaurants before finding herself in front of Quinn's hotel.

Without knowing if it was smart or right or even safe, she pulled in and parked. Ten minutes of considering options didn't clear her mind or give her any ideas.

Cursing both him and herself, she climbed out and headed for the three-story building. Minutes later she knocked on his hotel room.

The door opened. He'd showered since she'd last seen him, and had changed his clothes. But he hadn't recovered. There was still something dark and bruised lurking in his eyes.

He didn't speak. Nor did he shut the door in her face. Instead he stepped back to let her enter.

She did. When he closed the door behind her, she decided to be completely honest.

"I don't know why I'm here," she said.

He wore a T-shirt and jeans. He was lean, muscled and broken. She couldn't explain the latter, but she felt it down to her toes. Something inside of him had shattered.

The thought of his pain propelled her across the carpeting. She walked up to him, put her hands on his shoulders, raised herself on tiptoe and kissed him.

She couldn't explain her actions or predict his response. Before she could pull back or even call herself a name for being so stupid, his arms came around her and hauled her against him.

One second she was standing, the next she was pressed against him, her breasts flat against his chest, her fingers tunneling through his hair.

His hands were everywhere. Her back, her hips, her rear. Even as he tilted his head and swept his tongue across her bottom lip, his fingers brushed against her stomach before reaching higher.

She parted and he plunged inside. He circled her tongue, claimed it, then retreated and bit her lower lip. As she gasped with surprise and a jolt of passion, she felt his hands cup her breasts. He explored the full curves. Fingertips danced across her tight nipples. He flicked the tips with his thumb. At the same time he drew her lower lip into his mouth and sucked where he'd bitten her.

Wanting overwhelmed her. Her heart rate increased, as did the sound of the blood rushing through her body. Between her legs moist warmth invaded, making her slick, swollen and ready. She wanted to rub against him like a cat. She wanted to purr. Instead she ran her hands up and down his back, reveling in his strength, his maleness.

He tugged at the front of her shirt, his fingers quickly finding the buttons. Even as he kissed her jaw, her neck, then licked and bit her earlobe, he worked the buttons free. When he shoved the shirt down her arms and tossed it on the floor, he dropped his hands to her hips and drew her pelvis against him. He was aroused and he ground himself against her.

She caught her breath and found herself lost in his dark gaze. Passion tightened the lines of his face. He wanted her and his need increased her own.

Still staring at her face, he slipped his hands up her back to her bra. With nimble fingers he unfastened the clasp. The plain cotton bra fell down her arms, and she let it fall to the floor.

He dropped his gaze to her chest. She watched him watch her as he cupped her bare breasts in his hands. When he bent low, she braced herself for the sensual assault of his kiss. Seconds later firm lips claimed her right nipple. Liquid fire roared through her. Her head fell back as he licked and sucked her sensitive skin.

Her thighs trembled. She had to hold on to him to stay standing. Every cell in her body delighted in his touch and the promise of what was to come.

Without warning, he bent low and wrapped his arms around her legs. He picked her up and carried her the few feet to the bed. But instead of straightening after he set her down, he dropped to his knees and went to work on her jeans.

He quickly unfastened the belt, then undid the single button and the zipper. When he'd pulled the fabric down to her knees, he leaned in and kissed her flat belly.

D.J.'s entire body clenched. She couldn't part her legs, nor could she run. When he pulled down her panties, she stopped breathing. When he used his fingers to delicately open her, then touched her most sensitive place with his tongue, she had to grit her teeth to keep from screaming.

One stroke, then two. Muscles rippled. Heat grew. The need, oh, how the need filled her until it was impossible to think of anything else.

"Wait," she breathed, and sank back on the bed. "One of us is too formally dressed."

Quinn looked at her. Some of the darkness had faded from his eyes and he smiled. "Fair enough."

He stood and tugged off his T-shirt. While he worked on the rest of his clothing, she took off her shoes, socks, jeans and briefs. Kneeling on the bed, she reached for her braid and began to unfasten the thick plait.

Quinn swore.

She looked up and saw him standing, jeans open, feet and chest bare. His gaze roamed her body. He swore again.

She realized she was kneeling naked on his bed, her legs spread, her arms up. Aware of her vulnerability, she waited for apprehension to chill her enthusiasm, but it never came. Instead she felt proud that he found her attractive.

He shook his head. "You're a hell of a fantasy, D.J."

He shoved down his jeans and briefs as he spoke. His arousal sprang free.

He was large, thick and more than ready. She did her best not to think about what it would feel like when he was inside. Instead she finished loosening her braid, then tossed her head. He made a noise low in his throat and dove onto the bed.

He crashed next to her, brought his arms around her and pulled her down. Their mouths met in a hot, frenzied kiss that made her strain against him. He caressed her breasts, then slipped lower to the swollen wetness between her thighs.

The second he touched her there, she knew she was in trouble. The wanting was too great. Need made her whimper and squirm and surge toward him.

Just for a second, she told herself, trying to stay in control. She would let him do this just for a second. It felt so good. Too good to make him stop.

He moved slowly, as if discovering. When he brushed across her most sensitive spot, she caught her breath. He did it again and again. She could feel herself tensing, readying. So close. If he didn't stop, she wouldn't have a choice.

Deliberately she put her hand on his wrist and pushed him away. At the same time, she clamped her lips over his tongue and sucked until he shuddered.

Pulling back slightly she said, "Tell me you have protection with you because I don't."

"What?" His dark eyes were unfocused. He blinked, then grinned. "Sure thing, Daisy Jane."

She swatted his arm. "Stop calling me that."

"Why? It's your name."

He rose and walked into the bathroom. Seconds later he appeared with a box of condoms. He tossed them onto the nightstand, then returned to the bed. She knew what he planned even before he slipped his hand between her legs.

"Wait," she told him. "I want you ready."

Quinn started to protest, but before he could get up a head of steam, she bent down and took him in her mouth. He groaned low in his throat. As she teased him with her tongue, she reached for the box of condoms.

When he was breathing heavily and sagging against the bed, she raised her head and opened the box. He watched her slip on the protection.

Before he could shift toward her, she knelt over him and slowly settled on his arousal. He grabbed her hips.

"D.J., wait," he gasped. "I want you to—"

She sank lower. "I will," she told him. "Just let's get you going."

"I'm already there."

She smiled and slowly raised and lowered herself over his arousal.

He felt good, she thought, holding on to her control. Too good. It would be easy to give in to the feelings surging through her. But she couldn't. So she concentrated on letting him slip in and out of her, squeezing him with each stroke. The fingers on her hips tightened as he began to set the pace.

He moved one hand across her leg so he could reach her wetness. Even as she rode him, he rubbed his thumb against her swollen center.

Exquisite pleasure shot through her. She wanted to collapse against him, surrendering to the release. She was so close. Just a few more strokes. Just a few more…

No! She forced her mind away from what he was doing between her legs. Instead of letting go, she breathed his name. He opened his eyes and looked at her. While he watched, she gathered her hair and piled it on top of her head. The movement of her arms raised her breasts. She began to move faster and faster, pulling him inside of her. Her breasts bounced, her body rode him, she tightened her muscles, milking him until she felt him stiffen.

He swore again and replaced his thumb with two fingers. His pace matched hers. She was sliding over the edge. Control, she thought frantically. Control.

She dropped her hands to the mattress and pulsed her hips. The shift in her position forced his hand away and pulled him in deeper. At the apex of the thrust, she clamped around him and rocked.

He lost it.

Contentment filled her as she felt him shudder in release. His eyes sank closed, his body stiffened, then stilled. Between her thighs she felt the contractions slow, slow and finally stop.

She sighed and smiled. "Impressive," she breathed.

Quinn opened his eyes. For a man who'd just had what felt like an amazing climax, he didn't look happy. Instead of smiling back, he grabbed her and shifted so she tumbled onto her back. Then he loomed over her.

"What the hell just happened?" he growled.

Chapter 10

Quinn stared into D.J.'s face, but couldn't figure out what she was thinking. Her smile faded.

"What's wrong?" she asked.

She seemed genuinely confused.

He mentally grabbed hold of his temper. Okay, maybe he'd misread the situation. Maybe she hadn't done it on purpose.

"You had your way with me," he said, deliberately lightening his tone. "What's up with that?"

Her smile returned. "I wanted it to be good for you."

"What about you?"

"It was fine."

"Uh-huh."

He didn't believe her for a second. She'd held back. If he didn't know better, he would say she'd been damn close but had tried to distract him. Tried? She'd succeeded. But why?

To test his theory, he slipped a hand between her legs. She was wet, hot and more than swollen. He found the tight knot of nerves and rubbed it with his finger. Instantly her breath quickened and her pupils dilated.

But instead of letting him continue, she pushed his hand away and sat up. "Like I said—impressive."

She started to slide off the bed, but he grabbed her arm and held her in place. "What's going on?" he demanded a second time.

"Nothing." She narrowed her gaze. "Would you please let go of me?"

"When you tell me why this whole exercise was about me."

"Isn't that what you want?"

"No. I want it to be about both of us."

"It's sex, Quinn. Nothing more."

"I would have enjoyed sex. This was getting off."

She flushed and turned away. He released her arm and watched her stand up. She was more beautiful than he could have imagined. Strong, curved, completely feminine. From her high breasts to the triangle of dark curls protecting her femininity, she was erotic, sensual and pure fantasy.

She'd shocked him when she'd shown up at his door. He'd almost told her to leave, but he'd been tired of being alone. Then she'd kissed him and he'd realized why she'd come to see him. What she was offering. Somehow he'd assumed it would be for both of them.

He pulled off the condom and tossed it in the trash, then watched her gather her clothes. She pulled on briefs and her bra. As she stepped into her jeans, he tried to figure out what had gone wrong.

Her lack of reaction hadn't been about his technique.

He might not be God's gift to women, but he understood basic anatomy. He knew what went where and did his best to always make his partner see stars. But D.J. hadn't let him. Every time he'd been close, she'd pulled back.

"You're not leaving until this is settled," he told her.

She eyed him coolly. "You're going to keep me prisoner?"

"If necessary."

"Big talk from a naked guy." She shrugged into her shirt and fastened the buttons.

"Is it a control thing?" he asked.

She zipped up her jeans. "I have no idea what you're talking about."

"You could have climaxed. You were close. I could feel it. So what's the deal?"

She walked to the mirror over the dresser and finger combed her hair. "There's no deal."

Like he bought that. "Control?" he asked, speaking more to himself than her. "But what's the point? So you don't enjoy sex. How is that a win?"

She spun to face him. "You got yours, Quinn. Isn't that enough?"

"No." He stood and put his hands on his hips. "It's not how I do things."

"So if she's not screaming your name, you're not a man?"

"Something like that."

"Well, get over it. What happened today, or didn't happen, wasn't about you. It was about me. I don't—" she turned back to the mirror "—I'm not built that way. My body doesn't react."

He grabbed his jeans and pulled them on. "Are you

telling me you've never had a climax? That you're incapable?"

"Yes." She turned back to him. "It happens."

"Bull. You're more in tune with your body than anyone I've ever met. I felt you reacting, D.J. You were close. You deliberately pulled back."

Her dark eyes flashed with temper. "Maybe you're overestimating your skill in bed."

"I don't claim to be the world's greatest lover. I'm just a guy who wants to please the one he's with. What's so wrong with that."

She sighed. "Nothing. I appreciate the thought, but it's not necessary."

"It is to me."

"This isn't about you."

He crossed to her and touched her chin. When she looked at him, he smiled. "I've got all night. Let's get naked again and we'll see if I can prove you wrong."

She twisted away from him. "Thanks, but I'm not interested."

"Then why did you show up in the first place?"

"Good question. I'm having some second thoughts."

He frowned. None of this made sense. She'd arrived uninvited and had taken the first step. *She'd* kissed *him*. When he'd responded, she'd been more than willing. She'd wanted to have sex, but only if it was about him.

What was that?

She headed for the door. He got there first. "Answer the question," he said quietly. "Tell me why you won't let me make you climax and I'll let it go."

She sucked in a breath, then released it slowly. "I'm not interested in—" She shook her head. "You're so annoying."

"I know. Answer the question."

She looked at him. "I just don't. Okay? It's not that I can't, it's that I won't. Doing that…" She shrugged. "I won't ever let myself be that vulnerable."

If she'd screamed he wouldn't have believed her. But it was her soft words, the defensive set of her shoulders and the painful twist of her mouth that convinced him.

He stared at her. "Why do you hate men so much?"

"I don't. It's not about hating anyone. That implies way more energy than I'm putting into this."

She turned away and crossed to the bed. Once there, she sank onto the mattress.

"It's about not trusting them," she told him. "Sex does something to women. It makes them weak. They bond. And it doesn't seem to matter if the guy's a jerk or not. Or if he beats her. They connect. I don't want to be that weak, so I don't risk it."

Her words stunned him. "Not ever?"

"What's the point? You get weak, you get dead."

"That's ridiculous. You're extrapolating from an inconsequential statistical base. How many women get dead because they have sex?"

She sprang to her feet. "One woman is too many. You're a guy. You don't know what you're talking about."

"Then tell me. Help me understand."

She shook her head and crossed to the door. This time he knew he had to let her go. But she surprised him by laying her hand against the wood frame rather than the handle.

"My father beat my mother," she said, her back to him. "He was a mean drunk and even worse when he was sober. My earliest memory is of her screaming for mercy."

Quinn's stomach clenched. He'd wanted to know what had so terrified D.J. Now that he did, he wanted to rescind the request. Knowing didn't make it better.

"Sometimes he would go days, even a couple of weeks between attacks. I'd lie awake every night, wondering if it would start. When it would start. I was always afraid. What if he killed her? What if he turned on me, too."

She dropped her hand to her side, then shifted so she was facing him. "He waited until my seventh birthday. He got drunk, I spilled cake on the floor and he came after me. Sometimes he used a belt or his hand. He'd throw beer bottles at me. Then he'd pass out. When it was finally safe, my mother and I would huddle together on the sofa and make plans to escape. For a long time I believed that it was really going to happen."

Her dark eyes stared past him. Was she getting lost in the memories? Would she let him help her?

"She changed her mind," D.J. told him. "Every time. The next morning there were a thousand reasons why we couldn't go. The truth was, she loved him. Even when he broke her jaw, cut off her hair and called her a whore."

He wanted to go to her and hold her but knew she wouldn't want to be touched. Not now. Not when it wasn't safe.

She closed her eyes. "When I was eleven he came after me with a baseball bat. I can't even remember why. Just how bad it hurt. My mother took me to the emergency room. My arm was broken. The nurse there threatened to call the police and have me taken away.

My mother begged her not to. She said my father would kill me if the police got involved. The nurse said he was going to kill me anyway."

She opened her eyes and stared at him. "My mother took me home and told me it would be all right. The next day she made me go to school. I didn't want to. I was ashamed and in a lot of pain. But she insisted. The school nurse came and got me later that morning. After I'd left home that morning, my mother shot my father, then turned the gun on herself. She left a note. In it she said she couldn't let him continue to hurt me, but she couldn't live knowing she'd killed the only man she ever loved."

He swallowed hard. D.J. stood by the door, rubbing her left arm. He didn't doubt those bones had been the ones shattered.

He'd already guessed she'd been abused in some way, but he'd never thought it was that bad. No wonder she didn't trust men or love or sex. No wonder she held back.

"I'm sorry," he said. "I shouldn't have asked."

Her mouth twisted. "More than you wanted to know, huh?"

He stood. "There's nothing you can say that will shock me. I'm sorry for making you relive it."

She shrugged. "Old news. It doesn't matter anymore."

Of course it mattered. Her past dictated every aspect of her life. It was the reason she had to always be the best. He ached for her.

"D.J."

She held up a hand. "If you get all sloppy on me, I'm going to beat the crap out of you."

"Not a chance of that."

He crossed the room and reached for her. She shrank back, then stiffened and stood her ground. He'd seen men in battle, facing down their fear, but not one of them had shown the same courage as this woman. Every time he moved, she knew he could snap her in two. Yet instead of running for cover, she wanted him to teach her. When she could have walked away, she'd come over to help him heal. She had seen the nature of the darkness inside of him that morning. She'd watched him pulverize the punching bag, and she'd still shown up and offered herself.

"You're a hell of a woman," he said as he put his arms around her and pulled her close.

She was stiff as plywood. "I don't need a hug."

"Maybe I do."

She sighed heavily, as if this was *such* an imposition, then stood there while he ran his hands up and down her back. Gradually she began to relax. Her arms moved from her sides to his waist. Her fingers lightly rested against his back.

He breathed in the scent of her body, of her hair. She was tough, but still soft. He understood why she hadn't given in. He also finally knew why offering him sex in exchange for lessons had been so much easier than accepting a dinner invitation. Sex was just about the body. She could stay in control—although she'd come close to losing it with him. Dinner was more personal.

He also knew what had gone wrong between them today. She'd offered sex, and he'd accepted. Neither of them had been making love.

Quinn's chest tightened. Was that what he wanted? To make love with D.J.? Did he dare?

She pulled away and this time he let her go. She crossed to the door and let herself out without saying anything.

When her footsteps had faded, he moved to the window and stared out. He saw her walk across the parking lot and slide into her car. She moved with a grace that left him breathless.

He still wanted her, and he knew what it would take to get her. But could he risk it? He was the wrong man to try to save her. She might be on the edge, but he was already in the water and drowning.

She started her engine and drove away. Even after she was gone, he stayed at the window. Was it wishful thinking on his part to hope they could save each other? Were they both too far gone or did they have a prayer of finding their way back?

The next morning D.J. waited nervously for Quinn to arrive. Part of her hoped he wouldn't bother. That between what had happened—or not happened—in bed and their fight, he'd decided to forget it. His not showing up would make things easy for her. No more worries, no more questions, no more second-guessing herself.

She hadn't slept at all the previous night. Her feelings had fluctuated between anger, humiliation and frustration. She couldn't believe she'd simply blurted out the truth about her past. She never told anyone. Rebecca didn't even know. Oh, there had been hints, but she'd never actually sat down and spilled the whole sorry tale.

D.J. paced the length of her office, then returned to her desk and flopped down on the chair. Why had she told him? She wanted to say it was because he kept pushing and pushing, but she wasn't sure. Part of her wondered if she'd *wanted* him to know.

"Not possible," she said aloud. Him knowing only complicated an already difficult situation. Unless she'd been trying to scare him off.

She rose again and nodded. That was it. She'd wanted to send Quinn away.

Or had she wanted him to understand?

The question terrified her and she refused to consider it. No way. Not possible. Uh-uh. Him understanding would imply that he mattered, and he didn't. She'd proved that yesterday when they'd had sex. She'd held back the way she always did. The only difference was he'd noticed.

She crossed to the window and stared out at the street. Half the men she'd been with hadn't even wondered about her enjoying the process or not. A few had been worried, but she'd brushed them off. The rest she'd convinced that they'd simply missed her "event." Quinn had been the only one to push back.

She closed her eyes as she remembered his anger and his persistence. What he didn't know—what she would never tell him—was how close she'd come to giving in. She'd wanted to, and that realization scared her to death.

Her eyes snapped open. "What's up with all this Quinn crap?" she demanded of herself. "Stop thinking about him."

Good advice she couldn't seem to take. While his badgering had been annoying, she had to admit that it had been sweet of him to care so much. He'd—

She turned and glanced at the clock. It was nine. Maybe he wasn't coming.

She told herself she would be relieved if he didn't

show up. Better for both of them to end things now. Not that there was anything to end. But if there was, it should stop immediately. Yes, the lessons had been great but—

The front door opened. D.J. turned and ignored the sense of relief that swept through her when Quinn entered the room. Her gaze swept over him, taking in his easy smile, the athletic shorts and T-shirt, the flowers in his hand, the way he—

Her gaze snapped back to the flowers. Outrage filled her. "What the hell are those?" she demanded.

"Good morning to you, too," he said and put the dozen or so red roses on her desk.

She couldn't believe it. He'd brought her flowers?

"Of all the insensitive, stupid things you could have done," she told him, her temper growing by the second. "Flowers? You brought me flowers? Oh, right. Because they're going to make up for everything that's happened. Gee, I should have thought of that kind of therapy before. A few flowers will really heal my past."

She walked around the desk and glared at him. "Were you even listening to what I said yesterday? Don't you think this ridiculous gesture trivializes the story just a little bit? Or should I be grateful you thought about it at all? How like a man."

She wanted to squash him like a bug. She wanted to shove the roses in his face until he choked on them.

"You have no idea what I went through," she continued angrily. "You grew up in some perfect hometown where everyone knew your name. I was stuck in foster care because my mother killed my father and then herself. Imagine what the kids at school talked about when I walked into a room. The teachers kept waiting for me to explode or something, and there was an entire team of psychologists trying to make sure I was healed. Well here's a news flash. You don't heal from something like that. You learn to live with it and then you move on."

Quinn didn't move, didn't stop smiling at her, didn't say a word until she'd wound down enough to demand, "What?"

He nodded at the flowers. "They have nothing to do with your past. I always bring flowers after I see a woman naked. It seems like the polite thing to do. I ordered them just for you. They still have their thorns. I thought you'd like that."

D.J.'s mouth dropped open. She closed it, then felt herself flush.

She was an idiot. "Oh."

"Is that it?"

She shrugged.

"How about thanking me?" he asked. "The thorns are a pretty cool touch."

She smiled. "They are. Thank you."

Quinn shook his head. "Okay, I say we start the workout with you spending about twenty minutes jumping rope. You have way too much energy you need to burn off."

D.J. nodded and led the way toward the back. He followed. When they stepped into the workout room, he grabbed her hand and pulled her around so she faced him.

"Are we okay?" he asked.

He'd brought her flowers. No guy had ever done that before. Not that she *needed* flowers, but it had been sweet of him to go to all that trouble.

"I'm sorry I overreacted," she said.

"Is that a yes?"

"Yes."

"Good. But don't think apologizing gets you out of jumping rope." He released her hand. "Get going."

She grinned and headed for the equipment locker. Maybe telling him about her past hadn't been such a big mistake. Maybe everything was going to work out just fine.

A week later D.J. couldn't figure out if things were better or worse between herself and Quinn. While he'd never mentioned that night, the sex or her confession, she couldn't convince herself he'd forgotten anything that had happened or anything she'd said. Or maybe she was giving him more credit than he deserved. Maybe *she* was the problem. Because ever since they'd done the wild thing and she'd spilled her emotional guts, she'd been far too *aware* of him.

When they worked out, she noticed every brush of his hand, every whisper of masculine scent. When they talked, she studied his conversation for nuance and hidden meaning. Yes, she was getting stronger and learning more about keeping safe than she'd hoped, but she was also being driven to distraction by his presence.

"So stop thinking about him," she told herself as she turned in front of Rebecca's house and walked to the front door.

Her friend let her in before she could knock.

"I was watching for you," Rebecca said. "I sent the kids out with Austin, so it's just us for lunch." She smiled. "I thought about having doughnuts, in honor of our temporarily halted morning tradition, but that was just too strange for an actual meal."

"I wouldn't have minded," D.J. told her as she followed her back to the kitchen. "You know, you didn't have to stop coming by and visiting me."

Rebecca crossed the kitchen, pausing by the island where she'd already put out ingredients for salad. "Of course I did. Whatever we have to say to each other can wait until we get together for lunch or talk on the phone. This is the first time I've ever seen you interested in a man. I'm not getting in the way of that. You know where everything is. Help yourself to whatever you want to drink."

"Thanks." D.J. headed for the cupboard beside the dishwasher and pulled out a glass. "Just for the record, I'm not interested in Quinn."

Rebecca grinned. "Just for the record, you're lying."

D.J. ignored her and walked to the refrigerator. After filling her glass with ice, she opened the door and pulled out a diet soda.

Interest implied that she wanted something from Quinn, and she didn't. Not really. Okay, he confused her and she couldn't stop thinking about him, but that didn't mean he was important to her in any way. He was just…confusing.

"He's not sticking around," she reminded her friend. "His stay in town is temporary."

Rebecca cut up an avocado. "What does that have to do with anything?"

"If you're pushing for us to have a relationship, I'm telling you that it would have to be temporary."

"Not necessarily. He won't be staying in the military forever."

Good point. "He's not my type."

"You don't date enough to have a type."

Another good point. "Enough about me. Let's talk about you. How are the kids?"

Rebecca grated cheese over the salad, then handed the bowl to D.J. "Please take that to the table and don't for a second think you can change the subject. The kids are fine, Austin is fine, and I'm fine. Now, back to you and Quinn."

"There is no 'me and Quinn.' There's just me."

"So the fact that I see his rental car at your office every morning is insignificant?"

"Absolutely. He's working out with me, that's all."

Rebecca uncovered a plate of sandwiches and set them next to the salad. "Half-dressed sweaty bodies rolling around together? It sounds romantic to me."

"Then you need to work on your definitions." D.J. slumped down in a chair.

Rebecca sat across from her.

They couldn't be more opposite, D.J. thought. Rebecca wore a light, summer dress, jewelry and a flower in her hair. D.J. had pulled on khaki pants, a tank top and sandals. The closest she came to jewelry was the sports watch she sometimes remembered to strap on. Her hair was pulled back because that kept it out of her way. She felt as feminine and delicate as a machine gun.

Rebecca wore makeup, painted her nails, baked, sewed her kids Halloween costumes and acted as room mother in all her children's classrooms. D.J. had three black belts, no family and not even a houseplant to act as a pet.

Sometimes, not often, but sometimes, she wanted more. She wanted to be normal—like the other women she saw. Sometimes she wondered how her life would have been different if she hadn't grown up afraid. If she'd never learned that men couldn't be trusted.

"What are you thinking?" Rebecca asked as she scooped salad onto her plate. "You're looking fierce."

"I'm wondering how you can do all this without being afraid."

Rebecca frowned. "Of what?"

"Men. What they can do to women. How much stronger they are."

"I'll admit there are criminals out there, and bad men, but they're not a part of our everyday life. We don't live in a war zone, D.J. Sometimes I think you forget that."

"Maybe."

"You see the worst side of people. In your class you help women who have been abused or battered. While I admire what you do, it doesn't give you a balanced view of humanity."

"You want balanced? How about the percentage of woman who are beaten by their husbands? Or the kids who—"

Rebecca raised her hand. "That's my point. You live in a world of statistics. Of bad things. But most of us don't. We have regular lives with great guys. Oh, sure, they can be annoying but they're still honest, caring men. They're good parents and would rather cut off their own arms than hurt their wives or kids."

D.J. wanted to believe her. She knew in her head that most men weren't the enemy. The problem was, she didn't seem to run into many of them.

She wondered what her friend would say if she knew what had happened that night in Quinn's hotel room. Rebecca would be far more shocked by D.J.'s inability to let go than by the fact that she'd had sex. No doubt Rebecca assumed D.J.'s physical prowess extended into the bedroom. Most people probably thought that.

"There's too much surrender in marriage, and it all happens on the woman's part."

Rebecca bit into her sandwich and chewed. "I disagree," she said when she'd swallowed. "Both partners surrender. And with the right man it can be a wonderful thing."

"Oh, please."

"It's true. Being vulnerable and open to a man, while he's vulnerable and open to you, is the purest form of connection. Each of you can hurt the other, and you don't. That's what love is. Sharing secrets, trusting. Trust is the proof of love. Without it love doesn't exist."

"I'm not interested in love."

"Of course you are," Rebecca said quietly. "But the fear is greater than the wanting. I've always thought that was sad. I want you to find someone and be happy."

D.J. bristled. "I don't need some man to make me happy."

"Maybe not, but you need someone to crawl inside of you and prove that you can stop running."

D.J. poked at her salad. "This is a stupid conversation."

"Quinn's an interesting guy."

"None of this is about him."

Rebecca smiled. "Of course it isn't. As you said— he's leaving soon. Of course he would be someone good for you to practice on. So when the right one came along, you'd know what to do."

"There is no right one."

Rebecca's smile broadened. "For a woman who

thinks she knows everything, you're surprisingly ignorant of matters of the heart."

"What do you mean by that?"

"You're already falling for him, D.J. I can see it from here."

"No way. He doesn't matter." He didn't. He couldn't. She didn't let anyone matter. Not ever.

"Sell it somewhere else."

D.J. ignored her. There was nothing going on between her and Quinn. Okay—they'd had sex, but so what? It had been a week and he hadn't tried to do it again. Which was how she preferred things. The last thing she needed was some guy pawing her. It was disgusting. She much preferred being alone. At least she always had…until lately.

Chapter 11

"I can't believe we're doing this," D.J. told him as he held open the heavy glass door.

"I know. It's pretty special."

Quinn glanced around at the mall. He couldn't remember the last time he'd been in a suburban shopping center. Whenever he had to buy a gift—usually for his mother at Christmas or her birthday—he used the Internet.

The Glenwood Mall had been recently refurbished. Skylights flooded the two-story structure with plenty of light. While there were a few families out and about, most of the occupants seemed to be teenagers and retired couples. An interesting mix.

"You tricked me," D.J. said with a laugh.

Quinn turned his attention back to her and grinned. "I told you I was more than just a pretty face."

She rolled her eyes. "I wasn't kidding about shopping."

"That's fine."

"Won't going into a store give you hives or something? Don't all guys hate to shop?"

"I don't do it very often. I think I can survive any autoimmune-system reaction. If I don't, I'm sure you know first aid."

Her gaze narrowed. "Just don't expect mouth-to-mouth."

He snapped his fingers. "Bummer. I had this whole fantasy about keeling over in men's wear."

"I'm sure one of the burly guards would be happy to save your life."

"I'd rather you did it."

She shook her head and walked to the directory. Quinn followed. When he'd invited D.J. to dinner, he'd expected her to blow him off. But instead of refusing him outright, she'd said she had to shop for Rebecca's birthday. When he'd offered to accompany her *and* buy her dinner, she'd accepted. He'd been surprised and she'd looked a little stunned herself. Still, he considered her agreement progress. Not that D.J. made anything easy.

"You want to shop first or eat?" he asked.

"Where are we eating?"

"The food court."

She looked at him and blinked. "You're kidding?"

He put a hand on her arm. "I know it's going to be exciting for you, but try to control yourself. It gets embarrassing when you scream and jump all over me."

"The food court?"

"Sure. I'll let you have anything you want, and you can even have ice cream for dessert."

"I'm overwhelmed."

He grinned. "I thought you might be. And if any of the teenage boys try to hit on you, I'll scare them off."

She smiled. "I can't imagine anything more wonderful."

He tucked his hands into the front pockets of his jeans. "I do know how to show a lady a good time."

"Gee, with all that to look forward to, I guess we should shop first and let the anticipation build."

"That's my girl."

D.J. mumbled something under her breath. Quinn thought it best not to ask her to repeat it.

She led the way into a large department store. The main floor was a maze of cosmetics, women's shoes and jewelry. Quinn thought he caught sight of the men's department tucked into a far corner, but he wasn't sure and D.J. didn't head in that direction. Instead she circled the cosmetics, then hovered around the perfume counter.

"I never know what to get Rebecca," she admitted. "We had lunch yesterday and I kept looking at her, thinking we have absolutely nothing in common."

"So get something you'd hate, and she'll probably love it."

D.J. shook her head. "Gee, thanks for the advice."

She picked up a cut-glass bottle and sniffed, then grimaced and put it back down. Quinn understood her concern. From what he could tell the only thing similar about Rebecca and D.J. was that they were both female. But the relationship didn't surprise him. Rebecca provided D.J. with balance, although he doubted Miss Prickly would ever admit to it.

"She's so girly," D.J. muttered. "It's just…"

She didn't want to get it wrong. Quinn didn't have to hear the words to know what she was thinking. She might rag on Rebecca, but she cared about her. D.J. didn't let many people into her world, but when she did, they were in for life.

He wondered where he was on her radar. Not the inner circle. But someone she trusted—at least a little. She'd been willing to get naked with him, which meant a lot, even if she hadn't been willing to let herself enjoy the experience. Even more telling, she'd told him about her past.

Quinn still didn't know what to do with the information. Her old man was dead, so finding him and beating the crap out of him wasn't an option, although it had been his first response. He had no patience for those who preyed on the small and weak. If a man wanted to pick a fight, he should do it with someone his own size.

He knew that D.J.'s past had left her broken, and not just in her bones. He wanted to pull her close until she healed. Yeah, right. Because he was so mentally sound himself.

"Let's check out some of the boutiques," she said, leading the way out of the anchor store.

"What does Rebecca like?" he asked. "What about shoes? Aren't all women into shoes?"

D.J. raised her eyebrows. "Have you ever bought shoes for a woman."

"No."

"I suggest you never try."

"Fair enough."

He glanced down at her feet. She wore sandals. He liked looking at her bare feet. But with D.J. he pretty much liked looking at bare anything. Even in jeans and a tank top, which she had on tonight, she was sexy as hell. He wanted her naked, in his bed and screaming out her pleasure. As this was his fantasy and unlikely to happen anytime soon, he added the thrill of her grabbing him by the hips and begging him to take her.

"You're grinning," she said. "What are you thinking?"

"You really want to know?"

She sighed. "Probably not."

They passed a lingerie store. "What about something from here?" he asked. "I could get into that."

"How typical."

"Men are more visual than women. It's not our fault."

"Uh-huh." She paused outside a music box store. "They had a couple of things in here I saw last month, but I don't know."

Quinn moved behind her. The window display had been filled with music boxes. Everything from china dogs to dolls to carved wooden boxes.

"It seems like a Rebecca kind of place," he said.

D.J. shrugged. "The stuff in here is too impractical."

She started to walk away but he grabbed her arm. "Wait. Don't you want to look inside?"

"Maybe."

Her brown eyes darkened with something he didn't recognize at first. Then he recognized vulnerability.

He rubbed his thumb against her upper arm. "If it's from you, she's going to love it."

"You don't know that."

"Actually, I do. Rebecca loves you."

D.J. squirmed free. "We're friends."

"That's what I said."

She muttered something he couldn't hear and stalked into the store. Quinn wondered why the *L* word bothered her so much. As a guy he could understand not wanting to hear it in a romantic sense. There was the whole being-trapped feeling. Although he'd never minded the thought of one woman for the rest of his life. But weren't women supposed to be the warm nurturing ones? Didn't love come easy for them, especially between friends?

Then he reminded himself this was D.J., and while she might be sexy and the most challenging woman he'd ever met, she wasn't even close to easy.

He followed her into the store. She'd stopped in front of a display of tropical music boxes. One had a colorful cloisonné butterfly on top. She touched the edge of the wing.

"It's beautiful," he told her.

"It reminds me of Rebecca."

"I can see that." Oddly enough, it also reminded him of D.J., who was beautiful, but also tough. Like the butterflies who migrated thousands of miles each year.

She sighed. "I guess I'll get it. I mean, I don't see anything else I like as well."

She was acting like this was no big deal, but he'd already figured out the truth. D.J. had wanted to buy the music box for Rebecca from the moment she'd seen it. But for some reason she'd been worried it wasn't perfect. So she'd waited to get someone else's opinion. He was touched that she'd allowed him to be the one to help her decide.

"She'll love it," he said.

"I hope so."

Without thinking, he reached out and lightly stroked her cheek. She looked at him.

"What do you think you're doing?" she asked.

"Touching you."

"Why?"

"Because I want to."

Her eyes widened slightly. Tension crackled between them. Sure there was sexual awareness, but there was also something more. A connection. A possibility.

He waited for her to pull back, to protest, to slap his hand away. Instead she smiled.

"Okay."

D.J. set down her tray on the table and slid into a plastic chair. She'd chosen to have Chinese for dinner, while Quinn had picked Italian. He offered her a slice of garlic bread.

"Not with my orange chicken," she said, "but thanks for asking."

"Anytime."

When he'd invited her to dinner, she hadn't been sure she'd wanted to accept. Nor had she wanted to say no, which made no sense but was right in line with how her life was going these days. However, if she'd tried to figure out what would happen during the dinner, she would never have imagined them dining in the middle of the food court.

"Save room for ice cream," he told her. "I'm springing for two scoops."

"Be still my heart."

He grinned. "It's the flowers, isn't it? I brought you flowers and now you're getting all gooey on me. Not that I mind."

She blinked at him. "Gooey?"

"You know. Romantic. It's nice."

She grabbed her plastic fork. "I'm not getting romantic."

"Sure you are. We can hold hands while we eat, if you'd like."

She dropped her free hand to her lap. "I don't think so."

He winked. "I like that you're shy."

Shy? If she'd been drinking she would have spit. She might be a lot of things, but shy—

She glared at him. "You're teasing me."

"Uh-huh."

She tried not to smile, but felt the corners of her mouth curve up anyway. Damn him. How did Quinn do that? All her life she'd been out of the mainstream. Never just a regular teenager or young woman. She told herself she didn't mind being different, that she had a purpose. She needed to stay safe and keep others safe. But sometimes—rarely—she wanted to be like other women her age. Carefree. Unbound by the knowledge of how deadly the world could be.

When Quinn treated her like a regular woman, she could almost bring herself to forget.

He chewed a mouthful of ziti, then swallowed. "So I was thinking about the lingerie store," he said conversationally. "After dinner, we should go back and you can model some stuff for me."

"Excuse me?"

"You're excused."

Her warm fuzzy thoughts faded. "I'm not going to prance around in sexy lingerie for you."

"Technically, I never mentioned the word *prance*. See here's the thing." He leaned forward and dropped his voice. "I've been out in the jungle for a long time, serving my country. If you were to do this, you would be, in your own personal way, aiding the defense of our nation."

She chewed her orange chicken. "Does anyone really buy into your lines?"

He winced. "That was cruel. I'm being completely honest here. You would look great in sleazy underwear. And I'm in a position to know, what with having seen you naked."

D.J. didn't know what was going on. For the past week, Quinn hadn't mentioned that night she'd gone to his hotel room. She even wondered if he'd forgotten about it. Now, suddenly, it was a topic of conversation.

"Define *sleazy*," she told him.

He grinned. "Cut down to your belly button, up to your hipbones. Or topless. Topless works. Silk, lacy, see-through. I'm not real picky."

"I can tell."

She thought about the lingerie store they'd passed early. They carried more high-end inventory. She would describe their stock as feminine and erotic, but not sleazy. There's no way men would be allowed into the dressing room. Not that she was willing to give Quinn a fashion show for one. Still…

She remembered the bustier they'd had in the window, with some high-cut panties and a garter belt. She was too muscular to be thin, but her body had plenty of curves and definition. Some men liked that. Did Quinn?

Unhappy with the question, and with the image of herself wearing the bustier while Quinn moved ever closer, she attacked her dinner.

"I'm into cotton," she told him.

"Cotton could work. You would be hot in just about anything."

She glanced at him. Damn if the man didn't look sincere. And double damn if that sincerity didn't make her feel all warm inside. "Thanks."

"You're welcome. So you want to go back to that store?"

"Nope."

"What if I beg?"

She shook her head. "Explain the male fascination with the female body to me. I get why teenagers are interested, but once a guy hits his twenties, how can there be any mystery?"

He leaned toward her. "You're kidding, right?"

"No. I'm serious. I don't get it." She set down her fork. "During the war games, before I met up with you, there were three army officers. They were in their thirties, experienced soldiers. I sent Ronnie to circle around back while I used a frontal approach."

Quinn frowned. "You walked right up to them."

"Sort of. First I took off my shirt. I had a tank top on underneath, no bra. I twisted it and tucked it under my breasts so it was tight. Then I rolled down my pants to bikini level, loosened my hair and acted stupid. It worked perfectly." She took a sip of her drink. "I'll admit that it was cold and my shirt was damp, so the breast thing should have been mildly interesting, but they were so caught up in the 'girl thing' they got caught. What's up with that?"

"I have no idea."

"It's not as if each of them hadn't seen dozens of women's breasts before. They're *just* breasts. Why are men such saps? Can you imagine what would have happened if I'd been wearing a wet T-shirt and a thong? They would have probably told me state secrets. Frankly, anyone wearing a thong deserves that. I mean why would any rational woman want to have something tugging up her—"

D.J. noticed that Quinn's expression had glazed over. His eyes were slightly unfocused and he looked as if he was in pain.

"What?"

He made a noise low in his throat. "Change the subject."

"We can't talk about thongs at dinner? Why? You're the one who wanted me wearing practically nothing."

He reached over and grabbed her chair and pulled it several inches closer. Then he took her free hand and brought it to his crotch.

D.J. dropped her fork. He wasn't just hard, he was throbbing. She felt the length and breadth of his erection but didn't understand what had caused it.

"You're turned on by thongs?" she asked.

He groaned. "No. By you in one. Or nothing. We have to change the subject."

She slowly withdrew her hand. Several thoughts flooded her mind at once. They were, in no particular order, the realization that she was aroused, too. Somehow all the talk of being naked or almost naked, of him watching, of *sex,* had left her breathless and tingling. She also suddenly understood why he'd been angry after they'd been intimate. He was the kind of man who liked to share rather than just take. He'd trusted her and she'd violated that trust.

But the overwhelming feeling she had was one of awe. He wanted her, and he'd let her know. Even after what had happened between them, even after she'd refused to fully participate. Knowing she was difficult and that admitting to desire made him vulnerable, he'd done it anyway. What she didn't know is if he'd been afraid, or if it hadn't occurred to him to worry.

She could slaughter him with some verbal assault, but she didn't want to. Instead she found herself wishing he would pull her to her feet and drag her out to his car where he'd drive her back to his hotel and make wild passionate love to her.

"Don't look so shocked," he said lightly. "I'll survive."

She knew that. They would all survive. They would get by. But somehow that didn't seem like enough anymore.

"Quinn?"

"Don't sweat it, Daisy Jane."

Then he did the most amazing thing. He picked up her hand and brought it to his mouth where he pressed a soft, damp kiss against her open palm. Desire poured through her, flooding her until she wanted to plunge into the rising tide and never resurface.

The sexy, tender, erotic kiss made her want to curl up against him. She wanted to be held, and hold him. She wanted to touch, to be naked. She wanted to feel her body pressed against him and maybe, just maybe, let herself go. Just this once.

He stared into her eyes. She felt the connection down to her soul. If he didn't want to risk asking her back to his hotel, she could invite him to her place. Except she never brought anyone home. The only person who even knew where she lived was Rebecca.

So many walls, she thought sadly. She'd been so

concerned about keeping herself locked up and safe, she'd never considered who she might be keeping out.

"Ice cream?" he asked, breaking the mood and making her smile.

"Sure."

"Two scoops?"

"I always go for the gusto."

Quinn returned alone to his hotel room. He'd thought about inviting D.J. back with him, but the evening had gone so well, he hadn't wanted to risk ending it on anything but a positive note. Plus, he had a hunch she'd felt a tingle or two while they were together. Better to have her wanting. He was determined that the next time they were together, he would break through her barriers and seduce her into surrendering. In the meantime, he could tell there would be several cold showers in his future.

As he walked over to the bed, he saw the message notice on his cell phone.

He punched the number from memory, then waited for the answer.

"Banner."

Quinn heard the familiar voice of his CO. "It's Reynolds."

"There's been an unexpected development. I need a shooter. You interested?"

Quinn glanced down at the blank pad of paper. He'd been promising himself that he would make a list of the pros and cons of staying in his present job. But what was the point of that? He either wanted in or he wanted out.

If he left…then what?

He thought about Gage and Kari—their engagement, their marriage, their plans to have a house, kids, grandkids. He thought of Travis and Kyle, of Rebecca who loved her husband. Of the women like her. Could he have that?

"Quinn?"

"I'm still here." He shook his head. "No can do."

"This assignment or all of them?"

He thought of D.J. She didn't make it easy, but that was how he liked it. If he could have her...

"All of them. I want out."

His CO sighed. "You're going to be hell to replace. You've been the best."

"What does that say about me?"

"Good question. I'll need you to come in and formalize all this. No rush."

"I'll let you know when."

"Fair enough. Good luck."

"Thanks."

Quinn pushed the off button, then tossed the phone on the bed.

He'd just closed a door. Now he would wait to see what the view was like out the window.

"You reviewed the material, right?" D.J. asked, wondering why she was so edgy. She'd done this a thousand times before. Except she'd never done it with Quinn along. Could that make all the difference?

The man in question pulled the bag of supplies out of her SUV. "I looked it over several times. Relax."

"But you've never participated in this kind of a demonstration before." She led the way toward the elementary school. "I want to get it right."

He shook his head. "D.J., it'll be fine. Based on

what you told me, I don't even have lines. I'm just your punching bag."

She looked at him. "We're going to be demonstrating basic self-defense for these kids. If anyone tries to abduct them, this training may be all that stands between staying safe and getting kidnapped. I take that very seriously."

"So do I."

She nodded. "I know. It's just this is important to me."

"That's why I'm here."

His steady gaze reassured her. Normally she had one of the deputies from the sheriff's office help her out, but instead of calling Travis, she'd asked Quinn.

Really stupid, she told herself. Because it smacked of finding excuses to spend time with him. Which she really hated. Life had been a whole lot easier before the war games. Back before she'd known Quinn Reynolds existed.

"You're nervous," he said, sounding surprised.

"Of course I'm nervous," she snapped as they entered the school and headed for the front office to sign in. "I'm a person, not a machine. I have emotions."

"Most of the time you try to ignore them."

She stopped in the middle of the hall and glared at him. "This is a really bad time to psychoanalyze me, okay?"

He cupped her cheek. "You'll be fine."

She practically growled. "Of course *I'll* be fine. *I'm* not the problem."

"Meaning I am?" He dropped his hand. "Not true, Daisy Jane."

"Don't call me that."

"Hmm, so if it's not me and it's not you, then what has your panties in a bunch?"

She stalked to the front desk and signed both their names. "I could kill you right now," she muttered under her breath. "I have means and motive."

"So much violence."

He waited until they were out of earshot of the secretary, then leaned close. "Someone is just a little frustrated. Or is she worried that people might think she likes a certain someone? Are you afraid the kids will see that you want me to be your boyfriend?"

She grabbed the front of his shirt. "I do *not* want you for my boyfriend," she told him, her voice loud enough to echo in the empty hallway.

D.J. instantly dropped her hand and wanted to curl up in a ball. Embarrassment heated her cheeks.

"I'll get you for this," she told him.

He chuckled. "I can't wait."

Determined to ignore him, what he said, how he made her feel and every other thing about him, she walked toward the classroom. When she reached the door, she turned back to him.

"I expect you to behave in here."

"Yes, ma'am. But if I don't, are you going to punish me when we get back to my hotel?"

She rolled her eyes, then stepped inside the room.

The teacher smiled and greeted her, as did several of the students. Most of them she'd already met. When Quinn followed her in, she introduced him to the kids, and told them why they were here.

In the middle of her explanation, she saw Quinn

wink at one of the little boys. At the sight, the last of her nervousness faded and her heart gave a little squeeze.

Everything was going to be just fine.

Chapter 12

Quinn wasn't surprised when D.J. hopped out of the car as soon as he put it in Park. He figured her allowing him to drive in his vehicle was as much of a victory as he was going to get at one time. And it was enough.

He'd invited her to join him for a barbecue at Travis's house, and she'd accepted. Two weeks ago the mention of it would have sent her running, or put her into combat mode. She'd come a long way in a short period of time. He wondered if he was the only one who noticed, or if she'd seen the changes, too.

"Thanks for being my date," he said when he'd caught up with her.

She paused in midstep and looked at him. "Your what?"

Okay, so messing with her probably wasn't wise, but it was too much fun. She grabbed the bait each and every time. He liked how her eyes got all bright when she was riled and how she glared at him. As if she could really take him. She was tough and determined, and underneath that facade was a heartbroken woman desperate to be held.

"My date. I asked you to join me and you accepted. What would you call it?"

"Momentary lapse of judgment," she muttered.

He ignored that. "I know you want to compliment me on how things went at the school last week. You've been trying to figure out how to tell me I was brilliant."

She rolled her eyes. "You don't actually need me here for this conversation, do you?"

"Come on. Admit it. I was good."

She sighed heavily. "Fine. You were good. You made the kids feel comfortable and that's important."

The compliment surprised him. He hadn't expected her to go along with him. "You were great, too," he told her honestly. "You're real sweet with the kids. They trust you. You're giving them information that can save them. You get them to see it's important but you don't scare them."

She turned away. "Thanks," she mumbled, and kicked at the grass. "I want to keep them safe."

"I know."

He knew more than that. He knew she worried about them, and that some of her concern came from the fact that *she'd* never felt safe herself, growing up. He wished he could change that. He would like to go back in time and make her world right.

A burst of laughter caught his attention. For the first time he actually looked at the large house in front of them. It was a three-story Victorian on a huge lot. Half a dozen kids played in a side yard. Two young girls sat on the massive covered porch. There was a board game on the wood floor between them, and a tray with drinks and cookies.

He put his arm around D.J.'s shoulders and started forward. "Cops make more here in Glenwood than they do in Possum Landing," he said.

"I don't think so. This house, and the equally elegant homes the other Haynes siblings own are paid for by dividends from Austin's company. He's an inventor of heat-resistant polymers, or something like that. I can't remember. Anyway, they helped with the start-up money years ago and have been well rewarded for their faith. It's a great company. I bought a few shares myself."

He was pleased she hadn't pulled away from his embrace. Now he leaned close. "An amazing body, and money. You're quite the catch, Daisy Jane."

"You're the most irritating man I know."

"And yet you adore me."

She stopped at the foot of the stairs. "*Adore* is really strong. I'd be willing to admit to *tolerate*. Sometimes I tolerate you."

Coming from her, that was practically a confession of everlasting love.

"You think I'm sexy, too," he whispered, mindful of the girls on the porch.

She glanced down at the ground. "You are the most egotistical, arrogant, self-centered man—"

He silenced her with a quick kiss. She stiffened but didn't pull back. He considered that progress. When he raised his head, she looked stunned. Wanting lurked in her dark eyes, which pleased him. He'd spent the past couple of weeks in a constant state of need. There had been plenty of times when he could have ushered D.J. into his bed, but he wouldn't. Not until the moment was right. This time he wanted a very different outcome.

That condition would require her to trust him and need him. While he'd made progress on both fronts, he wanted to be sure. If they made love a second time and she was able to hold back, he knew that a pattern would have been established. The longer it went on, the more difficult it would be to break. Better to drown in cold showers than risk moving in too soon.

He took her hand and drew her up the stairs. They walked into the large house and were immediately plunged into familial chaos.

More kids ran through the front rooms. Travis and Kyle were talking, their wives at their sides. He saw Rebecca with a baby in her arms, Kari, Haley and Stephanie laughing together. Kevin and Nash shared a sofa. Family, he thought. His family.

Jordan spotted them first and called out a greeting. Suddenly Quinn and D.J. were surrounded by Hayneses, Reynoldses and Harmons. Quinn found himself shaking hands with the men and accepting hugs and kisses from the women. A couple of kids wanted to be picked up.

"Glad you two could make it," Austin said, as he put his arm around his wife. "We were wondering if you got lost."

"It was D.J.'s fault," Quinn said easily. "She takes so long with all that primping."

She shot him the death stare. "I was right on time."

As soon as the words were out, she pressed her lips together, as if she'd just realized she'd more or less implied they were together. A couple. His date, as he'd teased her earlier. Quinn waited to see if she would balk or distance herself. Instead she shrugged.

"But blaming it on the woman is so much easier, right?" she said.

He grinned. "Whatever works."

She glanced at him. The corners of her mouth quivered, then she smiled. He felt a tightness in his chest, but before he could figure out what it meant, Jill claimed D.J., then Gage walked over and the moment was gone.

"How's it going?" his brother asked him.

"Good. What about with you?"

Gage nodded at the crowd. "I hate to leave all this, but Kari and I are heading home in a few days. Kari promised to help Mom with her wedding to John, then we have to get moving on our own." Gage cuffed him lightly. "I'd like you to be my best man. Think you can swing it?"

"I'll be there."

Gage looked surprised. "Are you sure?"

Kari walked up and slipped her arm through Gage's. "Sure about what?"

"Quinn says he can make it home to be my best man."

Kari smiled at him. "I'm glad. Gage really wants you there, and I do, too. Think you can stand wearing a tux for a few hours?"

"Absolutely," Quinn told her.

"Good. Now that the family had expanded, the guest list just got a whole lot bigger. More people means more fun, right? Oh, that reminds me, I need everyone's addresses. I better get them now before I forget."

She kissed Gage's cheek and walked off. Gage turned and watched her go.

Quinn saw the happiness in his brother's expression. "You look like a man in love," he said.

"I am." Gage shrugged. "After all these years, I wasn't sure it was going to happen, but it did. She was worth the wait."

"How'd you know she was the one?"

"I just knew. I want to tell you that it was a gradual thing. That I figured it out in stages, but that's not true. When Kari came home, I still had some feelings for her, but I didn't know if they were about the past, or what. Then I found out about Earl Haynes being our biological father and nothing was the same. That was my own personal hell, and Kari was there. I finally got that I was better with her than without her. Imagining us together in twenty or thirty years was easy. I liked what I saw in our future."

"Sounds good."

"It is. I want to have kids with her. I want roots."

Quinn nodded. Roots had always been important to his brother. Gage had prided himself on being a fifth-generation Reynolds in Possum Landing. Learning that Earl Haynes was his biological father had changed everything, but he'd come through okay. Now Gage would create his own dynasty, pass on his own traditions.

"You've always known what you wanted," Quinn said.

Gage glanced toward D.J. "What about you? There's something going on. We can all see it."

Quinn didn't bother denying the obvious. He and D.J. *did* have something between them, but he wasn't sure what. She could be everything he'd ever wanted and needed, but what about him? Did he come close to being right for her?

"When I figure it out, I'll let you know," he said.

Travis walked over and slapped Gage on the back. "Did he tell you that he's heading back to Texas?"

"He did."

Travis shook his head. "I've done my best to talk him into staying, but he won't have any part of it."

Elizabeth joined her husband and slid her arm around his waist. "Honey, you've got to stop trying to get everyone in the family to move to Glenwood. We all think it's the perfect place to live, but Gage seems very fond of his hometown. You need to respect that."

Travis shrugged. "Can I help it if I want my brothers close?"

"I appreciate the sentiment," Gage told him. "You don't have to worry about us all losing touch. Now that we've found each other, you're stuck with us."

"I wouldn't have it any other way," Travis said.

Kyle walked up. "What about you, Quinn? You ever think about sticking around here? You could run for sheriff against Travis."

Quinn chuckled. "I don't think so. I'm not an election kind of guy."

"So challenge him to an arm wrestling match," Kyle said.

Travis shook his head. "Nope. He'd whip my butt."

"You're strong," Elizabeth told her husband.

"Quinn knows things," Travis said and kissed her. "But thanks for the support."

Quinn watched them. While he didn't begrudge them their happiness, seeing their contentment in their relationships left him feeling empty inside. As if he'd been missing out on something for a long time.

D.J. chose that moment to stroll up. She was on his side of the group, so he risked grabbing her wrist and pulling her close.

He half expected her to try to deck him. Instead she flashed him a startled glance, then stepped close enough for him to put his arm around her waist and rest his hand on her hip.

Travis and his wife looked at each other but didn't say anything. Gage grinned, as did Kyle. Quinn had a good idea about what they were all thinking. Let 'em, he told himself. No one's opinion mattered except for D.J.'s and his own.

"How long will you be staying in the military?" Elizabeth asked him. "If you don't have other plans, you could think about moving here when you get out. Even if you don't want to run for sheriff."

"Quinn always planned to stay in at least twenty years," Gage said. "That means another ten to go."

Quinn nodded. That had been his plan. Until a few days ago.

"I resigned last week."

Everyone looked surprised. Gage took a half step toward him. "What happened?"

As his brother asked the question, Quinn felt D.J.'s hand on his back. He glanced down at her. She didn't speak, but he could read the concern in her expression. He gave her a reassuring smile, then turned his attention back to Gage.

"I wasn't willing to be that person anymore."

There was a whole lot more to it than that, but no

one needed to hear the details. Later maybe he would discuss them with D.J., but not now.

Gage grinned. "Then you *will* be at my wedding."

"I said I would be."

Travis slapped him on the back. "You're welcome to stay here. Glenwood could always use another deputy."

"Or sheriff," Kyle said, then chuckled.

"I appreciate the offer. I don't know what I want to do, but when I figure it out, I'll let you know."

The conversation shifted to plans for the evening. Eventually people started drifting away. Quinn kept his arm around D.J. until they were alone, then he leaned against the wall and grabbed on to her belt loop and tugged her close.

"You've been quiet," he said.

"I'm still in shock from your bombshell. What made you change your mind?"

He shrugged. "I never liked what I did—even though I was good at it. There weren't enough rescues and there were way too many killings. That's not what I wanted."

"Makes sense."

He couldn't tell what she was thinking and it became important for him to know. Did any of this matter to her? Did she care that he was no longer going to be heading out of the country in a few weeks? Would she tell him the truth if he asked, and if she would, did he want to hear it?

"D.J.…"

She cut him off with a quick shake of her head. "I'm glad," she whispered.

Two words. Two little words that hit him with the power of a rifle blast at point-blank range. The air exploded from his lungs. His chest swelled and his heart rate doubled.

"Yeah," he said, trying for cool and not sure if he made it.

He glanced around and saw a small powder room tucked under the stairs. After making sure no one was watching, he took D.J.'s hand and drew her along with him. When they'd both squeezed into the tiny room, he shut the door behind them and gathered her close.

He'd thought she might protest but instead she melted into his arms. Even as he pressed his mouth to hers, she parted for him. Tongues swept against each other. Searching, hungry, deep kisses shredded his self-control and left him desperate with wanting.

He touched her hair, her back, then dropped his hands to her rear and squeezed. She arched against him, bringing her belly in contact with his erection. She seemed as eager, as ready. Her slender fingers touched his face, then explored his chest.

"I want you," he breathed against her mouth.

He cupped her face to hold her in place, then drew back enough to nibble along her jaw. When he reached her throat, she dropped her head, exposing her soft skin. He licked the sensitive spot just behind her earlobe and made her moan. Sucking the same bit of skin made her squirm.

She wore jeans and a tank top. Quinn grabbed the straps and pulled them down her arms. The knit fabric slipped over her breasts and pinned her arms to her sides. He knew she could free herself in a second, but there was the illusion of being trapped. Not exactly D.J.'s style.

"It's all right," he whispered as he unfastened the front of her bra. "I won't hurt you. I promise."

He kissed his way down her chest to her exposed breasts. As he took one tight nipple into his mouth, he teased the other with his fingers.

She tasted sweet and hot. He was so damned hard he could have lost it right there.

"So beautiful," he told her, moving to her other breast. "Perfect curves. Your nipples are so tight." He licked the hard tip. She jumped.

"I love how you react to my touch," he said, then opened his mouth and drew her in.

He sucked rhythmically. Her breath caught, then she shifted, freeing herself of the tank top. Quinn braced himself for her rejection. But instead of pushing him away, she buried her fingers in his hair and held him in place.

"Don't stop," she whispered.

They were magic words, he thought, both relieved and gratified by her response. She trusted him. Maybe not fully, but more than he'd hoped was possible.

While he wanted to push her up onto the narrow vanity and take her right there, he knew this wasn't the time or the place. When he next made love with D.J., he wanted privacy, a big bed and a whole night. Still, a man could dream, right?

He straightened. While keeping his hands on her breasts, he stared into her eyes and pushed his arousal against her. Her pupils dilated and her mouth parted. She shifted, parting her legs and then moving against him. Rubbing herself on his erection. Taking pleasure.

"I want you so much," he breathed. "Tell me you feel the same."

He was asking too much—he knew that. But he wanted to hear the words. *Needed* to hear them.

She pulled back a little. He kept his hands on her bare breasts.

"D.J., don't," he whispered, then kissed her.

He didn't know if he was telling her not to draw away, or giving her permission not to say the words. When she kissed him with the uninhibited passion of a woman desperate for a man, he told himself it was enough.

Eventually he became aware of his surroundings and lifted his head. "Someone's going to need this bathroom pretty damn soon," he said.

"I know."

He released her breasts and reached for her bra. "You're a terrific date."

She drew on the cotton undergarment and smiled. "You're not so bad yourself."

They both straightened their clothes. Quinn tried to adjust himself so his erection wasn't so obvious. D.J. watched, then grinned.

"You should probably stay close behind me until that goes away. Otherwise, the entire family will be talking."

"Good plan."

She reached for the door handle, then paused. "Quinn, I—" She shook her head. "I just… Hell."

She fumbled with the front of her jeans. Before he could figure out what she was doing, she unzipped them and took his hand in hers. Then she pushed his fingers down the front of her panties. He felt soft skin, softer curls, then a slick, swollen heat that made him groan.

"I do want you," she admitted, even as she turned away and fastened her jeans. "Just so you know."

Then she opened the door and stepped out into the hallway.

Stunned, aroused and more than a little awed by her courage, Quinn followed. And came face-to-face with a very amused Rebecca.

"Gee, after all this time, I would have thought you could manage the bathroom on your own," Rebecca said.

D.J. blushed. If Quinn hadn't seen it with his own eyes, he wouldn't have believed it.

"Nothing happened," D.J. told her friend.

Rebecca raised her eyebrows. "Too bad."

After the dinner, the men cleared the table, served dessert and made coffee. Quinn found himself in the kitchen, carefully cutting a large sheet cake into small pieces. Rebecca walked into the room.

"I brought you a cake server," she said as she set down a silver spatula-like device.

"Thanks."

He used it to transfer the first corner piece to a plate.

She leaned against the counter and watched Kevin pour coffee into a carafe. When he'd left, she turned her attention back to Quinn.

"I'm pleased that D.J. has finally let herself fall for someone," she told him.

Quinn was smart enough to recognize a mine field when he stepped into one. He carefully kept quiet.

Rebecca smiled. "Is the subject matter making you nervous?"

"Maybe."

"It shouldn't. You make her happy and that's good."

He scooped up another piece of cake. "Okay."

Rebecca sighed. "Fine. I'll talk. You can listen. That probably feels safer." She began putting plates on the tray. "I know there are a lot of dark secrets from D.J.'s past. Something horrible happened when she was still a kid. She doesn't talk about it, but I recognize the scars."

Quinn looked at her. She shrugged.

"I've been around orphaned kids for years," she told him. "Loss and pain are fairly universal. D.J. has a wounded spirit and it's not just because her parents are dead."

"Okay."

"There's a certain irony in all of this," she continued. "D.J. has done everything she can to stay safe. At least by her definition of the word. Then she goes and falls for the one man who will always be stronger, faster, more deadly. Maybe she recognizes something of herself in you. Or maybe you see a kindred spirit."

Quinn wasn't about to go there. He still hadn't decided if normal was in the cards for him. Although if it was, he put his money on D.J. being the one.

"She doesn't trust easily," he said.

"I know, but she's starting to trust you. When she pushes you away, and she will, take heart in that."

He handed her a plate. "What makes you think I'm worth it?"

"D.J. doesn't give her heart easily and never without the person earning the privilege of receiving it. Besides, I've met your brothers and I've spent time with you. You're one of the good guys."

Yeah, right. "Do you have any idea what I used to do for a living?"

"No. Why does that matter?"

"You wouldn't be alone with me if you had a clue."

"You're wrong," she told him. "It's not what you do, it's who you are."

"Haven't you heard that men are what they do?"

"Sure. And you just walked away from your job. I think there's hope, Quinn Reynolds. More importantly, D.J. does."

Rebecca was too trusting by half. "Maybe you should warn me off. Maybe you should tell me not to hurt her."

"I don't think you will. There's a part of me afraid she won't give you the chance. I hope she does. I hope she can open herself enough to be hurt, but I can't be sure. I wish—" Rebecca glanced at the doorway.

D.J. walked into the kitchen. "Don't stop talking on my account."

"I have to. We were talking about you. It's no fun if we can't do it behind your back." She tried to hand D.J. the tray. "Take this out to the dining room so we can go back to gossiping."

"No way. I want to hear what you two were saying."

Quinn finished cutting the cake. "Not even on a bet."

D.J. moved close. "I have ways of making you talk."

Their gazes locked. Quinn felt the heat slam into his body. The wanting that always lurked just below the surface exploded to life.

Rebecca sighed. "All this sexual energy makes me want to collect my husband, take him home and have my way with him. In fact I'm going to do just that right now. 'Night all."

She walked out of the room. Quinn didn't take his gaze from D.J.'s face.

"Not a bad idea," he said.

The drive back to the hotel should have taken fifteen minutes and probably did…but to D.J. it seemed to last a lifetime. Her mind raced with a thousand questions and not a single answer. Too many things had happened in too short a period of time. Quinn's announcement that he was leaving the military. While she had a good idea why he was doing it, she didn't know why it made her feel…hopeful. His employment had nothing to do with her. Leaving the military didn't mean he was sticking around in Glenwood, nor did she want him to. He would be leaving and she wouldn't be missing him when he was gone. Really.

So why did she feel so unsettled? Was it the kiss they'd shared? The intensity of the moment had humbled her. She'd wanted with a desperation she'd never felt before. Even more startling, she'd let him know.

She felt afraid, but also alive. More alive than she'd felt in years. Fear and desire. Which would be stronger?

They pulled into the hotel parking lot. Quinn stopped the car, then turned off the engine. When he pulled the key from the ignition, he dangled it between his fingers and glanced at her.

"I want you to stay," he said quietly. "Spend the night with me, D.J."

She didn't know what to say. The word *yes* hovered on her lips, but to speak it would require a level of courage she didn't possess. Quinn didn't know what he was asking.

He touched her cheek. "Stay," he whispered. "But know this. If you walk into that hotel room with me, it has to be different. You have to be willing to trust me."

She knew what he meant. He didn't want her holding back. Honestly, she wasn't sure she could. Last time she'd barely escaped. Now that he knew what she would try to do, he would work all that much harder to make sure she surrendered. Would she be able to withstand his sensual assault? Did she want to?

She told herself that walking away was the easiest and most sensible solution. Quinn was a great guy, but did she really want to take things any further with him? Why not keep it simple?

She actually reached for the door handle, but before her fingers could close on it, her heart cried out. The sharp, painful sound ripped through her, making her ache. She'd been alone for too damn long, she thought bitterly. Alone and empty. She'd devoted her life to protecting herself, and in the end, what did she have to show for it? Yes, she was alive, but was she living? She worried about broken bones, but what about blows to her spirit? Didn't she just once want to connect with another living creature? Didn't she just once want to be like everyone else?

She looked at him, at his familiar, handsome face, at his dark eyes and the steady set of his mouth. He wanted too much, yet how could she refuse? If she walked away, would she ever have the courage to try again?

"I can't promise it will work," she told him, forcing herself to meet his gaze when all she wanted to do was duck her head.

He smiled. "Agreed. But you have to promise to try." His grin turned cocky. "I can take it from there."

She thought about how it had been the last time they'd been together and what he'd made her feel just a few hours ago in that tiny bathroom. She thought of all the times he'd understood when she'd assumed no one ever would. She thought about how she looked forward to seeing him and how much he'd come to mean to her.

Slowly she stepped out of the car. Quinn did the

same. They stood on opposite sides of the vehicle. Her own SUV was just a few feet away. Easy escape, she thought. But at what price?

Then she straightened her shoulders and nodded. "Okay," she said. "I'll try."

Chapter 13

D.J. was shaking when they entered Quinn's hotel room, and it wasn't from desire. The need to bolt was nearly as strong as the need to keep breathing. Every cell in her body told her this was a really, really bad idea.

When he closed the door behind them, the sound echoed in her head. Since she'd last been in here, the space had shrunk to the size of a postage stamp. There didn't seem to be anywhere to move. She couldn't catch her breath.

"Hey," he said, taking her hand and leading her to the bed. "Looking like you're going to pass out isn't doing much for my ego. I'm a guy. If you mess with my confidence, this is going to fizzle."

She tried to smile at his humor. "I don't think your ego is the problem."

He sighed. "You're right. I'm just too good."

He sat and pulled her down next to him. She wanted to bounce right back to her feet, but resisted the burning need. Instead she laced her fingers together and concentrating on slowing her increasing heart rate. Be centered, she told herself. Be relaxed. Don't throw up.

All good advice, she thought, trying to find humor in the situation. But running out that door still sounded like the best plan.

"Lie down," he said.

The command stunned her. She turned to him. "What? Just like that? Should I spread my legs, too? You can do it in fifteen seconds and then I can be out of here. What a great plan."

He ignored her tirade and slipped back onto the mattress, then patted the space next to him. "Come on, D.J. Right here. Lie down and talk to me. That's all we're going to do. Talk."

Gritting her teeth against the need to continue her outburst, she kicked off her shoes and did as he requested. She hated stretching out next to him. She felt awkward and ungainly. All arms and legs, with nowhere to put them.

Quinn propped his head up on one hand and rested the other on her stomach. She jumped at the contact, then tried to slow her breathing.

"What?" she demanded, sounding more curt than she'd planned.

He didn't speak. Instead he slowly rubbed her belly. Around and around. Like she was some damn cat, she thought resentfully.

"Have you ever allowed yourself to climax while making love?"

That sure cut to the heart of the matter, she thought suddenly embarrassed. She closed her eyes and shook her head.

"Ever get close?"

Could they please stop talking and just do it? Except she couldn't say that and she still couldn't look at him, so she nodded.

"Sometimes," she whispered. "Not often. If I get too...interested, it's pretty easy to change direction."

"When you and I were together, I thought you were close," he said. "Was I right?"

She nodded. "It would have been easy to, um, you know."

"So none of this is about my abilities in bed."

She opened her eyes and glared at him. "Do you have to make everything about yourself?"

"Pretty much." He continued to rub her stomach. "It's okay that you're nervous. And scared. I understand that. All I want from you is the promise that you'll be open to the experience. Just lie there and let me seduce you."

He leaned close. "I'm going to touch you all over." He bent down and kissed her neck. "With my fingers, my lips and my tongue."

He demonstrated by lightly licking her skin. Instantly goose bumps erupted and her breasts began to swell. Anticipation grew, slowly pushing out the fear.

"I'm going to take off all your clothes," he continued. "When you're naked, I'm going to look at you because you're so beautiful. Then I'm going to work my way up from your toes. When I get here..." He moved his hands from her belly to that place between her legs.

"I'm going to touch you and taste you and pleasure you until neither of us can stand it. All you have to do is lie back and let me."

D.J. suddenly felt as if she were on fire. Her arms and legs felt heavy. Her brain wasn't working as quickly as usual, and she was already wet and swollen.

In the past she'd never allowed a man to do what Quinn was talking about. Everything about it made her feel too vulnerable. But suddenly she wanted to know what it would be like to experience that most intimate kiss. She wanted to feel his hot breath, his firm lips, his searching tongue.

She had to swallow before she could speak. "If I don't like it, will you stop?"

"Of course." He returned his hand to her belly. "You don't have to say yes, D.J. All you have to do is not say no. I'm going to wait for a count of three. If you remain silent, I'm going to start seducing you. Fair enough?"

She wanted. For the first time in her life, the need was greater than the fear. In fact she couldn't even find the fear anymore. She was hot and wet and shivering with anticipation. She needed him desperately. A small corner of her brain whispered that maybe she needed to trust more than she needed to experience sexual release, but she would wrestle with that issue another time. Right now she wanted to live the erotic image Quinn had planted in her brain. She wanted to lose herself in his arms and know what it was like to surrender to a man. To this man.

"One," he said slowly, his gaze steady on her face, his mouth curved slightly. "Two."

She reached up and wrapped her arms around his neck, then drew him close.

"Three," she whispered.

They met in an openmouthed kiss that sent her senses flying into the stratosphere. Liquid heat poured through her, making her ache and need with an intensity that took her breath away. His tongue swept inside her mouth, touching hers, teasing, tasting, taking and offering in a sensual combination that made her whimper.

He touched her back, her hips, her rear. He stretched out next to her, pulling her close, so she could feel him as well. The length of his legs, the breadth of his chest, the hardness of him.

He wanted her. If the fear returned, she would hang on to that one thought. He wanted her. He'd told her and shown her and his presence here, in this bed, reminded her this was important to him. He was willing to work much harder than most men she'd met. While she wanted to know why, she didn't ask the question. Not only because the answer would terrify her, but because she didn't want him to stop kissing her. Not now and maybe not ever.

His mouth still pressed against her, he shifted so he straddled her. His fingers tangled in her long braid, then slowly began to pull the strands free. When her hair was loose, he buried his hands in it and rubbed her scalp. Then he straightened and drew her tank top up and over her arms.

When he'd tossed the garment aside, he bent down and kissed her chin, then her jaw. He nibbled her earlobe, licked her neck and slowly moved down her chest to the edge of her plain, cotton bra.

His fingers made short work of the hook in front. She

felt cool air on her bare breasts, then his warm mouth settled on her left breast. His hand covered the right. Fingers and thumb teased her taut, sensitive nipple as his tongue matched the movements. Wanting poured through her. She reached for him, then let her hands fall back onto the bedspread as heat and passion made it impossible to move.

She could barely breathe. There was only the moment and the sensations. The tugging of her nipples, the ribbons of desire weaving through her pliant body. Quinn had talked of surrender. Right now she couldn't imagine anything else.

He shifted to one side and reached for the fastening of her jeans. When he'd lowered the zipper, he moved to the end of the bed and tugged them off. Her panties went along for the ride and when he knelt between her ankles, she was naked.

A vague uneasiness settled over her. This was the place she usually took control of the sexual encounter. Often she would shift the man onto his back, reach for the condom and make sure he didn't have a rational thought in his brain until he was finished.

Old habits died hard. But even as a part of her brain told her to sit up and get Quinn on his back, the rest of her remembered the promise to try. To let him seduce her. To let go…just this once.

The concept was foreign, but not so difficult to comprehend. Not when he lightly bit her ankle and made her giggle. He nibbled his way up her calf, then sucked on her knee.

"What are you doing?" she asked with a laugh. "That tickles."

She squirmed, but he didn't release her. Instead he transferred his attentions to her other knee and sucked on it. She writhed.

"I don't want to kick you in the teeth," she told him.

He raised his head and smiled. "An excellent philosophy I would encourage."

Then he ducked back down. But instead of returning to her knees, he began to work his way up her thighs.

He'd been more than clear about his destination, and his intent. She was nervous, apprehensive and more than a little excited by what he planned to do. Rebecca had talked about Austin doing that to her once. Her friend's dreamy expression had made D.J. feel more than a little left out. In truth, men had offered, but she'd never been willing to let them be that intimate.

Still, as Quinn kissed and licked and nibbled his way closer, she couldn't seem to keep her legs together. They fell open of their own accord and when she felt his hot breath on her waiting dampness, she didn't pull away.

"So beautiful," he murmured as he slipped his fingers into her swollen flesh.

A shiver rippled through her. The heat grew and for the first time she became aware of a rising tension. Her muscles quivered and contracted, her blood raced, and every part of her body focused on that one feminine place.

He reached for her hands, drawing them between her thighs and urging her to part for him. Despite the promise of pleasure, she felt exposed and vulnerable. Still, she'd said she would try, so she braced herself for the assault.

But instead of kissing her *there,* he nipped on one of her knuckles. She jumped and opened her eyes.

"What do you think you're doing?" she asked.

"Trying to keep things from being too serious." He sat up. "Pull your knees back."

She swallowed, then did as he asked, drawing her knees up and away, exposing herself even more.

"How are you doing?" he asked. "Nervous?"

He wanted to *talk* about it? "Do we have to have this conversation or can we just get to it?" she asked between gritted teeth.

"That's my girl," he said, and grinned. "Ever the delicate flower. It, D.J.? This isn't 'it.' We're making love."

Then, while she was still in shock from what he'd said, he lay back down on the bed and pressed his mouth against her.

She'd fought against that particular intimacy ever since she'd surrendered her virginity to Bobby McNare in her senior year of high school. As Quinn's tongue gently stroked her most sensitive spot and pleasure swept through her, she couldn't help wondering why.

He kissed her with a softness that left her breathless and needing. He moved over and around, sometimes fast, sometimes slow. She felt her control slipping as the need grew. Her body rebelled, wanting, striving. Tension spiraled to unbearable levels, settled there, then moved higher. Her muscles tightened. Her heels dug into the mattress. She parted her legs more, drew back her knees and pressed against Quinn's mouth.

More. She needed more. More of the slow licks, the leisurely explorations. When he lightly sucked on that one spot, she actually groaned. There was no doubting her body's destination, and if she was to pull back, this was the time. Maybe the last time.

But it felt too good. She didn't want him to stop. She didn't want to be swollen and frustrated. Just this once she wanted to let herself go. Just this once. Just with Quinn.

He loved her with his mouth. She knew now that this wasn't just sex. Not in the way she'd known it in the past. This was so much more. A man who actually cared about her and her response. A man who understood her in ways no one ever had before. She wanted to show him that his faith in her hadn't been misplaced, that she was worthy of his attentions. That—

He inserted a finger inside of her. Slowly, deeply, then pulled it out again. At the same time, he stroked her faster and faster. The combination of actions was too much. One second she was standing on the edge and the next…she fell.

Her climax caught her by surprise. Her entire body convulsed into mindless pleasure as powerful muscles contracted over and over. She cried out and shook and begged and still the waves of blissful release swept through her. It went on and on until the shudders slowed.

When she was finally still, she opened her eyes. He raised his head and looked at her. The fear returned, a cool trickling sensation that warned her she was in mortal danger. But Quinn didn't attack. Instead he kissed her palm, then shifted so he was kneeling between her legs, and smiled.

"Am I good in bed or what?" he asked.

If he'd said something emotionally significant, she might have bolted for the door. If he'd mocked her, she would have tried to kill him. Instead he made it all about himself, and made her laugh at the same time.

She grinned. "You're okay."

"Just okay? I would have thought I deserved at least a 'very good' for that performance."

"You were okay."

His smile faded and he lightly touched her knee. "Are you going to freak out on me?"

She might have a second ago, but now she felt fine. "Not unless you morph into an alien."

"That wasn't my plan. Instead I thought I'd rip my clothes off and have my way with you."

"That works."

While he undressed, she rose and walked into the bathroom where she found the box of condoms in his shaving kit and took one out. Before she turned to leave, she glanced at herself in the mirror.

She looked like a woman who had been well pleasured. Her hair was tousled, her mouth swollen, her skin flushed. She was naked and content. And happy.

The last surprised her the most. She wasn't afraid; she didn't want to run. Instead she wanted to feel Quinn inside of her, filling her, taking his pleasure in her. She wanted to be with him, bodies touching, straining. She wanted him.

Caught up in the delight of that thought, she turned and returned to the bedroom.

Quinn was on the bed. He'd stripped off his clothes and lay on his side, his arousal jutting out toward her. She tossed him the condom and slid onto the mattress.

"Take me, big boy. I'm all yours."

Her light, teasing voice touched him down to his heart. Quinn had been surprised and pleased by D.J.'s acceptance of their lovemaking, and thrilled when she'd allowed herself to climax, but it was her acceptance after the fact that gave him the most pleasure. She wasn't second-guessing herself or them. She wasn't pulling back. Somehow she'd decided to trust him, and there was no way he would do anything to violate that trust.

He slipped on the protection, then moved close and kissed her. When her breathing had increased and her hands roamed over his body with an eagerness that made control nearly impossible, he pushed her onto her back and knelt between her legs.

Eyes locked on hers, he moved into her waiting dampness. She stretched to accommodate him, then caught her breath as he slipped back out. Her mouth opened in a soundless gasp.

"What was that?" she asked, then grabbed him by his hips and pulled him in.

This time as he filled her, he felt a faint ripple. A tightness that sucked him in deeper. She arched toward him, her fingers digging into his rear.

"More," she gasped.

He plunged in again and again. Each time he felt the same tightening as her body shuddered. The faster he moved, the more she demanded. She wrapped her legs around him and drew him in deeper.

She was strong and powerful, yet the most feminine woman he'd ever known. Her surrender humbled him, even as the rippling contractions worked on his self-control until it shattered and he couldn't hold back anymore.

"I can't wait," he gasped.

Her eyes opened. "I don't want you to," she whispered and pulled him in deeper still.

He lost himself in the pleasure of his explosive release. As he did, he felt her body shudder and contract. She sucked in a breath, then screamed as she lost herself in release after release. Their gazes locked, their rapid breathing synchronized, he watched her face, her eyes, and saw down to the perfection of her soul.

D.J. awoke with the feeling that she couldn't breathe. The tightness in her chest propelled her into a sitting position. She recognized the symptoms immediately, but telling herself it was a panic attack didn't keep her from feeling that she was going to die.

She sat up and consciously fought her rising terror. As the covers fell away, she realized she was naked, and with that realization the events of the evening flashed through her mind. Suddenly the panic attack made sense.

Slowly, carefully, so as not to disturb Quinn, she crawled out of bed and made her way to the bathroom. When she'd shut the door behind her, she bent over at the waist and struggled to breathe. Determination battled the fight-or-flight response and slowly her rational side began to win. When the tightness faded and the panic was more manageable, she straightened and turned on the sink tap.

After washing her face with cool water, she grabbed a towel. The small nightlight illuminated her naked body. Not wanting to see that or think about what had happened, D.J. turned away from her reflection. But instead of returning to the bedroom, she leaned against the counter and fingered the white towel.

Last night…last night had been amazing, she thought. Terrifying and wonderful and awe-inspiring and horrible and life changing. Quinn confused her. He was so tender and caring, yet the man killed for a living. At least he had. How could he have lived through all that and still have a soul? How could he be so tender with her? How could he understand her?

She sucked in a breath. That's what got her the most. He *knew.* Somehow he'd figured out her fear and he'd worked to overcome it. Why? Shouldn't he be only interested in himself and his own pleasure? Why had he taken the time and made the effort. Why—

Her breath caught as an unexpected sob ripped through her. Even as tears filled her eyes and spilled down her cheeks, D.J. couldn't figure out what was going on. There was a second sob, then a third. She grabbed the towel and pressed her face into it to muffle the sound. What was wrong with her? She never cried. Never.

But this time she couldn't stop. The tears poured down her face as her body shook. Harsh, deep, painful cries tore at her throat. She didn't know why she was crying or why she couldn't stop. Her whole body ached, from the inside out. She felt as if she were being ripped into a million pieces.

The bathroom door opened, and Quinn stepped into the small space. Humiliation made her turn away. But there was nowhere to run. Not that he would have let her.

Instead he put his hands on her shoulders and turned her to him. He pulled the towel away and wrapped his arms around her body. As the sobs continued to choke her, he smoothed her hair and murmured softly. Not words, just comforting sounds.

Not knowing what else to do, she clung to him. He was warm and strong and safe in a spinning world she no longer recognized. The soft brush of his mouth on her forehead was comforting, although she couldn't say why. The steady beat of his heart calmed her. She cried and cried until she was nothing but a hollow shell, and still he held her.

Some time later, perhaps just a few minutes, perhaps as much as an hour, the crying slowed. D.J. was still unsure of what was wrong with her, but she had a feeling it was related to her sexual encounter with Quinn. Had her body's release somehow affected other parts of her being?

He continued to stroke her bare back. His large hands moved slowly along her skin. Suddenly the contact wasn't as comforting as it had been. She became aware of their nakedness, of his maleness pushed up against her belly, of her bare breasts flattening against his chest. Liquid heat filled her, then settled between her thighs. Her nipples got tight, her breathing increased.

Quinn didn't seem to notice. He continued to hold her with a tenderness that made her ache. But when she reached for one of his hands and brought it to her bare breast, the response was immediate.

He went from resting to ready in less than five seconds. She shifted so that she could sit on the edge of the counter, then parted her legs. He groaned. After fumbling in his shaving kit, he pulled out a condom and hastily tore the package open.

As he slipped on the protection, she kissed and nipped at his chest. She flicked her tongue over his nipples and smiled when they hardened and he shuddered. Then he was pushing in her and she couldn't think anymore, she could only feel.

Feel his hardness filling her. Feel the pressure building as he slid in and out. She wrapped her legs around him, pulling him close. He cupped her rear and drew her closer still. He pumped in and out, and with each aggressive thrust, she got closer and closer until all she had to do was keep breathing. The fall was inevitable.

Her first climax crashed over her like a hot wave of pleasure. The second was better and the third made her scream. Again and again, until she couldn't breathe, until he finally called out in guttural release. Until they were still.

The tears returned. Not the sobs, just silent tears spilling down her cheeks. She could no more explain them than stop them. But Quinn didn't ask. Instead, after tossing the condom into the trash, he gathered her close, picked her up and carried her into the bedroom.

When they were both under the covers, he simply held her close and lightly kissed her. She clung to him, even after the tears had faded. And when he told her to go to sleep, she closed her eyes and did what he'd requested.

D.J. woke with the sun in her eyes. She turned over and was stunned to find it was after nine. She *never* slept in—not even when she was sick. Even more shocking was the sight of Quinn up, showered, dressed and reading the paper. He'd done all that and she hadn't heard him?

"Morning," he said when he glanced up from the newspaper and saw her looking at him. "I ordered breakfast. It should be here in a few minutes, if you want to head into the bathroom first."

She blinked. "You made a phone call?"

"Yeah. I've tried placing orders using my powers of mental telepathy, but they usually get them wrong."

He looked exactly as he had the previous day. There was nothing different about his teasing, his smile, his dark eyes.

She braced herself for questions, but there didn't seem to be any. Was it possible he just accepted what had happened between them as normal? Didn't he want to talk about it?

"You probably have time for a shower," he continued. "There's shampoo by the tub. None of that girly stuff, though. This is macho shampoo."

She guessed the answer to her question was no. He didn't see the need. Which both pleased and terrified her.

She didn't want to get up and walk past him, what with being naked and all, but she really had to go to the bathroom. So she threw back the covers and stood up. As she walked by Quinn, he reached out and took her hand. He kissed her palm, then smiled at her.

"Thank you," he said.

That was all. Just thanks.

Her chest got tight, but not in a panic-attack sort of way. Her heartbeat got weird, too, and her skin felt all prickly. She bent down and hugged him.

"Quinn, I—"

But then she didn't know what to say. He stroked her cheek.

"I know, Daisy Jane. Me, too. Now go take your shower."

She straightened and headed for the bathroom. While she had no idea what she'd been saying, or what he'd agreed with, she felt happy and giddy and light enough to fly. She didn't even have to look out the window and check the weather to know it was going to be a very good day.

Chapter 14

"We had sex," D.J. said as she paced the length of Rebecca's kitchen.

Her friend smiled at her. "How was it? I would think that Quinn's finely honed hunter instincts would play very nicely in the bedroom."

D.J. glared at Rebecca. "This isn't funny. We're talking about my life here."

"If we can't find humor in our lives, what's left?"

D.J. shook her head. "I know. I'm being completely horrible and irrational, but if you knew what had happened. I mean what *really* happened." She stopped and pressed her lips together.

She didn't want to say anymore. There was no way she could confess the truth about *everything*. Not even to her best friend. But without some details, Rebecca wouldn't get how terrible everything was. How out of sorts she, D.J., felt.

She sucked in a breath and braced herself. "I cried."

Rebecca sat at the kitchen table and sipped her morning coffee. When she heard D.J.'s confession, she merely set down her mug and said, "Oh?"

D.J. stomped her foot. "'Oh?' That's it? I cried. Me. The emotionless one. The fighter. The brave, brash, fearless one. I sobbed my heart out and then we had sex right there on the bathroom counter."

"What I really want to know is, wasn't it cold to sit on tile, but I won't ask. I can see that wasn't your point."

D.J. felt like screaming. "You're not taking this seriously."

"I know, and I'm sorry. It's just that I can't figure out what the big deal is. We all cry."

"Not me. Not ever. And certainly not in front of some guy."

Rebecca rose and crossed to stand in front of her. "Quinn isn't 'some guy.' He's special. You care about him. You trust him. You're in love with him." She sighed. "Finally. I'd wondered if you would ever find the right one and you have. I think it's wonderful."

D.J.'s mind froze. Five words repeated themselves over and over in her sluggish brain as the icy cold seeped into her body.

You're in love with him.

In love? With a man? With the enemy?

"No way. Not now, not ever."

Rebecca shrugged. "Sorry. Even you don't get to pick and choose when it comes to matters of the heart."

Panic threatened, which was the last thing she needed. She already felt more fragile than a china doll. "I can't."

"You do. And for what it's worth, I think you picked

a great guy. Quinn is the right match for you. He's tough enough that you won't be able to walk all over him, but he's also tender and caring. You two have a lot in common. In fact, he's perfect. For you, I mean."

D.J. felt as if she'd been gut shot. She pressed a hand against her stomach and took an unsteady step back. Love?

"No," she said, and grabbed her keys. "I have to go."

"Wait," Rebecca called. "Don't be afraid. He's not going to hurt you. D.J.!"

D.J. was already running toward her SUV. When she reached it, she ducked inside and quickly started the engine. Love? No. She would never risk it. She couldn't. Not with a man like Quinn—a man who was faster, stronger and five times more deadly.

D.J. swung her foot out and connected with Quinn's arm. He was surprised by the force in the blow, but didn't say anything. She'd been edgy ever since he'd shown up for their practice, and after what they'd shared two nights ago, he couldn't blame her. He, too, was still trying to adjust to what had happened.

He'd set out to seduce her and he'd had high hopes for a night of hot sex. What he hadn't expected was the intimacy of sharing that with her. They'd connected on a level he'd never experienced before. If he was still putting all the pieces together, it made sense that D.J. was having the same problem.

She'd stayed for breakfast the previous morning and then had left. He hadn't seen her since. Last night he'd wondered if he should go talk to her, but he'd wanted to give her time. So he'd waited until their scheduled session this morning to see her.

She shifted her weight and kicked out again. This time he sidestepped the attack and she tumbled onto the mats. He bent over and offered his hand. She ignored the gesture, climbing to her feet by herself.

Typical, he thought, more amused than annoyed. When in doubt, retreat. It was a tactic he used himself, although he'd never had a chance to in matters of the heart. He'd never cared before. Still, with D.J.'s fears and her past, he understood her need to be wary. He understood a whole lot more than she knew. He'd even understood her tears.

They had touched him more than anything. More than her willingness to enjoy making love, more than her pleasure and the way she'd lost herself to passion. Her tears had been a reaction to years of holding herself apart. They'd exposed the vulnerability of her heart. He'd held her because he'd needed to be close as much as she had. All these years he'd wondered if he would find someone who could understand and accept him. He didn't care that she'd turned out to be prickly, difficult and scarred. He was scarred, too. They could heal together.

She circled around him and faked another kick, then punched with her right arm. The blow connected with his midsection. She might be a woman and at a disadvantage when it came to upper-body strength, but she punched like a guy.

As the air rushed out of his lungs, he took a step back. D.J. moved in closer and punched again. This time he batted her arm around. She turned and kicked.

During practice sessions she was always focused and determined. She never quit, never slacked off. But this was different. He had the feeling she was out for blood.

"We're done," he said, stepping off the mat.

"What? Why are you stopping? We're not through."

"I am."

He crossed to the small refrigerator and pulled out a bottle of water. Her reaction shouldn't surprise him. After what they'd shared, he'd thought she would back off. But not this much. He couldn't help being disappointed.

"It's because I'm getting good, isn't it?" she taunted. "You can't stand that."

He glanced at her. She stood in the center of the mats, her hands on her hips. He recognized the symptoms. She was flushed, bouncing with energy and ready for a fight.

"You're not here for a lesson," he said. "You're here because you're angry. Probably more with yourself than me, but I'm the easier target."

"I didn't realize you had a degree in psychology," she sneered. "Thanks for the analysis. So you're a gentleman killer. How new century."

He unscrewed the top on the water bottle and took a long drink. The action gave him time to access the damage her emotional hit had inflicted. Because after all this time, she knew exactly where to send in the warhead.

He was a killer. He could cover the truth with fancy words and patriotic stories, but that was the truth he couldn't escape.

"I'm out of here," he said, heading for the door.

"Because you can't stay to fight? What's the problem, Quinn? Afraid? But I'm just a girl. I can't be that much of a challenge for a professional like you. Come on, big guy. You can take me."

He stopped and faced her. "Why are you doing this? We had something amazing, D.J. Why do you want to destroy it?"

She walked toward him. "What I want to do is kick your butt. I want to beat you. I want to make you admit that I'm better."

She wasn't. She couldn't be, and they both knew it. So what the hell was going on?

Before he could decide what to do, she came at him. He shifted and batted away her kick. She tried to punch him. He put up his arm to block her just as she dropped her hands, and he accidentally came within inches of hitting her in the face.

Instantly he swore and stepped back. "What the hell was that?" he asked, feeling set up. "What are you playing at?" She'd deliberately faked him out, but why? So he would hurt her?

"Hit me," she yelled. "You know you want to." She rose on her toes and leaned toward him. "Do it."

He couldn't have been more horrified if she'd shot him. He swore silently and took another step back. Whatever this game was, he didn't want a part of it.

"Hit me!" she screamed.

And then he knew. All of it. The fury, the fear, the need to lash out and why he had to be the enemy. With the knowledge came sadness and a sense of loss. Both were bitter and metallic on his tongue, like blood.

He'd thought, he'd hoped…but he'd been wrong.

"I'm sorry," he told her, his voice quiet.

She practically vibrated with rage. "Don't be sorry, you bastard. Just do it!"

He shook his head. "I can't. I won't. But all of this—" He motioned to her, then to the room. "It's my fault. I thought if you saw what we could be like together, that it would be enough. But it's not. I can't fight your ghosts, D.J. And you won't."

"What the hell are you babbling about?"

"You. Us. Night before last we connected in a way that shook both of us."

She rolled her eyes. "In your dreams."

He ignored her. "I'm scared, too, but the difference is, I don't want to walk away from it. I'm willing to say that you matter to me. That *we* matter. That there's something special here."

"There's nothing here," she yelled. "Nothing."

"You're right," he said. "My mistake."

He reached out and took her hand in his. She tried to twist away, but he wouldn't let her. Still he was careful not to hurt her.

"You want me to hit you," he said, "because if I do, you can walk away. If I hit you, then I'm just like the rest of them, and you're right. You don't have to care."

He released her. "I'm going to make it easy on you, D.J. I'm not going to make you face your demons. I'm going to leave."

"Coward."

He shook his head. "Funny how all this time I worried about being good enough for you. I never saw you weren't good enough for me."

She went white but didn't speak.

He shrugged. Only a fool would expect more.

He started for the door, then paused and glanced back at her. "I haven't been in a fight since I was fifteen, and I sure as hell never hit a woman. But you already know that. You know I would never hurt you. But that doesn't matter because you made up your mind not to trust me before we even met. You won't trust anyone, and I'm the worst of the bunch. I'm faster, stronger and better trained, and you aren't willing to risk that."

"You have no right to judge me," she told him, her eyes narrowed, her mouth set. "You didn't live my life."

"You're not that eleven-year-old little girl anymore. Can't you see that?" He wondered why he was bothering. She wouldn't listen. But for reasons that weren't clear, he couldn't stop trying.

"You live your life in a emotional plastic bubble," he said. "No one gets in and you don't get hurt. But is that a life? Is that what you want? I'm willing to walk away from what I've known and start over. Why aren't you? I thought we could matter to each other. I thought we were each other's perfect match. But you don't want an equal. You want someone you can push around. You've lived in fear your entire life, avoiding men like your father. Well, guess what, D.J.? You haven't avoided him enough. You've turned into him. You're only interested in people you can bully, just like him."

D.J. watched him walk away. She couldn't speak, couldn't go after him, couldn't even breathe. Instead she sank to her knees as the blows that were his words attacked her. She felt ripped apart, exposed and left for dead. She curled up on the floor, pulling her knees to her chest and trying not to let the pain overwhelm her.

He was wrong, she told herself as she squeezed her eyes shut. He was wrong. About all of it. Most especially about her.

But there were too many fragments of truth for her to ignore. Too many whispers that he might be right. Too much shame for her to turn her back. Quinn had held a mirror up to her psyche, and she was stunned to find someone she hated staring back at her.

"My father used to beat me and my mother," D.J. said tonelessly, and recounted the story of her broken arm and the trip to the hospital. She spoke of how her mother had sent her to school the next day, then had killed her husband and herself.

Rebecca listened quietly. When D.J. finished, she shifted on the sofa so she could touch D.J.'s hand.

"I'm sorry," she murmured.

D.J. nodded. "But not surprised."

Rebecca shrugged. "You have scars. I've worked with enough wounded kids to have had an idea about how you got them." She leaned back into the cushions. "I don't understand people like that. People who abuse and abandon their children. What makes them do it? Why can't they see how sick they are and get help? And how dare your mother choose death over staying with you? She could have run." She frowned. "This kind of information makes me furious."

"Thanks for caring about me. It means a lot."

More than a lot, D.J. told herself. It meant everything.

She glanced around at her small living room—the place she'd once thought of as a sanctuary. Now it was little more than the place she paced the nights away. It was cold and dark, even with the sun shining. She had thought if she confessed the truth to her friend, she would find peace. But her heart still ached, and she knew she would never be warm again.

"I was wrong," she whispered, fighting back tears.

"I was wrong not to trust him. I was scared so I lashed out."

"You made a mistake. We all do. For what it's worth, Quinn was wrong, too." Rebecca smiled. "You're not a bully, D.J. You never were."

"I'm exactly like my father. I only want to be around people I can control."

Rebecca laughed. "Give me a break. In this friendship, I'm the strong one, not you."

D.J. nearly fell over in shock. "What are you saying? You're a…a…girl."

"I'm a woman who is content with her life and her place in the world. There isn't anyone more powerful than that."

D.J. understood. Rebecca lived her life out of love and hope, while D.J. existed in fear.

She'd spent the past week looking at herself and seeing ugly truths. She'd discovered the dark corners of her soul, and what she found there made her shudder.

"I don't know how to be different," she whispered.

"Yes, you do. You're already changing." She winked. "Daisy Jane."

"I can't believe I told you that."

"I'm impressed. And I can see why you go by your initials."

D.J. smiled. "Thanks for being so supportive."

"I want to do whatever I can to help, but this isn't about me, is it? It's about Quinn."

D.J. didn't want to think about him. It hurt too much. "He was right there. He said he cared about me. He showed it in everything he did. And I tossed it all back in his face."

Her eyes burned. She started to blink back the tears,

only to remember that she was done hiding behind a facade. She was going to be who she really was, even if that meant facing her demons head-on. She wasn't going to run anymore.

"I said some horrible things," she murmured as she brushed away the tears. "He'll never forgive me."

He'd probably already forgotten about her. It had been a week. Each day she'd wondered if he would get in touch with her. If he would try to make things right. But he hadn't. No doubt he didn't think she was worth the trouble. She couldn't blame him. He'd talked about finding a match. His match would be someone whole and loving. Not someone like her.

She shrugged. "I'll get over him."

"I guess that means you're not willing to admit you love him."

It had taken D.J. three days to be able to admit the truth to herself. Now she was about to admit it to someone else. Talk about scary.

She looked at her friend. "I *do* love him. I know that means the whole 'getting over' part is going to take a lot longer." A lifetime. "He's the best thing that ever happened to me, and I let him get away."

"You sure did. Bummer. So you figure he's long gone, right?"

"Yeah. I thought about getting in touch with Gage and asking him where Quinn went, but—" she swallowed "—I'm too scared."

"You know Gage is back in Texas, right?"

"Uh-huh. Travis told me."

Rebecca studied her nails. "Gage left with Kari, and Kevin and Haley are gone, too. Nash is staying, of course. You'd think Quinn would have blown this

Popsicle stand, yet he's still camped out at his hotel. I wonder why."

D.J.'s heart stood still. Hope filled her. It was scary and unfamiliar, but it was a whole lot better than loss and pain. She stood. "He's here? He's in town?"

"Yup. What do you suppose that means?"

D.J. pulled Rebecca to her feet, then hugged her close. "It means I have a chance. Doesn't it?"

Rebecca straightened and smiled. "I think it means you have a really good one. But a word of advice." She fingered D.J.'s stained T-shirt. "You haven't showered in days. You might want to take a second to clean up before you go try to win back your man. And wear something sexy. Guys like that."

Two hours later D.J. studied herself in the full-length mirror on her closet door. As much as she'd wanted to rush right over to Quinn's hotel room, she'd taken Rebecca's advice and showered. Then she'd agonized over what to wear. Now she was ready to leave and not sure if she had the courage to go.

Could she face Quinn and apologize for what she'd done and said? When she thought about some of the things she'd told him, she wanted to hide in a closet for the next twenty years. Except she'd spent the past sixteen years hiding—from her past, from what she was afraid of, from what she'd become. As Quinn had pointed out, she'd cut herself off from life. It was time to change everything.

Quinn was her world. She loved him. If she wanted a chance to prove that, she was going to have to start by seeing him.

She gave herself a once-over and wished she'd asked Rebecca to stay. She wanted another opinion. Did she look sexy or just stupid? Did it matter? She wanted Quinn, and if he wanted her, he was going to have to realize she didn't do the girl thing very well. But she was willing to learn. Not necessarily for him, but also for herself. She needed to explore the side of herself she'd been denying for so long. But first she had to figure out if Quinn was willing to give her a second chance.

Quinn tossed his T-shirts in the suitcase. He'd waited a week because he'd hoped D.J. would come around and see things as they were. She'd hadn't and there was no other reason to stay in Glenwood.

Travis had tried to convince him to take a job at the sheriff's office. While Quinn intended to join the mainstream, he couldn't do it here. Not with D.J. so close. Knowing she was in the same town, walking the same streets, seeing the same people—it would hurt too much. He'd finally found the one woman he could be with and she wasn't interested. Life had a hell of a sense of humor.

He crossed to the bathroom and collected his shaving kit. There was still an unopened box of condoms tucked inside. When he'd first met D.J. and had realized how much she turned him on, he'd practically bought out the drugstore's supply of protection. Optimistic bastard, he thought grimly. Now she was out of his life and all he had was—

A knock at the door made him turn. He dropped the box back into his shaving kit and walked into the bedroom. There was a second knock.

"Coming," he called and reached for the door handle. When he pulled the door open, he started to speak, then found he couldn't.

D.J. stood in the hallway. At least he was pretty sure it was her. His eyes saw and his brain registered, but neither body part believed.

She wore a black minidress, high heels and nothing else that he could see. Based on how high the hem came and how low the front dipped, he doubted there *was* anything else. Full, soft curls tumbled down her back. Makeup accentuated wide, frightened eyes. She was gorgeous. A sexual goddess. If she'd come here to seduce him, he was going to have a tough time telling her no.

She opened her mouth, then closed it. After shaking her head, she pushed past him and entered the room.

"I was wrong," she said, talking quickly. "About everything. You, me, my past. I was an idiot. Worse, I hurt you. I said horrible things and I'm sorry."

He closed the door. Both wary and intrigued, he folded his arms over his chest. "Go on."

"I shouldn't have taunted you that day," she said, her voice low. She swallowed. "I was scared and angry. What we'd done, what I'd felt—it terrified me. You were right about me living in an emotional plastic bubble. I kept the world at bay because caring to me was the same as dying. What I didn't see was that living alone was a different kind of death."

She laced her fingers together in front of her stomach. "You've been so patient with me and I don't know why. I mean, why did you bother? Why didn't you just walk away?"

"There aren't many out there like you," he told her. "You're tough and vulnerable. Feminine, strong and hell on wheels. How could I resist?"

Some of the fear faded from her eyes. "Really? I

thought maybe it was because I don't mind about your past. I understand what you've done and I'm okay with it. You're a good man. The best. What you did doesn't change that. I know you're stronger than me, and better and faster and all those things and it's okay. You'll never hurt me."

At her words, the tightness around his chest eased. He drew in a deep breath and moved close. They were so right for each other, he thought contentedly. She'd finally seen that.

"What are you saying, Daisy Jane?"

"That I agree with what you told me last week. That we're a match."

"I was telling you I loved you."

She smiled then. A bright, pure smile of happiness that nearly blinded him.

"I love you, too. I want to get free of my past so I can have a future with you. If you want me. I mean if you were talking about more than just a—"

He pulled her close and kissed her. Their lips met in a hot, hungry kiss that spoke of too much time apart and a lifetime of possibilities together.

"I was talking about forever," he said against her mouth. "I want to marry you." He chuckled. "If for no other reason than the minister is going to be saying your name out loud for the world to hear."

"I don't mind," she said, clinging to him. "Oh, Quinn, if you want you can join my business. We could expand and rescue more kids and maybe take on different projects. We could—"

He silenced her with another kiss. There would be plenty of time for business talk and details later. Right now he just wanted to be with the woman he loved.

"I can't believe I found you," he said as he touched the smooth material over her back.

"I found you, remember? That day in the woods. I captured you."

He smiled. "Yes, you did. All of me." He dropped his hands to her hips. "So is there any sleazy lingerie on under this dress?"

"Sorry, no." She kissed him. "There isn't any underwear at all."

He groaned. "You're my kind of woman."

Daisy Jane Monroe shivered with pleasure at those words. She'd come a long way toward healing, and she knew that all the pain and fear of her past was finally behind her. She'd learned to love enough to let go, and to hold on.

Quinn's woman. That was exactly who she wanted to be. He would be her man and together they would love each other for the rest of their lives.

* * * * *

Dear Reader,

I have just written my twenty-fifth book for Harlequin, and as I look back over the stories I have told, one thing stands out to me: I have an inordinate fondness for a tomboy heroine. Over the years I've written about a boxer, a mechanic, a chauffeur, a tattoo artist and a communications specialist in the army, all of whom were women of action and—mostly—strangers to high heels and frilly dresses.

Clearly, I have a thing about women who work in nontraditional roles! As a reader, I have always liked strong, independent women. When I was younger, George was always my favorite of Enid Blyton's *Famous Five*, and I pretty much thought Trixie Belden rocked. Obviously I have brought my love of these feisty, unconventional women into my writing career.

Hannah is one of my favorite tomboy heroines. She's a bit messed up after a painful family betrayal, and her confidence has taken a huge knock. The last thing she's looking for is a connection with the single father who's just moved in next door. It doesn't help that they get off to a bit of a bumpy start, either. But Hannah and Joe soon come to understand that sometimes love comes along when you least expect it.

I hope you enjoy this reissue of *Home for the Holidays*. I always love hearing from readers, so please drop me a line via my website, www.sarahmayberry.com, if the urge takes you!

Happy reading,

Sarah

HOME FOR THE HOLIDAYS

Sarah Mayberry

Thanks to *Neighbours* for inspiring this story.

Thanks to Claire and Helen for their wise advice
and thoughts on children.

And thanks, as always, to Chris.

You rock, in every possible way.

And last, but never, ever least, to Wanda.

She knows why.

Chapter 1

"Daddy, do you think Mommy will be able to find us in our new house?"

Joe Lawson paused a moment before answering his daughter's question. Ruby stared at him from her bed, her small, angular face anxious.

"I'll bet Mommy can find us no matter where we are," he said.

"That's what Grandma always says, but I'm not so sure. Melbourne is a long way from Sydney. It took us ages to drive here."

As he struggled to find an answer, Ruby sighed heavily and tugged the covers closer to her chin.

"I guess I'd better go to sleep. School tomorrow. I need to be fresh."

She rolled over onto her side and closed her eyes, apparently completely at peace now that she'd voiced her deeper metaphysical concerns.

The joys of being ten years old. If only he could dismiss her question as easily. Not for the first time, he wondered if he'd done the right thing moving the kids away from everything that was familiar to them so that they could be closer to the support his mother could provide.

Be honest. At least with yourself.

The truth was, he'd been more than happy to abandon the family home.

Pulling Ruby's door shut behind him, he walked up the hall to check on Ben. As he had suspected, Ben was out for the count, his bedroom light still on. Joe watched him for a long moment, noting how thin Ben had become over the past few months thanks to a growth spurt. Soon, his thirteen-year-old son would be able to look Joe in the eye. He tugged the duvet up over Ben's shoulders, flicked the light off then returned to the living room.

Boxes were still piled against the walls, filled with DVDs, books and God only knows what else, since he'd paid professionals to pack the contents of their former home. The kitchen was equally disastrous. In fact, the kids' rooms were the only spaces that were even close to being livable.

He stared at the boxes. He hated moving. Always had. Beth had claimed he was the worst packer in the Southern Hemisphere and always supervised him ruthlessly to ensure he was working up to her standards whenever they moved. He was pretty sure Ben had been conceived the afternoon they were packing to leave the small apartment they'd bought when they married. After a day of being dictated to, he'd rebelled against Beth's bossiness and seduced her on the kitchen floor.

She'd been laughing and protesting right up to the moment when he'd tugged her bra down and started kissing her breasts.

He shied away from the memory, as he had from all the other memories that had surfaced during the day. It was impossible not to think about her, though, when he was unpacking the life they'd shared together. The dinner set they'd chosen when they were married. The kids' finger paintings from preschool she'd saved. Even the damned side-by-side fridge reminded him of how excited she'd been the day it was delivered.

It had been two years. Everyone said time was the great healer—so why did he still burn with anger and grief when he thought about his dead wife?

He forced himself to cross the room and slit the tape on the top carton. The boxes weren't going to unpack themselves. He peered inside. Books. Good. Books he could handle.

He'd stacked half the contents onto the shelves of the built-in entertainment unit when he found the photo frame. It had been wrapped in several layers of tissue paper, but he recognized it by feel because of its chunky shape. Beth had made it herself as part of a framing workshop and even though it was just the slightest bit off center, it had always held pride of place on the mantel.

He folded the tissue back and stared at the photo inside the frame. They'd been on a family picnic and Beth had asked a passerby to take the shot. The kids were much younger—Ben eight or so, Ruby only five—and Beth's blond hair was long, well past her shoulders.

He stared into her face. Sometimes he forgot how

beautiful she'd been. How could that be when he still missed her like crazy?

His head came up as the low, throbbing rumble of an engine cut through the quiet of the house. A motorbike. A really noisy one. He waited for it to pass by, but the rumble grew louder and louder. Just when it seemed as though the bike was about to race through the living room, it stopped.

Unless he missed his guess, the owner of the world's noisiest motorcycle was also his new neighbor. Which meant he could look forward to the roar of a badly tuned engine cutting into his peace morning, noon and night.

"Great."

There ought to be a rule when a person bought a new house: full disclosure. The vendors should have to reveal everything about the house and the neighbors so there weren't any nasty surprises on moving day. Leaky roofs, yapping dogs, motorcycle gang neighbors, Peeping Toms.

It seemed unnaturally quiet after the racket of the bike. He put the frame to one side. He'd find a place for it later. He reached for more books, then tensed as the motorbike started up again. He gritted his teeth, waiting for the bike to roar off into the night. It didn't. Instead, the engine revved again and again, the sound so loud he guessed the guy must be parked inside his garage, the roller door open, the sound amplified by the space.

Over and over the bike revved and Joe grew more and more tense. His kids were asleep, but they wouldn't stay that way for long if this kept up. Surely the moron next door must have some idea that this was a residential neighborhood, a quiet middle-class suburb full of quiet, middle-class people who liked a little peace at the end of the day? Surely—

"For Pete's sake!"

He slammed the box shut. He was barefoot, but he didn't bother putting shoes on, simply threw open the front door and headed next door. As he'd guessed, the garage was open, light spilling out into the night. A motorbike stood propped on its stand toward the rear of the garage. A man squatted beside it, his back to Joe as he worked on something near the exhaust pipe.

Joe stopped on the threshold as he registered the guy's leather pants and long hair and the Harley-Davidson jacket thrown over the rusty frame of a second bike. It was every bit as bad as he'd suspected—he'd moved in next to a long-haired redneck. No doubt Joe had noisy, boozy parties, visits from the cops and loud domestic arguments to look forward to in the future.

Fantastic. Just what he goddamn needed.

"Hey, buddy, you want to keep it down?" he yelled over the roar of the bike.

The guy didn't even lift his head from whatever he was doing. Joe took a step closer.

"Mate!" he yelled. "You want to shut that thing off?"

Still nothing. Joe's temper began to burn. He didn't consider himself a short-fuse kind of guy, but he was tired and unpacking all the old stuff was tough and he needed this added aggravation like a hole in the head.

He strode forward and reached over the guy's shoulder for the ignition key. One twist and the bike fell silent. The guy jerked in surprise, then shot to his feet and spun around.

Joe took an involuntary step backward as he realized

that he'd miscalculated somehow. The leather jacket, the pants, the bike. He'd just assumed...

But he'd been wrong. Because his new neighbor was a *she,* not a he.

Her chin came up as she stared at him.

"Who the hell are you?"

She was tall—almost his height—with brown eyes and long, wavy brown hair.

He frowned. "I'm sorry. I thought... I called out but you couldn't hear me over the engine. I came to ask you to keep the noise down. My kids are asleep."

She blinked at him, then he saw comprehension dawn in her face.

"You're the guy who bought the Steveway place," she said.

"Yeah."

She tucked a strand of hair behind her ear. His gaze dropped to her breasts, then her waist. She had a good figure. Long legs, full breasts.

He looked away. He didn't care what kind of figure she had.

"I didn't realize you'd moved in," she said. "The Steveways were happy for me to work on my bike anytime."

"Then they must have been deaf."

He knew he sounded like a cantankerous old man but he couldn't seem to help himself. Her being a woman had thrown him off balance, one too many curveballs on what had already been a trying day.

"It isn't usually this noisy," she said. "There's a problem with the muffler."

"Maybe you should leave it to the experts to fix, then."

Her eyes narrowed. "Thanks for the advice. I know just what to do with it."

He'd pissed her off. Seemed only fair, since she'd roused him out of his home with her racket.

"So you'll pack it in for the night?"

"Like I said, I didn't know you'd moved in."

She put her hands on her hips and her T-shirt stretched over her breasts. Again he pulled his gaze away.

"Thanks, I appreciate the consideration," he said flatly.

He turned away.

"Welcome to the neighborhood," she called after him as he walked down the drive. She sounded about as sincere as he had when he'd thanked her.

He stopped in his tracks when he reached the privacy of his own driveway, a frown on his face, aware that he'd overreacted and not sure why. He stood there for a long moment, breathing in the cool night air. Then he shook off his unease and returned to his sleeping children.

What a jerk.

Hannah Napier pushed her hair off her forehead then grimaced when she remembered her hands were greasy. She wiped her hands on a rag then hit the button to close the roller door. She'd wanted to get to the bottom of the noisy muffler tonight, but it could wait until tomorrow. The last thing she needed was Mr. High and Mighty on the doorstep again with his attitude and impatience.

She'd met some chauvinistic assholes in her time, but her new neighbor was going to take some beating. The way he'd spoken to her like she was one of his kids.

The way he'd dismissed her with a quick once-over of his very blue eyes.

He'd almost given her a heart attack, sneaking up on her the way he had. She'd turned around and seen six foot plus of solid man standing over her and almost wet her pants. And not in a good way.

Not that he was unattractive. He had short, dark hair, and his face was deeply tanned. His shoulders were broad, his belly flat. Not bad, if your taste ran to bad-tempered, bossy men. She put him at mid-to-late thirties, then she remembered the deep lines that bracketed his mouth and the hardness in his blue eyes and upped her estimate to early forties. He'd been around the block a time a two, her new neighbor. Probably managed to piss off everyone he met along the way, too.

So much for her mother's hopes that the new owner of number twenty-four would be nice. Hannah grabbed her jacket and flicked off the lights as she used the connecting door to enter the house. Her work boots sounded loud on the tiled kitchen floor as she crossed to the fridge.

"Is that you, love?" her mother, Robyn, called from the living room.

"Yeah, Mom."

"Your dinner's in the fridge. And there's dessert, too, if you want it."

Hannah sighed. No matter how many times she told her mom not to cook for her, inevitably she came home to find a meal in the fridge, neatly covered with cling wrap. When she'd moved in with her mother six months ago, she'd done so on the basis that she wouldn't be a burden. She should have known that her mother would fight tooth and nail to defend her right to wash Hannah's dirty laundry and cook her meals. It was what her mother had always done, and it had been foolish to even think that things would be different because Hannah was twenty-eight now and had been living independently for nearly six years.

"Did you notice the lights on next door? The new neighbors have moved in."

"Yeah, I noticed." Hard not to when her new neighbor had just read her the riot act.

Hannah took the plate of chicken and salad to the living room and sat next to her mom.

"This looks great, Mom. Thanks."

Her mother dismissed her gratitude with the wave of a hand and leaned forward, her brown eyes dancing.

"So, don't you want to know?"

"Know what?"

"What he's like. The new neighbor. And you'll note I say *he*," her mother said.

"I don't need to know. I just met him."

"Really?" Her mother almost leaped off the couch. "How? Did he come over and introduce himself?"

"He was pissed about the noise, actually. Came over to give me a piece of his mind."

"That doesn't sound like a very promising start."

Hannah bit into a chicken leg, shrugging a shoulder. "Who cares? He's a dick," she said around a mouthful of food.

"Hannah! I thought he seemed very nice when I popped in earlier. His mother was helping him unpack, you know, and there was no sign of a wife."

Hannah scooped up a spoonful of potato salad. She could feel her mother watching her, waiting for Hannah's reaction. She concentrated on her plate, hoping her mother would get the hint.

"You didn't think he was good-looking?" her mother asked after a long pause.

Hannah put down her fork. "Mom. Give it up."

"All I want to know is if you think he's attractive."

She wanted a lot more than that but Hannah decided the best way to defuse this conversation was to answer the question and move on.

"I thought he was sad looking, if you must know. I thought he was about the saddest-looking man I've ever met," Hannah said. Those lines by his mouth, those hard blue eyes. All that anger bubbling just below the surface.

"Oh. Do you think?"

Hannah shook her head in frustration. "It doesn't matter, Mom. He could be Brad bloody Pitt and I wouldn't be interested. You know that."

Her mother eyed her steadily, her face creased with concern. "Don't be like this, sweetheart."

Hannah stood. There was no way she could eat the rest of her meal. She certainly couldn't endure another heart-to-heart with her mother.

"I need a shower. Thanks for cooking."

She scraped the remainder of her dinner into the garbage, rinsed her plate and slid it into the dishwasher. She spent ten minutes in the shower, washing and conditioning her hair and shaving under her arms. All the while, she reviewed the work she had tomorrow, prioritizing things on her to-do list. Anything to avoid thinking about what her mother had been suggesting.

As if she was going to start dating again. What a joke. A towel wrapped turban style around her hair and another around her torso, she made her way to her bedroom. She stopped in her tracks when she saw the long white box on her bed. A receipt was taped to the front of it, along with a note from her mother.

H, the dry cleaners called again today. They said if you didn't pick your dress up soon they'd consider it unclaimed goods and sell it. I knew you wouldn't want that.
Mom.

Hannah circled the box as though it was a wild animal. Even though she told herself she didn't want to look, that it didn't matter to her anymore, that it was all in the past, she reached out and slowly folded back the lid.

Intricate crystal beading sparkled in the overhead light. Her gaze ran over the shaped bodice, the pleating at the waist. The white silk skirt shimmered and she couldn't resist running a hand over it. She could remember the first time she'd seen the dress, the way it had felt sliding over her body when she put it on— cool and slippery and perfect. As though it had been made for her.

Anger rose in a hot flash. She shoved the box so hard it slid off the other side of the bed. She'd paid a small fortune to have it packed in acid-free tissue, but she didn't want it in her room. It was too pathetic—a wedding dress that had never been worn. Too, too sad.

She had a sudden vision of herself taking the box out into the yard, dousing it with gas and setting it on fire. All that pristine silk would burn bright and long. It would be good watching it all go up in smoke. Cleansing.

Almost, she was tempted, but she knew her mom would freak. Not to mention that it would be a huge waste of money. If she put the dress on eBay, there was a fair chance she could make back some of her money on the damned thing. After all, it had never been worn. That had to be a selling point, right?

She took a deep breath, then rounded the bed to pick up the box. The truth was, she didn't have the luxury of burning her wedding dress. Every dollar she could scrape together got her closer to her goal of being debt-free. And once she was debt-free, she could start planning for her around-Australia trip and get out of here once and for all. Leave it all behind her—the wedding-that-never-was, Lucas, Kelly, all of it.

She laid the box on the floor in the corner and sat on the end of her bed. More than anything she wanted to be gone. If she could close her eyes and make it so right now, she would. She wanted the road unrolling before her and the wind in her hair and nothing holding her back. She certainly didn't want to be sitting in her old bedroom, surrounded by her teenage memorabilia, living this life of quiet endurance and survival.

For a dangerous moment, tears threatened.

She stood and reached for the freshly washed jeans her mother had left folded in a pile on the end of the bed. Three minutes later she was fully dressed and tugging her work boots back on. Her hair was wet, but she didn't care. She could hear the television in the living room as she crossed the kitchen, but she didn't bother telling her mom she was going out. She would only want to know why, and Hannah wasn't up to fabricating an excuse for bailing again so soon after coming home.

In the garage, she tugged her jacket and helmet on then hit the button to raise the roller door. She was about to start the bike when she remembered the fun police next door.

She swore under her breath. For a moment she was tempted to start the bike anyway, then she recalled what he'd said about his kids sleeping. She rolled the bike down the drive and down the street, resenting every step. When she reached the corner, she slung her leg over the saddle. The engine started with a dull roar. She pushed down the visor on her helmet, leaned forward and opened the throttle.

She had no idea where she was going. As long as it wasn't here, she figured it would be good enough.

Chapter 2

"I don't want to go to school. Why can't I stay here with you and help you unpack?"

Ruby's face was beseeching as she looked at Joe across the breakfast table. He'd had a poor night's sleep and a headache building in the back of his skull but he did his best to give his daughter the reassurance she needed.

"I know starting a new school is scary, but once the first day is over you'll be fine."

"I don't want to go." Ruby pushed away her half-finished bowl of cereal.

She looked so small and defenseless sitting there. He stood and circled the table, squatting beside her chair.

"It's going to be okay, I promise," he said. He put his arms around her and pulled her close. She smelled of strawberries and talcum powder and she felt about as substantial as a baby bird in his arms. She burrowed her face against his chest, rubbing her cheek against his shirt.

"I want to stay with you," she said, her arms clinging to him.

He laid his cheek against her head and remembered the fierce, adventurous little girl she'd been only a couple of years ago.

"I'm not going anywhere," he said, drawing back so he could look into her face. She stared at him unblinkingly. "I promise I'll be waiting at the school gate the moment you step out the door at three o'clock."

She didn't say a word, but a small frown wrinkled her forehead.

"How about this? We'll make pizzas for dinner, from scratch like the old days," he said. "That way you've got something to look forward to all day."

Mastering the art of making pizza dough had been his one culinary achievement, and every Thursday night it had been a family tradition for Beth to put her feet up while he made the bases and the kids took charge of the toppings.

Ruby was silent for a long moment. Just when he was beginning to think he'd made a mistake suggesting they revive the tradition, Ruby smiled.

"Can I have three types of cheese on mine?"

Joe smoothed a hand over her fine blond hair, tucking a strand behind her ear. "Deal," he said.

"Okay, then I guess I can go to school."

Joe looked up as Ben entered the kitchen, his backpack already on his shoulders.

"Can I have some money for lunch?" Ben asked,

hands dug into his pockets. His gaze shifted around the kitchen, not settling on anything.

"Have you had breakfast yet?" Joe asked.

"Yes."

Joe hadn't noticed a bowl or plate in the sink, but he had no reason to think his son was lying.

"I thought we could pick up some sandwiches from the coffee shop on the way to school," Joe said.

He planned to get to the supermarket sometime this afternoon so he could make their lunches from here on in, but today he was winging it.

Ben frowned. "I don't want to be dropped off."

"Well, tough. It's your first day. I want to make sure you know where you're going." Joe said it with a smile but Ben's frown deepened.

"I already know where to go. I'm not stupid. I can work it out for myself."

"I know you can, but it won't be the end of the world to have a bit of help on your first day."

Ben pushed away from the counter, hands fisted by his sides. "I don't need help. I don't want it."

Joe stared at his son. Where had this sudden rush of anger come from? "Mate—"

"I'm walking to school," Ben said defiantly.

He stalked from the room. Joe sighed. Ruby was watching him expectantly.

"You should go after him," she advised.

"Thank you, Miss Bossy Boots, I was about to do that."

She grinned as he moved past her and into the hallway. He pulled up short when he saw Ben wasn't in his room. He checked out the window and, sure enough, Ben was on his way down the driveway.

Joe exited the house and took the porch steps two at a time.

"Ben!"

His son had reached the street and he paused, turning toward the house. He looked half afraid, half determined.

"What about a compromise? I'll drop you off up the block and you can walk the rest of the way on your own. How does that sound?" Joe suggested.

Ben shrugged, his mouth a tight line. Joe studied him, trying to understand what was going on. Was this simple first-day nerves? A reaction to the move?

"Is there something wrong, matey? Something on your mind?" he asked.

Ben screwed up his face in utter rejection of the idea. "No! Why would there be?"

Joe ran a hand through his hair. "It's just we've had a lot happening lately. Selling the house, saying goodbye to everyone, moving."

Ben shrugged. "So?"

Joe watched him for a beat, but Ben simply stared back, his face blank.

"Okay. Come inside while I get your sister ready," Joe said.

He managed to get them both to school on time without further incident but his gut was churning as he pulled away from Ruby's school.

This is my fault. I shouldn't have moved them. I should have taken Mom up on her offer to sell her place here and move to Sydney.

His hands tightened on the steering wheel. It wasn't as though he could undo the move. They were here now, they'd all have to make the best of it.

He checked his watch. If he hustled, there was just enough time for him to check out a few car dealerships before he was due at his lawyer's office. He'd bought their current sedan to replace the car Beth had been killed in, but for some time now he'd been thinking about getting something bigger. An SUV, or a wagon, maybe. Something that could absorb all of the kids' paraphernalia and still have room to spare.

He was taking a shortcut through the local Elsternwick shopping district on his way to the commercial strip along the Nepean Highway when he passed a shiny black SUV on the side of the road. He slowed when he saw the big For Sale sign in the back window. It was parked in front of an automotive garage and Joe hesitated a moment before pulling to the curb. Why the hell not, after all? Might as well see what the private market was offering before he hit the big car lots.

The SUV was a Mazda, only two years old with shiny alloy wheels. He did a lap of the car, peering in the window, checking out the panels. It was in good condition and a sign resting on the dashboard claimed that the car had been serviced since new at the garage and came with full records.

Joe turned toward the open bay of the workshop. A blue sedan was up on the hoist inside, a red coupe parked beside it. A middle-aged guy in grease-stained overalls was frowning at the underbelly of the sedan. Tinny radio music bled out into the street. The workshop floor was spotlessly clean, the walls freshly whitewashed. A promising start.

"Hey," Joe said, walking forward. "Have you got five minutes to talk me through the Mazda out the front?"

The man shook his head. "No point talking to me,

mate. You need Hannah. She's the manager." He jerked his head toward the other car and for the first time Joe noted a pair of legs sticking out from beneath the front of the coupe.

Right. A female mechanic. Apparently it was his week for finding women where he least expected them. In motorcycle leathers, beneath cars.

He moved closer to the coupe and squatted to make himself heard over the radio. "Excuse me. Any chance you could take me over the Mazda? I'm in the market for an SUV."

"Sure. Give me a sec to tighten this sump plug… There we go."

No sooner had she spoken than the mechanic slid out from beneath the car. He tensed. It was the woman from last night, the noisy biker with the attitude. She was smiling, but the smile froze on her face when she saw him. He wondered if his own surprise was as obvious.

There was a long moment of taut silence.

"Well, are you going to say it or am I?" she finally said.

She was still on her back on the mechanics' trolley. He hadn't noticed last night, but she had incredibly plump lips, the bottom lip rounded and full. Her sun-streaked brown hair was pulled back into a high ponytail, leaving her smooth cheekbones and small chin to speak for themselves. He'd noticed her curves last night, but it hit him suddenly that she was a very attractive woman.

"I guess it's up to me, then," she said. Her tone was heavy with irony when she next spoke. "We really have to stop meeting like this."

Because she'd caught him off balance again, his first

instinct was to retreat. He stood, sliding his hands into the front pockets of his jeans.

"I wanted to look at the car," he said stiffly.

She wiped her hands down the legs of her coveralls and pushed herself to her feet. He'd forgotten how tall she was. It was one of the reasons he'd been so startled to realize she was a woman last night—she'd been looking him almost squarely in the eye when she'd straightened and her face had been inches from his until he'd taken a step backward.

Now, she held his eye as she offered her hand.

"Hannah Napier," she said coolly.

Joe stared at her hand a second before taking it. "Joe Lawson."

Her hand was warm, her fingers firm. Her mouth quirked up into a lopsided, wry smile.

"Look at that—almost civilized."

She turned toward the parking lot and started walking. Of its own accord, his gaze dropped to check out her body. More specifically, her ass. It was pure instinct, imbedded in him since puberty, and as soon as he registered what he was doing he looked away—but not before he'd noticed she had a full, sweetly curved backside.

"It's two years old, one owner since new. I don't normally do this but he's a good friend and I wanted to help him out," Hannah said.

Joe lengthened his stride to come abreast of her as they neared the car. "Why's he selling?"

"Scored an overseas job. It's a good car. Bit greedy with gas, but safe, solid. You've got kids, right? There are built-in anchors for car seats."

He didn't bother telling her his kids were well out of

car seats. No point extending this encounter any longer than it needed to be.

"What's he asking?"

"Thirty. It's forty-five new, so it's a good deal. Full leather upholstery, six-stacker CD. Cruise control, tip-tronic transmission…" She glanced at him to check he was paying attention and his gaze got caught on the line of her cheekbone.

"Is this the model with the turbocharger?" he asked.

"Yep. It's got it all. Like I said, it's a good deal."

She lifted a hand to smooth it down the length of her pony tail and the neckline of her coverall gaped. He caught a glimpse of shadowy cleavage and white lace.

He took a step backward, frowning. He'd seen more than enough here.

"Right. Thanks for your time. I've really only started looking but I'll keep this in mind," he said politely.

She looked surprised. "You don't want to take it for a test drive, see how it handles?"

He made a big deal out of checking his watch. "I've got an appointment I don't want to be late for."

"Well, we're open till five if you want to come back later."

He nodded, already drawing his car keys from his pocket. Her eyes narrowed and she propped a hand on her hip.

"Be honest. You're not coming back, are you?" she asked.

He frowned.

"Right. Let me guess—you don't trust me," she said, contempt in every line of her body. "What could a woman possibly know about cars, right? What was it you said last night? *Leave it to the experts?* Was that it?"

She was bristling with aggression, her chin high. As he'd thought when he first set eyes on her, she was trouble with a capital *T*.

"Like I said, I've just started looking."

A muscle flickered in her jaw, then she swung back toward the car. As though he hadn't announced he needed to leave, she started talking.

"Tires have got another two years in them, depending on the kind of mileage you do. Suspension is independent, double-wishbone at the back. Brakes are discs all round, and it's fitted with ABS. It's a six cylinder, and with the turbocharger you're looking at zero to one hundred in about 9.8 seconds."

She moved to the front of the car. He remained where he was, arms crossed over his chest. She stopped and looked at him, defiance shining in her eyes.

Stubborn. And a pain in the ass to boot.

"Not real good at taking no for an answer, are you?" he said.

Something flickered in her eyes, then her face went utterly blank.

"You'd be surprised." She shifted her attention to the car for a second, then back to him. "You won't find a better car for the money."

It was possible she was right, of course.

"I'll think about it," he said again. He dipped his head in acknowledgment and walked toward his car. He could feel her watching him all the way, the awareness like a prickle on the back of his neck. Yet when he got to his car and glanced over his shoulder she had already disappeared into the workshop.

Right.

He gave himself a mental shake. He needed to get

going if he still wanted to check out the commercial car lots before meeting his lawyer. Then there was the grocery shopping to do, and the last of the unpacking—all before the kids were out of school at three.

He started the car and threw it into gear. As he had last night, he pushed his encounter with Hannah Napier out of his mind. She was nothing to him, the barest blip on his radar. Less.

Still, he glanced back one last time before he drove away, but Hannah was nowhere in sight.

Hannah was supposed to catch up with her friend Mikey for dinner after work, but he canceled on her at the last minute, leaving her at loose ends. She figured she'd head home instead and put in some hours fixing the muffler on the bike—quietly, of course. No doubt Joe Lawson would come after her with an elephant gun or a lynch mob if she dared disturb his peace again.

The memory of his dismissive attitude over the car had risen up to bite her on the ass all day. How she hated narrow-minded men like him. She'd seen it over and over—the cautious look in their eyes, the doubt as they listened to her tell them what was wrong with their cars. As though having breasts made her less qualified to understand the workings of the internal combustion engine. Please.

She was hungry and more than ready for a shower when she rode into the street. She stopped short of pulling into her mother's garage, however, her attention caught by the car sitting in Joe Lawson's driveway—a Mazda SUV, same model as the one she'd shown him today, dark navy instead of black. She switched off her bike and kicked the stand out before dismounting. She tugged her helmet off as she walked the distance from her mother's front yard to inspect the car. So much for *I've just started looking*. She'd been absolutely right—he hadn't been able to bring himself to buy a car from her.

She narrowed her eyes as she surveyed the rear of the SUV, then dropped into a squat to peer under the wheel arch. She did a slow lap, squatting once again when she reached the left rear wheel arch, craning her neck to confirm her suspicion.

"I assume you won't be billing me for the inspection?"

She started, then glanced over her shoulder. Joe Lawson stood there, one eyebrow raised. Her gaze dropped to his bare feet. No wonder she hadn't heard him sneak up on her.

"Did you get a warranty on this thing?" she asked, standing and jerking a thumb toward the car.

He crossed his arms over his chest but didn't say a word.

"I'm only asking because you're going to need it. This car's been in an accident," she said.

He glanced toward the Mazda. "It's been fully inspected by the automotive association."

"Which just confirms my opinion of those idiots." She gestured toward the wheel arch. "Take a look yourself. Something big ran into the back of this thing, ripped the chassis open. It's been welded back together, but you can see the repair if you look closely. And the shock absorbers are all new. No one puts new shocks on a two-year-old car unless they have to."

His hands dropped to his sides. He looked annoyed. Then, as though he couldn't help himself, he knelt beside the car and craned his neck to see under the wheel well. She knelt beside him and leaned in to point out the line of the weld.

"They've driven around a bit to dirty it up some, but you can still see it there."

"Shit," he said, so low she almost didn't hear him.

He was so close his shoulder brushed hers when he shifted his weight. She stilled, then stood, dusting her hands down her jeans.

"It's not going to fall apart or anything, but you'll probably have issues with panel fit and rattles. Once a car's bent out of whack, it's almost impossible for them to get it straight again even when they put it on the rack."

He stood. "I suppose I should thank you for sharing your expertise," he said grudgingly. She could tell it hurt.

"That's very gracious of you," she said dryly.

He crossed his arms over his chest again and widened his stance, as though he needed to brace himself for what came next.

"Thank you," he said more sincerely. "I really do appreciate the heads-up."

She smiled. She couldn't help herself. He was so damned truculent, like a surly teenage boy being forced to apologize. "Don't mention it. It was my pleasure."

He raised an eyebrow and she shrugged a shoulder as if to say, "Hey, what did you expect?"

"You should take it back," she said, turning to look at the car one last time. "Most of those big dealerships have cooling-off clauses in their contracts. Tell them you don't appreciate being ripped off and make them give your money back."

His chin lifted a little—not much, but enough to tell her that there was no way he was taking the car back. Not now that she'd told him to.

She could almost admire him for his dedication to his own point of view. Almost.

"Suit yourself," she said.

"Oh, don't worry, I will," he said. He beeped the car open, then reached into the back and collected a grocery bag. For the first time she noticed the long, curling scar that ran from the base of his left thumb, around the back of his hand and up his strongly muscled forearm to disappear beneath the pushed-up sleeve of his sweater. Where on earth did a man get a scar like that?

It hadn't occurred to her before to wonder what he did for a living, or why he'd moved into the neighborhood, but suddenly both questions were on the tip of her tongue. She bit down on them. As though he was going to answer anything she asked him when she'd made him look like a fool. She might not be an expert on men, but she knew that much.

He shut the back of the car with a firm click. The grocery bag rustled in his hand. She realized she was hovering for no good reason whatsoever.

"Anyway," she said.

"Yeah."

"See you around."

He didn't bother responding. She could imagine what he was thinking, though: *not if I can help it.*

He headed toward his house. She watched his shoulders rock from side to side with his long stride, then her gaze dropped to his butt. His jeans were faded and soft and they molded his ass faithfully. It was a good ass, too. Firm-looking, round. Quintessentially male.

Hannah registered what she was doing and swiveled on her heel. Who cared if he had a nice ass? It was attached to the rest of him, and that was arrogant and pigheaded and not-so-nice.

Still, she'd more than put him in his place tonight. He might have won this morning's skirmish, but tonight's battle was definitely hers.

Grinning, she headed into the house. Score: one all.

She was still smiling when she pushed open the connecting door from the garage and entered the kitchen. She could hear voices and guessed her mother was already in front of the TV, watching her soaps. Hannah rounded the corner, ready to regale her with the story of her two encounters with Joe Lawson.

"Hey, Mom, guess what just—" The rest of the words died in her throat when she saw who was with her mother. "What are you doing here?"

Her sister stood abruptly and smoothed a hand down her skirt.

"I was just going," Kelly said. She was very pale and her hands were shaking.

Hannah felt sick. She hadn't seen Kelly in months, not since the last confrontation when her sister had begged Hannah to forgive her, to understand, and Hannah had told her she couldn't.

Kelly started gathering her bag and coat.

"Hold on a minute," their mother said. She put a hand on Kelly's arm. Hannah looked at it, then at her mother. "Kelly is visiting me, that's what she's doing here. She's my daughter, too, Hannah, and I need to see her and know how she's doing, just as I need to know how you're doing."

Bile burned at the back of Hannah's throat. How long

had this been going on? How long had her mother been comforting her sister behind her back? Didn't Kelly have enough attention and love and adoration in her life?

Without a word, Hannah turned and started for her bedroom.

"Hannah." It was Kelly, her voice high with tension.

Hannah kept walking. She had nothing to say to her sister. Nothing that hadn't been said before, anyway.

"I came to talk about the apartment. We both feel really bad about you taking a loss on the sale. Please let us make it up to you," her sister called after her.

Hannah shoved her door closed, the echo of the slam loud in the small room. Arms folded over her chest, hands gripping her elbows, she crossed to the window and glared out at the backyard.

She couldn't believe her mother had been offering comfort to the enemy, and she couldn't believe her sister was still trying to foot the bill for the sale of the apartment she'd once owned with Lucas. It had been Hannah's place, hers and Lucas's. *Their* home, not her sister's. Kelly had had nothing to do with picking the decor, choosing the furniture, deciding which part of town they wanted to live in. Hannah was damned if she was going to let her sister reimburse her for her losses because she and Lucas had been forced to sell in a bad market. Kelly had stolen Lucas, stolen the dreams Hannah had had for her future with the man she loved. But Kelly couldn't take this one small thing away from Hannah: if it killed her, Hannah would pay off her share of the remainder of the mortgage, no matter what. Just to prove to herself and the world that it had happened, that it had mattered. That for a whole year and a half, Lucas Hall had been hers and not her sister's.

There was a tap on the door. Hannah tightened her grip on her elbows. If her sister dared to walk through the door...

"Hannah, it's me," her mother called.

"I don't want to talk."

"Fine, but you can still listen."

The door opened and her mother entered. Her expression was determined. "I think you should seriously think about your sister's offer."

Hannah made a disgusted noise. "Surprise, surprise."

Her mother held up a hand. "Listen for a minute, will you? You've been planning this trip around Australia for months. Years, really, since you put it off when you first met Lucas. If you take up your sister's offer, you can go now. I know that's what you want, what will make you happy. Why not do it?"

"Because I won't let her buy her way out of her guilt," Hannah said. Her sister had always made more money than Hannah in her high-end IT job. Kelly's yearly bonuses alone were sometimes triple Hannah's salary as a mechanic. Even with the global financial downturn Kelly was still hauling it in hand over fist.

"I don't think that's why she wants to do it. She wants you to be happy," her mother said.

"Then she shouldn't have stolen my fiancé."

"Would you really want to be married to a man who was in love with another woman? Do you think your sister should have stepped aside and let that happen, Hannah?"

"It should never have even been an issue. She's my sister and he was my fiancé. The thought should never even have entered her head."

"Or his head. But it did. Sometimes you can't stop yourself from falling in love with someone, sweetheart."

"Bullshit! I don't want to hear this, Mom. And I'm not taking her money. It was *my* apartment. Mine and Lucas's. I'll pay for my fair share of what's left of the mortgage. She can't take that away from me."

Her mother shook her head. "My God, you always were a stubborn one."

"Yeah, that's me—stupid, loyal, stubborn old Hannah." Her voice broke on the last word and her mother stepped forward, hand extended. Hannah jerked away from her. She was angry with her mother, unfairly or not. Kelly had hurt her, betrayed her utterly. It felt like a further betrayal to learn that her mother had been seeing her sister all these months behind Hannah's back.

"I need to work on my bike," Hannah said.

Chapter 3

Hannah didn't stop walking until she was safely in the garage, breathing in the smell of damp concrete and engine grease. She sank onto her upright tool chest, pressing her hands to her face. For a moment she was so angry and sad she could barely breathe.

I'm so sick of this. I'm so sick of feeling this way.

The problem was, she didn't know what to do with her anger. She'd thought that not seeing Kelly or Lucas for all these months would have made a difference, taken some of the heat out of her feelings. But she'd only had to look into her sister's perfectly made-up face to feel it all surging back. That, and seeing the pity in her mother's eyes…

Of course, her mother wasn't the only one who felt sorry for poor, jilted Hannah. It had practically become a national pastime once the wedding had been canceled. Their family, all of her and Lucas's friends, the neighbors, her customers—they'd all offered their condolences and shaken their heads. After all, it wasn't every day that a tomboyish older sister was cast aside for her younger, more glamorous, more beautiful sister. It was a classic tale of woe and everyone could relate. And more than anything—perhaps even more than the pain of betrayal and loss—Hannah resented being cast as a victim. It wasn't until her life had crashed around her ears that she'd understood how much pride she took in her independence and her unusual vocation and her own unique, take-no-prisoners view of the world. And now, thanks to Kelly and Lucas, she was simply poor Hannah, victim. Object of pity and sympathy.

And right now she was acting exactly like a victim, wallowing in her own messy emotional soup. No wonder her mother felt sorry for her.

Hannah surged to her feet and crossed to her bike. There was still an hour or so of daylight left and she might as well use it while she attempted to fix the muffler. Seizing the handlebars, she rocked the bike off its stand and pushed it down the driveway. After propping it on its stand again, she went back for her toolbox.

She deliberately focused on what she was doing, on what she needed to do next as she worked, and slowly she calmed. Later, she would apologize to her mother. Hannah knew she hadn't exactly been a dream to live with the past six months, and although she burned every time she thought about her mother listening sympathetically to her sister, she knew it was her mother's right to do what she thought was best. And Hannah was the first person to admit she was hardly unbiased in this situation.

Her stomach rumbled with hunger but she wasn't ready to go in yet. Instead, she grabbed a beer from the bar fridge she kept in the garage and palmed a handful of peanuts from the jar on the workbench. She'd downed half the beer when she became aware that someone was watching her.

She glanced across into a pair of big, intent blue eyes.

"What's wrong with it?" the little girl asked, toes hanging over the edge of the curb as she hovered near the bike.

Hannah had never been very good at guessing kids' ages, but the girl was small and skinny with a delicate, pointed face and Hannah figured she must be about eight or nine. Her very blond hair was caught up on either side of her head in pigtails, and her top featured lots of sparkles and stars in various colors of pink. When she clasped her hands in front of her tummy, Hannah saw her nails were painted with glitter polish.

"There's a hole in the muffler. I'm about to patch it," Hannah said.

"What's a muffler?" the little girl asked, taking a step closer.

Hannah pointed to the round tube at the head of the exhaust pipe. "It's this part here, in front of the exhaust pipe."

"What does it do when it's not broken?" She took another step.

Hannah could see the girl was aching to touch the shiny red finish on the gas tank and she nodded encouragingly. "It's okay, you can touch it."

"It's so shiny," the little girl said, glitter-tipped fingernails gliding over the paint.

"The muffler is supposed to stop the engine from

sounding so loud," Hannah said, answering the girl's earlier question. She tapped the motor. "When the bike is going, there's a whole lot of noisy stuff going on in here, and the sound has to escape somewhere. The muffler is supposed to turn the volume down."

"But yours has got a hole in it. Is that why it was so noisy last night?"

Hannah shifted guiltily. It didn't take a rocket scientist to work out that this was one of Joe Lawson's kids. She had his blue eyes, for starters. And there was something about the way she held her head... Which meant he'd been right last night—Hannah *had* woken his kids when she'd been fooling around in the garage.

"I'm sorry about that. I didn't realize you guys had moved in yet," Hannah said.

"It's okay. I didn't mind." The little girl thrust her hand forward. "I'm Ruby Lawson, by the way."

Hannah suppressed a smile. She held up her own hand, displaying the grease on it.

"I'm dirty, sorry. But I'm Hannah," she said.

"I don't care about dirt," Ruby said, and before Hannah could stop her she'd reached out and grasped Hannah's hand, her small fingers wrapping around Hannah's larger ones.

"Pleased to meet you," Ruby said solemnly.

It was impossible for Hannah to hide her smile then. "Pleased to meet you, too, Ruby."

Ruby smiled back, then looked at the bike. "Can I help you fix it?"

Hannah flicked a glance at Ruby's sparkly top and purple pants. She didn't exactly strike Hannah as the tomboy type. Still, Hannah wasn't about to discourage her—she'd been laughed at and sent on her way too many times when she was a curious kid to hand out the same treatment to another little girl.

"Sure. You can pass me tools when I need them, if you'd like."

"Okay. You might have to tell me which one is which, though."

"Deal," Hannah said.

They worked side by side for a while. Ruby was a fast learner, quickly working out how to tell what size the various spanners and wrenches were by checking the little markings on their sides. She took great delight in slapping each requested tool into Hannah's hand with vigor. Hannah figured the kid must have seen more than her fair share of medical dramas on TV over the years.

"My dad used to work with tools like this," Ruby said as they were refitting the patched muffler.

Despite herself, Hannah's curiosity pricked up its ears. "So your dad is a mechanic, is he?" It couldn't hurt to know a bit more about the man. He did live next door, after all. Might as well know what she was up against.

"My dad is an oilman. He works on the offshore rigs," Ruby said proudly. "He's done every job there is."

Hannah didn't know much about oil work, but she was pretty sure that offshore postings meant the person was away a lot. "You must miss him when he's working, huh?"

She knew she was being nosy, but she couldn't seem to help herself.

"He's been working in an office since Mommy died, and now he's going to be a businessman."

Hannah froze for a second.

A dead wife. It went a long way to explaining the look in Joe's eyes.

Suddenly she felt as though she'd invaded her new neighbor's privacy. She was almost one hundred percent certain that he would hate for her to know about his sad personal life.

"You know what? I think we're about done," she said. She stepped back from the bike and Ruby did the same, copying Hannah's hands-on-hips posture.

"Do we start up the motor now, see if it works?" Ruby asked. Her eyes were wide with excitement when she looked at Hannah.

"Absolutely. You want to do the honors?"

Ruby's eyes went even wider. "Really?"

Hannah simply handed over the keys. Ruby vibrated with anticipation as she stood on tiptoes and slid the key into the ignition. With an encouraging nod from Hannah, Ruby twisted the key and the bike roared to life. Ruby gave a little squeal and jumped backward. Hannah laughed, then immediately bit her lip when Ruby gave her a reproachful look.

"It just took me by surprise, that's all," the little girl said.

"I know. It startles me all the time, too," Hannah said.

Ruby cocked her head to one side. "Is it fixed? It still sounds very loud."

She was right; the bike was still too noisy. Ideally, the bike needed a new muffler, but Hannah couldn't justify the expense when she was still paying off the personal loan she'd had to take out to cover what was left of the mortgage after they'd sold the apartment.

"Well, it's not perfect, but it's going to have to do for now," Hannah said. She reached out and switched the bike off again.

"Can we go for a ride?"

Hannah smiled. She'd been waiting for that one. "I don't think your dad would appreciate us doing that."

"He wouldn't mind."

"Hmm. I'm not so sure about that."

Ruby pressed her hands together and gave Hannah a limpid-eyed beseeching look. "Pretty please?"

As pitiful pleas went, it was very effective. Hannah wondered if Ruby had practiced in the mirror. "Sorry, sweetheart. You can have a sit on it, though, if you'd like."

Ruby considered for a moment. "I guess that would be okay," she said grudgingly.

Hannah wiped her hands on her jeans and helped boost Ruby onto the saddle. Ruby's legs barely straddled the seat and she wobbled and clutched at the handlebars, a worried frown on her face.

"Hang on a minute," Hannah said. She slung a leg over the bike so that she was sitting behind Ruby, holding the little girl's hips with her hands. "Is that better?"

"Yes. Can I rev the engine?"

"Sure, why not?"

Hannah twisted the ignition key and the bike rumbled to life beneath them. Ruby giggled.

"It's all bouncy," she said.

Hannah laughed. She vaguely registered the sound of a door slamming shut in the background as she leaned forward to twist the throttle.

"See? You grip this and twist it slowly forward. But not too much—you don't want to push it too hard."

Ruby reached out, fingers spread wide.

"What the hell do you think you're doing?"

Hannah nearly fell off the bike as Joe stalked across the sidewalk, his expression livid.

"Are you out of your freaking mind?" he demanded. He grasped Ruby around the waist, plucking her from the bike as though she weighed less than a feather.

"No, Daddy. Hannah was just going to let me rev the engine," Ruby protested.

Joe set her on the ground and put a hand on her shoulder. "I want you to go inside."

"No! We weren't doing anything wrong. We were just sitting there," Ruby insisted.

Hannah could see the little girl was getting herself worked up. She could also see that Joe was in no mood to listen to reason. She met Ruby's gaze.

"It's okay, sweetie," she said reassuringly. "You do what your daddy says."

The small exchange only made Joe angrier. He forcibly turned Ruby around. "Inside, now!" he barked.

Ruby's bottom lip stuck out and her eyes filled with tears but fear won out over valor. Hannah didn't blame her—Joe Lawson in full-blooded fury was a pretty damned intimidating sight. With one last glance over her shoulder, Ruby raced toward the house.

Joe waited until his daughter was well out of hearing before turning on Hannah. "What kind of a reckless idiot takes a kid for a ride on a motorbike without a helmet? You want to answer me that?"

"You're overreacting. If you calmed down for one second—"

"Don't tell me to be calm, lady." He shoved a finger in her face. "You had no right to risk my daughter's life. Did you even stop to think—" He broke off, unable to articulate his fury.

Hannah held his gaze, pride demanding that she not waver for a second in the face of his misplaced righteousness.

"Are you finished?" she asked calmly. "Any more insults you want to throw at me?"

He gave her a scathing head to toe. "Stay away from my daughter." He turned on his heel and strode toward his house.

Hannah let out the breath she'd been holding.

Wow. That had been exactly what she hadn't needed—a big, shitty cherry on top of an already shitty day.

She started gathering her tools and was dismayed to see her hands were shaking. She squeezed her hands into fists, willing them to steady. She hadn't done a single thing wrong. She refused to let him get to her.

When she opened her hands again, the shaking was barely discernible.

Good. That was the way it should be. Back straight, she wheeled her bike into the garage.

Joe paused outside Ruby's bedroom door to take a deep breath and consciously relax his shoulders. His blood was still pounding in his head, but Ruby didn't deserve his anger. She was just a kid, going with the flow. It wasn't her fault that Hannah Napier was reckless and irresponsible.

He lifted his hand and rapped on the door.

"Rubes, it's me," he called.

She didn't say anything but he pushed the door open anyway. She was stretched out on her bed, her face buried in her pillow.

"I'm sorry for yelling at you like that," he said as he

crossed to the bed and sat beside her. He laid his hand on her shoulder. He could feel the agitated heat coming off her body. "I didn't mean to frighten you."

Hell, he was the one who'd been frightened. Seeing his little girl perched on the bike like that, realizing what Ruby had been up to while he'd been kneading pizza dough in the kitchen... He'd seen red. If Hannah Napier had been a man, for sure he would have grabbed her by the scruff of the neck and shaken her till her teeth rattled. Luckily for her, she'd been protected by her gender. Just. For a few seconds there, it had been a close-run thing.

"What happened wasn't your fault, okay?" he said. He stroked Ruby's rigid back. "But I need you to promise that you will never, ever go for a ride on a motorbike again without talking to me, okay?"

Ruby lifted her head and he could see she'd been crying. "No!"

He frowned. "I know they look like a lot of fun, but they're dangerous, sweetheart. There's a whole bunch of special equipment you should be wearing before you even think of riding one of those things."

His voice caught as he imagined what could have happened to her if something had gone wrong. Ruby was so small, so bloody fragile....

"No, Daddy, you've got it all wrong. Hannah didn't take me for a ride and now you yelled at her and she'll never let me help her again."

Joe frowned. "Ruby, I saw you on the bike. I know you're only trying to protect your new friend—"

"She didn't take me for a ride! I asked her to but she said no. Then she said I could sit on the bike if I wanted to and she was really nice and lifted me up and held me when I thought I was going to fall," Ruby said in an urgent rush.

Joe stared at his daughter. Ruby held his gaze unflinchingly, her blue eyes drenched with tears. The tight, uncomfortable feeling in his gut told him his daughter was speaking the truth.

Damn.

He closed his eyes for a long moment as he reviewed his reaction through the filter of this new information. Over-the-top? Just a little.

"Hannah's going to hate me now," Ruby said miserably.

Not half as much as she hates me.

"I'm sure she doesn't hate you, Rubes. You didn't do anything wrong. I was the one who made the mistake."

"I tried to tell you, but you wouldn't listen. I asked and asked Hannah to take me for a ride, but she said you wouldn't like it. I even said you wouldn't mind, but she said she thought you would."

Just in case he didn't feel enough of a heel already.

"Yeah. The thing was, Rube, I saw you sitting up there, and the bike was running, and it looked like you guys had come back from a spin around the block."

Dear God, could he sound any more defensive?

Ruby gave him a level look. "You should have listened when I tried to explain."

"You're right. I should have. And next time, I promise I will."

Ruby sniffed loudly, then knuckled her eyes dry. "It's okay. I forgive you," she said magnanimously.

"Thank you."

"But we should go next door right now and apologize to Hannah," Ruby said. She was already wriggling toward the edge of the bed and she looked at Joe expectantly.

He nodded. "That's a good idea."

Even though it was going to make him squirm.

"Oh, I know what we should do!" Ruby grabbed the front of his sweater she was so excited. "We should invite Hannah over for pizza! She won't be able to stay angry with us if we make her pizza."

Want to bet?

"It's a lovely idea, Rubes, but I think we might leave the pizza for another night. Hannah probably doesn't want to have dinner with us just now."

"Then we should take her one for her to eat on her own. I'll make it for her and we'll take it over together and explain how you got it wrong and how you're sorry for yelling at her."

For a moment Joe was tempted to agree to the idea, but he knew that taking Ruby with him was the coward's way out of the hole he'd dug for himself. There was no way Hannah would give him the verbal smackdown he deserved with his daughter standing beside him.

"I tell you what. Why don't you make a pizza for Hannah, and I'll take it over to her on my own and apologize?" he said.

Ruby studied him. "Don't be embarrassed because you made a mistake, Daddy. You only got upset because you love me. I know that."

Joe smiled. Maybe he *should* take his daughter with him, after all. There wasn't a jury in the land that would convict him with her on his side.

He tugged on one of her pigtails. "How did you get to be so wise?"

Ruby smiled and shrugged. "Just lucky, I guess."

They went to the kitchen to create a pizza especially for Hannah. Ruby insisted on putting every single topping available on it, since they didn't know what Hannah liked or didn't like.

"This way, she can pick off the bits she doesn't want," Ruby reasoned. "But if the bits aren't there in the first place, she can't put them back on."

Ben had a bit to say about his sister's logic, but finally Joe had a pizza in his hand and a speech roughed out in his mind.

He'd apologize straight up, not offer any excuses. And when she let fly at him, he'd take it. The way she'd taken it when he dished it out to her.

He felt like a kid going to the principal's office as he walked up the front steps to Hannah's house. Gritting his teeth, he rang the doorbell.

There was a rattle of a door chain being removed, then Mrs. Napier opened the door.

"Oh, hello, Joe. How are you doing? How did the big move go?" Robyn said, a welcoming smile on her face.

"I'm good, thanks. And the move was pretty smooth, all things considered."

"Did you want to come in? Or were you after something? Goodness, is that a pizza?"

"Um, yes, it is. I was actually wondering if I could have a quick word with Hannah?"

Robyn's smile widened. "Of course you can. Why don't you come in and I'll go grab her?"

Joe stepped into the foyer as Robyn disappeared up the hallway. He glanced around as he waited, taking in the fussy wallpaper and antique hat stand in the front hall. Interesting. Not the kind of furnishings he'd imagined a woman like Hannah favoring.

There was a family portrait hanging next to it, a photograph of Robyn and two young girls. He moved closer and recognized the oldest girl as Hannah. He guessed she must have been about twelve or thirteen when it was taken. Her hair was cut short and she wore jeans and a football sweater. She had her arm wrapped protectively around her younger sister and there was a challenge in her eyes as she smiled down the barrel of the camera.

Full of attitude, even at thirteen. It figured.

A door closed somewhere in the house and Joe turned away from the photograph just as Hannah entered the foyer wearing a pale green satin bathrobe. Her hair was wrapped in a towel and she had her arms crossed defensively over her chest as she stopped in front of him. She glanced at the pizza and arched an eyebrow.

"It's for you. Ruby made it," he said awkwardly.

She looked different without her coverall or biker gear. Softer. More vulnerable.

"To say thank you for the motorbike ride I didn't take her on, I assume?" Hannah asked coolly.

He squared his shoulders. "Yeah, about that. I owe you an apology. I jumped to conclusions. I should have let you explain before I barged in."

"Yep, you should have."

He shifted his weight. He hadn't expected her to make it easy for him, but he couldn't remember the last time he'd felt this uncomfortable. "I can't remember exactly what I said, but I was out of line and I'm sorry."

"Let me see if I can refresh your memory. *Reckless idiot*, I think you called me."

He winced. "I'm sorry."

She eyed him for a moment, then her gaze dropped

to the pizza. "Ruby made this for me—is that what you said?"

"Yes. It's a Ruby superspecial with the works. Home-made base and everything."

She held out her hand and he passed the pizza over. Now that her arms weren't crossed over her chest, he could see the outline of her breasts against her robe. The soft shape of her nipples was clearly visible beneath the silk, and he realized that she must be naked beneath it.

For a moment he got caught on the thought, his mind filling with images of soft skin and even softer curves.

Where the hell did that come from?

He shoved his hands into his pockets. Then he cleared his throat. "Before I go, I wanted to thank you for taking the time to talk with Ruby. I know she probably got in the way. It was kind of you to let her help."

Hannah gave him a scathing look. "It wasn't kind. She's a good kid. Smart, funny. A minor miracle, considering who her father is. But I won't hold that against her."

She stepped forward and opened the front door. "Tell Ruby thank you for the pizza," she said.

His audience was over. He stepped over the threshold and turned to face her. "I will. And I just want to say again—"

The door closed in his face. He blinked, then slowly turned away. Despite everything, a reluctant smile curved his mouth.

Hannah Napier was a handful. He'd got that much right about her.

And despite that, he wanted her.

The realization killed his smile. He hadn't felt a thing for another woman since Beth died, yet for some

crazy reason every time he looked at his new neighbor he found himself thinking things he had no business thinking.

*It's only sex. You haven't touched a woman in two
years. You're only human.*

All true, but somehow not enough to ease the tight
feeling in his gut. He didn't want to be attracted to another woman. He wasn't over Beth yet, not by a long
shot.

Chapter 4

The following afternoon, Hannah pushed through the double doors to The Watering Hole, the local pub and her favorite after-work hangout. It was the kind of pub that used to dominate the suburbs of Melbourne before slot machines were introduced—scuffed and dented around the edges, friendly vibe, no pretense about it. She loved the cream and burgundy tiles behind the bar and the dusty memorabilia hanging on the walls.

Her mate Bugsy raised a hairy arm in greeting when he saw her. "Napier. Took your time."

She smiled. She didn't know what she would have done without her biker buddies over the past few months. Bugsy and Grunter and the rest had quietly circled the wagons when the wedding fell through. No one had said a word, but she knew they'd felt for her and she'd appreciated their silent support.

She slid onto a stool beside Bugsy and accepted the beer he pushed toward her. "Cheers," she said, raising her glass.

"Straight back at you."

She took a long pull from her beer. There was nothing better after a long day at work. She rested her elbow on the counter and smiled at Bugsy. "Gonna let me whip your ass on the pool table?" she asked.

"You can try, little girl."

She laughed. Then she caught sight of a man out of the corner of her eye and did a double take.

Joe Lawson.

Man. Was it too much to ask for her to have a moment's reprieve from the guy? She felt as though he'd invaded her life since he'd moved in.

He was talking to Mandy, The Watering Hole's longest-serving waitress. Hannah hoped she was giving him directions to someplace far away. Hannah had come here to relax and she was pretty damn sure she wasn't going to be able to do that with him sitting across the bar.

He glanced up and caught her staring. His expression didn't change but his shoulders shifted. For a moment they stared at each other, then his focus returned to Mandy.

"What's wrong?" Bugsy asked.

"Nothing," she said. She took another mouthful of beer. "Let's go play pool."

She slid off the stool and grabbed her jacket with one hand, her beer with the other. Bugsy led the way to the seen-better-days pool table in the back corner, but she couldn't help glancing over her shoulder as she followed him, just to check on where her nemesis was. She almost walked into the cigarette machine when she saw Mandy ushering Joe behind the bar. What the hell…?

Mandy was gesturing toward the spirits lined up on the shelves behind the bar. Joe nodded, asked a question. Mandy turned and pointed to the beer taps along the front edge of the counter.

"You coming or what?" Bugsy called from behind her.

Hannah tore her gaze away and walked the final few steps to join him.

Why was Joe Lawson being invited behind the bar? If she didn't know any better, she'd think Mandy was giving him an orientation tour.

Shit. What if he'd taken a job at The Watering Hole? It was possible, after all. He was new to the area, and Ruby had said he'd retired from the rigs. He must need to work. Still, this was the one place she could relax and not worry about anything, the one place where she felt utterly comfortable. She didn't want to have to run the gauntlet of her surly neighbor every time she wanted a beer and a game of pool.

Hannah was distracted as Bugsy set up the table then flipped a coin to see who would break. She kept glancing across to the bar to check what Joe was doing. Sure enough, he'd started pulling beers for customers.

"Bloody hell."

Bugsy broke and started sinking balls. Hannah tried to concentrate, but she was too thrown to really follow the game. When Mandy sailed past with a tray full of empty glasses, Hannah called after her.

"Mandy. You got a minute?" she asked.

The older woman paused and smiled at Hannah. "Sure. You guys want another round?"

"We're all right for now, thanks. I was just curious about the new guy."

Mandy rolled her eyes and fanned herself with her free hand. "I know, isn't he gorgeous? Talk about dumb luck, huh? When Arnie told me the news I was sure it was going to suck big-time, but now that I've met Joe I've got to say, I'm definitely coming around."

Hannah frowned, confused, but Mandy just kept talking.

"And the great thing is, the way he's talking, Joe's not going to change anything. He's definitely not going to put in slot machines or try to turn the place into one of those slick yuppy hangouts, thank God. So even though it'll be sad saying goodbye to Arnie after all these years, I think I can live with it."

Hannah blinked as she deciphered Mandy's ramblings. "He's *bought* the place?" Hannah hoped against hope that she'd gotten it wrong.

"Yeah. Didn't you see the notice?" Mandy pointed to a handwritten note stuck near the till. "Sale was finalized yesterday, but apparently they've been negotiating for over a month."

Hannah swallowed the four-letter word on the tip of her tongue. "Well. How about that."

Mandy wiggled her eyebrows suggestively one last time before moving off. Hannah tried to come to terms with what she'd just learned.

Joe Lawson, arrogant, judgmental neighbor extraordinaire, had purchased the one place left on earth where she felt like a normal human being. What were the odds?

She was seized with the sudden urge to march across the bar and demand he undo the sale, that he choose some other pub to invest in. This was her home away from home. She'd already lost the apartment she and Lucas had lived in, the future they'd planned. She'd narrowed her life to working hard and paying off her debts so she could escape. The Watering Hole had been her solace.

And now Joe Bloody Lawson had taken that away from her, too.

She should walk out the door and never come back. She didn't like him, he didn't like her. He made her uncomfortable. There were plenty of other places she could play pool and drink beer with her mates. But leaving felt like admitting defeat. Even if he owned the place now, she'd been here first. She'd been coming here for years, for Pete's sake. There was no way she was going to let him run her out of town, so to speak.

"Your shot," Bugsy said.

Hannah dragged her gaze away from where Joe was pouring shots for a group of university students. Jaw set, she took up her cue. Lining up a ball, she took her shot. The ball sped straight into the pocket with a satisfying thwack.

"Aw, man," Bugsy complained as she started to clean up the table.

She wouldn't back off. She would come here after work two or three times a week, same as she always had. Joe was nothing to her. Less than nothing.

Absolutely.

Two weeks later, Joe let himself into the house to find his mother dozing on the couch. He tried to be quiet but she started to wakefulness as he entered the room.

"Joe! You scared me."

"Sorry. I tried to be quiet."

She sat up and ran her hands over her hair.

"My goodness, it's after eleven. I didn't mean to fall asleep, but television was dreadful tonight. All that horrible reality TV just celebrates the absolute worst in humanity. What happened to good old-fashioned dramas like *Dallas* and *Dynasty?*"

"Joan Collins got old and J.R. got sick," he said. He dropped his keys onto the coffee table and stretched out his back. "How were the kids? Did Ben get through his homework okay?"

Joe had been making a point of being home when the kids got in from school most days, only heading into the pub after they'd had their dinner. His long-term plan was to hire a night manager, but his mother had been good enough to cover the evenings while he learned the ropes at The Watering Hole in these early weeks. Tonight, however, he'd had to delegate all child care to his mother while he dealt with a staff crisis. Not a big deal, but annoying given that the whole point of buying the business had been to offer his kids a more stable home life.

"He told me he did it. I'm not sure what that means anymore," his mother said.

He ran a hand over his hair. He knew exactly what she meant. Ben had become increasingly incommunicative lately. He spent a lot of time alone in his room listening to his iPod or playing on his handheld game, and no matter what Joe said or did he couldn't get more than a shrug and a handful of words from his son.

"Have you had that talk with him yet?" his mother asked.

"Yes. He said school is fine, he's making friends. He

likes the new house. I couldn't get anything more out of him." He sat on the couch beside her. "I should have stuck it out in Sydney."

"Maybe, but you're here now. And once Ben and Ruby settle, things will even out, you'll find new rhythms and routines."

"I guess."

"How's the pub going?"

"Good. Still getting used to being on my feet most of the day." He gave her a tired smile. "Got soft over the past few years, being a desk jockey."

He'd given up his work on the offshore oil rigs when Beth died and taken a desk job so he could be around for the kids. It had been more than enough to prove to him that suit-and-tie stuff was not for him. Hence the purchase of the pub. It had always been Beth's dream that they buy their own place and run it as a family.

"You look tired," his mother said, her eyes concerned.

"I'm okay."

"I know it must be hard. You and Beth always planned on doing this together."

He shrugged. He had to do something with his life now that he could no longer do the rig work he loved. He'd decided to go ahead with Beth's dream because he hadn't had one of his own and she'd always said that when he gave up offshore work he'd go stir-crazy if he tried to take on a nine-to-five job. The past two years had more than proven her right.

Just for a moment he allowed himself to wonder what she'd think of The Watering Hole. He hoped she'd like its old-fashioned wooden bar and beat-up floor, the scratched and scarred tables and chairs and the chalkboards dating back to the 1930s. She'd always talked about buying a traditional place, a pub where families could get a reasonably priced meal and where the locals came to spend time with each other. No slot machines, no loud bands to scare people off. A neighborhood place.

His mother stood and started collecting her things. "I'd better get going. I'll see you around dinnertime tomorrow, okay?"

He looked at her. "I appreciate this. You know that, right?" He'd never been great with words, but he hoped she understood how much he valued everything she'd done for him and his kids.

"I do. And you don't have to keep thanking me. Ben and Ruby keep me young." She squeezed his hand and stood on her toes to kiss his cheek. "Get some sleep."

He walked her to her car and waited until she'd rounded the corner before turning back to the house. He glanced at the Napier place as he walked up the front path. The light was on in the garage, illumination leaking out around the edges of the roller door. He could hear the radio playing. Hannah was obviously in there, tinkering away at something. He didn't need to check his watch to know it was late, well past eleven. What the hell did she have to do in there that couldn't wait until morning?

Over the past two weeks he'd watched her at The Watering Hole. He hadn't wanted to, but he'd been unable to help himself. The moment she walked in the door she exerted a gravitational pull on his senses that he found impossible to ignore. She came in twice, maybe three times a week. She had a beer, sometimes two, played a couple of games of pool with her biker friends, then she left. She never got drunk, never flirted, never let the guys win to make them feel good about themselves. Watching her interact with them, he was almost certain she wasn't sleeping with any of them. Although why that was any of his business he had no idea.

She'd let Ruby help her twice since his knee-jerk reaction. Both times Ruby came home with greasy fingernails and clothes and conversation peppered with lots of "Hannah saids." Through his daughter he'd learned that Hannah was restoring an old Triumph Thunderbird, that she planned to take off on a round-Australia road trip as soon as she had enough money saved, and that Hannah couldn't stand Brussels sprouts, turnips or radishes.

He couldn't work her out. She was gorgeous, yet she spent most of her time alone, up to her elbows in oil and grease. He'd finally discovered that her mother owned the house next door and that Hannah was living with her, and not the other way around. Yet Hannah didn't strike him as the kind of person who would cling to her mother's apron strings.

She was a mystery. One that his mind kept mulling over, again and again.

He climbed the steps to the house, shutting out thoughts of his provocative neighbor along with the cool night air as he closed the front door. He had no business speculating about her, just as he had no business fantasizing about what she looked like naked or how her skin would feel against his own. It was a dead end, and he didn't have time or energy to waste on dead ends.

He locked the door then did his nightly check on the kids before heading to bed. Ben's door was closed, but Joe eased it open and stepped into the room. His son

looked much younger than his thirteen years when he
was sleeping, his face more rounded, his chin less determined. Joe backed out silently then made his way to
Ruby's room. Her door was ajar and he swung it open
quietly. Unlike her brother, Ruby was twisted in her
quilt, one hand flung up near her head on the pillow. He
crossed to the bed to untangle her and frowned when he
saw the damp patch on her pillow. Her eyelashes were
spiky with moisture, her cheeks flushed. She'd been
crying, had cried herself to sleep, in fact. That was a
blow to his solar plexus. It was one thing for him to be
around while his daughter cried, to be able to comfort
her and talk to her, but it was another thing entirely to
know she'd been huddled in her bed, crying her misery
into her pillow all on her own.

He wanted to wake her and reassure her and make
her world right again. Instead he crouched beside the
bed and smoothed the hair from her forehead. She
looked more and more like Beth every day. She was
going to be beautiful like her, too.

Because there was nothing else for him to do, he
straightened her quilt, making sure she was warm
enough. His fingers encountered something where the
bed met the wall and he pulled out a crumpled ball of
paper. He waited until he was in the hallway and the
door was closed before smoothing the page. It was a
flyer, sent home from Ruby's school.

Elsternwick Primary School invites entries for its
annual Mother and Daughter Fashion Parade. All
funds raised will go toward the new gymnasium…

Joe swore under his breath and let his hand drop to his side. No wonder she'd been crying.

"Damn."

Life was going to be full of moments like these for his children. Casually delivered school notices, other children's birthday parties, a myriad of other social and community events centered around families. He couldn't protect Ben and Ruby from them all, no matter how much he wanted to. But God, how he wanted to.

He walked slowly to the kitchen and placed the flyer on the counter. He stared at it, trying to work out how to handle the situation. Wait until Ruby brought it up? Mention it himself? Did the fact that Ruby hadn't said anything to his mother tonight and instead chose to cry alone in her room mean he should tackle this more vigorously or give her more space?

He was truly clueless. He rubbed a hand over his face. Then he folded the notice in half and slid it into the junk drawer. He would talk to Ruby in the morning, see if she mentioned the fashion parade. If she didn't... He would cross that bridge when he came to it. If she did, he would offer what comfort he could. Maybe his mother would be an adequate substitute. Or maybe he could offer to do something special with her the night of the parade and turn it into a father-daughter event instead of an occasion of sadness and grief.

Maybe. It was becoming the most overused word in his vocabulary.

The next day, Hannah exited the workshop and waited for a pause in the traffic before crossing to the small group of shops opposite. She could see there was already a queue forming in the bakery, but she knew Ian would bitch and moan all day if she didn't bring him back the doughnut he'd requested for morning break.

Resigning herself to a long wait, she joined the line and dug her hands into the pockets of her coveralls, jingling her change in the palm of her hand. She was glancing idly out the front window when she saw a dark-haired boy walk past with a couple of taller, older kids. She'd have to be blind not to recognize the younger boy as Joe's son—she'd seen him coming and going from the house often enough.

She checked her watch. It wasn't even close to lunchtime, which meant Joe's kid had no legitimate reason for being on the street during school hours.

Unless he was ditching, of course.

She turned her attention to the menu board behind the bakery counter and concentrated on choosing between a Danish and a vanilla slice for herself. So what if Joe's kid was sneaking off from school with what looked like older, meaner kids? It was none of her business.

It was harder to stick to her decision when she exited the bakery and spotted Joe's son emptying his pockets near the corner while the older kids inspected his haul. It had been a while, but Hannah recognized the classic signs of shoplifting when she saw them. The furtiveness, the repressed excitement and fear. She could imagine how it had worked, too—the older kids distracting the shopkeeper while the younger, more innocent-looking kid played mule and stuffed his pockets.

She hesitated on the curb, watching the smaller boy shake his head in response to something one of the older kids said. Joe Junior or whatever his name was looked a lot like his old man—same dark hair, same blue eyes. No doubt he'd grow up to be as big and strong, too. As though he felt her regard, Joe Junior looked up and for a moment they locked gazes. He looked away first, but not before she saw the sadness in him. Another thing in common with his father.

She crossed the street and reentered the workshop, tossing Ian the bag with his doughnut in it.

"Thanks, boss lady," he said with a grin.

"Just don't blame me when you have diabetes."

She leaned her butt against the rear workbench and bit into her Danish, frowning fiercely as she chewed. For the life of her, she couldn't get the little scene from across the road out of her mind. The way Joe's son had hunched his shoulders when the older kids were talking to him, the patent unhappiness in his eyes—he hadn't looked as though he was having a good time to Hannah. He was new to the area, too. Who knew what kinds of pressure he was experiencing at his new school and what he felt he had to do to fit in with his new peers?

"Shit."

She screwed the remains of her Danish up inside the bakery bag and tossed the lot in the garbage. She couldn't believe she was about to do what she was about to do.

"Ian, I'm heading out for half an hour or so. Cover the phones, okay?"

"Sure. Don't forget Mrs. Lockhead wants her wagon back by three."

"Yeah, I'm on it."

She didn't bother to check her hair or change out of her coverall. This wasn't a social call, after all. She walked around the corner, and down the block to The Watering Hole. It was dim inside after the brightness out of doors so she stopped on the threshold and blinked, waiting for her vision to clear.

It was quiet, since it was only half past ten. Staff were busy cleaning tables and stacking glasses. The smell of beer and fried food hung in the air.

Second thoughts bit hard. She had no business being here. Then Joe exited the office, a stack of papers in hand.

Fine. Get it over with if you're going to be a do-gooder.

She took a deep breath and crossed to the bar. "You got a minute?"

Joe's head came up and his eyebrows lifted. He didn't bother pretending to look pleased to see her. They didn't have that kind of relationship.

"What's up?"

Hannah glanced at the bartender pouring ice into a bucket nearby. "Is there somewhere more private we can talk?"

She figured he wouldn't be thrilled to have his staff learn about his renegade son. Not that he was going to be thrilled at all, of course.

There was a short pause before he gestured with his head for her to follow him. She kept her eyes on the back of his neck as he led her into the manager's office. Boxes of supplies were stacked along one wall and a battered desk filled the corner. He turned to face her, eyes wary.

"If this is about Ruby, if she's been getting in your way when you're trying to work, just say the word and I'll find something else for her to do."

"You have a boy, right? Dark-haired, same eyes as you? I've seen him in the street."

"Yeah, Ben. Why? What's happened?"

"I just saw him at the local shops."

Joe frowned. "He's supposed to be at school."

"I figured." She hesitated a moment, unsure how he was going to take her next bit of news. "I think he was shoplifting."

"What?" He straightened, took a step forward.

She held up a hand, all too familiar with his temper. "Before you start turning green and busting out of your clothes, you might want to hear me out."

She could tell he didn't like the reference but he nodded to signal she should continue.

"He was with a couple of older kids, and it looked like they were using him as their mule, if you know what I mean. That's why I figured you ought to know, since maybe he wasn't doing it because he wanted to do it but because he felt like he had to to make friends."

If she hadn't been looking into his face she would have missed the flash of pain in his eyes. She would have only seen the way his body tensed and heard the anger in his voice.

"How long ago was this? Where were they? Can you show me?" He was already striding for the door.

"They're long gone by now. They were splitting up the booty when I left them ten minutes ago. They've probably gone to the mall to play video games or to some kid's house where there are no parents home." She could see her words sink in. Some of the urgency went out of him. He turned to face her, ran a hand through his hair.

"Bloody hell."

"Yeah, well." She looked away from the confusion and concern on his face. "I thought you'd want to know."

"Thanks." He made an effort to pull himself together. "I appreciate you taking the time. Especially considering I haven't exactly given you a lot of reasons to want to be a good neighbor."

"It's no big deal."

His blue eyes were searching as he looked at her. "It's a big deal to me. My kids are all I have."

She didn't know what to say to that. Apparently she could only handle this man when he was having a go at her. Fill his mouth with civilized conversation and take away his frown and she was reduced to shrugging and discomfort.

She made a show of checking her watch. "I really should get back to the workshop. Good luck with it."

"Let me know next time you're in and I'll shout you a meal."

"Sure." There was no way she'd ever take him up on the offer, but he didn't need to know that.

She got all the way to the door before her conscience bit her. She could only imagine how tough it was bringing up two kids solo, trying to be mother and father to them, trying to anticipate and manage all the little things that could go wrong in life.

Her steps slowed and she closed her eyes and made an impatient noise. Then she swiveled and marched back to his office.

He was leaning against his desk again, head lowered, rubbing the bridge of his nose. For a crazy moment she had to fight the urge to go to him and put her arms around him and draw his head onto her shoulder. As though he wanted her sympathy. He'd probably charge her with assault, given their track record.

She cleared her throat and his head came up. "I have

this friend. He's a cop. I'm sure if I asked him, he'd be happy to come around and have a little chat with Ben. If you wanted to go down that route, that is."

He stared at her and she suddenly felt incredibly self-conscious. She was about to apologize for interfering when he spoke up.

"I was just sitting here racking my brains for ways to handle this."

"I always remember the police making a pretty strong impression when I was a kid."

His mouth quirked a little and she realized he'd almost smiled. A minor miracle.

"Me, too."

She pulled her cell phone from her pocket. "Give me a second and I'll see what I can line up."

Andrew answered on the second ring and she filled him in briefly before handing the phone over to Joe. She watched as he added a few details then confirmed his address and a time for Andrew to visit that evening.

Joe eyed her curiously when he handed the phone back. "He obviously thinks a lot of you."

"We went to school together. And I helped him rebuild his 1970 Capri a few years back."

"Ah."

Her phone was warm from where he'd held it. She slid it into her pocket then shifted her weight awkwardly. "I'm sure Andrew's visit will nip this in the bud. If Ben's anything like Ruby, he's a good kid."

"Despite having me for a father." He was utterly deadpan, but she was almost certain he was joking.

"Took the words right out of my mouth," she said.

His gaze instantly dropped to her mouth. "Ruby tells me you're restoring an old Triumph."

The comment came from so far out of left field it took her a moment to realize what he was doing: making small talk.

"Um, yeah. It's a Thunderbird, 1955."

"Original electrics?"

She narrowed her eyes. "They were redone in the seventies. You know your bikes."

He shrugged. "I had a few growing up. Always wanted a Thunderbird. Anyway, I'm holding you up." He offered her his hand.

As usual, hers were covered with grease and oil and she showed them to him. "Occupational hazard, sorry."

"I don't mind a bit of dirt."

She smiled, couldn't help herself.

"What's so funny?" he asked.

"Ruby said almost exactly the same thing when I first met her."

He smiled, the corners of his eyes crinkling. "A chip off the old block."

All of a sudden she was struggling to form a reply. He looked utterly different with a smile on his face. Younger, lighter—and so attractive she had trouble breathing properly.

Yeah, right. Like you hadn't noticed before.

But she hadn't. Not consciously, anyway. Men simply hadn't been on her agenda. Certainly Joe hadn't been.

He offered his hand again and this time she had no choice but to take it. His hand was bigger than hers—no small feat, since she wasn't exactly a shrinking violet.

She pulled her hand free as soon as she could and shoved it into her pocket. She jerked her head toward the door. "Gotta go."

He nodded and she hustled out. She didn't slow her

pace until she was outside, breathing in the cool spring air. She pressed a hand to her chest, feeling the fast thump-thump of her heart against her breastbone.

Crazy. She had no business getting flushed and flustered over her new neighbor. And over a *handshake,* for Pete's sake. For starters, she didn't even like the guy. And beyond that, she was months, perhaps years off being ready to date again after what Lucas and her sister had done to her.

She let out a bark of laughter as she registered her own thoughts. As if Joe Lawson wanted anything to do with her. As if dating him was even an option.

Absurd. Utterly, completely absurd.

Telling herself she was relieved, Hannah headed back to work, her small moment of madness forgotten. Almost.

Chapter 5

Joe kept an eye on the clock that night, watching the minutes tick toward six. Ruby was next door, hanging out with Hannah again. He wasn't sure how he felt about that, and how much of his discomfort came from his inability to deal with his attraction to his new neighbor. A lot, he suspected.

When the doorbell rang a few minutes later, he glanced to where Ben was doing homework at the kitchen table. "Would you mind getting that, mate?"

Ben had been quiet all night. Joe put it down to guilt or maybe fear. But the truth was he had no idea, and he hated that most of all.

Joe waited until Ben had left the room before moving to the kitchen doorway, one ear cocked to hear what was happening at the front of the house. He heard the door open, then the sound of a man's voice. He couldn't quite make out the words, but there was no missing the high note of fear in Ben's voice when he announced that he would go find his dad. Joe crossed to the fridge and collected two beers. Ben appeared in the kitchen, his face ashen.

"The police are here. They want to talk to you," Ben said. His hands were trembling.

Joe laid a hand on his shoulder. "You okay?" he asked.

Ben nodded quickly. "I might go finish my homework in my room."

"Why don't you hang around here for a minute?"

Ben swallowed audibly. Joe steered him toward the front door. Hannah's police buddy stood on the doorstep, resplendent in full uniform. Joe offered his hand.

"Joe Lawson. I appreciate you coming around like this."

"Andrew Bower. And like I said, it's not a problem. I owe Hannah, big-time."

The other man was tall and athletic looking with dark blond hair. Joe guessed he was in his early thirties, maybe a little younger. Ben was looking from the policeman to his father with dawning understanding. Joe met his son's eyes.

"Why don't we all go into the kitchen?"

He led the way and slid a beer in front of Andrew.

"You're off duty, right?"

"On my way home," Andrew confirmed as he twisted off the cap.

Ben stood between them, rigid with fear. Joe put his hand on his son's shoulder again. "I know what happened today at the corner store. You and I are going to talk more about how that all came to pass. But I asked

Constable Bowers if he wouldn't mind having a word with you about how the law treats shoplifters."

Ben swallowed again. He hung his head, then sniffed mightily. After a long moment, Ben lifted his head. Joe was proud of the way his boy squared his shoulders.

"Okay," Ben said. He couldn't quite look the policeman in the eye, but he drew up a chair at the kitchen table and sat dutifully.

"So, Ben, I thought it might be good if we talked about Mr. Balas," Andrew said.

Ben's forehead wrinkled. "Who's he?"

"He's the man who owns the corner shop. He and his family moved here from India ten years ago because they wanted better opportunities for their children. The whole family works in the store and lives in the house out the back.

"They work every night and every day. And every time someone steals from them, they have to work a little harder and a little longer."

Ben shifted uncomfortably.

"I'm guessing you probably didn't think about them when you were stealing all that chocolate?" Andrew said.

Ben shook his head.

"That's the thing about stealing. About most crimes, actually. Most of the time, you're hurting someone else. A lot of people don't take the time to think about that."

Joe could see Ben was really listening to what the policeman was saying.

Over the next half hour Hannah's friend shared what happened to shoplifters when they got caught, and the kind of trouble he'd seen other kids get into. After the policeman had gone, Joe talked some more with his son. It became clear that Ben had been having trouble making friends at his new school and he'd fallen in with the older kids because they were the only ones who'd shown any interest in him.

"Now I know why," Ben said darkly as he sat at the kitchen table. He looked up at Joe, trepidation in his gaze. "Are you going to ground me? Take away my Nintendo?"

"No. I think it might be best if we leave it up to Mr. Balas to decide how he wants you to make this up to him."

Ben's face went chalk-white. "No. No way. I'll do anything, anything you want, but not that," Ben said, blinking rapidly.

"Ben…"

"He'll think I'm a no-good thief, Dad," Ben said, the words wrung out of him.

Joe took his son's hand. "I'll go with you, okay? We'll do it together. But you need to face up to what you did."

For a moment Ben struggled with tears. Then he took a deep breath and sniffed. "Okay. Can I go to my room now?"

"Sure, matey."

Joe was sure Ben was going to his room to shed the tears he couldn't let himself cry in front of his father.

For a moment, he was besieged by doubts. Every word, every decision was a minefield. He had no idea if he was helping steer his son in the right direction or scarring him for life.

He missed the support and reassurance of having Beth to talk things over with. The reality was, however,

Beth was gone. He'd wasted enough time willing it to be otherwise. He needed to get on with living his life.

He pushed to his feet and crossed to the front door. It was time for Ruby to come in for dinner. He ran a hand through his hair and straightened his shirt before he realized what he was doing—primping for Hannah Napier.

Stupid. And completely pointless, for so many reasons he couldn't even be bothered enumerating them.

He could hear Ruby chattering away as he entered the Napiers' garage. She was telling Hannah about the dog they'd had when she was younger and he could hear Hannah laughing.

"Time to come in for dinner, Rubes," he said.

Ruby's expression instantly became mulish. "But we're not finished yet. We've only pulled apart one wheel."

He saw they'd been working on the Thunderbird, the disassembled pieces laid out on an old sheet.

"I'm sure it can wait. We need to get you fed and washed and into bed."

Ruby opened her mouth to protest but Hannah beat her to it.

"I'm about to call it quits, anyway. We've done more than enough for one night."

She met his eyes and he saw the question in them. He nodded slightly to indicate things had gone well with her friend.

"Why don't you head inside and set the table?" he said to Ruby.

She moaned some more before finally saying goodnight to Hannah. Joe waited till she'd gone beyond hearing range before speaking.

"Andrew was great. Thanks for arranging for him to come over. Ben and I had a good talk."

Hannah smiled. "I suppose Ben's grounded for the rest of his natural life?"

"Nope. I'm taking him to apologize to Mr. Balas tomorrow. Mr. Balas can decide how he wants Ben to make it up to him."

She winced. "Ouch. That's gonna sting. But he's never going to forget it, either."

She squatted to place another piece of the bike on the sheet. Her jeans pulled tight across her thighs and he had to work hard not to stare. She had great legs. Firm and strong looking.

He looked away.

"I meant what I said about letting me know the next time you're at the pub. I'll shout you dinner," he said, mostly because he didn't know what else to say. Certainly not any of the entirely inappropriate things that were suddenly floating around his head.

She stood, shrugging dismissively, a gesture he was becoming increasingly familiar with. He remembered the fierce, protective look in her eyes in the family portrait in her mother's foyer. He bet she was the kind of person who struggled to let anyone do anything for her while bending over backward to help other people out.

He pointed a finger at her. "You're going to eat that dinner."

"Yeah? Who's going to make me? You and whose army?"

A smile was tugging at her mouth. He wondered how those plump lips would feel beneath his. They looked so damned soft...

"Don't forget, I have a secret weapon," he said.

She raised an eyebrow in silent question.

"Ruby. I bet you wouldn't say no if she asked." He was aware that he sounded more than a little smug and that he was starting to enjoy himself.

"A child. You'd be willing to stoop that low?"

"Hell, yeah. When there's a point of honor at stake."

They both grinned at his twisted logic. A wariness came into her eyes after a few seconds, however, and she dropped her gaze to the rag in her hand.

"I'd better start cleaning up." She glanced around, almost as though she'd rather look anywhere else than at him.

"I'd better make sure Ruby isn't trying to cook again. Last time it was not pretty."

He raised his hand in farewell and she nodded an acknowledgment before turning away and starting to load tools into a rolling tool chest.

He walked slowly back to the house. If he were a younger man, with less weighing him down… But he wasn't. He definitely wasn't.

After dinner, Ben went to his room to finish his homework and Joe ran Ruby a bath. As usual, he had to go roust her out after half an hour.

She was splashing happily when he entered the bathroom. She'd molded her hair into a bubbly bouffant on top of her head and was singing to herself as she made shapes in the strawberry-scented bath foam.

He smiled. At least he still had a few more years before he had to worry about shoplifting, surliness and silence where she was concerned.

"How you doing in here?"

"Good. You should try some of this strawberry bubble bath, Daddy. It smells good enough to eat."

"Hmm. I'm not sure if strawberry is really me, sweetheart."

Ruby shrugged with one shoulder, the gesture oddly familiar. Then he realized she'd stolen it from Hannah.

As though she could read his mind, Ruby suddenly piped up. "Daddy, do you think Hannah's pretty?" She watched him from beneath her eyelashes, trying to appear disinterested in his answer.

"I don't know, I haven't really thought about it," he lied.

"Do you think she would like to dress up and have fun?"

Joe had a feeling he knew where this was leading. And though he thought it was sweet—if disconcerting—that his daughter was trying her hand at matchmaking, he wasn't about to encourage it. Even if he had just been wondering what it would be like to kiss his prickly next-door neighbor.

"I'm sure Hannah has lots of people she likes to have fun with," he said. "It's time for you to get out now. You want to wash your hair and get into your pj's?"

"It's just that there's this thing happening at school. And I was thinking that maybe Hannah wouldn't mind being my partner in it. But I wasn't sure if she would want to or not," Ruby said in a rush. Her hands were twisted together and she was watching him uncertainly.

He stilled as he understood what she was referring to: the mother and daughter fashion parade. He'd waited for her to bring it up this morning, but she'd been so chirpy and bright over breakfast he'd struggled to find a way to introduce the subject into their conversation.

He'd been planning to tackle it tonight before Ben's misadventures had intervened.

He moved into the bathroom and sat on the edge of the tub.

"I saw the flyer for the mother-daughter fashion parade. Is that what you mean?" he asked.

She nodded. "Do you think Hannah would like to be my partner?"

Joe took a moment to choose his words carefully. "I'm not sure. I know she seems to enjoy working on her bikes with you. I was thinking that maybe we could ask Nana Angela to do it with you."

Ruby squashed some bubbles with her hands. "Nana Angela is going to Queensland with her friend next month. Remember?"

Damn. She was right—his mother was attending a rose-lovers convention on the Gold Coast in early October. Which explained why Ruby had cried in her room last night rather than share her misery with her nana. Ruby was smart enough to know that her grandmother would cancel her trip in a blink if she felt either of her grandchildren needed her. His mother was all too aware that Beth had been an only child and that because Beth's parents were deceased, Angela was the extent of their extended family.

For the second time that night he was filled with a fierce pride in his children. They were good kids, despite the shit life had thrown at them. Despite his own shortcomings.

"So do you think I should ask Hannah?" Ruby prompted.

Joe frowned. What were his options here? Say no because he was wary of further entangling his life with that of his compelling neighbor and disappoint his daughter? Or risk a messy situation in order to ensure Ruby didn't miss out on something she wanted very badly?

It was a no-brainer. When push came to shove, his own discomfort or wariness was nothing compared to his daughter's needs.

"I'll have a word with her tomorrow," he said. "Leave it to me."

Ruby slapped both hands down into the water.

"Really? Really, truly?"

"First thing," he promised.

Ruby surged out of the water and flung herself, bubbles and all, against his chest.

"You're the best, Daddy."

He knew he wasn't. Not even close. But he was doing what he could. Even if it meant spending more time with a woman he had no business being attracted to.

Hannah was about to head off to work the next day when she had the distinct sensation of being watched. She was astride the bike, the engine running, but she pushed up the visor on her helmet and glanced over her shoulder. Ben stood on the curb in front of his house, his face impassive as he watched her.

They locked gazes for a moment and Hannah felt an absurd stab of guilt when she saw the accusing light in his eyes. She'd only done what was best for him, but she was sure he didn't see it that way. He probably thought she was a squealer of the highest order.

She switched off her bike and tugged her helmet off. Yesterday had been a big day for him and she'd played a part in it. It seemed only right to acknowledge that.

"It's Ben, isn't it? I'm Hannah."

"I know who you are."

"Because of what happened yesterday."

"You ratted me out."

"I did. I was worried about you. You didn't look like you were having a great time with those older kids."

"I can look after myself."

"Sure. The thing is, I don't know you, so I had no idea what you were up for. All I saw was those big kids standing over you, and I figured I'd better talk to your dad about it."

She could see the play of emotions across Ben's face. Surprise, thoughtfulness, wariness. She let the silence stretch for a moment.

"I need to get to work, but I'll see you around, Ben," she said.

He frowned, then he nodded. She slid her helmet on and started the bike. She checked the mirror before riding off and saw him starting up the street, hands deep in his jeans pockets, schoolbag on his back. He looked as though he had the weight of the world on his shoulders.

Not your problem.

She knew it was true, but she couldn't help feeling for Ruby and Ben. Losing their mom so young must have been scary and hard.

She shook the thought off. Her first impulse was right—it wasn't her problem.

They had a busy day scheduled and she threw herself into work the moment she arrived at the garage. She'd just finished flushing the fuel injector on a Honda Civic when something made her look up and she saw Joe walking toward her, his long stride eating up the ground. She quelled the impulse to slip into her office and let Ian deal with his enquiry, whatever it was. She'd never backed down from a challenge, even one as annoying and confusing as Joe.

"Hey," he said as he stopped in front of her. "You got a minute?"

She glanced at the clock. "If you don't mind talking while I work. We're under the hammer today."

"Okay."

She crossed to the Honda. Joe followed but didn't say anything immediately. For some reason she was all fingers and thumbs as she bolted the injector rail back onto the engine. The silence stretched and finally she glanced up at him.

"Is this a quiz? Am I supposed to guess what you want?" she asked lightly.

He met her gaze and she realized he was nervous.

Huh.

"It's about Ruby. Her school is holding a mother-daughter fashion parade."

She winced. "Just what she needs."

"Yeah. I was hoping my mother could do it with her, but she's going to be away."

"Right." She had no idea where he was going with this and she propped an elbow on the rocker cover, waiting for him to get to the point.

His gaze flicked up to hold hers, then quickly flicked away again.

"Ruby and I were talking last night and she suggested that maybe you wouldn't mind doing it," he said, his tone absolutely neutral.

Hannah straightened so quickly she knocked her shoulder on the hood of the car. She rubbed it absently, staring at him.

"You want me to go in a fashion parade?" she asked incredulously.

"Not me. Ruby. And I absolutely understand if you're not up for it. It's a hassle, and you've already been very kind to Ruby—"

"My God, you're really serious, aren't you?" She couldn't quite believe it.

"Well, yeah. Ruby's not something I usually joke about."

She laughed and slid the spanner she was holding into the pocket of her coverall. "Sorry. I'm not laughing at you. It's just the idea of me in a fashion parade... It's pretty funny." She gestured toward her attire. "I couldn't tell you the last time I wore anything except jeans."

"Does that mean you're not interested?"

"It means I'm probably not a great choice. Surely there must be someone else? A family friend?"

His face was utterly impassive as he nodded briefly.

"Sure. I'm sure we'll think of someone." He glanced at his watch. "Thanks for your time, anyway. I appreciate it."

He headed to his car.

She watched him, feeling as though she'd let him down. Worse, she felt as though she'd let Ruby down. But the idea of her in a fashion parade... It was absurd, it really was. Surely Joe could see that? She barely knew how to put on mascara and lipstick, and she'd practiced for weeks before the wedding so she'd be able to walk down the aisle in her stiletto heels. She was so not what Ruby needed.

And yet Ruby had thought of her and sent her father to ask her. And Joe had swallowed his pride and God knows what else to give his daughter what she wanted.

"Damn it."

She took off after Joe, catching him just as he was sliding into the front seat of his SUV.

"Wait a minute."

He looked at her, his hand on the door, waiting.

She shook her head, still unable to quite get her head around it. "It's not that I don't want to do it. It's just… Are you sure? I mean, does Ruby have any idea how much of a handicap I'll be?"

"Ruby thinks you're the bee's knees."

"Which shows how much she knows," Hannah said, but she could feel heat rising into her face.

She was so tragic. It wasn't as if he'd said she was beautiful or anything—he'd compared her to insect appendages, for Pete's sake. What was there to feel self-conscious about in that?

"When is it?" she asked to cover her embarrassment.

"A week from Friday."

She took a deep breath. "Okay. If Ruby wants me, I'm all hers. God help her."

The tight look left his face but his eyes were still wary. "If it's too big a deal, it's fine. Like I said, I'm sure there's someone else."

She gave him a look. "Didn't anyone ever tell you to quit while you're ahead, Lawson? You just got me to agree to wearing high heels and makeup. My advice is to drive away like a bat out of hell before I come to my senses."

She was smiling, suddenly feeling unaccountably goofy. Slowly his mouth curved into a smile. Just like last time, it almost knocked her back on her heels.

"Okay. Thank you. I'll tell Ruby after school. She'll be dancing on the ceiling, no doubt."

"That's because she hasn't seen me in a dress yet," Hannah said darkly.

"I was going to take her shopping on the weekend. I guess maybe we should all go together, make sure your outfits coordinate. That's the way it probably works, right?"

She held up both hands helplessly.

"You're asking a mechanic. But you're probably right. What time do you want me to meet you at the mall?"

"Seems stupid to take two cars. Why don't we plan to leave at around ten or so and meet out the front of your place? Does that suit?"

"Sure. Wait till Mom hears about this. She'll be in heaven."

They finessed the details for their outing then Joe drove away. Hannah remained where she was for a good minute or two.

A cocktail of thoughts and emotions swirled inside her. Warmth that Ruby wanted her to be her partner in fashion crime. Surprise at herself for saying yes to such a ridiculous proposal. And something else. A sort of strange, foreign excitement that she wasn't quite sure she even wanted to name.

Brow furrowed, she strode to the workshop. Hopefully Ruby wouldn't have cause to regret her decision.

Chapter 6

Ruby was so excited about the shopping trip that Joe had to send her back to bed three times on Friday night. She was almost jumping out of her skin Saturday morning as he made pancakes for her and Ben.

"Can I wear a tiara in the parade, like my Barbie doll?" Ruby asked.

"Sure. If that's what you want and we can find one. Remember, though, that you and Hannah need to complement each other in some way."

They'd gone over the guidelines for the parade when they filled out their entrance form the previous night, but Ruby was too caught up in the prospect of shopping to remember the rules.

"There's no way Hannah's going to wear a tiara," Ben said.

Ruby shot him a dirty look. "How would you know? She's my friend, not yours. You hardly know her."

Ben squeezed a small bathtub's worth of maple syrup onto his pancakes. "I don't need to know her. She rides a motorbike. There's no way you're going to get her to wear some stupid tiara."

Even though Joe privately agreed with his son, he had the good sense not to say so out loud.

"I think we should wait until we see what we can find at the mall before we start worrying about stuff like that," he said diplomatically.

Ben must have caught something in his tone because he looked at Joe suspiciously. Joe couldn't resist winking, and Ben hid a smirk behind his fork as he lowered his head. The small moment of connection almost made Joe grateful for the shoplifting incident. Ever since their trip to Mr. Balas's corner store earlier in the week, Ben had been smiling more and actually volunteering conversation rather than having to have it dragged out of him monosyllable by monosyllable.

Not that the apology had been a walk in the park. Far from it. Ben had been so nervous beforehand he'd been trembling. Joe had kept his hand reassuringly on the back of his boy's neck throughout the whole encounter, squeezing occasionally when he could feel Ben's wiry body tensing with anxiety. Mr. Balas had been stern but fair as Ben explained his part in what had taken place, offering his apology in a shaky but clear voice. Joe had offered to repay Mr. Balas whatever he was owed for the stolen items, in addition to whatever punishment he deemed fit for Ben. The shop owner had surprised them both by refusing the money. Instead, he'd offered Ben the chance to work off his debt by helping out in the store after school.

Ben's relief had been palpable when the ordeal was

over. Even though Ben had avoided hugs for the past few years, he didn't resist as Joe pulled him into his arms once they exited the shop.

"You did good," Joe had said. Ben had let his head rest on Joe's shoulder for a few seconds, his arms tightening around him. Joe had had to exercise real self-control to avoid squeezing his son too fiercely.

This morning, Joe slid another stack of pancakes onto a plate and sat next to Ruby.

"What time do you finish at the shop this afternoon?" he asked as Ben helped himself to a second helping.

"One o'clock, I think. Mr. Balas said he only needs me to help sort out the milk delivery and crush the boxes, then I can go."

This would be Ben's third shift. So far, so good.

"We'll be back by then to pick you up. If not, I'll call you."

"Three hours isn't long for shopping, Daddy," Ruby said reprovingly.

"It's going to have to be. We can't chew up all of Hannah's weekend. She might have other things she needs to do."

For all he knew she might have a hot date tonight that she needed to prepare for.

Joe frowned as he sliced into his pancake. What Hannah did in her spare time was nothing to do with him. He didn't even know where the aberrant thought had come from.

"I'm going to go wait out front for Hannah," Ruby said, her chair legs scraping across the floor as she pushed her chair back.

It was still only a quarter to ten, but he figured there was no harm in letting her wait outside. Kicking her heels for a few minutes might even calm her down a little.

He should have known better. He'd just finished rinsing the fry pan when Ruby banged her way back into the house.

"Daddy, we're ready to go now. Hurry up, slowpoke."

He turned to find Ruby had dragged Hannah into the house behind her. His gaze ran over Hannah's damp hair, pulled back into a ponytail.

"Ruby, I hope you didn't hassle Hannah to come early," he said.

Ruby closed her eyes for a long blink before shaking her head, a sure sign she was prevaricating. "No. Hannah was already up and dressed, weren't you, Hannah?"

Hannah smiled and pinched one of Ruby's earlobes. "Barely, grease monkey. But it's okay, I'm ready to go now."

Her gaze flicked around the kitchen, and he was immediately aware that the room needed to be painted and that he'd been meaning to do something about the pile of mail stacked on the end of the counter.

"I guess we should go, then," he said.

There was a moment of awkwardness as they sorted out the seating arrangements in the car. Ruby automatically moved to one of the rear doors when they exited the house but Hannah quickly intervened.

"No, sweetie, you should sit up front with your dad," she said.

"I don't mind," Ruby said. She slipped into the back of the car and buckled her seat belt.

Joe met Hannah's eyes over the roof of the car for a brief second before she opened the front passenger door. He was acutely aware of her sitting beside him as he started the SUV and backed into the street. He could see her long, jeans-clad legs out of the corner of his eyes, her hands resting on her thighs.

For Pete's sake, you're not fifteen.

He only felt that way. Which boded well for the day.

It wasn't until they had entered the first clothing store that he realized how tense Hannah was. She was frowning, her shoulders very square, her generous mouth pressed into a thin, straight line as Ruby circled the racks, pulling out frilly dress after frilly dress. Hannah's eyebrows rose when she saw how short the skirt was on one of the dresses and she visibly flinched when Ruby selected a shiny Lycra thing in vivid pink.

"What do you think?" Ruby asked.

"Um. Well. I guess. Is this the sort of thing you were thinking of?" Hannah asked.

Ruby nodded. "My Barbie doll has one just like this."

"Your doll?"

"Yep," Ruby said. She started walking toward the change rooms. "We have to hurry because we've only got three hours."

Hannah closed her eyes for a few seconds and he heard her say something under her breath. Then she followed Ruby to the change rooms.

"I'll wait out front," he said.

"No, Daddy, you have to stay with us. We need a boy's opinion," Ruby said bossily.

"I don't know how much help I'll be, Rubes. This isn't really my area of expertise."

Hannah gave him a dark look. "It's not mine, either, but you don't see me trying to wriggle off the hook."

He gave in, partly because Ruby was watching him with big, expectant eyes and he knew that if Beth was here she'd be all over this shopping trip, and partly because he was curious to see what Hannah looked like in a miniskirt.

Spectacular. That was how she looked. Her legs were long with well-defined muscles. Her waist was small. Her breasts... Well, he'd already done his fair share of staring at them. She filled out the minidress like a supermodel, but even Ruby couldn't help but notice how acutely uncomfortable Hannah was in it. She tugged at the neckline, she plucked at the hem, she pulled the fabric away from her middle. She looked about as happy as a cat being forced into a bath.

"You need to stop fiddling with the hem," Ruby said. "It's hard to see how the dress looks when you keep doing that."

"I don't think this one is a goer," Hannah said. "This hot pink color will be really hard to match when we try to find your dress, and I think blue would probably suit you better."

She slipped back into the change room and whisked the curtain closed.

Ruby sighed. "All right then. But remember, we've only got three hours."

Hannah refused to even open the curtain when she'd changed into the next dress. Ruby finally negotiated her way into the change room, and Joe couldn't help overhearing their conversation.

"The top on this dress looked much bigger on the hanger, didn't it?"

"Yes."

"It looks really small now. Really small."

Joe cleared his throat, his imagination going haywire.

"Here." Ruby stuck her head outside the curtain and

thrust two dresses into his hands. "None of these are any good."

One of the dresses—the indecent one, he guessed—was still warm from Hannah's body. His fingers slipped through the fabric as he stepped onto the shop floor.

"Here, let me help you with those," a sales assistant said.

Joe returned to the change rooms in time to see the curtain whisking closed on Hannah as she vetoed the third dress. He caught a glimpse of gauzy floral fabric, spaghetti straps and a deeply ruffled hem.

"No good?" he asked.

"No!" Hannah said adamantly from beyond the curtain.

"I thought you looked beautiful," Ruby said wistfully.

"It's too tight. I think we need to find a winter dress. Something with sleeves."

"What do you think, Daddy?"

Ruby pulled the curtain open before Hannah could object. Hannah lifted her hands as though she wanted to cover herself, then let them drop to her sides helplessly.

"It's terrible, isn't it?" she said.

The dress had a low, rounded neck that sat over her breasts in soft folds. He was sure there was a technical name for it—all he knew was that the draping fabric did a great job outlining the high, round shape of her breasts. The waistline was fitted and the skirt hugged the lines of her thighs until it reached just below her knees, where it merged into a froth of ruffles which ended just above her ankles.

He shoved his hands into his pockets. "I think this should definitely go on your short list."

Hannah's eyes widened. "No way. It's terrible. I look like a kid playing dress-up in her mom's closet."

He frowned, studying her face. She avoided his eyes, her cheeks flushed.

"Daddy likes it, and I get a vote, too, so it's on the short list," Ruby said triumphantly. She herded Hannah back into the changing cubicle. "Now get changed and we'll go to Myer's. They have lots of nice things."

Ruby started gathering dresses at the speed of light once they hit the big department store, once again going for what he could only describe as couture à la princess. Hannah accepted the hangers with a resigned stoicism that would have been funny if it didn't come from genuine discomfort. When Hannah disappeared into the change room with Ruby's selections, he caught his daughter's elbow before she could follow Hannah inside.

"Rubes, wait a minute. I think maybe we need to re-think the fashion direction a little."

Ruby's face wrinkled with confusion. "What?"

"I don't think Hannah's very comfortable in the dresses you're choosing for her."

"But she looks so good in them. She looks like a supermodel."

"Yeah, but you've got to remember she's used to wearing jeans and T-shirts most of the time. I think maybe all the pink and frills are a bit too much for her."

Ruby stared at him as though he'd grown another head. "But they're pretty."

"I know. What I was thinking was, maybe we could find an outfit that was somewhere in between what you like and what Hannah likes. That way you'd both be comfortable."

"But Hannah said I could choose whatever I wanted. She said I was in charge of the fashion decisions." Ruby was starting to pout.

He touched her cheek. "You are. But Hannah isn't going to have much fun if you choose something for her that she's not very comfortable in, is she?"

Ruby's forehead puckered into a deep frown as she thought it through. "No more pink?" she asked after a long moment.

"Maybe a little less pink."

"No more frills?"

He held his thumb and forefinger an inch apart. "Just a few, not too many."

Ruby finally nodded. "Okay. If you think it will make Hannah more comfortable."

"I do."

A martial light in her eye, Ruby disappeared into the change rooms. A few seconds later, she reappeared with a pile of dresses in her arms. Hannah trailed after her, looking both confused and relieved.

"You don't want me to try them on anymore?"

"I've decided that maybe you should pick something. So I know what you like," Ruby said.

"Ruby, honestly, whatever you want is fine with me," Hannah said.

Ruby darted Joe a hopeful look, but he shook his head subtly. Ruby sighed. "No, it's better this way. Let's look around together."

Ruby looked to him again and he gave her a thumbs-up. She smiled. Then she slid her hand into Hannah's and led her into the ladies' department.

"Maybe we should look at the trousers," Ruby said.

Joe hung back for a moment, smiling at his daughter's handling of the situation. Just before they disappeared amongst the clothing racks, Hannah glanced over her shoulder. For a second their gazes met and held. Then the moment was gone and he'd lost sight of her behind a display of coats.

Hands shoved into the back pockets of his jeans, he started after them.

"What about these? You'd look great in these," Ruby said.

Hannah surveyed the white jeans the girl was holding up. Sequins and embroidery glittered under the shop lights. They were the kind of jeans Mariah Carey might wear, dripping with bling and sex appeal.

Dear God. Was this morning never going to end? She felt as though she'd been ushered into her own personal version of hell.

"Wow. They're… great," Hannah said.

She'd hesitated just a moment too long. Ruby's bottom lip pouted. "You don't like them." It wasn't a question.

"But you do, sweetie, and I'm happy to wear them if you love them," Hannah said. Especially if it meant she got out of wearing one of the microdresses Ruby had been keen on initially and it meant this shopping expedition was over.

"No, *you* have to be comfortable," Ruby insisted stubbornly. "Daddy said you have to be happy, too."

Hannah frowned. "When did he say that?"

"Before, while you were in the change room. He said you didn't like pink and that you wouldn't have fun if you had to wear something you didn't like."

Hannah was nonplussed. How on earth had Joe

picked up on her reluctance? She'd thought she'd been turning in an Academy Award-winning performance yet he'd been perceptive enough to register her discomfort. Further, he'd taken steps to remedy the situation.

"Come on, let's take a look around some more," Ruby said, not giving Hannah a moment to dwell on the realization.

They found the navy linen pants in the corner. Wide-legged, they featured a cute row of buttons across the front, giving them a stylized nautical appeal. Hannah pulled them from the rack and considered them briefly before putting them back. They were way too plain for Ruby's flamboyant taste.

Her pint-size shopping companion stepped forward and took the pants off the rack again.

"Let's try these on," she said.

Even Hannah was surprised by how good she looked and felt in the beautifully tailored pants. They made her butt look high and firm and were so long she'd have to have them taken up a little, a rarity indeed for a five-foot-eleven-inch woman. She stepped out of the changing room feeling good, a sensation that only intensified when she saw the look on Joe's face. His gaze went straight to her legs, lingered around her hips and thighs, then finally made it to her face.

"Okay?" she asked, smoothing a hand down her hip.

"Ah, yeah. You could say that."

He could have just been being polite, but she didn't think so. There was something in his eyes as he looked at her, something dark and intense…

The day was a downhill run once the pants had been given the thumbs-up by all parties. The moment they stepped into the children's department Ruby spotted a cute sailor dress in navy and white, complete with matching hat. Given the nautical feel of Hannah's trousers, it was love at first sight. Another hour was spent looking for a shirt to complete Hannah's outfit, then matching shoes for both her and Ruby. By the time Hannah was ready to pay for her share of the booty, she felt as though she'd run a marathon.

"This shopping business is exhausting," she said in an aside to Joe as they waited to be served.

"Tell me about it. And she's not even a teenager yet."

His tone was wry but the expression on his face was indulgent. Hannah felt an odd squeeze in her chest as she looked at him.

He was a nice man. They'd gotten off to a bad start, but now that she knew him a little better she understood that while he might be taciturn sometimes and stubborn as all hell, Joe Lawson had a big heart and a fierce determination to do right by his kids. Coupled with his undeniable physical attractions, he was a pretty compelling package.

She ducked her head and fished in her wallet for her credit card, thrown by her own thoughts. She wasn't interested in packages, compelling or otherwise. She was heartbroken, angry, bitter.

Right?

She slid her credit card from its slot and held it in readiness as the cashier began to key in her sale.

"Uh-uh. No way. I'm getting this," Joe said.

"What? No, you're not buying me clothes."

"Hannah, come on. You've already given up your Saturday for Ruby, and I saw the look on your face when you tried on those high heels. You're never going to wear them once the fashion parade is over."

"I might. I might go out to dinner one night or something. I'm not a complete scruff, you know."

"Nobody called you a scruff."

"Yeah, but you were thinking it."

He waited a beat before responding. "You have no idea what I'm thinking."

There was a low, slightly rough note to his voice and she jerked her head up and caught the intent look in his eyes again. Her heart did an odd little two-step. She suddenly felt overheated, as though she'd been working over a hot engine for too long.

While she was staring at him like a landed fish he reached out and plucked the credit card from her fingers.

"Hey!"

"You can have it back afterward."

She protested some more, but he was immovable, and afterward he insisted on buying her and Ruby an ice cream each, as well. Only then did he hand her credit card back to her.

"You were born about five centuries too late, you know that?" she grumbled as she put the card back in her wallet. "You need some serfs and peasants and whatnot to boss around."

"Shut up and eat your ice cream," he said mildly.

Ruby sucked in a shocked breath at his deliberate rudeness then pressed her fingers over her mouth to smother a giggle. Hannah couldn't stop the smile curving her mouth, either. She knew it would only encourage him in the mistaken belief that he knew best, but she couldn't seem to help it. He grinned back at her. It was the most relaxed she'd ever seen him, the deep lines by his mouth not so obvious, his big body loose.

"I'll just leave the money in your mailbox," she said.

"Then I'll give it back to you."

"I don't think you have any idea how determined I can be when I put my mind to it."

"I have a fair idea. And I guarantee you I'm more stubborn."

"There's no need to sound so proud of it."

"Oh, I'm not. I know it's a curse. Sometimes it stops me from being gracious when I really should be."

Hannah paused mid-bite, her gaze locking with his. His blue eyes were dancing with mischief and challenge.

"If you think being called ungracious will shame me into giving in, you've got another think coming. I've been ungracious all my life," she said.

"I bet."

She choked out a laugh, couldn't help herself. She pointed her ice cream at him.

"You want to wear this?"

He simply quirked an eyebrow as if to say "I dare you." Hannah stared at him, unable to stop smiling, sorely tempted to follow through with her threat.

"Dad? Don't we have to pick up Ben at one o'clock?"

Hannah blinked, suddenly aware that they were in the middle of the food court, people brushing past them, Ruby watching them quizzically.

"That's right. We do, don't we? Thanks for the reminder, sweetheart."

Joe moved away from Hannah then and the loss of his attention and charm was like the sun disappearing behind a cloud. Hannah blinked, then gave herself a firm shake.

What is wrong with you?

But she had a fair idea, although she didn't want to

acknowledge it. Her life was complicated and messy enough without adding any new problems to the mix.

And Joe Lawson was definitely a problem—a big, broad, tall one.

"Hannah, you need to sit still or I'll never get this done."

Joe hid a smile at the frustrated note in Robyn's voice. She'd volunteered to help both Hannah and Ruby with their hair for the fashion parade, but he figured she'd planned on working on a serene, calm model and not the fidgety, nervous recalcitrant in the chair.

"You've been at it for hours. Surely it's done now? You didn't spend this long on Ruby's hair," Hannah said.

"That's because I didn't move around so much," Ruby said.

Hannah's mom had curled Ruby's hair so that it sat in fat spirals on her shoulders. Once she donned her sailor's hat she was going to look exactly like Shirley Temple, minus the dimples.

Joe watched her, enjoying the light in her eyes and her air of suppressed excitement. By hook or by crook, he'd managed to ensure she took part in the parade. It felt like a minor victory.

In the week since their shopping expedition, Ruby had disappeared before dinner most nights. Each time he'd had to collect her from the Napiers' garage where the Thunderbird was now spread in all its many parts on the sheet. He found it not a little baffling that his daughter could be so interested in fashion and dolls yet revel so much in getting dirty alongside Hannah. Maybe, as his mother said, Ruby was simply exploring different aspects of herself, trying on the mantle of tomboy for a while without completely forgoing her love of sparkles and frills. Lately she'd taken to wearing jeans more, and he'd dodged more than one not-so-subtle suggestion that her wardrobe would never be truly complete without her own leather jacket. Biker style, naturally.

Joe glanced at Hannah's profile as she submitted to a final blast of hair spray. He wondered what she thought of her little shadow, whether she'd noticed Ruby's hero worship or not. His gut told him no. She was completely unaware of the power and appeal of her own personality. No doubt she thought that Ruby was simply a little mechanic in the making.

"All right. That's your hair done," Robyn announced.

"Thank God."

Hannah stood, shaking her head as though she could shake off the last few minutes.

"Don't do that! The pins will come out!"

Hannah's mother sounded so exasperated Joe grinned.

"Sorry. Can we go now?" Hannah asked.

"I guess I could put on the rest of your makeup at the school," her mother said, starting to pack things away into a hefty-looking makeup bag.

"I was kind of thinking I could wear some mascara and lipstick," Hannah said. "Let the clothes do all the talking, you know."

"Well, you were thinking wrong, weren't you?" Robyn said crisply.

Hannah rolled her eyes and Ruby giggled. Joe figured it was time to step in.

"How about we start loading up the car?" he suggested.

An hour later, he stood in the audience beside Robyn,

waiting for Ruby to have her moment in the sun. His slim-line digital camera was tucked into his front pocket, and he was under strict instructions from Ruby to take lots of photos. Ben shuffled restlessly at Joe's side as he checked the camera battery one last time.

"How long is this going to take? Do we have to stay for the whole thing?"

Joe took pity on him and gave him some money to buy a drink and something to eat from the refreshments table at the rear of the school gym. When he turned back to the runway, he noticed Robyn was twisting and turning the bracelet on her wrist, her gaze darting back and forth between the clock on the wall and the curtained-off area behind the runway.

"They're running late, aren't they?" Robyn said. She sounded worried.

"I'm no expert, but I'm guessing that with that many women and only a limited number of mirrors there's a pileup."

Robyn didn't so much as crack a smile at his small joke.

"I hope everything goes okay. Hannah needs something to boost her confidence," she said. "She took such a blow when the wedding was called off...."

Joe couldn't hide his surprise. "Hannah was engaged?"

She was so prickly and independent, he couldn't imagine her letting anyone close enough to propose.

Robyn bit her lip, obviously debating whether she should say more or not.

"It's okay. I don't want to pry," he said quickly. Even though he did. Big-time.

"Oh, it's not like it's a state secret or anything. Everyone knows. I guess that's part of the problem. Lucas swept her off her feet, romanced her till she was so dizzy she didn't know which way was up. She was so happy…. And then Kelly came home from her job in the U.K. and everything went bad from there."

Joe wanted to ask who Kelly was, but he was afraid to interrupt Robyn's train of thought. Hannah's mother shook her head as she remembered something.

"I should have seen it coming. I mean, Lucas and Kelly had so much more in common. They both worked in the IT industry, they shared so many opinions and dreams and ambitions. If only they had handled things better, told Hannah how they felt sooner rather than leaving it so late…."

Robyn was tearing up. He reached into his back pocket for the handkerchief he always carried.

"Here."

"Thanks." Robyn dabbed at her cheeks. "You'd think after six months I'd be a little more resigned to it all, but it's so damned hard watching my two girls torn apart when they used to be such great friends. Kelly didn't mean to hurt Hannah, I know that, but she did. And Hannah feels so hurt and angry and betrayed. Honestly, I don't see how this thing will ever resolve itself."

Joe stilled. Was he getting this straight? Had Hannah's *sister* stolen her fiancé? Could that possibly be right?

It was such a huge betrayal that he couldn't get his head around it. No wonder she preferred working alone in the garage at night to going out and partying or dating. Suddenly every encounter he'd ever had with her was cast in a different light. Her defensiveness, her silent stoicism, her uncertainty.

Before he and Robyn could talk further, music blasted out of the speakers and the lights dimmed. The crowd turned toward the T-shaped runway as one of Ruby's teachers, a tall, slim woman in her fifties, took up her post behind the podium to the far left of the runway.

"Welcome, ladies and gentleman. Elsternwick Primary wants to thank you all for your time and for your generous donations tonight. We've got lots of excited models backstage, so I'm going to dive straight into things. We hope you enjoy our parade as much as we enjoyed putting this night together for you."

She turned toward the stage, then consulted a sheet of paper in her hands.

"Our first models are Melinda and Liana. Let's give them a big welcome."

The crowd dutifully clapped as the first mother and daughter stepped onto the runway. Joe was too busy thinking about what he'd just learned to pay them much attention as they walked to the top of the runway to pose and turn and pose some more while the MC described their outfits.

He could only imagine how humiliated Hannah must have felt to be rejected by her lover in favor of her younger sister. And from what Robyn had intimated, the rejection had come late in the day. He stared blindly at the stage as he wondered how late. Had Hannah bought her dress? Chosen the menu for the reception? Booked the honeymoon?

What kind of an asshole would do that to a woman

he'd been prepared to marry? What man could claim to have ever loved her, only to hurt her so badly? As for Hannah's sister…

"Our next models are Hannah and Ruby. Don't they look great?"

Joe lifted the camera, yet he could do nothing but stare. Something warm and primitive expanded in his gut as he stared at the woman holding his little girl's hand. She looked amazing. With her hair piled on top of her head and her eyes done in smoky makeup, Hannah's beauty was undeniable. The navy trousers clung to her long legs as she and Ruby began walking, the fine fabric of her ruffled, sleeveless white blouse betraying the sway of her breasts. But it wasn't simply her many physical attributes that held his gaze, it was the way she lifted her chin as she walked, the look in her eye as she took on the challenge of the fashion parade. She'd rather be anywhere else, he knew, was probably nervous and self-conscious as hell, but she was doing Ruby proud because she'd said she would.

What man could ever walk away from you?

The thought should have been disturbing since it had no place in his world, but it wasn't.

"Hannah wears a pair of Trent Nathan tailored trousers teamed with an Alannah Hill blouse and Marc Jacobs shoes," the MC said. "Ruby wears a sailor dress by Osh Kosh B'Gosh and shoes by Petit Shoes."

Realizing he had yet to take a single shot, Joe lifted the camera and hit the shutter button.

Hannah and Ruby got to the end of the runway and performed the little crossover maneuver he'd seen them practicing the past week. Ruby stuck her left hip out and propped her left hand on it, then Hannah followed suit. Then, unexpectedly, they saluted one another with their right hands, in keeping with their nautical theme. Joe was surprised into laughter, as was the rest of the audience. Hannah's smile was genuine as her gaze swept the audience. For just a fraction of a second their eyes caught and held as he lowered the camera. Then she and Ruby strutted their way back up the runway, Ruby clearly having the time of her life. One last wave, and they disappeared behind the curtains.

Joe could hear Robyn sniffing beside him as he flicked the camera off and tucked it back into its case. She gave him a rueful smile when he glanced across to check if she was okay.

"At least I'm getting good mileage out of your handkerchief," she said.

"I think they both had a good time."

"Oh, I know. That's why I'm crying," Robyn said. She laughed at her own logic.

The next mother and daughter team stepped onto the stage. Joe consulted his program. There were twenty entries in all, and they weren't even a quarter of the way through. He checked his watch, then made a decision. He leaned toward Robyn.

"I'm going to go backstage and check on Ruby. If Ben comes back, would you mind…?"

"Sure. I'll keep an eye on him."

He flashed her a grateful smile and started angling his way through the audience toward the back of the hall. Hannah and Ruby had attended a rehearsal on Wednesday evening and he knew that models who had walked the runway waited in a separate area to those yet to go on. One of the organizers pointed him in the right direction. Ruby leaped out of her seat when she saw him and practically bounced into his arms.

"Did you see, did you see?"

"I did. You were wonderful," he said.

Hannah remained seated, her expression unreadable as she watched them.

"Did you like our salute? That was Hannah's idea and I wasn't sure but everyone seemed to like it." Ruby's cheeks were pink, her sailor's hat tilted on a rakish angle.

"Everyone loved it," he said. "You were both beautiful. The stars of the show."

One of the organizers stepped into the holding area.

"Ruby, we need you to come line up with the other students now," she said.

"Oh, okay." She turned to Joe. "Just us kids are going to do our thing again at the end of the parade so I have to go now."

"Off you go, then," he said with a smile. "I'll keep an eye out for you up front."

"And take lots of pictures."

"Lots of pictures," he promised.

She ran off, curls bouncing. When he turned to talk to Hannah, her chair was empty. He frowned. Then he caught sight of her disappearing through a side door.

He followed her, finding himself in a dimly lit corridor. She had a head start on him, her high heels echoing loudly on the concrete floor as she walked briskly toward the exit sign at the end of the corridor.

"Hey. Wait up," he said, lengthening his stride to catch her.

She stopped, but even in the bad light he could tell she didn't want to.

"Where are you going?" he asked when he reached her side.

She gestured toward the exit sign. "Outside. It's too hot in there."

She fanned her shirt and a waft of something sweet and spicy hit him. With her high heels they were eye to eye and his gaze was drawn to her mouth. She was wearing gloss and her bottom lip looked very full and soft.

"Did you want something?" she asked, and he realized he'd been staring.

"I just wanted to say thanks. You did a great job out there. And Ruby loved every minute of it."

She shrugged. "Honestly, it was no big deal. And it was fun."

He couldn't stop himself from looking at her mouth again. "I also wanted to tell you how great you look."

She made a rude noise. "It's okay, you don't have to suck up to me."

"I wasn't," he said. "You look beautiful."

She frowned and shifted uncomfortably. "Well, don't be fooled. Underneath I'm still the same old grease-stained Hannah Napier."

"Maybe that's what's so good about it."

She stared at him. She looked deeply uncertain. Almost afraid. "I need some fresh air," she said in a subdued voice.

She started to leave. He didn't want her to go. He moved his body to block her path. Didn't think about it, or where it might lead. Just did it.

He felt the warm brush of her body against his side.

"Hannah," he said, but words failed him as he caught another waft of her perfume. "Hell," he said. And then he was leaning toward her.

She gasped with surprise as his mouth found hers. Her lips were incredibly soft against his. His tongue dipped briefly inside her mouth and he tasted her for the first time. Sweet and fresh. He went back for a second taste and after a small hesitation her tongue slid along his, tentative, searching.

Hot desire exploded in his belly and thighs and chest. He crowded her against the wall, his body pressing against hers, hip to hip, chest to chest, as his arms wrapped around her. He angled her head back, deepening the kiss. Her hands grabbed his shoulders as her tongue met his, stroking and challenging and tasting him as avidly as he tasted her. Her hips pressed forward and he could feel her breath coming in fast pants. He slid a hand down her back to her backside, his fingers gliding over the taut, round curve of her ass cheek.

She felt good. So firm and strong. He curled his fingers into her backside and used the grip to pull her more closely against his hips. She made an encouraging sound in the back of her throat. He left the sweet heat of her mouth to taste the skin of her cheekbone and explore the intimate whorls of her ear. She shuddered as his tongue dipped inside her ear, then she grabbed his hand from where it was clamped on her shoulder and dragged it down to her breast. She arched her back, filling his palm, her breast warm and heavy, her nipple already stiff with desire. He ran his thumb over her nipple once, twice, then rolled it between his thumb and forefinger. She shuddered and her hands slid onto his butt, guiding his hips closer as they kissed and caressed and rubbed against each other in the dark.

He was so hard it hurt. He wanted to get her naked and he wanted to be inside her. His frantic, horny mind started making plans. They could go out to the car. Or find a dark, private corner somewhere. Anything, anywhere, as long as he could satisfy the need building in his body.

She seemed to have the same thought. One of her hands slid from his ass to start fumbling with his belt. He found the buttons on her blouse and slid one free, then another, then another. He slid his hand into the gap and found warm, rounded flesh cupped in lace and satin. He pushed her bra aside and groaned as he felt the slide of her silky skin against his hand. She finished with his belt and popped the button on his jeans, reaching for the tab on his zipper. He got harder still as he imagined her hand on him, sliding up and down his—

Music and light blasted into the corridor as the door to the hall opened. Two women approached, talking and laughing. Joe jerked his hand from inside Hannah's shirt. Her hand slid from his waistband. They moved apart and she angled her body toward the wall as she fumbled with her shirt buttons.

Joe pasted on a polite smile and nodded as the women passed, aware he and Hannah probably looked as guilty as hell. God knows what the women were thinking, but he didn't really care. He was too busy trying to understand what had happened.

One minute they'd been talking, the next he'd been ready to throw Hannah over his shoulder and go find a handy cave.

It seemed to take a long time for the two women to

reach the exit. He waited until he and Hannah were alone again before speaking.

"I'm sorry. I didn't mean for that to happen."

"It's no big deal."

They were both lying. She couldn't look him in the eye, and he'd wanted to kiss her, touch her from the moment he first saw her, even if it had taken him until this moment to admit it to himself.

He didn't know what to do, what to say. He simply hadn't been looking for anything like this. He'd loved Beth and he'd believed his capacity for this kind of need had died with her. Apparently it hadn't.

"I'm sorry," he said again because he didn't know what else to say.

"You already said that. I get it," Hannah said. "Let's just forget it ever happened."

Before he could respond, she walked away, heading for the exit.

Forget it ever happened.

It was a great idea, in theory. In practice, he knew it was going to be a long time before he was able to forget the feel of Hannah's breast in his hand and the sound of her breath in his ear and the feel of her long, strong body pressed against his.

The door opened and she was silhouetted against the night sky for a handful of seconds. The door swung shut, throwing him back into darkness. After a long moment, he turned and walked the other way.

Chapter 7

Hannah was still reeling from Joe's kiss when she woke the next morning. She lay in bed and stared at the patterns the morning sun made on her ceiling and relived the feel of his big shoulders beneath her hands and the slide of his tongue inside her mouth.

God, she'd wanted him. Right there, right then. Even with Lucas she'd never gotten so hot and heavy so quickly. With him sex had always been more fun and playful than hot and fiery. Lucas had never rubbed her the wrong way as Joe did, either. But maybe that was part of it. Maybe the rub was part of the tension, part of the heat.

She shook her head, trying to shake the memory loose. It had been a mistake, a big one. They'd both agreed that was the case. So there was no point closing her eyes and remembering how hard he'd felt through his clothes, how much she'd wanted to press her lips to his skin and slide her hands over his body.

She shifted in the bed, feeling hot and sticky all over again.

All those years out on the oil rigs had given him a fantastic body. There had been no softness to him, no hint of weakness in his broad shoulders and muscular arms....

Hannah threw back the covers. Lying in bed fantasizing about Joe Lawson was the biggest waste of time under the sun. What had happened had been a freak occurrence, never to be repeated, brought about by too much makeup, a dimly lit hallway and a pair of well-cut trousers. And even if it hadn't been, there was no future in it. He was a widower with two kids, and she was about to set out on a round-Australia trip.

She dressed in her usual jeans and T-shirt after her shower then entered the kitchen. Her mother was making tea and she gave Hannah an assessing look as she poured milk and spooned in sugar.

"You were very quiet last night after the parade. Did you enjoy yourself?" Robyn asked.

"Sure. Ruby had a great time and I didn't take a dive into the audience. What was not to like?"

Hannah collected the cereal box and a bowl, hoping all the activity would hide the slow tide of warmth she could feel creeping up her face. She could only imagine what her mother would say if she knew Joe had kissed her. And that she'd kissed him back and the only reason things hadn't gone any further was because they'd been interrupted.

God, what if we hadn't been? What would have happened if those two women hadn't come along?

"Hannah! You're getting corn flakes all over the floor."

Hannah blinked and realized she was pouring cereal into an already full bowl.

"Sorry. Must have inhaled too much hair spray last night."

Her mother sighed and put down her teacup. "Was it so horrible, getting all gussied up for a change?"

Hannah thought about the way she'd felt when she looked at her made-up face and hair last night—like an impostor, a fake.

"It's not me, all that stuff. You know that," she said. "I know you wish I was more girlie like Kelly, but I'm not, Mom."

Her mother's face clouded. "I don't wish you were like Kelly. I love you the way you are."

"Right."

"I just want you to feel good about yourself, Hannah. I don't care how you do it."

Hannah scooped the spilled cereal into the box, using the small task to buy some time. She wanted to tell her mother that she did feel good about herself, that she knew she was a good mechanic and a good person, but she knew that wasn't what her mom meant. The truth was that Lucas's betrayal had knocked her already fragile sexual confidence. She'd never been very good at playing the man-woman game. She didn't know how to flirt. Pretending she was helpless or that she needed a man had never been her style. And she'd never been adept at working out when a man was interested in her or not.

Case in point: Joe Lawson. Until the moment he'd blocked her body with his own and leaned toward her, she'd been almost one hundred percent certain that he considered her a nuisance to be tolerated because his daughter had formed an attachment to her. But then he'd kissed her and she'd realized that the awareness she felt when she was around him wasn't one-sided. Not by a long shot, if his heated response was anything to go by.

"Hannah?"

Hannah glanced up and saw her mother was frowning at her. She'd zoned out again, thinking about Joe. What on earth was wrong with her? It wasn't as though she'd never been kissed before, for Pete's sake.

"Sorry, did you say something?"

"I did." Her mother hesitated a moment, studying Hannah's face. "Lucas called earlier. He'd like to speak to you."

Hannah waited until she'd finished pouring milk on her corn flakes before responding. "What does he want?"

"I'm not sure. To talk to you, I suppose."

Hannah could feel her mother watching her. She crossed to the fridge and put the milk away. What on earth could Lucas have to say? He'd already apologized. She'd refused to take his money more times than she could count. What more was left?

An insidious, dark thought wormed its way into her mind. What if he and Kelly had had a falling-out? What if he'd decided that he'd made a big mistake, choosing her sister over Hannah?

What if he wanted Hannah back?

A few months ago, the thought would have made her heart thump with nervousness and a twisted form of hope. Today, it made her frown.

She didn't want Lucas back.

She froze. When had that happened? When had the wishing for what-once-was faded away to nothing?

She had no idea, but it felt good. As though she'd shed a weight. Without giving herself a chance to think, she walked to the phone and picked it up.

"What's his number?" she asked.

Her mother's eyebrows rose toward her hairline, but she reeled off the number without comment. Lucas picked up on the third ring.

"Lucas speaking."

"It's me. Hannah."

"Hi." There was a short pause. "Thanks for calling." As always, he sounded uncomfortable. Awkward. Regretful. One of the many reasons why she'd gone out of her way to avoid any contact with him or her sister. She didn't want Lucas's pity.

Apparently she didn't want his anything anymore.

She was still getting used to the feeling.

"Mom said you wanted to speak to me."

"I did. I mean, I do. Would it be okay to meet for coffee?"

Her mother was making a big show out of pouring more water into the teapot, but Hannah knew she was listening.

"Can't you just say what you need to say over the phone?"

"I'd rather do it in person. I can meet you at The Watering Hole or wherever you like," Lucas said.

"Not The Watering Hole," she said instantly. The last thing she wanted was to see Joe again so soon. There was no way she'd be able to look him in the eye without blushing from head to toe.

"What about the coffee shop near the workshop? Ten minutes?"

"Twenty. I need to finish my breakfast."

"Okay."

Her mother deliberately talked about every other subject under the sun while Hannah finished her cereal, but she gave Hannah an extra-fierce hug goodbye when Hannah stood to leave.

Lucas was waiting at an outside table when she pulled up, his sunglasses resting on the table before him. He was looking the other way, his foot tapping restlessly, but his gaze swung around when he heard the rumble of her bike.

He stood when she approached the table. He was wearing jeans and a white linen shirt and he needed a shave.

"Hannah."

"Lucas."

They both sat at the same time.

"Thanks for coming at such short notice."

Hannah put her gloves on the table and shrugged out of her leather jacket.

"What's up?" she said, meeting his eyes squarely.

He laughed self-consciously. "You never did beat around the bush, did you?"

"Nope. Life's too short."

"Yep." He rubbed his hands down the front of his jeans and for a moment she worried that she'd guessed right, that he really was trying to find some way to reconnect with her.

"I wanted you to be the first to hear. Your mom doesn't know yet, or my parents. Only me and Kelly. She's pregnant. We're having a baby."

Hannah blinked, waiting for the old pain to reignite in her chest. Kelly was having Lucas's child, something Hannah had once dreamed of doing herself. She'd had it all planned—two children, eighteen months apart. She hadn't cared what sex they were, as long as they were healthy and as long as they had Lucas's deep green eyes.

But the pain didn't come. Slowly her shoulders relaxed. At long last, after six months of dragging her ass around, she'd finally let go of some of her anger and hurt and pain.

"Congratulations," she said after a short, intense silence. "When is she due?"

"The end of March."

Hannah did some mental arithmetic.

"So she's only eight weeks?"

"That's right. We found out yesterday. Like I said, I wanted you to be the first to know."

She looked at him, really looked at him, for the first time in six months. Apart from his obvious nervousness and discomfort at meeting with her, he looked well.

"Are you happy?" she asked suddenly.

"About the baby? Of course. You know I've always wanted kids."

"I meant in general. Are you happy with life, with Kelly, with everything?"

He glanced down at his sunglasses, clearly struggling to find the right thing to say.

"Just tell me the truth, Lucas."

He met her eyes. "Yes. I'm happy. I wish it hadn't been at your expense, but I love Kelly."

His declaration stung a little, but that was more pride than anything else.

"Did you ever love me?" She wasn't going to go

home and cry over the answer, but she'd always wanted to know.

"Yes. I still do. But it's different with Kelly. I can't explain it. It's just…right. With you, it was like we were best friends and you happened to be a woman. It was comfortable. I'm never comfortable with Kelly."

She stared at him, trying to understand. "And that's a good thing?"

He smiled and focused on something over her shoulder for a second or two, thinking it over. "Yeah, it is."

She looked away. "Well, I guess we're all better off, then."

Lucas focused on her again. "There's no excuse for what we did to you, Hann. It was the last thing you deserved. If I could change it, I would."

She smiled faintly. "No you wouldn't. Not if it meant giving up Kelly."

He looked as though he was going to argue for a moment, then he shrugged. "More of that Hannah Napier no-bullshit honesty. I miss it."

"Well, you know, I'm happy to be honest with you anytime you like," she said drily. He laughed and she found herself joining in.

Incredible. She was sitting with her ex-fiancé at a coffee shop on a Saturday morning and *laughing*. She wondered if she should pinch herself, to make sure this was real.

Lucas relaxed into his chair, the smile still playing around his mouth. "You going to have a coffee with me?" he asked.

"You paying?"

"Yep."

"Then I'll have a large mochachino. And a piece of orange poppyseed cake."

His smile broadened. She stretched out her legs as he called over a waitress and placed their order. He waited until the girl was gone before leaning forward and putting his elbows on the table.

"There's something else I wanted to talk to you about," he said.

"Let me guess—the money." In the past six months she hadn't had a conversation with him or Kelly that didn't include some mention of her debts.

"Yes." He pulled a piece of paper from his back pocket and put it on the table between them. It was a check, and when he folded it open she saw it was made out to her for $20,000.

"Let me cover the loss we took on the apartment," he said.

She opened her mouth to speak but he held up a hand.

"Before you rip my head off and stuff it down my neck, let me say my bit. It's my fault this mess happened. The moment I realized I felt something more for your sister than I should have, I should have put the wedding on hold. But I didn't. I let things play out because I couldn't believe that what I was feeling was real and that Kelly felt the same way. And because I knew I was going to hurt you."

He paused as the server delivered their order. Once they were alone again he leaned forward, elbows on the table, expression intense.

"I'm the one who screwed things up. Why should you suffer? Why should you carry the can for my mistake? Give me one good reason."

Not so long ago, Hannah would have had half a

dozen good reasons, all of them angry and bitter. She looked at the check and thought about what a difference it would make to her life. She wouldn't have to delay her road trip any longer. No more scrimping and saving. No more feeling trapped. She could hit the road and follow her dream. North first, to the New South Wales coast. Then on to Canberra to see the nation's capital. Sydney, Byron Bay, Coffs Harbour—there were so many places she'd circled on her map. And that wasn't even including the less-traveled parts of the country. The red heart, the small bush towns, the tropical communities at the northernmost tip of the continent.

"It won't put it right. It won't come close to making it up to you, I know that. But at least it will make life easier for you," Lucas said.

She turned away from him, trying to think and unable to do it properly while he was watching her with those familiar green eyes. Was she letting her sister and her ex off the hook by taking the money? Or was she being smart, looking out for herself?

A dark navy SUV pulled up at the curb. Joe swung out of the driver's seat, Ben exiting the passenger side. Joe slung his arm around his boy's shoulders as they walked toward the Balas's corner store, bending to say something that made Ben laugh and squirm out from under his father's arm.

She told herself to look away, but she couldn't take her eyes off Joe. There was so much arrogant masculinity in the way he walked. As though he owned the world. It made her remember the way he'd pushed her against the wall last night, the utter solidness of his body pressed against hers.

Just before they entered the store, Joe turned his

head. He was wearing sunglasses, but she knew he'd caught her watching him. She jerked her gaze away, but not before he'd nodded his head in acknowledgment.

"So, what's it going to be, Hannah?" Lucas asked.

Her hand closed around the check without her even willing it. She folded it in half and slid it into the front pocket of her jeans. Lucas smiled.

"Thank you," he said. "You have no idea what this means to me. And to Kelly."

She looked him dead in the eye. "I'm not doing it for you. I'm doing it for me."

"I'm just glad you're doing it."

She took a mouthful of her coffee. Lucas looked as though he was ready to break into song and skip up the street. He hadn't been lying when he said he was relieved.

She searched her heart and realized she was relieved, too. She'd cut the last tie that bound them all together. What happened next, she had no idea. But she was sick of living in the past.

Joe tried to concentrate on what Mr. Balas was saying, but his mind was outside, wondering what Hannah was doing with the blond-haired guy in the white shirt. Was he a friend? A customer?

He kept thinking about the way the guy had been watching her, as though right at that moment she was the most important thing in the world to him.

So not a friend, then. Something more.

It took Joe a moment to recognize the emotion burning in his belly as jealousy. It had been a while since he'd had reason to be jealous of anyone.

"So, Dad, I'll see you after two, okay?" Ben said.

"Sure, no problems. Call my cell if you finish early."

He kept his gaze on his car as he exited the store, but he could still see Hannah and her friend out of the corner of his eye. They were talking, leaning toward one another. He told himself what she did and who she did it with was none of his business. It didn't make any difference to the burn in his gut.

Ruby was having a playdate with one of her friends from school so Joe had the house to himself when he got home. He tidied the kitchen, then threw on a load of washing. By the time he'd straightened the living room and cleaned the bathroom, he was all out of busywork. He did a lap of the house, walking from the living room to the kitchen and through the hall to the bedrooms, restless energy and a vague sense of dissatisfaction gnawing at him. Finally he came to a halt in his bedroom doorway.

The bed was a mess, a tangle of sheets and quilt, a couple of pillows thrown on the floor. He'd had a bad night's sleep, tossing and turning, his mind full of images and sense memories: Hannah's breast, full and warm in his hand; the taste of her in his mouth; the feel of her firm, rounded ass. Somehow, somewhere in the dark hours, Hannah and Beth had gotten mixed up in his dreams and he'd found himself looking into Beth's face but pressed against Hannah's body, guilt and desire twisting inside him until he didn't know which was which. He'd woken sweaty and agitated, the sheets wrapped around his legs in a confining snarl.

Now, he sat on the end of the bed, thighs wide, hands on his knees, his unfocused gaze on the carpet.

When Beth had died, the emptiness she'd left in his life had seemed so profound, so all-encompassing that he hadn't been able to see past it. He hadn't been able to imagine ever wanting another woman again, let alone taking the risk of loving someone again.

And then he'd met Hannah.

He'd tried like hell not to notice her, but his body had had other ideas. She fascinated him and aggravated him in equal measures. She made him laugh. And she made him want things he had no business wanting. He wanted to touch her, slide his skin against hers, lose himself inside her. He wanted to make her smile. He wanted to tease her, just to see her rise to the bait. And he wanted to chase away the shadows in her eyes.

He didn't know how to reconcile all that want with his memories of Beth and what they'd once had together. The reality was that he and Hannah hardly knew each other. There was a physical attraction. There was the potential for more, maybe. But he had to take the next step to find out. And he wasn't sure if he was ready to do that.

By the time he'd stripped all the beds and remade them and put on yet another load of laundry, it was time to collect the kids.

"I've decided what I want to get for Hannah," Ruby said the moment she climbed into the car.

They'd discussed buying Hannah a thank-you gift on the way home from the parade last night, in between Ruby scrolling through the photos he'd taken with the digital camera.

"Okay. What did you come up with?"

"Perfume. Carly's mom has this really pretty stuff in a bottle shaped like a lady's body, but with no arm or legs or head."

"Right. Well, perfume it is, then. We can swing by the mall after we pick up Ben."

Once they got to the mall he sent Ben off to prowl the video game shop while he and Ruby hit the department store. Ruby sampled almost every perfume on display until she spotted one with a bottle shaped like a shiny red apple. Joe suspected it could have smelled like insect repellent and she'd still have chosen it.

"Can we take it to her now? Please?" Ruby pleaded in the car on the way home.

"Sure, if she's home."

He wasn't sure if he wanted her to be or not. He still didn't have his head on straight after last night. But he also wanted to see her.

What are you doing, man? What are you thinking? She kissed you, that was all. You have two kids and so much baggage it's ridiculous. You're not exactly a great catch.

But apparently that didn't matter, because when they pulled into the street and he saw Hannah in the garage at her mom's place, his gut tightened and his palms got sweaty.

What are you, a teenage girl?

Ruby was out of the car in a flash, running next door to the Napiers'. Joe followed more slowly, Ben trailing behind him. Hannah was holding the wrapped gift in her hands by the time they reached the garage.

"You didn't have to do this," Hannah said, but the smile on her face said she was pleased.

"I wanted to. I had such a good time last night and we had the best clothes in the whole parade and no one else looked as good as we did," Ruby said.

Ben made a rude noise at his sister's shameless vanity.

"Ah, the modesty of the young," Joe said.

Ruby frowned. "But it's true, Daddy. None of the other women looked even close to as good as Hannah did."

Hannah gave Ruby's shoulder a light nudge. "I think you might be a little biased there, sport."

"No, I'm not. You're beautiful," Ruby said.

Deep color stained Hannah's cheeks. She didn't seem to know what to say and she shot him an anguished, self-conscious look.

"Open your present," he said, a little amused and a lot touched by her reaction.

She seemed grateful for the diversion. She ran her thumb under the tape and pulled the paper open carefully. Not a ripper, like his kids, Joe noted. But her spotless workshop and attention to detail showed that she was a woman who appreciated order and workmanship.

"Oh, wow, this is lovely, Ruby," she said as she discovered the perfume.

Ruby was bouncing on her toes, thoroughly enjoying her moment of generosity. "I picked it because of the bottle. It's shaped like an apple."

"Cool. I can't wait to try it."

"You should put some on now," Ruby said.

"Okay." Hannah glanced at him quickly from under her lashes before she pried the box open. He wondered what she was thinking, if she was remembering last night.

The smell of sweet toffee apples and something more floral filled the air as Hannah sprayed her wrists.

"Mmm, that's really nice. Thank you so much for

such a great present, Ruby," she said. She pulled Ruby close for a hug.

Warmth spread through Joe's chest as he watched the way Ruby hugged her back, her small hands clenching Hannah's T-shirt.

Ben had been lingering on the threshold, but now he stepped inside, drawn to the bike parts laid out on the garage floor. He touched a rusty mudguard with his toe, curious, and the piece of metal teetered for a few seconds before falling over with a loud clang.

"Sorry," Ben said, starting guiltily. "I didn't mean to break it."

Hannah shrugged. "There's nothing you can do to hurt that big old lump of rust. I've got a lot of work to do before it's worth anything," Hannah said. "Go ahead and check it out all you want."

Ruby tugged on the hem of Hannah's tank top to regain her attention. "We got lots of pictures last night. Do you want to see?"

"Sure," Hannah said.

"Okay." Ruby promptly turned and bolted for home.

"Nothing like an instant response," Joe said drily.

"I'd better make sure she doesn't break the camera," Ben said.

Hannah was smiling as she watched him go, but the moment their eyes met she sobered.

It was the first time they'd been alone since the kiss, and Joe was acutely aware of it. Hannah seemed just as uncomfortable, shuffling her feet and reaching for a rag to clean her already-clean hands. He watched her twist her hands in the soft cloth and wondered if he should apologize for what had happened between them. He'd initiated it, after all. He'd been the one who pushed her against the wall. But she'd hardly been a reluctant participant.

The memory made his blood heat. He shoved his hands into the front pockets of his jeans and did some foot shuffling of his own.

"Listen, about last night," he said.

Hannah's gaze flew to his face. "I know, it was a mistake. It was stupid—"

"It wasn't a mistake," he said before he could edit himself. "That wasn't what I was going to say."

"Oh." She reached for her ponytail, combing her fingers through the ends of her hair for a beat or two. Finally she met his eyes again. "What were you going to say?"

"Come out with me?"

She looked as surprised as he felt. Hadn't he decided this morning that whatever he was feeling for Hannah was too hard, too confusing, too much for a man in his position?

"You mean on a date?" She said it as though he'd suggested they attempt nuclear fission rather than share a meal.

"Yeah. You, me, no kids. The usual kind of thing."

"Why?"

She was asking him that after last night? But he could see she was serious and he reminded himself what her mother had told him last night. Hannah's confidence had taken a huge knock recently.

"Because I like you."

"Oh." Her gaze dropped to her feet, but he could see the corners of her mouth curling into a smile.

"What's so funny?"

"Um, I think I like you, too," she said.

"You *think* you like me?" he asked lightly, something inside him relaxing at her words. She was going to say yes. He could feel it.

"Yeah. But we don't really know that much about each other, do we, to know if we really like each other?"

He knew enough. He knew that she was sexy and strong and too damned appealing for his peace of mind, which was why he was standing in her garage despite his many misgivings.

"That's what dinner would be about. Getting to know each other a little better, no distractions."

"But—" She didn't finish whatever it was she'd been about to say, instead lapsing into a frowning silence.

He took a step closer. "But what?"

She lifted her head and looked straight into his eyes. In an instant all the heat from last night was there between them. He could feel himself growing hard, just from a look.

"Okay. Yes." She sounded a little breathless. She licked her lips. "I'll go out with you."

She looked as dazed as he felt. But she'd said yes. He smiled, and she smiled back at him.

She'd said yes. Now he only had to worry about what the hell that meant, and what happened next.

Chapter 8

Hannah couldn't believe she'd said yes. What had she been thinking? Even if she hadn't still been grappling with the aftermath of her failed wedding, there was the small matter of her imminent trip around Australia and the fact that Joe had two children to consider. Not exactly your ideal dating scenario.

And yet she'd said yes.

You like him. At least be honest with yourself. You like him, and you think he's sexy.

Which was why she shaved her legs for the first time in months on Sunday night, and why she chose her best underwear and sprayed on a generous amount of her new perfume. She balked at spending too much time on makeup, however. The Hannah he'd kissed at the fashion parade was not the real her. If he wanted that woman—and she was almost convinced that must

be what was going on, since he'd never grabbed her
and pressed her against a wall when she was in her
work coverall—then he was in for a rude awakening.
She chose jeans and a shirt for the same reason, refusing to pretend to be anything other than who she was.
She'd played that game with Lucas—grown out her hair,
worn more makeup, bought more dresses. Then her
sister had come home and cast Hannah well and truly
into the shade.

She hadn't told her mother about the date. She didn't
want Robyn jumping to conclusions or assuming anything. Probably it would be a one-off. No point getting
her excited over nothing.

Good advice, Napier. How about taking it yourself?

Because there was no denying the anticipation tap-
dancing in her belly. She was half scared, half excited
about the prospect of spending a whole evening with
Joe. Sitting across the table from him. Talking to him.
Thinking about that kiss.

Even if it was probably only going to be a one-off.

She gave herself a quick head to toe. Fitted black
shirt with tiny black flowers embroidered on it. Her
good dark denim jeans. Her favorite black boots with
the Western heel. Her hair was long and loose and she
was wearing a touch of mascara and lipstick. She looked
about as good as she was ever going to.

She shrugged into her leather jacket and grabbed
her wallet. Her mother was chopping vegetables at the
kitchen counter and she looked surprised when Hannah appeared in the kitchen doorway.

"You're going out?"

"Yeah. Sorry. I meant to tell you, but it kind of
slipped my mind," Hannah fibbed.

Her mother took in her loose hair and good shirt in a single glance. The corners of her mouth twitched for a second before she returned her attention to the chopping board. "Not a problem. Have a nice time."

Hannah suspected her mother knew exactly who she was going out with. She hovered for a moment longer, trying to decide if she should address the issue or not. But her mother didn't look up again, so Hannah simply shrugged and headed for the door. Joe was waiting by his car already, his hair damp from the shower. He looked good in a dark brown shirt and black jeans. Maybe a little too good—one look at him and her palms got clammy.

"Hi," he said.

"Hi."

"You look great," he said, his gaze running appreciatively over her body.

She shrugged, unsure what to say. She'd never known how to handle compliments. Probably through lack of practice. Guys tended not to tell you how nice you looked while you were helping them strip a carbie or beating them at touch football.

"Shall we get going? I booked us a table at an Italian place," he said.

"Okay."

She rolled her eyes as she walked to the passenger door. Could she be any less sophisticated? So far she'd managed two words and a shrug. Next she'd be grunting in response to his questions.

She stopped in surprise when she realized Joe had rounded the car to open her door for her.

She muttered a disconcerted thanks as she slid into the car. She wasn't used to having men wait on her.

She concentrated on securing her seat belt, but she was very aware of his aftershave as he got in beside her and started the engine. Something spicy and mellow that made her think of wood and leather.

She smoothed her hands down her thighs. "So where is this place you're taking me, anyway?"

"It's called Il Solito Posto. It's in a laneway off Collins Street. One of the guys at work recommended it."

"Cool."

"If it sucks, you can help me come up with a suitable punishment for him."

She laughed. "That'll teach him to recommend anything."

"Exactly."

The restaurant turned out to be partly underground, with windows high in the wall that offered glimpses of the legs of passersby in the bluestone alleyway outside. They were seated in a corner, the fat candle on the small wooden table casting a warm light over them.

"You want something to drink to start with?" Joe asked as they scanned their menus.

Hell, yeah.

Maybe some alcohol would make her feel less stiff and on edge. "That sounds good."

He ordered a bottle of red for them to share and a plate of antipasto. She chose gnocchi for her main. He chose osso bucco. With the ordering out of the way and wineglasses in front of them, they stared across the table at each other.

"This is nice," she said lamely.

Good one. Hit him with more of that sparkling banter, Napier.

"Yeah. Place seems good." He took a hefty slug from his wine then shifted in his chair.

He was regretting his decision. She could see it in every line of his body. He'd asked her out on impulse, maybe because he had been misled by all that hair and makeup the other night, maybe because he'd felt grateful on Ruby's behalf. And now he was willing the minutes to pass.

"Listen," they both said simultaneously, leaning forward.

Hannah laughed awkwardly. "You go first," she said.

Joe cleared his throat. "I was just going to say sorry if I'm a bit rusty. Haven't done this sort of thing for a while."

Dull color traced his cheekbones.

Huh. So she wasn't the only one flailing around here. The knowledge helped loosen the band of tension around her chest. "Well, in case you hadn't noticed, I'm not exactly a social butterfly myself," she said drily. "I've kind of been keeping a low profile lately."

She took a deep breath, then let it out again. She hated telling anyone about the wedding, but he was bound to hear it from someone eventually. The whole neighborhood knew about it, and if he heard it somewhere else first then he'd think she'd kept it secret on purpose, which would give the wedding far more importance than it deserved.

"I was engaged last year, but the wedding was called off at the last minute," she said before she could change her mind.

There was a short pause before he answered. "That must have been tough."

She checked to make sure he wasn't giving her the

pity look. She'd seen it often enough over the past six months to be able to spot it at ten paces. But he simply looked straight at her, his deep blue eyes giving nothing away.

She tightened her grip on her wineglass. Might as well reveal the full horror. "It was called off because my fiancé fell in love with my sister."

His expression didn't change; he simply ducked his head in acknowledgment. She narrowed her eyes.

"You already knew, didn't you? Who told you?"

"Your mom."

She sat back in her chair, expelling her breath on an exasperated sigh. "Bloody hell. Is nothing sacred?"

"Not where moms are concerned. Talk to mine long enough and she'll tell you I took twice as long to toilet train as other kids and that when I was fifteen she caught me with my hand up Sally Perkin's blouse."

She smiled, even though she made a mental note to have a word with her mother on the subject of discretion. "I guess there's not much left for me to confess, then."

"Was that who you were talking to yesterday at the coffee shop? Your ex?"

"You don't miss much."

"Used to work on an oil rig. Keeping an eye on what's going on around me is pretty much a survival skill."

"Hmm. You know, in a woman that would simply be called plain old nosiness," she said.

He smiled. "Lucky I'm not a woman, then."

Her gaze ran over his shoulders and broad chest. He was *definitely* not a woman. "Lucas wanted to tell me my sister is pregnant."

Joe went very still, then swore under his breath. "I hope you told him where to get off."

She liked that he was angry on her behalf. "Not exactly. I congratulated him. I'm not going to waste the rest of my life being angry with them."

"You a Buddhist or something?"

"Nope. Just sick of feeling like I want to punch something."

He smiled and she found herself smiling in return. They both sat back as the waiter put a large white platter on the table between them. Hannah surveyed the tempting array of antipasto. Her mouth watered.

"Yum," she said.

Joe laughed. Then he lifted his glass and tilted it toward her in a toast.

"You're a gutsy woman, Hannah Napier. But I guess I already knew that about you."

Because she didn't know what to do with the warmth in his eyes and tone, she reached for the serving tongs and started filling his plate.

"Thanks," he said when she'd finished.

She shrugged and slid some stuffed mushrooms onto her own plate.

"So, Ruby tells me you've got a big trip planned. Any idea when you're going to hit the road?" Joe said as he picked up his knife and fork.

"Soon." Hannah thought about the check she'd deposit first thing Monday morning. "Sooner than I thought, actually. I really only need to wait for the owner of the garage to find someone to take over from me, buy some gear then I'm off."

There was a small silence. When she glanced up he looked…disappointed. That was the only way she could describe the mix of frustration and regret she saw in his eyes. Then he blinked and it was gone.

"Ruby's going to miss you," he said, spearing a chunk of fried polenta with his fork.

What about you? Will you miss me?

She shook the thought off. They hardly knew each other. How could he miss someone he barely knew?

"I'll miss her, too. She's been a fantastic help with the Thunderbird."

"You won't get to finish restoring it."

"No. I guess I won't."

Their gazes met across the table.

"So, where are you heading for first?" he said, breaking the small silence.

Hannah spent the next twenty minutes doing her bit to clear the platter of delicious Italian morsels while detailing her planned route to him.

"So you're going to camp most of the time?" he asked.

"If I can. The weather is good and I think it's the best way to see the country."

"Not going to miss hot and cold running water and all the mod cons?"

She cocked her head and raised an eyebrow. "Not a fan of the great outdoors, Joe?"

"Me? I love it. Always have. Beth couldn't stand it. Had to have a roof over her head, air-conditioning, running water, you name it."

The name came out of his mouth so casually, so naturally, but they both stilled. It was the first time he'd ever mentioned his wife to her. He fiddled with the stem of his wineglass for a few seconds. "Beth was my wife," he said.

She nodded. She could see this was hard for him, and she guessed that it wasn't something he talked about very often.

"How did she die?" she asked, trying to make it easier for him since he seemed determined to address the issue.

He frowned slightly. "How did you…?"

"Ruby."

"Ah."

"Seems the family telegraph has been working for both of us," she joked. Anything to ease the desolate look that had come into his eyes.

"It was a car accident. I was up north on the rig and she was driving to collect Ben from karate practice. A driver ran a red light, smashed into her car."

His knuckles were white, and she was afraid he was going to snap the stem in half. She reached across the table and laid her hand over his.

"It's okay. We don't have to talk about it."

He stared at her, his expression bleak. Then something in him seemed to relax. "It's more that I'm out of practice. It's been two years. And people don't exactly line up to talk about it."

"I can imagine," she said drily.

"The worst of it was that she didn't die straightaway. She had massive head and internal injuries. They operated while I flew down to Sydney from the rig. She died before the plane landed."

She tried to imagine the torture of sitting on a plane, hoping against hope that her loved one would survive, willing the plane to fly faster, get there sooner, only to arrive to the worst possible news.

"I'm so sorry. That must have been a terrible thing to come home to."

"Yeah. Worst flight of my life. I was almost too scared to turn my cell phone on when we landed. Then my mom called."

He blinked a few times and her chest ached for him. She had no words of comfort to offer. What was there to say, after all? If she knew him better, she would have simply stood and rounded the table to put her arms around him. But she didn't, so she sat quietly while he took a swallow of wine.

"Sorry. Like I said, out of practice," he said.

"Tough memories."

He nodded.

The waiter cleared the platter and their side plates. Hannah took advantage of the moment to pull herself together. Watching the grief on Joe's face, it had suddenly hit her that he was still hung up on his dead wife. And that meant that anything that happened between them was, by definition, doomed to failure.

Hello? You're about to hit the road. What does it matter if he's over his dead wife or not? It means nothing to you. He means nothing to you. One kiss does not give you the right to feel disappointed.

But the fact was that she couldn't help looking at Joe and seeing a world of what-ifs. What if they'd met at another time, when she'd been less angry and he'd been less hurt? What if either of them had been prepared to take the risk of loving someone again? Because she had the feeling that Joe Lawson was a man it would be very easy to love.

The buzz of a cell phone interrupted her thoughts. Joe pulled a face and reached for his back pocket.

"Sorry. I told the sitter to call if there were any problems."

"Of course."

She hadn't dated a man with children before, had never really thought about all the extra complications and problems a woman would have to be prepared to take on. It would be daunting, becoming part of an instant family. A real baptism of fire.

She fiddled with her cutlery, not wanting Joe to think she was eavesdropping, but it was hard to avoid overhearing his conversation even though he was talking quietly. It quickly became obvious from his tone and what he was saying that he was talking to Ruby.

"The spider's not going to hurt you, honey," he said. "It's probably more afraid of you than you are of it."

Joe flicked her an apologetic glance, but she shook her head to indicate she wasn't fussed. His kids needed him. She had no issue with that.

"Well, if it ran under the bed, it's probably not going to come back out again." Joe smiled as he listened to his daughter. "Okay, how about this? You bunk down on the couch and I'll check your room out when I'm back from my meeting? How does that sound?"

Meeting?

Joe said good-night to Ruby and ended the call. "Sorry. Ruby had a spider in her room. It only sounds like a huntsman, but she's terrified of the things."

Hannah nodded. She told herself to ignore what she'd heard, but she couldn't help herself. "You didn't tell her about our date?"

He looked uncomfortable for a moment, then he shrugged. "I haven't dated anyone before and I wasn't sure how she'd react. I know she loves you, but I didn't want her getting the wrong idea."

Hannah stared at him, wondering what he thought the *wrong idea* was. Then she thought about the sad, awkward little confessions they'd just made—her failed wedding, his dead wife—and her planned trip and his fierce protectiveness and sense of duty toward his kids.

She shook her head slightly. "Who are we kidding?"

He raised his eyebrows. "Sorry?"

She gestured toward the table, the candle, the wine. "All this, what happened the other night… I'm about to head off for months. You've got your kids. We're both walking wounded. This was never going to happen."

He looked arrested for a moment, then his shoulders visibly relaxed. "You're probably right. I'm not exactly the best catch at the moment."

"Second only to me, owner of a never-worn wedding dress." She raised her wineglass. "To a bold attempt."

His eyes were warm with appreciation and humor as he lifted his own glass. "To bad timing."

She laughed and Joe joined in.

The rest of the evening flew by. With the possibility of anything romantic developing between them well and truly put to bed, the tension dissolved and conversation flowed freely, ranging from childhood anecdotes to favorite movies to most coveted vintage car. Joe had a dry, quick sense of humor and he loved to tease her, his blue eyes dancing as he threw a contentious comment onto the table and waited for her to take the bait. He had a great laugh and she found herself doing everything she could to amuse him. She told him stories from her apprenticeship, shamelessly embroidering them so she could see the corners of his eyes crinkle and his mouth curve into a grin. He countered with his adventures as a young roustabout on the rigs, and they wound up comparing scars on their hands and forearms.

"This one was completely my fault," Joe said, tracing the wicked-looking curling scar she'd noticed when she first met him.

"Let me guess—you were juggling knives?"

"Close. A couple of guys and I were fishing off the platform one afternoon—"

"You can fish off an oil rig?"

"Hell yeah. Fish love it around a rig. They're like shipwrecks, covered in barnacles below the water. Once you've got barnacles, you've got fish."

"Huh. Sorry, I interrupted. You were explaining how your tomfoolery scarred you for life."

He let her gibe pass. "We'd been out there for a few hours when I got a big tug on the line. A beauty, a giant trevally, looked about a hundred and eighty pounds."

"*Looked about?* Uh-oh, I sense a bad ending to this fishy tale."

"Yeah, well. He was a big boy, and it took me ages to bring him in. The other guys were hooting and hollering. When I finally landed him he was all snarled up in the line. Mick told me to let him be awhile before cutting him free, but I was too impatient. So I grabbed my fishing knife and knelt down to cut the line, and the fish bucked like a bronco. I nearly took off my hand as well as cutting through the line. Meanwhile, the trevally slid off the platform and back into the ocean without so much as a goodbye and good luck."

"Selfish bastard. How many stitches did you need?"

He shrugged. "Enough to learn my lesson."

"Which was what? Never take a knife to a fish fight?" she asked, deadpan.

"Anyone ever told you you've got a mouth on you, Ms. Napier?"

"Frequently and at great length."

"I bet."

They shared a dessert and lingered over coffee. By the time they were walking back to Joe's car, Hannah was feeling warm with goodwill and the mouthful of hazelnut-flavored liqueur she'd had with her coffee.

"Definitely you shouldn't sack him," she said as they walked along the Paris end of Collins Street—so-called because of the ornate European-influenced buildings lining either side of the road.

"The guy who recommended the restaurant?" he asked.

She smiled. She liked that he'd been able to follow her chain of thought without her explaining. "Yep. He did good."

"I know. I'm thinking of giving him a raise."

She spluttered out a laugh. "It wasn't that good."

"Speak for yourself."

She nudged him with her elbow. "You're easily pleased."

"You have no idea."

She laughed again, aware that he was flirting with her but knowing it was meaningless. They'd both agreed that there was no future in the attraction between them. What was a little harmless flirtation between friends, after all? It had been a while since she'd felt this light and frivolous and had so much fun.

They bantered some more in the car on the way home, the radio playing softly in the background. She was surprised when the car pulled into their street.

"We're here already," she said stupidly when he pulled into the driveway of his house.

"Seems like it."

"Huh." She reached for her seat belt and slid it free. She started to frame a thank-you in her mind, but she didn't want the evening to end yet. If she wasn't living at her mother's place, she'd invite him in for coffee. But she was. And he had kids and a sitter at his place....

"Well, I had a great night. Thanks," she said.

"We'll have to do it again sometime."

"Yeah. Although I'll probably be pretty busy getting stuff ready for my trip."

"Right. I'd forgotten about that for a moment."

His face was in shadows and she couldn't read his expression, but there was a note of regret in his voice. Or maybe she was imagining it, because suddenly she was wishing all over again that things could be different between them.

She shook her head minutely. Stupid to wish for things that were never going to happen.

"Anyway, thanks," she said again.

"It was my pleasure."

She didn't consciously think about her next move, she simply leaned across to press a quick kiss to his cheek. Except he turned his head, and instead she found herself kissing the warmth of his mouth. She pulled back a fraction and for a moment the car was very still, then Joe made an unintelligible sound—or maybe it was her—and they came together again, hands reaching for shoulders, heads angling, mouths pressing together and opening.

He tasted of coffee and hazelnuts and the touch of his tongue against hers sent a thrill all the way through her body. In no seconds flat her heart was galloping and her body was on fire.

His fingers slid into her hair, the pads of his fingers pressing into her skull as he urged her closer. She was only too happy to oblige. She wanted to taste him until the craving inside her was gone. She wanted to slide her hands over his body to discover if he really was as hot and hard as he looked. She wanted him to touch her, and she wanted to answer the question that had been echoing deep inside her ever since she'd first met him: what would it be like to be skin to skin with this man? To have him inside her?

She made an encouraging noise as his hand slid down her shoulder to her breast. Her nipple was already hard and he rolled it between his thumb and forefinger. Desire pierced her, so sweet it made her shudder. She felt a tug as he opened her shirt and then his hand was sliding inside her bra to cup her bare flesh.

"Yes," she whispered against his mouth.

He pulled her closer and the hand brake pressed into her belly. She broke their kiss long enough to throw a leg over the center console and scramble over it. Then there was nothing between them as she straddled Joe's lap.

His stubble rasped against her as he trailed kisses up her neck. She gasped as he tongued her ear. She could feel how aroused he was, his erection a thick, hot presence pressed against her wide-open thighs. She rotated her hips and it was his turn to groan. Hungry for more, she slid a hand beneath his shirt and pressed her palm against the firm muscles of his belly. He felt incredibly hot, and she slid her hand up to cover one of his firm, rounded pecs, her thumb finding his nipple.

He tugged on her shirt some more until he was pushing it open, his gaze taking in her breasts with a single-minded intensity that made her feel like the most desirable woman on the planet. He lowered his head and ran his tongue along the lacy edge of her bra, then he used his teeth to pull her bra cup free even as his hands were busy behind her, undoing the clasp. His mouth closed over her nipple, hot and wet and she lost all power of thought. She wanted. That was all. The rest of the world ceased to exist.

She slid her hand between their bodies to grasp the thick, long ridge of his erection through his jeans. His body tensed and his hips pressed upward encouragingly. She began to stroke him while he suckled and teased first one breast then the other.

She was panting, mindless. His body was bowed toward her, tense with desire and need.

"Hannah," he said, his voice low and deep.

"Yes. Please," she said. "Hurry."

He reached for the stud on her jeans and she leaned backward to help him out. The sound of the car horn cut through the night like a siren. They both started and Hannah jerked away from the steering wheel.

"Shit," she whispered.

A porch light came on. She had a sudden vision of a sleepy-eyed Ruby or Ben coming out to see what was keeping their father from coming inside.

Joe must have shared her vision because they both scrambled for her shirt buttons at the same time.

She threw a leg over the console and slithered awkwardly into the passenger seat, twisting around so she was facing the right way even as her fingers worked furiously at her buttons. By the time the front door was opening she was decent, even if her bra was hanging loose around her rib cage.

"The babysitter," Joe said as a young girl stepped onto the porch and looked curiously toward the car.

"Grace Melville," Hannah said, recognizing the teenager from across the street.

"Yeah."

Joe gave Grace a reassuring wave and the girl ducked back into the house. He ran a hand over his face and exhaled loudly.

"Probably just as well," he said after a moment.

She nodded.

"It's not like it was ever going to go anywhere," he added.

"No."

"And we're both too old for car sex. So, really, being interrupted was a good thing."

"I wouldn't go that far," she said drily.

He looked at her, startled. She didn't bother trying to hide how frustrated she was, how much she still wanted him. His mouth crooked into a faint smile. "Yeah, well, there is that."

They stared at each other for a long moment. She held out her hand.

"I had a nice time. Thanks."

"Nice?" He raised his eyebrows, clearly unimpressed with the lukewarm adjective.

"Parts of it were exceptional, but I'm marking you down for failure to complete."

"You're the one who sat on the horn."

"Don't I know it."

He laughed at her double entendre. At last he took her

hand. His fingers closed around hers, warm and firm. "There we go with the bad timing again."

"And then some."

She slid her hand free. "Good night, Joe."

"Good night."

She exited the car, closing the door quietly. She let herself into the house and walked on her toes across the tiled floor, in case her mother was still awake. She didn't want to talk right now. She was still buzzing with arousal, disappointment and frustration. She reached her bedroom and eased the door closed. For a moment she simply stood there, her back pressed against the door.

She felt as though she'd just had a glimpse of something wonderful and impossible. Something good and real.

Her gaze fell on the road atlas she'd been using to plan her route and she straightened.

They'd already agreed at dinner: it wasn't going to happen between them. Too many problems, too many obstacles, too much baggage. A handful of great kisses and some heavy-duty lust didn't change any of that, no matter how much her frustrated body wanted it to.

Heavy with regret, she got ready for bed.

Chapter 9

Joe felt like a kid. A horny, dumb, inarticulate kid. It didn't matter how many times he told himself that Hannah Napier was a dead end, he couldn't stop himself from wanting her. He slept badly after their interrupted tryst in the car and the next day he kept one eye on the door of The Watering Hole for most of the afternoon until he realized he was waiting for her to enter. As soon as he acknowledged his own subconscious desire he also acknowledged that she wouldn't be coming into the pub that day, not after what had almost happened between them. She wasn't the kind of woman who played games. She was going away, he was staying. There was no point pretending otherwise, even if the physical chemistry between them was hot enough to launch a rocket. He appreciated the clear-cut honesty of it, of her. But he still wanted her.

That night when Ruby asked if she could go next door to help Hannah with her bike, he found himself making the short walk next door alongside his daughter. Hannah was hunkered down cleaning the rusty front forks of the Thunderbird with some steel wool and she glanced up with a smile when Ruby said hello.

"I was wondering if I was going to see you tonight," she said. Her gaze flicked to him and away again, but the extra color in her cheeks told him she was every bit as aware of him as he was of her and that last night was still on her mind.

"I was thinking you might need an extra pair of hands," he said.

Her eyebrows rose. "You want to help me strip rust off old bike parts?"

"Sure. Why not? Ben's doing his homework, I'm finished at the pub for the night. And like I told you, I always wanted one of these things."

And he wanted to be around her, even if it meant nothing and went nowhere.

He had the good sense not to say the last part out loud.

"Okay, sure. Grab some steel wool." She darted a sideway glance his way as he helped Ruby tear off a chunk of fine-grade steel wool, but she didn't say anything more.

"Maybe we could do this bit together, Daddy," Ruby suggested, pointing to the rear wheel rim.

"That sounds like a plan."

Ruby sat cross-legged on the concrete and began to attack one end of the once-shiny rim. He squatted and began working on the other side.

"Guess what we did at school today, Hannah," Ruby said.

"Um, reading? 'Rithmatic? 'Roo wrestling?" Hannah guessed.

Ruby laughed. "None of those things. We had to make a car of the future in art class."

"Wow. I bet you a million dollars egg cartons and pipe cleaners were involved." Hannah was smiling, her attention on her work.

"How did you know?" Ruby asked, eyes wide.

He laughed and Hannah glanced up and met his eyes. For a moment something warm and bittersweet unfolded inside him.

I could get to really like you, Hannah Napier. I could get to really admire your salty wit and your take-no-prisoners attitude and that sexy, curvy body of yours.

Too bad she was going away.

He helped Ruby and Hannah out again on Wednesday after dinner but when he was about to slip next door on Thursday night Ben looked up from his Nintendo game with a frown.

"What's so good about next door, anyway?"

"Why don't you come with us and see? I'm sure Hannah would welcome the extra pair of hands."

"That would be so cool. If we all work together we can finish the bike really quickly," Ruby said enthusiastically.

Ben scowled at the TV screen, his thumbs twiddling aimlessly with the game controls.

Joe stepped into his son's line of vision. "Come on, it'll be fun."

Rolling his eyes, Ben tossed the game controller onto the couch. "This had better be good," he said as he slouched toward the front door.

Joe suppressed a smile and followed his kids out into the street. Hannah looked surprised to see her new recruit, but she quickly recovered. "Excellent. More slaves to do my bidding. Hope you like grease, Ben."

Ben shrugged, eyes downcast. Hannah didn't let his manner put her off. Over the next hour, she checked in with him regularly as they all worked at cleaning bike parts. Joe watched surreptitiously as Ben slowly thawed and relaxed. By bedtime Ben was laughing at Hannah's jokes and trying out a few of his own.

Joe lingered for a moment after he'd packed the kids off to clean up and brush their teeth. "You handled him just right."

"I treated him like any other apprentice."

"Ah. Is that how you see us? As your apprentices?"

She shot him a look from beneath her eyelashes. "Not all of you. Some of you have more than your fair share of experience."

He grinned. "I'm going to take that as a compliment."

She frowned. "There's no need to look so pleased about it."

"I can't help it. I've been staring at the ceiling all week thinking about Sunday night. It's good to know I'm not the only one it left an impression on."

She smiled ruefully. "Yeah, well, next time we decide to quit while we're ahead, let's quit while we're ahead."

She stooped to collect some discarded steel wool, and Joe stepped in front of her when she straightened.

She looked at him steadily. There was wariness in

her eyes as well as frustrated desire. He couldn't help himself—he ran his thumb along the slope of her cheekbone. Her breath caught, and her eyelids swept down over her eyes, hiding her reaction from him. But he knew. If he kissed her right now, it wouldn't take much to get either of them back to the same hot, heavy place they'd been in his car the other night.

If only she wasn't going away...

It was on the tip of his tongue to ask if she really had to go, if maybe she couldn't delay her departure, hang around and explore this feeling between them.

But she'd been planning this trip for a long time. She'd told him over dinner how she'd already put it off once for her ex-fiancé. He couldn't ask her to put it off again for him. What did he have to offer, after all? Neither of them had any idea what the future held. He couldn't ask her to delay her dream on the chance that things might work out between them. And what were the odds of that? Her broken heart, his blighted one. His kids. Plus all the usual misapprehensions and problems most couples dealt with. It would be a miracle if they lasted a week.

She took a step backward.

"It's not that I don't want to kiss you again, but I'm really not into self-flagellation. I'm trying to be smart here," she said.

"Yeah, I know." He turned and started down the driveway. "Good night."

"Thanks for the help with the bike," she called after him.

He simply raised a hand in acknowledgment and kept walking. It wasn't like he had much of a choice.

* * *

When Ben and Ruby went next door the following evening, Joe stayed behind, pleading bookwork for the pub as an excuse. It was too hard being near Hannah and not being able to touch her or look at her the way he wanted to.

He was hunched over the calculator, trying to reconcile the hard spirits inventory when he heard the front door open. He finished adding a column of figures, then glanced up to see Ruby standing in the doorway to the living room, her face twisted with emotion.

"She's going," she said. "She's leaving next week!" She hurled herself across the room and into his arms, pressing her face into his neck.

He closed his arms around her and cupped the back of her head with his hand.

"It's okay, Rubes."

"I don't want her to go."

"I know. But we always knew Hannah was heading off on her big trip, didn't we?"

"But I didn't think it would be for ages and ages. I don't want her to go."

He didn't know what to say. He couldn't make promises on Hannah's behalf. He had no idea when she planned to come back, or if she planned to come back at all. He suspected Hannah didn't know herself. That was part of the appeal of the open road.

He heard the sound of the front door opening again and a couple of seconds later Ben entered the living room, Hannah hard on his heels. She looked stricken when she saw Ruby in his arms.

"Oh, man," Ben said, his voice filled with brotherly disdain for his sister's tears.

"She'll be all right," Joe said to Hannah. "I think you just took her by surprise."

"I didn't mean to upset you, Rubester," Hannah said. "I thought you knew I was going soon."

Ruby spoke into his shirtfront. "I did. But I don't want you to go."

Hannah met his eyes over Ruby's head.

"I wish I could stay, sweetheart. But this is something I've dreamed of doing ever since I was your age. I've been collecting maps and tourist guides for years and years."

"I know. You showed them to me, remember?" Ruby said.

"That's right. I forgot. Look, it's not like I'll be gone forever. I'll come back. My mom lives right next door— I have to come back or she'll kill me."

He glanced down and saw that Ruby was smiling a little now.

"Will you send me postcards?"

"Every week," Hannah said. "I promise."

Finally Ruby pushed away from his chest. He loosened his arms and she turned to face Hannah.

"What's going to happen to the Thunderbird while you're gone?"

"I'm going to pack the parts away so that I can take them to be rechromed when I come home. You can help me put it together when it's all done, if you like. That's if you're not too busy doing your nails and going shopping by the time I return."

"I can do both," Ruby said.

"Good. Because I'd miss having my ace right-hand woman working beside me." Hannah paused to eye Ruby carefully. "So are we okay?"

Ruby shrugged her shoulder in perfect imitation of Hannah. "Yeah." She walked across the room and wrapped her arms around Hannah's waist, laying her head against Hannah's hip. "It's going to be weird without you."

Hannah blinked rapidly. "Yeah."

Joe became aware of Ben standing to one side, the expression on his face an odd mixture of scorn and envy as he watched Hannah embrace his sister. Joe had a sudden memory of Beth sitting on the couch, Ben snuggled in her arms as she read him a book. She'd been a very demonstrative woman, warm and affectionate. Kisses and cuddles before bedtime, the casual brush of a hand over one of her children's heads when they passed in the hallway, tickle wrestling on the living room rug.

Ben missed being held by his mother, just as Ruby clearly craved a woman's touch. For a moment Joe felt heavy with regret. There were so many losses he could never hope to replace, too many gaps in their lives for him to even come close to filling them all.

"I was thinking that maybe before you go I could go for a ride around the block on your bike," Ruby said. She kept her voice carefully innocent, but she knew what she was asking.

For a second he locked eyes with Hannah. Her lips twitched into a smile, and he couldn't help but respond.

"Nice try, sweetheart," Hannah said.

"I couldn't have put it better myself," he said.

"You are such a doofus, Ruby. No way is Dad going to let you go on a motorbike," Ben chipped in, but even he was smiling at Ruby's opportunistic audacity.

"It was worth a try." Ruby's grin was cheeky.

"Yes, it was," Joe agreed. "Now, who wants a hot chocolate before bed?"

"Me. But I want double marshmallows," Ruby said, twisting away from Hannah and racing for the kitchen.

Ben wasn't far behind her. "I'm measuring out the cocoa. You mucked it up last time."

Joe looked to Hannah. "Can we tempt you?"

She was silent for a shade too long. "Thanks, but I'd better go. Maybe another time."

"Sure."

He pushed his disappointment aside. Hadn't he decided to minimize his contact with her before she left for the sake of his own sanity? And yet here he was, leaping on the first opportunity to prolong her visit. He was as bad as Ruby, a desperate opportunist.

He followed Hannah to the door. "I take it you're leaving next weekend?" he asked.

She nodded. "Saturday."

"Right."

Another long silence.

"I'd better go," she said.

"Okay."

When she turned away, her movements were jerky, almost as though it had taken an effort to drag herself away.

He closed the door after her, staring at the wooden surface blindly.

One more week, then she'd be gone.

Damn.

The following Friday night, Hannah checked her camping gear one last time before strapping it to the accessory rack she'd bought for the back of her bike.

Her mother stood to one side of the garage, arms crossed tightly over her body.

"I can't believe you're really going. You've talked about this for so many years, and now this is finally it," her mom said.

"Yep."

"What time are you leaving tomorrow?"

"Ten. Traffic should be fairly light heading north."

Her mother pressed her lips together, but Hannah could see she was close to tears.

"Mom, I'll call every week, I promise."

"I know. It's just been lovely having you back home again."

Hannah hid her smile. She'd hardly been the most gracious houseguest, but her mother was feeling sentimental and there was no point letting the facts get in the way of a good farewell.

"It's been great being here. You've been a lifesaver, Mom."

Her mother waved a hand dismissively, but Hannah could see she was pleased.

"I must admit, I was holding out hope that something might happen to give you an incentive to stay."

Her mother's gaze was assessing. Hannah busied herself checking the oil level on the bike.

"Fine," her mother said. "Make me come right out and ask, then. Is anything happening with Joe or not?"

"He's got two kids to consider and I'm hitting the road. What do you think?"

"I think you should hang around and see what happens."

Hannah screwed the cap back on the oil tank. "I can't."

"Australia will still be out there in six months' time."

Hannah turned on her mother. "And what if it doesn't work out again? What if I'm not the woman Joe thinks I am or something else goes wrong? Am I supposed to pick myself up and dust myself off all over again?"

"You're scared." Her mother said the words as if they were a huge revelation.

"Of course I'm scared. I'd be stupid if I wasn't. We're supposed to learn from past mistakes, aren't we?"

Hannah's mother smiled sadly. "Loving someone is always a risk, sweetheart. That's why it's so exciting and terrifying all at the same time."

"Right now I'm willing to pass on the excitement if it means I don't have to put up with the terrifying."

"If you could see the way Joe looks at you when you're not watching…"

Hannah's chest tightened. She took a deep breath. "Mom, I don't want to talk about it. I've made my decision, I've said my goodbyes. I'm leaving tomorrow."

Her mother flinched and Hannah knew she'd hurt her feelings.

"Okay. Well, I'll leave you to it and I'll see you in the morning."

"Mom…"

"It's okay, Hannah, I understand."

Hannah kissed her good-night and gave a sigh of relief when her mother had disappeared into the house and she was once again alone. She couldn't wait to be on the road, all of this far, far behind her.

Maybe that made her a coward, but so be it. She wasn't ready to risk her heart again. Especially with a man who almost definitely hadn't come to terms with his grief for his dead wife.

She checked a few more last-minute things then went in to the house. She'd written out a detailed outline of her proposed route and a bunch of contact numbers for her mother, and she stuck the page to the fridge with a magnet. Then she went to her bedroom and sorted her rucksack. She was traveling light by necessity: a few pairs of jeans, underwear, a swimsuit, T-shirts, a couple of warm sweaters. If she needed anything else, she'd simply buy it on the road.

Satisfied she had everything in order, she shed her clothes, brushed her teeth and crawled into bed. She wasn't even close to being able to sleep, however. Her thoughts kept circling around tomorrow, her last good-byes, the first hours on the road. She planned to camp at Albury her first night before making her way to Eden on the New South Wales coast. She'd check out the scene there, spend a few days fishing and swimming, then head north again.

It would be good. Free, easy. At last she'd get a chance to see the country the way she'd always wanted to.

She rolled onto her side and stared into the darkness.

I wish he'd never kissed me. I wish he was just a man with two kids and a dead wife who happened to live next door.

But Joe had kissed her, and he'd become more than her neighbor. A lot more.

"So stupid," she muttered.

She'd known she was going on this trip, so why on earth would she start feeling something for a man she was always going to leave behind? It was dumb, plain old dumb.

Eventually she fell asleep but she woke feeling gritty-

eyed and grumpy. Her stomach was tense with nerves
and she had to force herself to eat a decent breakfast.
As ten o'clock drew closer she grew more and more nervous, her gaze darting to her watch every few minutes.

Ruby had made a point of saying she'd be over at ten
to see her off. Hannah was dreading saying goodbye
to her little buddy. She was also terrified Ruby would
be accompanied by her father. She didn't trust herself
not to say or do something embarrassing and revealing.
Like throw herself at him and ask him to tell her to stay.

She was in the garage tugging on her leather jacket
when Ruby appeared. Joe was with her, and Ben. A
lump formed in the back of Hannah's throat.

"Hey," she said. Somehow her voice sounded normal, even though her throat felt constricted.

"We bought you a going-away present," Ruby said.

"You didn't have to do that." She looked to Joe,
frowning. "You guys have given me enough already—
the perfume, all the help with the bike."

Joe lifted a shoulder. "Don't look at me. It was Ruby
and Ben's idea."

"Here," Ruby said, holding out a neatly wrapped
parcel.

Hannah accepted the parcel. "You guys," she said,
shaking her head in admonishment.

Ruby moved closer and Hannah could feel the little girl watching and waiting for her reaction. Hannah
eased the tape free of the paper and didn't have to feign
appreciation when she saw what they'd bought her: a
pair of beautiful leather motorcycle gloves, complete
with high-end carbon knuckle guards.

"Thank you. These are wonderful."

Ruby looked at her brother. "You were right," she

said, resigned. She turned back to Hannah to explain. "I wanted to get you more perfume but Ben thought you'd prefer these."

"Perfume would have been lovely but these are perfect, Ben. Thank you."

Ben's cheeks were a fiery red as he shuffled his feet, the picture of teen discomfort. "It was just an idea, that's all."

"A great idea. I love them. They're miles better than my old gloves."

She ceremoniously picked up her old ones and flung them onto the workbench at the back of the garage. Ruby and Ben both looked thrilled by the gesture. Joe simply watched, his face utterly impassive. She flicked him a quick glance, then looked away again.

"I have something for you guys, too. Nothing fancy, but I thought it might be fun for you to keep track of where I'm going on a map."

Hannah collected the small bag of supplies she'd put together and offered it to Ruby.

"There are some pushpins in there and a big map of Australia. I figured each time one of my postcards arrive you and Ben could stick a pin in the map and keep track of my progress."

Ruby clutched the bag to her chest. "Thank you."

Hannah sank to one knee and opened her arms and Ruby stepped into them for one last hug.

"You've been great. The best apprentice ever," Hannah said.

Ruby sniffed and nodded her head. With a shuddery sigh she stepped back, using her forearm to wipe her eyes.

Hannah glanced at Ben but his body language told

her he wouldn't welcome a hug the way his sister had. She held out her clenched hand instead and they bumped fists.

She flicked another look at Joe. He was staring at the ground, his mouth a firm, straight line. There was no way she was hugging or kissing him in front of his kids. There was nothing platonic or friendly about their relationship.

Because she didn't know how to say goodbye to him, she zipped her jacket and reached for her new gloves.

"I guess I'd better get this show on the road."

Her mother came out of the house, a wad of tissues clutched in one hand.

"Don't start, or you'll set me off," Hannah said. "I'll call you from Albury, okay?"

"Don't forget. And I want weekly updates."

"I promise."

Hannah flexed her hands in her new gloves, smiling to show Ben and Ruby how much she appreciated them. She slid her helmet on, pushing the visor up. "Okay. I'm as ready as I'll ever be."

Ruby moved closer to her father, reaching for his hand. Hannah turned the key to start the bike. The engine fired and she rocked the bike off its stand.

She was acutely aware that she and Joe had barely exchanged a word. She had no idea what he was thinking or feeling, if the uncertainty and regret she felt were one-sided or shared. For a moment she hesitated, gripped by the urge to say something, anything to connect with him.

But he wasn't rushing forward to talk to her. Hadn't even offered her his hand or his best wishes.

She twisted the throttle, and the bike rolled out of

the garage and into the street. Joe and his kids and her mother walked after her. She paused for a moment, one foot on the ground, and glanced over her shoulder. She lifted her hand in a last farewell. Her mother mopped at her tears with the tissues. Ben stood off to one side, a frown on his face. Ruby had turned her face into her father's belly, her arms wrapped around his waist. Joe's attention was on his daughter. He didn't so much as glance up.

Well, I guess that answers that question. No good-byes, no regrets. Time to haul ass, Napier.

She turned away and eased the throttle open. The bike took off down the street. She told herself not to look back again, but she couldn't resist a glance in the rearview mirror.

Her mother was turning toward her house, but Joe and Ruby and Ben still stood watching her. For the first time she saw emotion on Joe's face—disappointment, frustration, regret. Then the road demanded her attention and she turned the corner and they were gone.

For a moment her grip eased on the throttle and the bike slowed.

He feels it, too. The pull of what might have been.

But she'd made her decision. As she'd told her mother last night, she wasn't prepared to gamble with her heart again, and she was at the beginning of a lifelong dream. There was nothing to do but look forward.

Joe went over and over those last few minutes with Hannah during the following weeks. He should have said something. Given her his best wishes. Made a joke, at the very least. Instead, he'd stood there and let her ride away.

He told himself it was for the best. Safer. Easier. But when he came home at night and saw the garage door at the Napier house firmly down, he remembered what it had been like to make Hannah laugh, and how soft her skin was and how kind she'd been to his children. It was the same at work—every time a slim, brown-haired woman walked into The Watering Hole his gut got tight, then he'd blink and realize it wasn't Hannah and that she wasn't coming back anytime soon.

For the first time in two years Beth was absent from his dreams. There was only Hannah, her body firm and warm under his hands, her taste in his mouth. Teasing him, then walking away. Or staring at him expectantly, waiting for him to say or do the one thing that would make her stay.

The first postcard arrived on the Wednesday after she left. It was from Eden and showed a fishing fleet sailing out into the ocean, an arc of golden sand marking the shore. Hannah wrote that the weather was fine and that she'd stopped on the way north to help a couple with a broken-down car on the freeway. She missed Ruby and her new gloves were the best she'd ever owned. Lastly, she asked Ruby to say hello to everyone for her.

Ruby read it out loud three times before solemnly pressing the first pin into the map. She'd mounted it on the cork bulletin board on her bedroom wall and every time he tucked her into bed he saw that lone pushpin and thought of Hannah.

"Do you think she's thinking of us the way we're thinking of her, Daddy?" Ruby asked exactly one week after Hannah had departed.

"She sent you a postcard. That means she must be thinking of you," he said.

Ruby stared hard at the map. "Do you think she'll be back by Christmas? I really want her to be home for my birthday."

"I don't know, sweetheart. It's three months away, but Australia is a big country, there's a lot for her to see. You probably shouldn't bank on it."

He felt like a complete fraud since he'd been doing the exact same calculations in his head. How long till she reached Queensland? How long till she'd traversed the Northern Territory? How much time to explore Central Australia? When would she head west? And, finally, when would she make her way home again?

Might as well ask how long a piece of string was. Part of the appeal of this trip for Hannah was the freedom of the road, the ability to move at her own pace and explore at her leisure. She'd explained it all to him over their one-and-only dinner, her eyes alight with excitement and anticipation. If she found somewhere she loved, she planned to stay awhile, get some casual work, get to know the locals. If she heard about an amazing place that wasn't on her route, she'd divert and go find it. This was her dream. He was just the idiot she'd left behind.

The second postcard arrived like clockwork a week after the first. Sydney this time, a classic shot incorporating the Harbour Bridge and the Opera House. Ruby pressed another pin into the map. He told himself that soon he would stop thinking about Hannah. They'd had one date and shared a handful of kisses. It was stupid to be so hung up on someone and something that had never really happened.

But it seemed he was destined to be stupid. He

wanted her, and her being gone didn't seem to make a damn bit of difference to that fact.

Three weeks after her departure from Melbourne, Hannah stood on the beach in Townsville in Northern Queensland. A strong offshore breeze blew the hair off her face and pressed her clothes against her body. She squinted her eyes against the brightness of the rising sun and told herself how lucky she was to be here, seeing this, experiencing this moment.

After a few minutes, she started back to the campground where she'd pitched her tent last night. It was going to be another stinker of a day, with the mercury predicted to hit forty degrees. The beach would soon be filled with tourists and locals keen to claim their patch of sand. If she wanted to, she could put on her swimsuit and take a towel and a book down to the water to join them. There was no work to get to, no one else's needs or desires to consider. She could laze the day away and work on her already impressive tan.

The problem was, she didn't want to. She'd woken this morning with Joe's face in her mind and her hands clenching the fabric of her sleeping bag. This was supposed to be her dream, but every day she'd had to remind herself how lucky she was, how beautiful the landscape was and how much she'd looked forward to finally seeing all the places she'd circled on the map over the years.

Her heart wasn't in it. That was the truth of the matter. Her dream had changed.

The realization had sat like a lead weight in the pit of her belly for the past few days. Her heart—her stupid, inconvenient, badly house-trained heart—was back in

Melbourne, fixated on a tall, dark-haired man with sad eyes and the most incredible smile in the world.

Every postcard she'd sent to Ruby had taken her hours to compose. She'd told Ruby about her adventures and the people she'd met. She'd made jokes at her own expense and included tidbits of history and local lore. And all the while, the only thing she wanted to write was: *Does he miss me? Does he think about me? Does he feel the same way I do?*

She had no idea when she'd become so involved, so enmeshed with Joe Lawson. Somewhere between him chewing her out for working on her noisy bike at night and the moment she'd turned the corner and left him standing in the street with his children on either side of him. It was crazy. They'd had one date, shared one meal. She didn't know half the things she used to think were important to know about someone. His birthday, whether his childhood had been happy, what political party he voted for. And yet she knew how to make him laugh. She knew he felt deeply and loved with everything he had to give. She knew he was a great dad, even though he suffered doubts over some of his decisions. She knew he was honest, even if the truth was sometimes hard to hear. She knew that he was as scared to love again and trust another person as she was, even if he was motivated by very different reasons. And she knew that when she'd ridden away from him and Ruby and Ben she'd made what was possibly the biggest mistake of her life.

She stared at her meager campsite—the tent, her bedroll, her rucksack of clothing. She turned and squinted toward the rising sun. She thought about the years she'd planned this adventure. Then she knelt and began to pull the tent pegs from the ground. Within twenty minutes she had the tent packed away. Half an hour later her worldly goods were once again strapped to the back of her motorcycle. She didn't look back as she rode out of Townsville.

Chapter 10

Joe woke early. He rubbed his tired eyes and stared at the ceiling. So much for the blissful escape of sleep. Hannah came to him every night, and every night he wrestled with his subconscious for control of his dreams. If he could make his dream go the way he wanted it to, if he could just hold her and say the things he wanted to say… But he never seemed to find the words to stop Hannah from walking away.

He had half a dozen sleeping tablets left from the time after Beth died. If he'd wanted to, he could have taken one and slept the night through, deep and dreamless. That was the worst part of the whole mess, because, as tired and irritated and frustrated as he felt dreaming of chasing Hannah and never catching her every night, he'd choose the dreams over nothing any day. He knew it made him a tragic, laughable figure of the highest order, but there it was. If he couldn't have the real Hannah, he'd settle for a dream of her, even if it was driving him slowly crazy.

You pathetic bastard.

He glanced at the alarm clock. Just after 6:00 a.m. Great. The kids had stayed at his mother's last night since it was a Friday and he'd had to work late due to staffing problems at the pub. He'd arranged to pick them up at midday, which left him with a whole six hours to fill.

There was laundry to do—there was always laundry—and a host of other domestic chores. Maybe if he really threw himself into the housework he'd stop his mind from running in a continuous loop, thinking about Hannah then reminding himself how pointless it was.

He rolled out of bed and reached for his jeans. He smoothed a hand over his hair as he walked up the hallway to the kitchen. Pizza boxes were stacked beside the counter, even though he'd asked Ben to put them out at least twice during the week. He flicked the kettle on and picked the boxes up, making a mental note to have a word with Ben about doing his chores.

Barefoot and bare chested, he made his way to the carport where the recycle bin lived, then walked to collect the newspaper from the mailbox. He was scanning the front page when he heard the low rumble of a motorbike engine in the distance. His head came up and his muscles tensed.

Which was stupid, because there was no way it was Hannah.

The engine noise grew louder as he started toward the house. He glanced over his shoulder, his pace slowing. Sure enough, a motorbike turned into the street.

His hand tightened around the newspaper. He stopped in his tracks and turned and stared as the bike slowed and then stopped in front of his house.

It was her. It had to be.

He barely stopped himself from breaking into a run as he made his way down the driveway, dropping the newspaper on the concrete behind him. Hannah slid off her helmet, shaking out her hair. He stopped in front of the bike.

"You're back," he said, then gave himself a mental kick. Talk about stating the obvious.

"Yeah."

She dismounted and placed her helmet on the seat. He couldn't take his eyes from the long line of her jeans-clad legs. She was so bloody sexy. How had he ever kept his hands off her?

Belatedly it occurred to him that something pretty serious must have happened to bring her home so early.

"Is everything all right?" he asked. "Is Robyn okay?"

"She's fine. I came back because I forgot something."

There was a look in her eyes….

"What did you forget?"

She held his gaze and stepped closer, so close the front of her leather jacket brushed his bare chest.

"This," she said. "I forgot to do this."

She reached up and curled a hand around the back of his neck and pressed a kiss to his lips. Her body leaned into his, the leather of her jacket supple and warm against his skin. For a moment he was passive, blown away by her return, by the fact that she was kissing him, that this was real. Three weeks of dreams. Three weeks of calling himself an idiot for letting her go without even trying to get her to stay...

Hunger and lust and relief rose inside him in equal measure. He wrapped his arms around her, sliding his palms across her back, hauling her close. Her mouth opened under his.

She tasted of sunlight and ocean breezes. She tasted like salvation, a new beginning. Hope.

He slid his hands into her hair, grabbing handfuls of it as he angled her head to deepen their kiss. She spread her palms flat against his back and pressed her length against him. She felt so good. So warm and alive.

After long, breathless moments they broke apart to stare at each other.

"Come inside?" he asked.

She flicked a glance toward his house. He knew what she was thinking, what she was worried about.

"The kids are with Mom."

She huffed out a sigh of relief. "Thank God, because I don't think I can wait a minute longer."

He laughed, loving the boldness of her. When had Hannah ever given him less than the truth? "Come on." He slid his hand down her arm to weave his fingers with hers.

He started toward the house, towing her after him. His mind sprinted ahead to the bedroom, imagining peeling her out of her clothes, seeing her for the first time, exploring her soft curves. His body swelled, growing even harder. He quickened his pace, almost dragging her over the threshold.

"Where's the fire?" She laughed.

"I'll show you in about ten seconds."

Then they were in his bedroom and she was standing in front of him, a smile on her face.

"If you had any idea how many times I've imagined being here like this with you…" she said.

He reached for the tab on her jacket zipper.

"In *my* fantasies, you're always wearing a lot less," he said.

Her smile turned into an outright grin as he tugged her zipper down and pushed her jacket open and down her arms. Underneath she was wearing a tight-fitting black tank top. He stared at her breasts for a moment, simply appreciating the sweet perfection of her.

"You're good for my ego," she said.

"Baby, I haven't even started."

She laughed and reached for the hem of her top, pulling it over her head in one smooth move. Her eyes locked with his, she reached behind her back for her bra clasp.

"Next time, we'll go slow. But I've been thinking about you, about this, for too long to wait," she said.

He didn't respond because he couldn't. Her breasts were bare and all rational thought fled his mind. He ached to taste her, to shape her with his hands. Instead, he reached for the stud on his jeans. The soft denim gave easily and within seconds he was pushing his jeans down his legs, his erection springing free.

"Oh, man," she said, her gaze on his groin. Her movements became frenzied as she tugged at her belt and shoved her own jeans down her legs. She kicked her shoes off and at last they came together, skin to skin, mouth to mouth.

"So good," she murmured against his lips.

"Tell me about it."

He slid his hands onto her backside and snugged her hips against his, his erection pressed against her belly. She made an approving noise and circled her hips. He ducked his head and kissed the smooth valley between her breasts, scattering kisses across the curves until he found a nipple and pulled it into his mouth. She shivered, then her hand slid between their bodies and down his belly until she was curling her hand around him.

He lost track of time for a while. The world became only her and him and soon they were on the bed, touching one another, exploring, encouraging, discovering.

"Joe," she whispered after a while, her body trembling in his arms. "Please."

He was only too happy to oblige. He took a moment to protect them both, then he slid inside her. She made a small, satisfied noise in the back of her throat. He clenched his hands into the sheets on either side of her body. For seconds neither of them moved, both of them marking the moment. Then he shifted his hips and she moved with him and soon they found their rhythm.

Her hair was spread across the pillow, her eyes dreamy and unfocused. He kissed her, riding high inside her, feeling how much pleasure she took from his body. She started to pant, her hands clutching at his back and his butt, one leg wrapping around his waist as she urged him on.

Pleasure rushed through him and he tried to hold off, but it had been so long and he'd been dreaming of this for weeks. He pulled back, wanting to ensure her pleasure, determined to make it last. She shook her head against the pillow, her hands on his hips urging him to move harder, faster, deeper. He felt her quiver around him. Her head dropped back, then her body arched as she found her release. His breath rushed out as he pressed his face into the soft skin of her neck. He shuddered as his own climax hit him, one hand gripping her hip, the other lifting her so he could bury himself deep inside her.

He dropped his head onto the pillow beside her for a few beats afterward, his breath coming fast, a bead of sweat trickling down his spine. Hannah smoothed a hand around his shoulder to the nape of his neck, her fingers kneading the muscles there. He felt her belly muscles tense as she lifted her head to press a kiss to his shoulder. He closed his eyes, swamped by a swell of emotion. It had been a long time since he'd held anyone or been held.

"I missed you," he said.

"I could tell."

He lifted his head so he could see her face. She was smiling, but her eyes were serious. He curved a hand around her cheek and caressed the soft skin of her temple with his thumb.

Thank God she came back.

She lifted a hand and traced his lips with a finger.

"You have the best smile. When I first saw it my knees literally went weak."

"When I first saw you, I thought you were a man," he said.

She gasped and punched him on the shoulder. He laughed and caught her hand.

"Let me finish. I thought you were a man for about half a second. Then you stood and turned around and I realized I'd made a huge mistake and I couldn't get out of there fast enough, because I was afraid you'd bust me staring at your breasts like a randy schoolboy."

"No one would ever mistake you for a schoolboy. Believe me."

He kissed her, and things soon became heated all over again. Afterward, she fell asleep in his arms, her head a welcome weight on his shoulder. He must have drifted off as well because he woke to a gentle nudge in the ribs, finally opening his eyes when Hannah bit his shoulder gently.

"Wake up, sleepyhead," she said. "What time did you say you had to pick Ben and Ruby up?"

He rolled on top of her so quickly that she could only laugh and weakly try to fend him off.

"Midday. And I was only sleeping so I could recover from being woman-handled twice in a row," he said.

"Well, it's eleven. And if you're complaining about the woman-handling, there's a really quick and easy cure."

"I'm not complaining. Not by a long shot. Handle away," he said.

"You have no idea how tempted I am. But there is no way I'm making you late for picking up your kids. Not exactly the best way to start out," she said.

She rolled toward the edge of the bed. He watched as she stood, the long muscles of her legs rippling. If he was about ten years younger, he'd drag her back onto the mattress and make it three for three. But he wasn't, and she was right about his kids. For the first time he allowed himself to think beyond the here and now and the demands of his body.

"Ruby will jump out of her skin when she hears you're back," he said.

"Yeah? I wondered if she might have gotten over being a grease monkey while I was away."

"Nope. She's been bugging me to show her how to change the oil in the Mazda."

"Really?" She looked delighted.

He watched as she pulled on her underwear.

"How do you think she'll feel about this?" she asked, her gesture taking in the rumpled bed and him lying in it.

He frowned, thinking about how his kids might react to the news he was dating Hannah. Ruby adored her, but that didn't mean she'd warm to the idea that Hannah was dating her daddy. He'd learned enough about the possessiveness of women over the years to know that. As for Ben… Joe had no idea how his son might react. Things had been better between them since the shoplifting incident, but Ben was still not the open, happy boy he'd once been. Maybe some of that could be laid at the door of hormones and puberty, but Joe figured a lot of it was about Beth dying. Was Ben ready to accept that his father might want and need another woman in his life?

"I don't know. This isn't something we've been through before."

"I kind of guessed," Hannah said.

"That obvious, huh?"

"No. But I knew there hadn't been anyone since Beth."

His wife's name seemed to hang in the room for a long beat. He shifted on the bed. "Probably the best thing for us to do is take things slowly," he said.

She nodded. "Sure."

"Maybe you should come out for dinner with us tonight. Let the kids get used to you being around again."

She smiled.

"That sounds good."

She zipped her jeans and tugged her tank top on. He stared at her, barely able to believe that the past few hours had really happened, that she was here. That she'd come back for him. For a moment, all his doubts and uncertainties fell away.

Hannah was home. The rest they could make up as they went along.

Hannah was nervous as she got ready that night. Sweaty palms, queasy stomach, shaking hands—the works, basically. All for a casual dinner at The Watering Hole.

The thing was, she'd thought about Joe and his kids the whole of her journey south. She'd thought about the way Ruby looked at her with so much trust, and she'd remembered the wary curiosity and interest in Ben's face when he'd worked with her on the Thunderbird. They were both good kids. She enjoyed their company, and she hoped they enjoyed hers. But the fact remained that her parenting experience was zero and they'd lost their mother in shocking and sudden circumstances just over two years ago. If things worked out between her and Joe, she would be stepping into some pretty big shoes, and it would be foolish to assume that everything would go smoothly.

She pressed a hand to her nervous stomach. She couldn't believe she was standing in her mother's house thinking about becoming a stepmom. It seemed so presumptuous.

Then she thought about the way Joe had looked standing in the street this morning wearing nothing but his low-slung jeans. The look on his face, the hope in his eyes... This was about more than sex. This was real. And more than anything she wanted it to work.

Her toes curled in her boots as she thought about the way he'd made love to her. He'd been insatiable, attentive, passionate, demanding—everything she'd ever fantasized about and more. He'd made her feel beautiful and sexy and precious.

Which was why she'd come home, after all. And why she was standing in her bedroom freaking out over having dinner with his children.

A knock sounded on the door and her mother popped her head in.

"I thought you might need a little jacket or something in case it got cold," her mother said. She offered a black woolen shrug to Hannah. "This would look so nice with your jeans."

Her mother knew Hannah had about a million jackets she could wear to ward off the coolness of an October night. The truth was, her mother was excited and she wanted in on the action. She'd burst into tears when she'd seen Hannah on the doorstep, her hands pressed to her chest.

"I knew you'd come back! I knew you were too smart to throw away something so good," Robyn had said, throwing her arms around Hannah.

Now, she helped Hannah into the shrug and turned

her to face the mirror. "There. Doesn't that look nice? Not too overwhelming, but it will keep your arms warm."

Hannah met her mom's eyes in the mirror. "Thanks for being so patient with me, Mom."

"I had a feeling about Joe the moment I met him," Robyn said. "He's a good man. I think you can make each other happy."

"I hope so."

"And those children need you so much, Hannah."

"They have to get used to their dad dating me first."

"I'm sure they'll be fine with it. It's not like you're some stranger he's bringing into the home."

"Maybe. Anyway, we're going to take it easy to start with."

Her mother frowned. "What does that mean?"

"We're not going to ram it down their throats. Like tonight—I'm meeting them for dinner as a friend, that's all."

Her mother's frown deepened.

"You mean you're going to lie to them?"

"No. We're going to give them a chance to get used to the idea of me being around, then we're going to tell them."

"But they're already used to you being around. You live next door. I don't see why he needs to lie to them about you."

"He's looking out for his kids, Mom. What if things don't work out between us? He doesn't want his kids investing in something that might not go the distance."

Her mother made a rude noise. "You gave up your dream for him, Hannah. You traveled halfway across the country for him. What more does the man want?"

Her mother looked so fierce, as though she was ready to wade into battle on Hannah's behalf.

"It's okay. Really. I understand his kids have to come first."

Her mother eyed her for a long moment, then she shrugged. "All right. I just hope for your sake that this isn't a sign of something else."

"Like what?"

"There's a reason the man hasn't dated anyone else in two years, Hannah. He obviously loved his wife very much."

"Yes, he did. But she's dead, Mom. And Joe deserves some happiness in his life."

"I didn't say he didn't, darling."

Hannah growled in the back of her throat. "Unbelievable. Five minutes ago you were ready to marry the guy yourself," she said.

"Forget I said anything. I'm sure you and Joe will sort things out. You've managed to muddle your way through up until now without me sticking my oar in."

Hannah grabbed her purse.

"Fine. I'm going now," she said, her tone a little on the sharp side.

Her mother stepped forward to brush some lint off her shoulder. "I want you to have everything you deserve, sweetheart. That's all."

Hannah softened as she saw the concern in her mother's eyes. "Don't wait up for me, okay?"

"I won't."

Joe and his children were waiting for her at a corner table when she arrived. Ruby was sitting on the edge of her chair and she shot to her feet like a jack-in-the-box the moment she saw Hannah. Her small body rocketed into Hannah's with force, her arms wrapping around Hannah's waist.

"Hey," Hannah said, bending to return Ruby's embrace.

"You're back," Ruby said.

"That's right."

"And you're not going away again?"

"Not that I know of."

Ruby's arms tightened even further and Hannah had to blink back tears. It wasn't until that moment that she'd realized exactly how much she'd missed her little helper.

"I missed you, too, sweetheart," she said.

Ben had remained with his father, but he offered her a shy smile when she and Ruby finally made their way to the table. Ruby practically sat in her lap as Hannah explained that she'd come home because she'd been homesick. Every time she met Joe's eyes she flashed to the hours they'd spent in his bed that morning and had to look away again, sure that what was going on between them must be obvious even to the uninformed eyes of two prepubescents.

By contrast, Joe was the most relaxed she'd ever seen him, his blue eyes warm with good humor, his mouth curved at the corners as though he was constantly on the verge of smiling. She very badly wanted to lean across the table and kiss him or simply slide her hand into his. For the first time she had an inkling of how hard it was going to be to play his public friend while being his private lover.

"I thought you'd planned your trip for years," Ben said, his forehead wrinkled with a frown. "I thought it was your big dream."

Hannah met Joe's eyes for a moment before looking away. "It was. But it turned out that I'd outgrown that old dream. I realized I wanted to be here more than I wanted to be there."

Ben bounced a glance between her and Joe, a wary look on his face. "Seems like a waste of a good trip."

Hannah stirred in her seat, sure that any second now Ben was going to ask a more pointed question.

"Can I have French fries *and* a pizza?" Ruby asked.

The conversation shifted to food and Hannah let out a silent sigh of relief. Under the table, she felt a nudge as Joe's leg slid between hers. It wasn't sexual, more reassuring. She pressed her leg closer, letting him know she appreciated the contact.

Despite the awkwardness of having to keep a close guard on herself in regard to her behavior toward Joe, she enjoyed the meal. Ruby and Ben were bright, articulate kids, and they enjoyed teasing and being teased by their father. She found herself laughing a lot and copping her fair share of mock abuse and razzing.

She'd thought the evening was going really well until Joe and Ruby left to check out the cake display and Ben turned and nailed her with a disconcertingly direct stare.

"Are you and my dad going out with each other?"

Hannah blinked, her mind a complete blank for a long, long moment. She'd always been a crappy liar, one of the many reasons why she preferred sticking to the truth. She felt particularly bad lying to Joe's child. No matter what she'd said to her mother about Joe protecting them from the potential failure of their relationship, it felt wrong.

"Wow. Where did that come from?" she finally said.

"I know you like him," Ben said. "You look at him all the time."

Hannah could feel warmth climbing into her cheeks. Good grief, was she that obvious?

"I think your dad's a really good guy. But we're just friends at the moment," she lied.

It was what Joe had asked her to do, after all.

Ben stared at her for a moment longer before shrugging. "Okay. Whatever."

The wrinkle between his eyebrows relaxed, however. He believed her. And he was relieved.

Useless to pretend that it didn't sting a little to know he was glad she wasn't seeing his father. She and Ben hadn't gotten off to the best of starts, but she'd thought they'd developed a friendship during their sessions with the Thunderbird.

His mother died, Hannah. Of course he doesn't want to replace her. Get a grip.

She shook the moment off. This was why she and Joe had agreed to keep things low-key initially, after all—to give the kids time to adjust.

When they walked out to the street after their meal, Joe let the kids go ahead and caught her hand in his in the darkness.

"How're you doing?" he asked quietly.

"Good. How about you?"

"All good."

She took a deep breath. "You should probably know—Ben asked if we were dating when you and Ruby went to check out the cakes."

There was a short silence.

"What did you say?"

"That we were just friends."

"Thanks for that."

She shrugged. "It's what we agreed to."

They were nearing the car and he released her hand. She was surprised by the sense of loss she felt.

"Well, I'll see you guys later," she said.

"Can I come over tomorrow to work on the bike?" Ruby asked.

"Sure, sweetheart."

Ruby kissed her goodbye. Ben gave her a wary nod. Joe raised a hand in farewell.

She walked to her bike and took her helmet from the storage box beneath the seat. Joe's Mazda pulled away from the curb and drove off. She stared after his fading taillights.

So. Their first family dinner, if it could be called that. She wasn't sure if she should label it a success or not. She'd known she'd be taking on a lot, dating a man with children, but she hadn't expected to feel so…left out.

It's day one, Hannah. Give it a chance. This is new for everybody.

She knew it was true, but it didn't change the way she felt. When she got home, Joe had slipped a note beneath the garage door.

Meet me out front at 10:30?

She had no way of replying, but it wasn't as though she was going to say no. She'd driven thousands of miles to be with him. She'd take whatever she could get.

She'd been waiting for five minutes when she heard Joe's front door close later that night. She straightened from her position leaning against the tailgate of his car. He smiled when he saw her.

"You came."

"Yep."

He stepped closer and slid his arms around her. They kissed long and slow, taking their time, but soon hands were gliding over backs and breasts and hips and bellies.

"You taste good," Joe whispered near her ear.

"So do you."

They fooled around a little more until they were both hot and bothered. Finally Joe broke their kiss and let his forehead rest against hers.

"The kids go to school at eight-thirty on Monday," he said. She could hear the frustration in his voice.

She smiled. Any doubts she had faded away in the face of his very evident desire for her. This was right. Not perfect, but definitely good. They would make it work.

"You wouldn't happen to be setting up a booty call, would you, Mr. Lawson?"

"I'm interested in a lot more than your booty."

She kissed the line of his jaw. "Monday seems like a long way away."

"Tell me about it."

He tucked her hair behind her ear, his fingers caressing her neck.

"Thank you for tonight. For your patience. I know it's not easy—"

She pressed her fingers against his lips. "Don't. You don't have to apologize or explain. This is going to be tough for Ben and Ruby. I get that."

"Yeah. But maybe we need to rethink holding off on

telling them. Ben's obviously picked up on something."
He was frowning, clearly troubled.

"Whatever you think is best," she said.

He focused on something over her shoulder, his gaze
distant. "It's so hard to get a read on him lately. I have
no idea what's going on in his head half the time."

She could feel the uncertainty in his body. He was
such a good man. So determined to look out for his
kids, even if it meant sacrificing his own happiness
and comfort.

She pressed her palm flat against his chest. "We'll
work it out."

His gaze returned to her, warm with appreciation.
"Have I mentioned yet how happy I am that you came
home?"

There was a serious note to his voice. Suddenly she
felt very exposed, very vulnerable. As unspoken decla-
rations went, returning early from a lifelong dream trip
so you could get busy with a man was right up there.
Not much Joe Lawson didn't know about how she felt
about him now.

"It's good to be back," she said, mostly to fill the
silence.

"Hannah." Joe lifted her hand to his mouth and
kissed her knuckles.

Her chest seemed to swell with emotion as she looked
into his eyes. She waited for him to say something more,
but he didn't. Instead, he lowered his head and kissed
her again.

"You drive me crazy, you know that?" he said.

For the second time that night she felt a stab of disappointment. She wasn't sure what she'd expected or

wanted Joe to say. That he loved her? It was too early for that. For both of them. Right?

She pushed her stupid thoughts aside. All that mattered right now was that she was in Joe's arms, and he was kissing her as though his life depended on it.

Chapter 11

Joe tried to gauge his son's mood as they ate breakfast the next morning. Ben was quiet, chewing away at his cereal mechanically, his gaze fixed on the tabletop. Joe cleared his throat, determined to get this right with his children.

"So how are things at school these days? Everything good?"

Ben shrugged a shoulder. "It's okay."

"Any new friends?"

"A couple."

"Hey, that's great." Joe winced. He sounded like a freaking game show host, stiff and artificial.

This is bullshit. Just tell him the truth and deal with whatever happens.

His gut said it was the right decision. He pushed his cereal bowl away and focused on his son. "There's something I wanted to talk to you about."

Ben fiddled with his spoon. "What did I do wrong now?"

"You didn't do anything wrong." Man, he hated that his son's default position was to assume he was in trouble. Had he really been riding him that hard? "This is about me and Hannah."

Ben's gaze flew to his face. "What about her?"

"Well, she and I have gotten to know each other. And it turns out we both like each other. So, we've decided to start dating." He sounded like a game show host again, but he had no idea how he was supposed to sound when discussing his sex life with his thirteen-year-old son.

Ben's eyes burned with intensity as he stared across the table. "What about Mom? Don't you love her anymore?"

"Of course I still love her. But it's been two years, mate, and sometimes it's nice to have someone to go to the movies with and dinner and stuff."

Ben's lip curled. "You're not going to the movies with Hannah. I'm not stupid. You're *doing it* with her."

"We're dating," Joe said firmly. "I wanted to give you guys a chance to get used to Hannah being back before I told you about us, but she told me you asked her about it last night."

"Yeah, and she said you were just friends."

"Because I asked her to. Like I said, I wanted you kids to have a chance to get used to her being around first."

Ben stood. "Is that all?"

"Do you have any questions? Anything you want to talk about?" Joe asked.

Ben simply stared at him for a long moment. "No."

There was no mistaking the anger and hurt in his face.

"Ben…"

"I've got homework to do."

Ben strode for the hall. Just before he exited the kitchen he ducked his head and dashed his forearm across his eyes. Then he was gone.

Shit. Joe sat back in his chair for a second. That had gone well. Not.

He sighed, wondering if he should go after Ben or give him time to cool down and vent and cry a little.

The doorbell rang, the sound echoing through the house, and he pushed himself to his feet.

"I'll get it," Ruby called. He heard the thump of her feet on the floor as she ran to the door.

He was halfway up the hallway when he heard Hannah's voice.

"Hey there, grease monkey. I came over to see if you wanted to get started early."

A smile curved Hannah's mouth when he entered the entrance hall and she saw him.

"Hi."

Before he could respond, Ben strode between them and pointed a shaking finger at her.

"You're a liar. A bloody liar," he said.

"Ben!" Joe said, startled by the belligerence in his boy's voice.

Ben shouldered his way rudely past Hannah and out the front door. Joe made eye contact with Hannah.

"Sorry." Then he went after his son.

"What's going on?" he heard Ruby say as he took the porch steps two at a time.

Ben hadn't gone far. He stood beside the mailbox, his head bowed, his shoulders hunched. Braced, Joe guessed, for his father's disapproval.

Joe stopped in front of him. "I asked Hannah to keep what was happening between us private. That's why she told you we were just friends last night."

"Then you're a liar, too."

"Yes, I guess I am, in this one case. But do you understand why I made that choice?"

Ben hunched a shoulder.

"Mate. Look at me."

Ben slowly lifted his head. His face was filled with so much misery Joe's chest ached.

"This doesn't change anything between you and me and Ruby. It doesn't mean I love your mom or any of you any less. It only means that Hannah and I are going to spend some time together."

Ben broke eye contact and returned his gaze to the ground.

"Now, I want you to come apologize to Hannah."

Ben stiffened. "No way. I didn't do anything wrong. She's the one who lied to me."

"Because I asked her to. I thought you liked Hannah."

"That was before she was screwing you."

Joe flinched at the ugliness in Ben's tone. Ben shot him a half afraid, half defiant look, clearly expecting his father to come down on him like a ton of bricks.

Joe leveled a finger at him. "I don't want to hear

that kind of language from you. Especially not toward women, and especially not toward Hannah. She's been a good friend to our family."

"She's not my friend. You can't make me like her."

"No, but I can make you apologize. Right now."

"Joe."

He turned to find Hannah standing behind him, a concerned frown on her face.

"It's okay," she said.

"Ben needs to apologize to you."

"He's allowed to have his feelings," she said. "I understand."

Joe wavered, uncertain if he was setting a bad precedent by letting Ben get away with such disrespect. Hannah had a point, however. He'd brought much of this on himself by trying to protect his kids. And Ben did have a right to his feelings.

"I want you to go to your room," he said to Ben.

"Fine."

Ben speared Hannah with a burning look as he strode past her.

"I'm sorry. That was my fault," Joe said.

"It's all right. I'd be angry if I was in his shoes, too."

Ruby appeared on the doorstep, a frown on her face.

"I need to talk to Ruby," he said.

"I think she's heard enough to have a fair idea of what's going on."

He shook his head. "What a screwup."

"Yeah, well, it could have been worse."

"How so?"

"They could have walked in when we were going at it like monkeys yesterday morning."

He couldn't help but laugh. "There is that."

"Let me know if there's anything I can do, okay?" she said.

"Will do."

She gave him a small smile before turning to wave to Ruby and walking away. He watched her for a moment, admiring the swing of her hips.

Then he took a deep breath and went to talk to his daughter.

Later that night he fielded a call from his mother.

"I thought you should know that Ben phoned and asked if he could come live with me," she announced.

Joe swore.

"That's not going to solve anything," his mother said.

"Thank you, I know that." He took a deep breath and let it out again. His mother hadn't done anything to earn his anger. "Sorry."

"What's going on? Did you two have a fight or something?"

"I've started dating someone. Ben doesn't approve." He filled his mother in briefly.

"Oh, Joe. You've made a real mess of things, haven't you?"

He bit his tongue. She was only speaking the truth, after all.

"I'm open to suggestions," he said.

"Who is this woman, anyway? How come I haven't heard about her before?"

"She lives next door."

"The girl Ruby has taken such a shine to?"

"She's hardly a girl."

"She sounds very young to me from what Ruby has told me."

"She's in her late twenties." He was thirty-six. He figured it was a respectable age difference, nothing to get outraged over. Certainly he'd never given it a moment's thought.

"But she rides a motorcycle, is that right? And didn't she take off on some big road trip recently?"

"She came back. And she's hardly a biker moll. She's a mechanic and she's into restoring old bikes."

"I see."

"I thought you'd be happy I was seeing someone."

"I am. But it's not like you only have yourself to think about. It's not enough that you're attracted to this woman. You have children to consider."

No shit. He rubbed the bridge of his nose.

"I know all this, Mom. The kids already have a relationship with her. And I wouldn't have gotten them involved if this was just some fling."

"Well, that's good to hear. I only hope she feels the same way."

"What's that supposed to mean?"

His mother's sigh filtered down the line. "You're asking her to take on an awful lot, stepping into a ready-made family."

"Hannah knows who we are."

"And is she ready to become an instant mother to someone else's children?"

He tipped his head back and reached for patience.

It had all seemed so simple when Hannah had ridden back into his life yesterday. He'd been thinking about her so much, had been kicking himself for letting her go without saying anything, and it had felt right and good to take her to bed. But it hadn't taken long for reality to intrude.

As his mother said, he wasn't a man alone. He had two children who depended on him utterly for everything. And they had to come first, no matter what.

"Look, it's early days. All I know is that she's great with Ruby and she's been incredibly patient with Ben."

"And what happens when the novelty wears off and the going gets tough? Is she going to stick around?"

"She's not like that, Mom."

"I'm not saying she's a bad person, Joe. I'm just saying that you're asking her to take on a lot. And it's going to take a special kind of woman, a very generous woman, to do that."

He stared at the wall. It wasn't as though he'd never considered the issues his mother was bringing up. But he'd let desire and need override his common sense and caution.

Had that been a mistake?

He flashed to the hot and sweaty hours he'd spent in bed with Hannah the previous morning and the contentment and peace he'd found lying with her in his arms afterward. There hadn't been a doubt in his mind then. He had to hang on to that feeling, to that belief.

"Hannah *is* special," he said.

"I hope you're right. What do you want to do about Ben? And how is Ruby taking the news?"

"She couldn't be happier. She told me she'd been wishing for Hannah to be my girlfriend because she thought we were both lonely."

Despite everything, the memory brought a smile to his mouth. At least one of his kids was happy.

"Hmm. Out of the mouths of babes."

He decided to ignore the skepticism in his mother's tone.

"I'll talk to Ben," he said.

"Maybe he should come stay with me for a couple of days, let him cool down."

"No. We're a family. He can't opt out when it suits him. We have to work this through."

"Good to hear."

"Glad you approve of something," he said drily.

"Joe…"

"I know. And thanks for the call. I appreciate the heads-up. And the lecture."

"Anytime," his mother said, and he knew she was smiling.

They talked a little more before he ended the call. He sat for a moment, going over the conversation again in his mind. Then he pushed himself to his feet and made his way to Ben's room.

His son was lying on his bed, his iPod plugged into his ears. His eyes flicked toward Joe then away again.

"Could we talk for a minute?" Joe asked.

Ben ignored him. Joe walked to the bed and tugged the earphones from Ben's ears. "I asked you a question."

"I didn't hear you."

Joe decided to let the lie slide. "I just got off the phone with your grandmother. She told me you wanted to come stay with her."

"That's right."

Joe cocked his head and studied him for a moment.

"Is that really what you want? You don't want to be here with me and Ruby anymore?"

Ben shrugged, avoiding eye contact. "At least Nan doesn't lie to me."

"I've explained to you why I felt it was best to hold off on telling you and Ruby what was happening between me and Hannah. You're old enough to understand that there are different kinds of lies. If you tell a lie to hurt someone, or to cover up something bad, that's wrong. But what I did was to protect you and your sister."

Ben simply stared at him, unresponsive. Joe sighed. Clearly there would be no getting through to him tonight.

"Look, all I can say is that I love you kids and you're my first priority, always. I'm sorry if what I did hurt your feelings. But that doesn't mean you can milk this forever. You're not going to your grandmother's, okay?"

Ben looked as though he was going to say something for a moment, then he shrugged and reached for his earphones again. "You're the boss."

He stuck his earphones back in his ears and made a point of focusing on the football poster at the end of his bed.

Not the most satisfactory conversation Joe had ever had, but it would have to do. He couldn't force his son to feel one way or another. He would simply have to wait him out. Ben had liked Hannah before Joe had started dating her, and Joe was confident his son would come around eventually. It would take time, and patience. He crossed his fingers that Hannah was prepared to ride out the storm with him.

If she runs screaming for the hills, then you'll have your answer, won't you?

He told himself it was his mother's voice he was hearing in his head, advising caution, casting doubts. But the fact remained that most of what his mother had said was true: he was asking Hannah to take on a lot.

Two weeks later, Hannah waited on the front porch of Joe's house for him to return from dropping the kids at school. He was running a little late and she checked her watch. If she got the job she was interviewing for this afternoon, it would mean the end of their early-morning meetings.

She stared glumly out at the empty street. Well. They would have to find another way to spend time together without further upsetting the delicate balance in his household. So far, Ben had showed no sign of thawing toward her. She'd come over for dinner on the weekend and he'd steadfastly ignored her through the whole meal. On Tuesday night they were all supposed to go to the movies together, but Ben had claimed he had study group at a friend's place. And last night he'd answered the phone when she'd called and said not a word once he recognized her voice, simply passing the phone to Joe.

She was officially persona non grata where he was concerned, and as much as she told herself he was young and full of grief and entitled to his feelings, she wasn't immune to his tactics. It was hard to take pleasure in the time she spent with Joe and Ruby when she understood that at the same time she made Ben unhappy. She kept telling herself that it wasn't personal, that he'd feel this way about any woman Joe was dating, but that argument was wearing thinner and thinner.

She'd been hoping for some sign of a thaw by now. Anything—some eye contact, a mumbled word of greeting. Hell, she'd even take a belch if it sounded friendly enough. But Ben was sticking staunchly to his guns, with no sign of a cease-fire in sight.

The sound of a car engine brought her head up and she smiled as Joe pulled into the driveway.

"Sorry, I got held up with one of Ruby's teachers," he said as he exited the car.

He kissed her deeply, his palm curled around the back of her neck. She leaned against his broad chest, savoring the contact. This was the one thing in her world that was absolutely right: being with Joe, holding him, touching him, being touched by him. She'd never had a more considerate or passionate lover.

"You okay?" he asked when he broke the kiss.

"Yeah, of course."

The concern and warmth in his eyes made her chest hurt. Every time she saw him, he asked her the same question, his first thought for her and how she might be feeling. He already had the world on his shoulders, and yet he was prepared to take on her problems and doubts and fears, as well. He had a generous heart.

"As long as we haven't scared you off yet." He said it lightly, but she couldn't help wondering if he wasn't also fishing for reassurance. Did he think her feelings were so small and malleable that Ben's resistance would tip the balance out of his favor?

"I'm hard to scare. I thought you knew that by now."

And I love you. I'm not going anywhere.

The words formed in her mind and were almost out of her mouth before she caught them.

Well. She hadn't wasted any time, had she?

She ducked her head, buying a few seconds to pull herself together and deal with her realization. Apparently she hadn't ridden halfway across the continent only to see what Joe was like in bed. Apparently she'd fallen in love with him, somehow, somewhere. Go figure.

He tilted her chin up and kissed her again, one hand sliding onto her backside. Familiar heat raced through her body. She flashed to the last time they'd made love, the way he'd kissed her all over and made her crazy using only his hands and his mouth. Thinking about it made her feel liquid with longing again.

He made a frustrated noise as he broke their kiss.

"I've got an appointment at ten o'clock with my lawyer," he said.

She checked her watch. It was nine-thirty.

"How long do you need?" she asked, looking up at him from beneath her eyelashes.

She loved how quickly he hustled her inside. She loved how avidly he gazed at her breasts and belly and thighs as he stripped her. She loved the way he savored her, his eyes closed as he teased her breasts with his mouth then kissed his way down her stomach. She loved everything about him, and as he slid inside her she had to bite her lip to stop herself from saying the words out loud.

She had no idea if her feelings were reciprocated, and he had enough on his plate without having to deal with a badly timed declaration from her. She knew he fancied her like crazy, that he loved sex with her. She knew he laughed at her jokes and appreciated it when she challenged him. But he'd been married for fifteen years to a woman he'd loved passionately, and there was every chance he would be slower and more careful before giving his heart away than Hannah was. She figured she'd already shown her hand enough by returning to be with him—there would be other times to let him know how much he meant to her.

"We're on the clock, pay attention," he said as he moved inside her.

She pushed her thoughts away and followed instructions. Within a handful of minutes she was clutching at his back, his shoulders as he drove into her. Rippling pleasure washed through her and her body clenched his as she climaxed.

"Hannah," he whispered, then he came, too, his cheek pressed against hers as his body tensed and shuddered.

He pressed a kiss to her jaw afterward, one hand curled possessively over her breast.

She traced the arch of his right eyebrow with her fingertip then repeated the gesture with the left.

"I love your eyes," she said, mostly to stop herself from saying something else.

He smiled. Then he tensed as he caught sight of the clock on the DVD player.

"Shit. I'm going to be late," he said. He rolled off the couch and onto the floor.

Hannah laughed as she helped him round up his underwear and shoes, buckling his belt for him as he pulled on his shirt. He left her to lock up the house, kissing her one last time before bolting for his car. She finished dressing and was about to head out the door when she paused.

It was the first time she'd been alone in Joe's house. Feeling somewhat guilty, she crossed to the family portrait propped on a shelf near the TV.

She'd never had a really good look at Beth before. She'd passed the portrait a dozen times but never lingered, for obvious reasons. Now she picked up the frame and studied the photograph. It was an informal shot. The family was gathered on a picnic blanket, the kids sprawled like puppies at their parents' feet, Beth leaning back against a smiling Joe. Joe's wife was small and blonde, with wide blue eyes. She wore a white dress with little yellow flowers on it, and a pair of high-heeled yellow espadrilles had been kicked off to one side. She was beautiful in a fragile, feminine way.

Utterly different from Hannah. She stared at the photograph, trying to understand if what she was feeling was envy or jealousy or something else altogether.

It must be every woman's nightmare not to live to see her children into adulthood. The thought of not being there to guide them through crises, to kiss things better or deliver a serve of tough love...

Looking into the other woman's smiling face, Hannah decided that she felt sad for Beth Lawson, nothing else. She'd had a life, a family, a good marriage. She'd loved and been loved. And it had all been taken away in a split second.

If it was me, I'd want Joe to be happy. I'd want him to find someone else to love, for someone else to love my children.

Hannah placed the frame back on the shelf.

Making peace with Beth had given Hannah new clarity. She loved Joe, and she fell more and more in love with his children every day. Ben could ignore her all he liked, but he couldn't stop her seeing his little-boy's heart or understanding he was hurting. She could wait him out. He needed her. They all did, just as she needed them. At the end of the day, that was what family was about, right?

I want this. I want them.

It was that simple. Now all she had to do was win Joe's son's trust and hope that Joe could find the courage to love another woman the way he'd loved his wife.

Small potatoes, right?

Over the next week, Joe swung between two states—stupid, bemused happiness and deeply frustrated sadness.

It seemed crazy to him that both states could coexist, but it was the reality of his life. When he and Hannah were alone, he felt invincible. She was sexy, strong, gutsy, smart—she made him feel seventeen again, the way he couldn't stop thinking about her. If he wasn't careful, one day soon he'd come out of a daze and find he'd etched her name in his desk at the pub. He was that obsessed, that involved.

Then there was Ben. Angry, silent, rude. And that was on a good day. It had been three weeks since Hannah had returned and he'd told the kids they were dating. Ruby was as happy as a clam. Each night she trekked next door to help Hannah with the Thunderbird. Sometimes he joined them, sometimes he didn't. Ben never did. He'd taken to spending time in his room, except when Joe forced him to join them at the dinner table. He'd also had to intervene in more than one row between Ben and his sister, Ben's anger spilling over into other aspects of his life. Joe was waiting for the inevitable phone call from school to tell him Ben had been in a fight—it seemed a logical extension of his son's behavior.

The worst thing was that Joe felt so powerless. He'd tried patience. He'd tried communication. He'd tried bribery, to his shame. Nothing got through to his sullen son. Ben had effectively withdrawn from the family.

Every time Ben turned his back on Hannah or glared at her or avoided spending time with them as a group, Joe remembered his mother's words. *You're asking her to take on an awful lot, stepping into a ready-made family.* Even though his gut told him Hannah would stay, that she would never have entered their lives if she hadn't intended to go the distance, a part of him was afraid that he would lose her just as he was beginning to understand how bloody lucky he was.

The tension within him came to a head when Hannah was over for dinner Tuesday night. Ben opened the door to her knock and walked away without acknowledging her at all.

"Ben!" Joe said sharply, but his son just kept walking up the hallway.

Joe took one look at Hannah's dismayed face and his temper flared.

"That's it. I've had enough." He moved toward the hallway, but Hannah caught his arm.

"Wait five minutes before you go after him and say something you might regret."

"Something has to give," he said. She might not want to acknowledge it, but Ben's attitude was getting worse, not better. He was becoming openly, aggressively rude, something Joe would not tolerate. Ben didn't have to like what was happening between Joe and Hannah, but he had to respect his father's decision, and he needed to respect Hannah.

"I know. But two angry Lawson men aren't going to get us anywhere."

She was right. He knew she was right. "Okay. I'm counting to a hundred."

"Make it two hundred," she said.

Which made him laugh. She always knew how to get to him.

Before he could stop himself, he reached out and tugged her close, kissing her briefly on the lips. She kissed him back and he had to remind himself his children were in the house. Sure enough, when they pulled back he became aware of Ruby standing in the kitchen doorway, a drink in her hand. They'd been very circumspect with physical stuff to date, hand-holding being the limit of their displays of affection in front of the children. Ruby's eyes were wide, as though she'd just spotted a real-life fairy, or some other mystical creature at the bottom of the garden.

Hannah cleared her throat, her cheeks a little pink. "Um, hi, Ruby."

"When are you going to stay the night?" Ruby asked, her small face avid.

Hannah made a choking noise.

"Ruby," Joe said, amused despite himself. She was incorrigible—and he much preferred her this way to the nervous, anxious little girl she'd been when they first moved from Sydney.

"I'm only asking what everyone else is thinking," Ruby said matter-of-factly.

"Everyone? Who's everyone?" Joe asked. Too late he realized he'd been foolish to buy into the discussion.

"Grandma, and Aunty Robyn next door."

"Not quite everyone," he said.

"Close enough," Hannah murmured.

"Staying the night isn't something people should rush into," Joe said.

"Why not? I thought you liked each other. It would be cool to have Hannah here for breakfast," Ruby said.

There was a sound from the hallway and Joe swung around to see his son standing in the living room doorway, his angry gaze fixed on Ruby.

"What is wrong with you?" Ben snarled. "Why are you trying so hard to replace Mom?"

Hannah visibly flinched and Ruby went pale as she stared at her brother.

"I'm not. I'm not trying to replace Mommy," she said. She looked to Joe, stricken.

"Yes, you are. Wanting Hannah to be in that mother-daughter thing with you, always sucking up to her and trying to get Dad to like her more. What do you think Mom would say if she could see you?"

Ben was white with anger, his hands curled into fists by his sides.

"Mate," Joe said, stepping forward.

Ben swung toward him. "You're just as bad. Don't you care that she's not here? Don't you even think about her anymore?"

"Of course I do, we all do—"

"No, you don't. You just want to do it with Hannah all the time and forget about everything else. You don't even care that she's dead."

"You know better than to talk like that," Joe said.

"Don't think I don't know what you do when Ruby and I go to school." Ben's face was red and he was shaking, but he didn't take his fierce gaze from Joe's.

Hannah stepped forward. "Ben, the last thing I want to do is try to take your mom's place. My dad left when I was about Ruby's age, and I know it's not the same as dying, but I missed him like crazy."

Ben refused to even look at her, keeping his gaze fixed on his father.

"I don't want to try and take away your memories of your mom or replace her or anything like that, I promise," Hannah said. "I just like spending time with you and your dad and Ruby."

Joe watched carefully, trying to read his son's response, not sure if he should intervene or not.

"You want more than that," Ben said. "I'm not stupid."

Hannah held up her fingers in a classic Scout's pledge. "I swear, I just want to hang with you guys. No agenda. I like you. Where else am I going to get such cheap labor for the Thunderbird?"

Ben shot her a confused look. Hannah took another step forward and reached out to place a reassuring hand on his shoulder. "Couldn't we at least try to be friends?" she asked.

Ben looked at her, and for a moment Joe caught a glimpse of something desperate and needy in his son's face. Then Ben scowled and shrugged his shoulder, roughly brushing Hannah's hand away. "I told you, you're never going to be my mom."

Ruby was across the room in a flash, throwing herself between Ben and Hannah, reaching out to push her brother away.

"Stop it! You're going to ruin everything! You're going to make Hannah hate us and then she'll go away and we'll never see her again."

"You're a traitor," Ben yelled. "A stinking traitor." He shoved Ruby with all his might. She staggered backward, wildly off balance, then fell awkwardly onto her outstretched left arm.

Her wail of pain made the hairs on the back of Joe's neck stand on end. He was at her side in seconds, cradling her as she hugged her arm to her chest.

"It hurts. It hurts so much," she sobbed.

Grim, he gently tested her wrist joint. Ruby yelped with pain.

"I think it's broken," he said.

Ben stood frozen, so pale Joe thought he was going to pass out. "I didn't mean it. I didn't mean it." Ben bolted for the door.

"Ben!" Joe bellowed. It was dark outside and the last thing he needed was to have to chase Ben down when they had to get Ruby to the hospital.

But Ben was gone, the door banging loudly behind him.

"I'll go after him," Hannah said. "You need to get Ruby to a doctor."

He nodded briefly, giving Ruby a reassuring squeeze. Hannah headed for the door, her stride long, and he gave his daughter all his attention.

"Daddy's just going to go grab a bag of peas from

the freezer for you, sweetheart. It'll make the pain a bit better. You keep your arm still and don't move."

By the time he had Ruby in the car and ready to go, Hannah had returned.

"No sign of him. I'm sorry, I have no idea how he disappeared so quickly," she said helplessly.

He stared out into the night. He hated the thought of Ben roaming the streets, upset and alone, but there wasn't much he could do about it right now. He couldn't be in two places at once.

"I need to go," he said.

"I'll find him," Hannah promised.

He looked at her, remembering his mother's warning that once the novelty had worn off and the going had gotten tough, Hannah might want to opt out. He figured tonight definitely qualified under the tough category, but she showed no signs of flinching.

"Thank you," he said.

She simply shook her head. "You don't have to thank me."

He could see what she wasn't saying in her eyes and even though he had a million worries pressing down on him, he couldn't stop the words from rising up inside him.

"Love you," he said, stepping close to press a quick kiss to her lips before turning to slide into the driver's seat.

She looked flustered for a moment, then her mouth lifted at the corner. "Nice timing."

"Figured I'd better get in while the getting was good."

She looked as though she wanted to say more, but

she pushed his car door closed. "Call me from the hospital, let me know how Ruby is."

"I will."

She stepped back from the car as he reversed into the street. The last thing he saw was her standing in his driveway, arms crossed over her chest, her stance strong and sure.

Love you.

Joe's words echoed in Hannah's head as she walked the streets of Elsternwick, eyes peeled for a slim thirteen-year-old boy in baggy jeans and a white T-shirt.

How typical of Joe to blurt it out like that. She'd been biting her tongue for days, waiting for the right moment to declare herself, and he'd just thrown his own declaration at her as casually as goodbye or hello or have a nice day.

Okay, it hadn't been *that* casual. But he'd definitely caught her by surprise. And she'd been very aware of Ruby in the backseat, her face creased with pain. Hardly the moment to tell him the feeling was mutual and that she adored him, body and soul.

She checked her watch. She'd been searching for nearly forty minutes now. She'd checked the school, The Watering Hole and the local shops. She'd run out of obvious options, so it was time to start thinking not so obviously. There always seemed to be a bunch of kids hanging out at the twenty-four-hour convenience store near the highway. Maybe Ben had taken refuge with them. And it might be worth checking in with the Balases. Ben had formed an attachment with the Indian shop owner over the past few months.

Her phone buzzed in her pocket. Joe's name was illuminated on her screen.

"How is she?" she asked as she took the call.

"Broken scaphoid bone in her wrist. When she fell on her arm like that I was pretty sure that'd be the case. Seen it a few times out on the rigs."

"But she's okay?"

"She's fine. Getting a cast put on as we speak, lapping up the attention and the lollipops."

"I was about to check out that twenty-four-hour place over near the highway," she reported. "He's not at the school or the shops or the pub."

"All right. I'll come join you once I've got Ruby home."

"Mom's there to look after her."

"Good, that'll save me calling my mom."

Might as well say what they were both thinking.

"If we don't find him soon, we should probably think about calling the police," she said.

"Yeah, I know." His voice was heavy with worry.

They agreed to touch base again once he was close to home, then Hannah ended the call. She got her bearings and struck out in the direction of the highway. She was passing the local playground, the equipment reduced to vague shapes in the darkness, when she caught a flash of something out of the corner of her eye. She stopped in her tracks. Ben had been wearing a white T-shirt. Was that what she'd seen in her peripheral vision?

She peered into the park. Slowly the vague shapes took form: a swing set, a slide, monkey bars, a flying fox.

"Ben? Are you there?" she called.

She held her breath, waiting. Nothing but silence

greeted her. She walked farther into the park and saw there was a log bridge situated beyond the swing, the kind made from two mounds of earth placed on either side of a large section of concrete pipe with a bridge built over the top.

Her heart gave a huge, painful thump of relief when she saw a pale shape huddled in the darkness inside the big pipe.

Ben. It had to be.

She ran the few steps to the bridge and dropped to her knees.

"Ben. Thank God. Are you okay?"

As she'd half expected, he flinched away from her. "Go away."

"I can't do that, I'm sorry. Your dad's worried sick about you."

Silence from the pipe. She could barely see the pale oval of Ben's face.

"Ben, why don't you come out and we can go home and talk? No one's angry with you, if that's what you're worried about."

Ben hiccuped softly, and Hannah realized he was crying. Had been crying for a while, judging from the hiccups.

"Ben, it's okay," she said.

She crawled a few feet inside the pipe so that she was sitting next to him. She wanted to put her arm around him very badly but doubted he'd tolerate it.

"Are you worried about Ruby? Is that it? Because I just spoke to your dad and he said she was going to be fine."

Ben's sobbing increased.

"Come on, let's go home," she said again. "Don't you want to go home?"

He was crying so hard she almost didn't hear what he said.

"Can't."

"Why can't you come home, Ben?" She felt woefully out of her depth, but Ben was so miserable she had to try.

His voice was broken and small and Hannah had to strain to hear his reply. "Because it's my fault. They'll all hate me once they know."

She frowned. She might be inexperienced with kids, but her gut was telling her that there was a whole lot more going on here than reaction to the incident at the house.

"I haven't known your dad and Ruby as long as you have, but I know that there is no way they could ever hate you, Ben. They love you. Absolutely they love you."

Ben pressed his hands to his face. "That's only because they don't know."

"I'm sure that whatever it is, it's not as bad as you think."

"It is. It's the worst."

A shiver raced up her spine. Had something happened to Ben? Had someone taken advantage of him? "Would it help if you told me? Maybe you'd feel better if you got it off your chest."

He shook his head.

"What if I promised not to tell anyone else unless you gave me permission? Would that make a difference?" She held her breath, banking on the fact that Ben was clearly aching to tell someone what was on his mind.

Ben sniffed a few times, thinking her offer over. "You can't tell anyone."

"I swear it will be our secret."

There was a long silence. When Ben spoke, his voice was barely above a whisper. "The day Mom died, I was supposed to get a lift home from karate with George Simpkin's mom, but George and I had a fight during class and I called Mom and asked her to come get me."

Hannah closed her eyes, guessing what was coming next.

"If I hadn't asked her to pick me up, she wouldn't have been in the accident. It's my fault she died," Ben said brokenly.

Bloody hell.

For a moment Hannah was swamped with a huge, vast sadness. Joe's son had been carrying this misplaced guilt around with him for two long years. No wonder he'd been so angry and sad and withdrawn.

"See. You hate me now. And Dad and Ruby will hate me if they find out."

Tears pricked the back of her eyes at the depth of his fear and hurt. For a moment she felt overwhelmed. Then she shuffled around so she was facing him. "Ben, I want you to look at me."

His head came up. His face was streaked with tears and his bottom lip trembled with emotion. She held his eye.

"What happened was not your fault. It was an accident. No one could have known that it would happen."

"But she wouldn't have even been there if it hadn't been for me."

Hannah wondered how many times he'd lacerated himself with the exact same thought. "Someone ran a red light. That's why your mom died. You didn't do a thing wrong."

She could see how much Ben wanted to believe what she was telling him. It was bad enough that he had to live with the grief of losing his mother, but to believe he was to blame… It was the sort of misconception that could ruin a life.

"Accidents happen all the time, for no reason," she said. "I know that's kind of scary to think about, but it's true. You can't take responsibility for an accident."

Ben frowned into the darkness. She wished she knew the handful of magic words that would convince him, but she suspected there were none. He'd been living with his mistaken belief for two years, and it was going to take time to convince him he was blameless.

He shifted and sniffed mightily, wiping his nose on the sleeve of his T-shirt.

"Has anyone ever told you how gross that is?" she said lightly.

As she'd hoped, it shocked a laugh out of him. "Yeah. Grandma. All the time."

"You do that in front of your grandma? You're a brave man."

Ben sniffed again, but the look he flashed her was marginally less miserable.

She pulled out her phone. "I'm going to call your dad, let him know I've found you so he can stop worrying. Okay?"

She kept the call short, letting Joe know they were on their way home. When she ended the call, she simply sat in silence for a few seconds.

"You ready to go?"

"I guess."

They crawled out of the pipe. Ben looked so small and young, Hannah had to clench her hands into fists to stop herself from hugging him.

They were both silent as they walked through the park to the street. Ben didn't speak up again until they were about to turn into their street.

"Are you going to tell him?"

"Your dad? No. I promised you I wouldn't, and I won't. But I think you should."

Ben stared at her mistrustfully. She stopped walking to give him her full attention. "What have you got to lose?"

"Only everything."

"And that would make you really miserable and you wouldn't want to hang out with anyone or make new friends and you'd probably spend most of your time in your room on your own listening to your iPod. When you weren't yelling at your sister or ignoring your dad, that is. Does that sound about right?"

Ben blinked. "You're saying I'm already unhappy."

"You tell me."

They both started walking again, Ben's face screwed up in concentration as he thought over what she'd said.

"I guarantee he won't hate you, Ben," she said as they turned onto their street and saw Joe's house, light spilling out of every window, the Mazda parked in the driveway. "I know it's hard, but I think you need to start telling people how you're feeling instead of keeping everything locked up inside all the time."

Ben glanced at her out of the corner of his eye.

"If you want me to, I could tell him with you. Would that make it any easier?" she said.

Ben didn't respond. She bit her lip. She was about

out of strategies. They walked toward the house. She could feel the heat coming off the SUV as she passed the hood. Joe must have just gotten home.

"Okay," Ben said, so quietly she almost didn't catch it.

She glanced at him as Joe walked out onto the front porch. Ben stopped in his tracks and the two Lawson men stared at each other across the space of a few feet. A knot lodged in her throat as she saw the fear and longing on Ben's face.

"You okay?" Joe asked, his voice rough with emotion.

Ben nodded. Joe started down the porch steps and Ben made a choking sound before flinging himself into his father's arms.

Hannah sniffed noisily as she watched Joe comfort his son. Lucky she wasn't the kind of woman who wore a lot of makeup or tonight would have left her looking like a panda.

"I'm sorry. I didn't mean to hurt Ruby," Ben said, his voice muffled by Joe's shirt.

"Your sister is fine, although she's probably going to drive you crazy asking you to sign her cast."

Ben made a sound that might have been a laugh. Then he pushed away from his father's embrace. He shot Hannah a quick, nervous glance, then focused on his father and took a deep breath.

"There's something I need to tell you. It's about Mom," Ben said.

Joe's face remained carefully neutral. "Okay. Why don't we go inside?"

He started to herd Ben toward the door, but Ben hung back and glanced over his shoulder.

"Hannah, too," he said.

It was the smallest of shifts, but it pierced her heart.

"It's okay, I'm coming. Try keeping me away," she said with a watery smile.

Then she followed Joe and Ben into the house.

Chapter 12

Joe paused in the hallway as he shut the door to his son's room. It was late, past one in the morning, and for a moment he felt immeasurably heavy, weighed down by the sadness his son had been carrying for so long.

He closed his eyes and rubbed the bridge of his nose. He should have pushed harder earlier, asked the right questions. He should have somehow seen that Ben's misery went deeper than simple grief.

He walked slowly to the living room. Hannah was on the couch and she looked up when he entered.

"How's he doing?"

"He's asleep."

"No wonder. It's been a big night."

"Yeah."

"Come here." She patted the floor. "Sit between my legs."

He sat on the floor and allowed her to draw him back against the couch, her legs on either side of his shoulders. She began to massage him, her thumbs working at the tense muscles in his back and neck.

"Don't give yourself a hard time," she said quietly.

He shrugged. She found a knot in his neck and worked at it diligently for a few seconds.

"You're a great dad, Joe. One of the best. But you're not a mind reader."

"You didn't know him before the accident. I should have seen it was something more than Beth dying."

"Tell me, how is a grieving kid supposed to act? Moody, angry, incommunicative? Until Ben was ready to tell someone what was going on in his head, you didn't stand a chance of working it out on your own. And blaming yourself isn't going to get anyone anywhere or do Ben any favors, by the way."

Typical Hannah, calling it as she saw it, like always. Despite his weariness and sadness he smiled. "You're a real ball breaker, you know that?"

"You wish."

"You saying I want my balls broken?" He twisted his neck to look at her, one eyebrow raised.

"I'm saying you'll take any attention down there that you can get."

"Really?"

"Really." She raised a challenging eyebrow back at him.

He moved quickly, twisting and hooking an arm behind her neck and hauling her onto the floor. He didn't stop until she was beneath him, her arms pinned to the carpet.

"Thank you for making my point," she said.

He kissed the smile off her lips. "You can break my balls anytime."

"Aren't you supposed to whisper sweet nothings like that in my ear?" she said.

She was such a smart-ass.

He pulled her earlobe into his mouth and bit it gently.

"How about this? I love you, Hannah Napier," he whispered against the soft skin of her neck.

She went very still, and he released one of her hands so he could lever himself up on an elbow and look into her face.

"Something wrong?" he asked, trying to keep his tone light despite the flutter of nervousness in his belly. He thought he understood her, knew what was in her heart. But he could be wrong. He could be way off base.

"No. You just keep taking me by surprise, that's all."

"You mean it's a surprise to you that I'm crazy about you?"

And here he thought it had been as obvious as hell, that he might as well plaster it on a billboard and shout it to the world.

"Yes. No. You know what I mean. I've been biding my time, trying to find the right opportunity, the right moment, and you just threw it out there...."

It took him a moment to understand what she was saying. He smiled, warmth unfolding in his chest. "Let me get this straight. I'm in trouble because I beat you to the punch?"

"Not in trouble. Just stuck with me for the foreseeable future."

She still couldn't say it. He had her ex-fiancé to thank for that, he suspected. He cupped a hand to his ear, pretending to be hard of hearing.

"Sorry, was that a declaration I just heard, Ms. Napier?"

She stared at him for a moment. Then she took a deep breath, her eyes very serious as she looked into his. "I love you, Joe Lawson. Happy now?"

"Yes."

He wrapped his arms around her and pulled her close, his cheek resting against hers, her scent in his lungs, her heart beating next to his. He thought about the past few weeks, the trials she'd endured, and he squeezed her closer.

"I love you," he said again, just to hear the words out loud.

"I love you, too. So much."

"Let's go to bed."

She hadn't stayed the night before, but he needed her tonight. Needed her body against his, the simple comfort of having her near.

"Not really the best timing for such a big move," she said regretfully.

He knew she was right, but it was hard not to feel frustrated. And it wasn't about sex. It was about intimacy. Belonging. Comfort. Security.

She traced a finger along his jawline. "What if I just lie down with you for a while? Then I'll go home."

It was something, better than nothing.

He led her to his bedroom and she took off her shoes and jeans and climbed into bed beside him wearing her T-shirt and underwear. He pulled her into his arms and she rested her head on his shoulder, their legs tangling. She felt good, smelled even better. He closed his eyes and pressed a kiss to the top of her head.

Almost immediately his brain circled to the problems of the evening, to his troubled son and his daughter with her arm in a cast. He smoothed a hand down Hannah's arm over and over, wondering what more he could have said to put Ben's mind at ease, if there was something else he should be doing.

"He's going to be all right, Joe. He's a smart kid. He'll work it out."

Somehow, she knew he was fretting again.

"I hope so."

She turned her head to look at him. "I was thinking it might help to find someone for him to talk to. Someone who specializes in kids. What do you think?" She said it hesitantly, as though she was unsure of his reaction. Trust Hannah to have a game plan when he was still floundering and trying to find his feet.

"Good idea. I'll talk to our doctor tomorrow, see if he can recommend someone." He'd make the call first thing and do whatever it took to get Ben to open up.

"He'll be okay," Hannah said again.

"Yes."

She smiled at the conviction in his voice and lay her head back on his chest. "I'm just going to close my eyes for a few minutes. *Do not* let me fall asleep."

"I won't."

"Because I can't stay the night yet."

"I know."

"Not until Ben is absolutely okay with all of this."

"Yes."

It was one of the many things he loved about her, the fact that she put his kids' welfare first and foremost, always.

"Just a few minutes," she reminded him drowsily.

He smiled to himself. In all likelihood she would fall

asleep, and he would let her. Then he would wake her in an hour or two, and if he was very lucky, they might make love before she went home.

And maybe, one day soon, she wouldn't have to go home, and he'd have the pleasure of waking to find her next to him, her brown eyes hazy with sleep, her beautiful mouth curving into the first smile of the day.

Getting a little ahead of yourself, buddy.

But for the first time in a long time it felt okay to dream a little, to believe that maybe they'd turned the corner and that things were going to improve.

And right now he had Hannah in his arms, even if for a few hours. It was enough to be going on with.

"Hannah, over here. Come and look at this one."

Hannah looked up from the doll-themed pajamas she was inspecting and saw her mother was knee-deep in the women's lingerie department, a flashy red bra and pantie set dangling from one hand.

"Mom, we're not shopping for me. Or you, for that matter," she said.

It had been nearly six weeks since Ben's big blowup, or what she and Joe now referred to as The Turnaround. Christmas was just around the corner and she was still trying to find a few must-haves for Ben and Ruby. The Nintendo game he'd requested was proving impossible to find, and even though Ruby claimed that with her eleventh birthday looming in late December she was "over dolls," Hannah knew better. Ben had taken it upon himself to do an inventory of his sister's accessories so Hannah would know what not to buy, and Hannah was determined to take home a haul of pink, spangly stuff if it killed her.

She smiled as she remembered Ben's earnestness as he handed over his list to her. He'd been seeing a counselor for about a month and the change in him was nothing short of miraculous. It was as though a huge burden had been lifted from his shoulders—which, of course, it had. Every time he laughed or teased his sister or looked to his father for approval, Hannah's chest ached to see him so changed. Best of all was when he looked at her, or laughed at her jokes, or came over to help her put the finishing touches on the newly chromed Thunderbird. Joe didn't know it yet, but she was giving it to him for Christmas, and both his children had been excellent coconspirators in helping her trick the bike out to suit his tastes. She and Ben had finished buffing the mudguards just last night, in fact.

"It's so beautiful, Hannah," her mother called again. "At least come and look at it. If I had your figure I'd buy it in a snap."

Everybody in a five-mile radius could hear what her mother was saying and see the red bra and panties. Hannah rolled her eyes, knowing there was only one way to shut her up.

"It's one of those sexy balconette things," her mother said, thrusting the bra into Hannah's hands the moment Hannah joined her. "And feel how soft the silk is."

Hannah dutifully rubbed the silky fabric between thumb and forefinger. As her mother had said, it was very soft. And even though she wasn't particularly into girlie underwear, the red silk and black lace was actually pretty saucy up close.

"Joe loves red," she said absently. He'd commented on her one, rather pedestrian red bra a number of times.

She checked the price tag and almost choked when she saw how much the pair would set her back.

"Get out of town," she said, putting the underwear back on the rack. "No way am I paying so much for so little."

"I'll buy it for you. My Christmas present to both of you." Her mother gave Hannah a cheeky wink.

Somehow, despite her objections, Hannah found herself being herded into the change room.

"We need to go to the men's department next," Hannah said as she started undressing. "I want to get Joe that cashmere sweater we saw last week. I should have bought it at the time."

"I thought you were giving him the bike?" Her mother's disembodied voice floated over the curtain.

"I am. But I want to get him a few other things, as well. He'll be suspicious if there are no parcels for him under the tree."

She was a little embarrassed about how much she was looking forward to Christmas Day. They were going to have a big sit-down dinner with her mother, Joe, the kids and his mother. Between them, she and her mom and Joe's mom were going to cook the meal. It was going to be a real family day, her first Christmas with Joe.

She fumbled the clasp on the new bra and fiddled with the straps until they were comfortable. She laughed a little when she saw how outrageously sexy the bra looked when it was on.

"How does it look?" her mother asked, sticking her head inside the curtain. "Oh, Hannah. Isn't it wonderful!"

"That's one word for it. I don't know if this is really me."

She had a veritable shelf of breast in front of her, packaged in silk and lace.

"Joe will love it. Not another word, I'm buying it," her mother insisted.

Hannah shrugged. She knew her mother well enough not to bother arguing. She reached behind her to undo the clasp and felt a stab of pain near her left armpit.

"Ow!" She tugged the bra away from herself and saw the culprit: the tiny safety pin holding the swing-tag to the bra had popped loose.

"Stupid thing."

She pulled the bra off and soothed the scratch with her hand.

"Give it to me and I'll take it to the register," her mother said.

Hannah frowned as she felt something small and firm beneath her fingers.

"What's wrong?" her mother asked.

Hannah met her mother's eyes in the mirror. "There's a lump."

The smile faded from her mother's eyes. "Are you sure?"

"Yes. It's probably nothing. Hormones or something."

"Let me feel."

"Mom." Hannah wasn't about to let her mother feel her up in a public change room.

"Let me. I have more experience with this than you. My breasts are twenty-five years older than yours."

Hannah sighed and turned so her mother could poke

the side of her breast where it tapered into her armpit. "Can you feel it?"

"Yes."

Her mother was frowning now. "When did you check your breasts last?"

"I don't know. Five months ago? Six?"

"Hannah," her mother said reprovingly.

Hannah started pulling on her own bra. "I'm twenty-eight. Hardly in a high-risk group," she said when she caught sight of her mother's worried expression.

She wished she'd never said anything, or that she'd been alone when she tried on the bra. Her mother would be all over her now to get it checked out, and it was probably nothing. Breast cancer was an older woman's disease.

As if she could read Hannah's mind, her mother started counting names off on her fingers. "Kylie Minogue. Christina Applegate. Anastacia. Belinda Emmett. Don't think young women don't need to be careful. I want you to get this checked out, Hannah."

Hannah sighed and tugged on her T-shirt. Clearly, she was never going to hear the end of this until she'd made an appointment with her doctor.

"Fine. I'll go see Dr. Nelson."

Her mother pulled out her cell phone. "I'll see if she can fit you in tomorrow."

"Mom. Will you stop being such a panic merchant? Unbelievable."

"Consider it your early Christmas present to me— peace of mind."

Hannah listened resignedly as her mother spoke to the receptionist at the medical center, making an appointment for during her lunch break tomorrow. She'd found a new position as senior mechanic with a big, progressive workshop three weeks ago and was glad her mother at least understood that she couldn't afford to take time off so early into the job.

"Happy now?" she asked when her mother ended the call.

"Not yet. But I will be."

The next day, Hannah greeted her doctor with a self-deprecating smile.

"I feel stupid even mentioning this," she said when she'd explained about finding the lump. "I mean, I'm twenty-eight. Like it's going to be anything to worry about, right?"

"It probably isn't, but you were right to come in. Any changes are worth investigating. The sooner we catch anything, the better," Dr. Nelson said. "Why don't you step behind the screen and take your bra and top off and we'll take a look."

Hannah did as instructed then eyed the examination couch.

"How do you want me?"

"On your back, with your arm behind your head, elbow out."

Hannah lay down and Dr. Nelson pushed the screen back and stepped toward the examination table.

"Sorry if my hands are cold," she said before laying her hands on Hannah's breast.

"I've had worse."

Dr. Nelson smiled. She became more serious as she concentrated on palpating Hannah's breast. Hannah tensed as her doctor located the lump and felt around it.

"Okay, it's definitely a discrete lump. Is there any tenderness when I press it?"

"No, not at all. That's good, right?"

Dr. Nelson's small smile was sympathetic and slightly worried. "Accepted theory is that breast cancer lumps are not generally painful. But there are always exceptions to the rule, especially in younger women."

Hannah frowned. "So is it good or bad that I have no pain?"

The doctor's eyes were unfocused as she concentrated on palpating the rest of Hannah's right breast. "I suspect it's neither here nor there. I'm just going to check your lymph nodes."

Hannah lay still as Dr. Nelson checked her armpit and neck, then examined her left breast.

"Well, Hannah, I'm going to send you for an ultrasound. There's no doubt in my mind that this lump is new and therefore worthy of investigation."

Hannah's stomach was suddenly hollow. "Okay. Um. When should I book the test?"

"I'll ask my receptionist to arrange one for you with a radiologist we have a relationship with. They usually keep a few appointments free for cases like this."

Cases like this. What did that mean?

Dr. Nelson obviously read the uncertainty in her face because she put her hand on Hannah's shoulder. "We're being safe, that's all. Don't hit the panic button just yet. And remember, if we find something, there's an enormous amount we can do."

"Sure."

Hannah dressed in a daze, her cold hands fumbling with the catch on her bra. She'd expected to be reassured and sent home, not sent off for tests.

It's nothing. Dr. Nelson said it herself—she's just being safe.

But the words didn't make the panicky, fluttering feeling leave her stomach. Hannah waited tensely in the reception area for the receptionist to get off the phone with the radiologist.

"They can fit you in first thing tomorrow. How is that?" the receptionist asked.

"I'll have to be late for work, but that should be fine," Hannah said. So much for not looking bad in her new job. She would have to make up the time at the other end of the day.

The receptionist wrote down the address for the radiology clinic and Hannah tucked the card into her pocket. Her first impulse when she stepped outside the clinic was to phone Joe. She hadn't told him about finding the lump or her appointment, hadn't thought it worth mentioning, but now she needed to hear his voice, deep and reassuring. She pulled her cell from her pocket, then remembered that he had a huge function booked for The Watering Hole tonight. An office Christmas party, with over two hundred guests. She didn't want to dump bad news on him when he had to work all night. He'd simply fret and worry, and for what? Tomorrow she'd have her test and get the all clear.

She was about to get on her bike when her cell vibrated in her pocket. It was her mom, surprise, surprise.

"How did you go?"

Hannah hesitated a moment. "Good. Dr. Nelson said not to worry," she lied.

"Oh, that's good. Thank God. You must be relieved."

Hannah closed her eyes. "Yeah, I am."

"And I suppose you're cursing me for making you get it checked out."

"Something like that."

"Well, I'm not sorry. I'd never have stopped worrying otherwise."

Hannah made an excuse to end the call. She had no idea why she'd just lied to her mother. She simply hadn't wanted to say the words out loud. *The doctor's sending me for tests.* It sounded so ominous. Scary.

She went back to work and spent the evening watching DVDs with Ruby and Ben. It was good to force her worries from her mind and give herself over to the here and now of being with Joe's kids. Ruby insisted Hannah sit on the floor so Ruby could sit behind her on the couch and braid her hair. By the time Brendan Fraser had finished journeying to the center of the earth, Hannah had a head full of slightly wonky plaits.

"If you leave them in overnight you'll wake up and your hair will be all kinky," Ruby said.

"And this is a good thing?" Hannah asked.

"Oh, yes. People pay a fortune to have kinky hair," Ruby said knowledgeably.

She hustled the kids to bed at eight-thirty, aware they had school the next day. Ben wanted to read for a little while and she left him to it, figuring he'd probably pass out with his book in his hand and she could swing by in twenty minutes and turn the light out. Ruby wanted to talk, and Hannah sat on the side of her bed and listened to her plan her birthday party.

"Some people think it sucks having your birthday so soon after Christmas, but it's good," Ruby confided. "People always worry that you feel hard done by and you get extra stuff."

"I've never thought of that."

"The only thing is, you have to wait a long time with no other presents to break up the year. Ben's birthday is in June, so he gets presents every six months. But I only get them once a year."

"That is definitely a bummer. Maybe we should move your birthday, what do you think?"

Ruby laughed. "You can't move a birthday, silly."

"So what else are you going to have at this party of yours? Lions and tigers, dancing horses?"

Ruby rolled her eyes at Hannah's silliness but she was smiling. "No. We're going to have pass the parcel and musical chairs. And blindman's buff. And little sandwiches cut into triangles."

"Mmm. And ice-cream cake. We always had ice-cream cake for our birthday parties."

Ruby's face clouded. "My mom used to make our cakes. She had this cookbook with lots of different cakes in it and each year me and Ben were allowed to pick the cake we wanted her to make. I've had a castle, a turtle, a pony and a puppy. The puppy was the best." Ruby's hands plucked at the edge of the sheet as she remembered.

"I bet they were great cakes."

"They were. They were the best."

Ruby's voice had dropped to a whisper and she blinked rapidly. Hannah patted her knee. "Why don't you squish over and I'll lie down with you?"

Ruby shuffled over without a protest and Hannah kicked her shoes off and lay down beside her, sliding an arm around the little girl's middle so she was snuggling her from behind.

"You give good cuddles," Ruby said.

"So do you."

They were both quiet for a few minutes.

"Hannah?"

"Yes?"

"I'm glad we moved in next to you."

"Me, too, sweetheart."

Slowly Hannah felt the tension leave Ruby's body as she drifted toward sleep.

Hannah started to ease away from her, but Ruby shifted restlessly.

"Don't go. I don't want you to go."

Hannah subsided and waited until Ruby was breathing steadily before sliding out of the bed.

Joe came home late, tired and smelling of beer and cigarette smoke. She swallowed the urge to spill all her doubts into his lap as she listened to him detail the small dramas of the evening. He was tired, and she knew he would be worried if she told him what was happening. It seemed pointless and selfish to do that to him when she would probably get the all clear tomorrow.

Because that was what was going to happen, definitely.

So instead of telling him, she went home to stare at the ceiling and count the hours till morning.

The radiologist was a friendly older woman who patiently explained the ultrasound procedure to Hannah before asking her to undress and lie on a table with her arm behind her head. Cool gel was smoothed over Hannah's skin and the ultrasound wand pressed against her breast. Hannah watched the screen intently, trying to understand what she was seeing.

"So is this what you guys do now instead of mammograms?" she asked.

"Oh, no, mammograms are still very much in use. But when we're looking at younger breasts, ultrasound is often more helpful. Younger breast tissue is much more dense and not so easy to look at with X-ray."

"Oh, right."

The radiologist paused as she ran the wand over the area near the lump. Hannah watched the screen, her heart in her mouth. "Is there something there?"

"There's an unusual mass, yes," the radiologist said slowly.

Hannah had to swallow before she could speak again. "Is it cancer?"

"I'm afraid I can't tell you that just by looking. We need to take a biopsy. But we can do that now."

Hannah nodded dumbly. She'd stand on her head if only this woman would give her the all clear.

The radiologist started to assemble a tray with needles and swabs and other medical paraphernalia. After a local anesthetic, she used the ultrasound to target the lump in Hannah's breast and then drew some cells out of it using a fine needle.

Hannah watched as the woman smeared the cells onto a glass plate.

"These go off to the lab now. You should have the results within forty-eight hours."

More waiting. Hannah tried to smile and failed. She dressed slowly and rode to the garage. For the rest of the day she threw herself into her work, trying to drive fear and uncertainty away through sheer willpower.

She was supposed to have fish and chips on the beach with Joe and the kids for dinner but she called and told him she thought she was coming down with a cold. She couldn't look into his eyes and not tell him what was going on. And she wanted to, so much. Wanted his support. His concern. But she'd already decided to spare him the worry she was going through. Joe had been through enough.

She was inspecting the shock absorbers on a Range Rover when her phone vibrated in her pocket the following day. She closed her eyes when she heard her doctor's voice. Dread thumped in her belly. There was no reason for her doctor to call her before her scheduled appointment tomorrow afternoon unless there was bad news.

"Hannah, I'd like you to come in today if possible," Dr. Nelson said. Her voice was calm but serious.

"Oh, God."

"Can you make it this afternoon? Let me know and I'll shuffle appointments around."

A great rush of fear surged up inside Hannah and she pressed her forehead against the cool metal of the car.

"Hannah?"

"I'm still here." Just. Barely.

"Can you come in?"

"Yes. I think so. I need to talk to my boss."

"Look, why don't you just come when you can. We'll work around you."

Hannah nodded, then realized Dr. Nelson couldn't see her. "Sure."

"Hang in there, okay?"

Hannah ended the call. She felt dizzy. Her stomach was tight; it was hard to breathe.

She had cancer. That was the only reason Dr. Nelson could possibly want her to come in so urgently.

She couldn't think. Her brain was resounding with

the shock of it. Adrenaline was surging through her body, but there was nothing for her to fight or flee from. Whatever was attacking her was inside her body, inescapable, unavoidable.

After a few minutes she took a deep breath and forced herself to push away from the car. She concentrated on the short-term goal of getting to the doctor's. That was the most important thing right now.

Her boss took one look at her bloodless face and gave her the afternoon off, no questions asked. She rode to the clinic and the receptionist notified Dr. Nelson the moment Hannah announced herself. Within five minutes she was sitting opposite her G.P.

"As you've probably guessed, your tests have come back positive. Hannah, you have what's classified as invasive ductal carcinoma. It's the most common form of breast cancer. Basically, it means the cancer started in one of your milk ducts and has spread into the surrounding breast tissue."

Hannah's hands were clamped to her knees, her knuckles white. "Am I going to die?"

"You're young, the lump is small, there are some excellent treatments for breast cancer. You have every chance of surviving," Dr. Nelson said.

Hannah stared at her. She'd been looking for a one-word response: no. She hadn't gotten it.

"I'm referring you to an excellent surgeon. He works at the Peter Mac Hospital in the city. He's very highly regarded."

Hannah tried to marshal her thoughts. There were things she ought to ask, but for the life of her she couldn't think of what they were.

"Hannah, is there someone I can call for you? Maybe someone who can come and give you a lift home?"

Joe's face filled her mind and her eyes flooded with tears. She blinked a few times, then straightened her shoulders. "I'll be fine. I just need to get my head together."

"Are you sure?"

"Yes."

By the time she left the doctor's office she had an appointment to see a surgeon on Monday of the following week. Dr. Nelson explained that they would want to operate quickly as breast cancer in younger women could sometimes be more aggressive than in older women.

"And we'll want to test you for the breast cancer gene. That might make a difference to your treatment. But Dr. Minton will go over all of that with you."

Hannah rode home, but instead of parking her bike and going inside to tell Joe and her mother and the rest of her world that she might be dying, she rode straight past.

She wasn't ready to go home yet.

She rode hard and fast down the highway until she hit the beach. Then she parked her bike and strode the length of the St. Kilda Pier. She stared out at the ocean and took in big gulps of fresh air, her hair tangling around her face in the breeze.

After a while she sat and leaned her back against one of the weathered wooden pylons. Tears leaked from the corners of her eyes as she watched the ever-moving blue of the ocean. A ship crawled slowly across the horizon. Seagulls flew overhead.

It's not fair. I'm too young. I just found Joe.

The three thoughts looped through her mind as she cycled from anger to despair to fear and back.

Her life had just started coming together. She had a future planned out, with Joe and Ben and Ruby at her side. This wasn't supposed to happen.

Finally her thoughts settled. She hugged her knees to her chest, willing herself to calm. She didn't have the luxury of wallowing in self-pity. She needed to get her shit together. She was about to take on the battle of her life.

And she was going to have to do it alone.

She choked on a sob as she consciously acknowledged her decision for the first time. She wasn't sure when she'd made it. When she decided not to tell Joe about the lump on that first day? When she lay in bed next to Ruby the other night? It didn't really matter. The fact remained that there was no way she could put Joe and his kids through the trauma of surgery and chemo and God knows what else. No. Way.

Joe had barely recovered from the loss of his wife. Ben was seeing a counselor to help him come to terms with his grief and guilt. And Ruby needed someone to make her feel safe, not a woman who may or may not be around to see her next birthday.

She couldn't do it to them. That was how much she loved Joe Lawson and his children.

She huffed out a humorless laugh. She was so freakin' noble it made her sick.

No matter how much she needed Joe or wanted Joe, no matter how much she wanted to be a part of his children's lives, she had to face the fact that she had now become a liability. Joe could not afford to have someone like her in his life. Certainly his kids couldn't. It simply wouldn't be fair to expect them to take this journey with her.

She pressed her knuckles into her eyes, willing the tears to stop. She had to stop crying. No matter how scared and sad and angry she was, throwing a pity party was not going to get her through this. She was going to have to be tough. She was going to have to stand her ground and then some.

She waited until the tears dried on her cheeks, going over and over what had to happen next in her mind. Finally she scrubbed her face with her hands and stood.

It was time to go do what had to be done.

Chapter 13

Joe stepped from his car, the heat of a Melbourne summer's day hitting him like a wall after the air-conditioning in the SUV. He frowned when he saw the kids hadn't drawn the curtains to keep the afternoon sun out as he'd asked. Great. Now the living room would be like a sauna all night.

"Hey, Daddy," Ruby said when he entered the living room.

The kids were sprawled on the floor with Hannah playing cards, all of them stripped down to shorts and tank tops. He tried not to stare at Hannah's long, tanned legs.Maybe there were advantages to having a hot living room, after all.

"Hannah and Ben and I have been playing poker and Hannah says that cheating is wrong but I can't win otherwise," Ruby explained.

"She's right. Cheating is wrong," he said.

Ruby pouted.

"Told you," Ben said triumphantly. "You want to win, you got to play smarter, that's all."

Joe sensed an argument brewing and decided to head it off at the pass. He reached for the envelope in his back pocket.

"I have something I wanted to discuss with you guys," he said, his gaze taking in all of them.

Ben and Ruby stared up at him, their faces expectant. Hannah's face was lowered as she fiddled with her cards.

"Is this about Christmas?" Ruby asked.

"No, this is about Easter. How do you guys feel about a trip to Movie World and Sea World on the Gold Coast?" he asked.

He knew they'd been disappointed they weren't going away for Christmas, but the pub was too busy to leave at this time of year. The Easter trip was his way of making it up to them.

Judging by the shocked delight on their faces, he'd done all right.

"For real?" Ben asked, his face splitting into a big smile.

"Yeah, for real. Got the plane tickets right here. Four of them." He glanced at Hannah to check her reaction. There was a look on her face he couldn't quite define.

Ruby and Ben whooped with delight. He cocked his head in enquiry as he caught Hannah's eye. What was going on?

"Surprise," he said wryly, waiting for her to smile.

She didn't. Instead, she frowned, then lowered her head and fiddled with her cards some more.

Ben and Ruby were too busy enthusing over the holiday to notice. As they enumerated to each other the rides they'd go on and the sights they'd see, Joe sat on the couch and nudged Hannah gently with the toe of his shoe.

"Too much of a surprise, huh?" he asked lightly.

She glanced up at him, her expression unreadable. "The trip sounds great." But there was a definite lack of enthusiasm in her voice.

"I know it's not camping and it's not the hidden byways of the country you want to explore, but I thought it might be fun...."

"It's a nice idea," she said, still not meeting his eyes.

She straightened her cards into a neat little stack and returned them to the deck, making sure they were all lined up.

"You okay?" he asked.

She met his eyes briefly. "We need to talk."

There was something heavy in her words.

"Okay." He stood, gesturing for her to join him in the kitchen.

She shook her head. "Later. When the kids are in bed."

He stared at her for a long moment, then nodded. It was going to be one of those kinds of talks.

The next hour crawled by. He watched Hannah out of the corner of his eye, trying to get a read on her. She'd been a little withdrawn the past couple of days. And she'd canceled dinner with him and the kids the other night. He hadn't thought anything of it at the time, but now he wondered if he should have.

We'll work it out, whatever it is.

One of the things he loved about Hannah the most

was that she was such a straight shooter. If there was something wrong, she'd let him know and they'd sort it out.

He sent the kids off to brush their teeth at eight-thirty. He tucked Ruby into bed and confiscated Ben's flashlight so he couldn't read under the covers. Then he returned to the living room.

Hannah sat on the couch, her elbows on her knees, hands gripped together. She was staring at a spot on the carpet, her mouth grim. She looked like a soldier about to go into battle.

Not a great sign.

He stopped inside the doorway and she looked up at him. They stared at each other for a long moment.

"What's going on?"

"I can't go to Queensland with you," she said.

"I know I should have checked with you first—"

"It's not about that."

She took a deep breath and he realized she was shaking. Whatever was bothering her, she was really worked up about it. He crossed the room to sit beside her.

"Hannah." He started to slide his arm around her shoulders, but she caught his hand and held it in both of hers. Her fingers were cold, her grip tight.

"I got a call from my G.P. today. I had some tests this week…" She shook her head. "Man, this is hard." She whispered the words, almost as though she was talking to herself. Her chest lifted as she took a deep, long breath. Then she looked him in the eye.

"I have breast cancer. I'm scheduled to see a surgeon on Monday."

He stared at her, barely able to comprehend what she was saying. "What…?"

Cancer. *What the hell?*

"You're too young," he said.

"Apparently not."

She winced and he realized he was squeezing her hand so tightly his knuckles had turned white.

"Jesus, Hannah," he said. He didn't know what else to say so he obeyed the impulse of his heart and dragged her into his arms. She held on for dear life, her cheek pressed against his. He could feel the fear in her trembling through her body, and he held her even tighter, trying to marshal his thoughts.

Cancer. Hannah had cancer, and she was terrified.

That one thought helped him to push his own fear and dread and shock to one side.

"You'll be okay," he said.

She huffed out a breath that was almost a laugh. "Can I have that in writing?"

"You will. They can do amazing stuff these days. And you're young."

She turned her head to kiss his cheek then eased away from his embrace. "That's what my doctor said. But there are no guarantees, Joe."

"But you've caught it early, right?" He'd never felt a lump or anything unusual in her breasts and he figured he'd made a pretty thorough study of them.

"Yes. I think so. But they won't know anything until they've operated and seen what they're dealing with."

"You're seeing the surgeon on Monday, is that what you said? I've got a meeting with the bank, but I'll shift it so I can come with you."

Her eyes filled with tears, and she blinked rapidly until they were gone. "That's really sweet of you."

He frowned. He didn't have to be a genius to hear the unspoken *but* in her tone.

"You don't want me to come with you?"

"It's not about what I want. I don't think it would be smart."

"What do you mean? If you're worried I'll hassle the doctor or ask stupid questions, I promise to sit there quietly. Whatever you need from me."

She brushed her fingers along his jaw, her touch gentle, her eyes sad. "You're such a good man."

There was something very final in her words. He stared at her, understanding slowly dawning.

"No." He shook his head.

"I don't think we should see each other anymore," she said, confirming his guess.

"Hannah…"

She held up a hand. "Hear me out. You're a good man, so your first impulse is to stand by me. And I appreciate that, I really do. But you didn't sign on for this. I'm going to get sick, Joe. Chemo, radiation therapy… I'm probably going to lose my hair and I'm almost certainly going to lose my breast."

"I don't give a shit about any of that stuff."

"I know. But I do, and I refuse to put you through it."

"Isn't that my decision to make?"

"And what about Ruby and Ben?" she asked. "Is it their decision, too? I might die, Joe. You really want to put your kids through that?"

He flinched. "That's not going to happen."

"I appreciate the vote of confidence, but no one knows that. And I will not be the person who brings more sadness into your children's lives."

He stared at her. He couldn't believe they were even

having this conversation. Just this morning he'd bought tickets for the four of them to holiday in Queensland together; now Hannah was telling him she might be dying.

"No," he said again, shaking his head.

"Once you've thought about it you'll realize I'm right. Your kids need certainty and safety and love. They don't need to watch me fight for my life, and neither do you. And it's in my power to make sure you don't have to, and that's what I'm going to do."

She stood. He stared at her.

"Where are you going?"

"Home."

"Like hell. We haven't even begun to discuss this," he said, shooting to his feet.

"How long have we known each other, Joe? A few months? Not long enough for you to have to come on this journey with me. Not nearly long enough. If we end things now, we can all walk away and get on with our lives."

"That's bullshit, Hannah, and you know it. You can't define what we have in terms of weeks and days."

"I'm being smart. This is the best thing for your kids, Joe." She turned away.

He grabbed her arm. "I get a say in this, too."

"No, you don't. This is my fight, and it's my decision. And I choose not to do this to any of us." There was absolute steel in her voice and her face. Then her expression softened and she covered his hand where it still lay on her arm. She lifted it free, turning it so his palm was up. She pressed a kiss into the center of his hand.

"For what it's worth, it's been amazing. A gift. Thanks for sharing your family with me."

He was about to demand that she stay when the low sound of Ruby's voice floated up the hallway.

"Daddy? Daddy, I had a nightmare."

Hannah gestured toward the hallway. "You'd better go to her. She needs you."

Before he could say another word, Hannah was gone, the front door clicking closed behind her. He stared at the spot where she'd stood for long seconds, a thousand thoughts and feelings churning inside him.

Hannah had cancer. And she'd just cut him loose.

"Daddy?"

He stirred himself. "I'm coming, sweetheart."

He went to Ruby's room. She was huddled in bed, her favorite bear clutched to her chest.

"What's going on?" he asked, struggling to keep his tone light.

"I had a bad dream."

"Ah. Too much cheese."

It was his standard response to nightmares and she smiled. "I knew you were going to say that, Daddy."

"Did you? When did I get so predictable?"

He talked to Ruby for a few minutes, soothing her back to drowsiness. All the while his mind was on Hannah.

Finally he left Ruby and walked to the living room and simply stood there, staring at nothing.

Hannah had cancer.

For the first time he allowed himself to feel the full impact of the news. Fear and grief twisted through him. He lowered his head, closing his eyes against the ugly enormity of it.

They'd just gotten their shit together. Ben was finally talking and laughing again. They'd started building the foundations for a new family, a new way of living. They'd barely started to enjoy one another.

He was gripped with a sudden rush of rage, so powerful he wanted to slam his fist into the wall.

She deserved better. After what her sister did to her, Hannah deserved happiness. Hell, so did he. He'd buried his wife, his kids had buried their mother. Didn't they all deserve a freaking break?

Without stopping to think, he strode out of the house. He stopped only when he'd arrived at her front door. He hammered a fist against the door, anger and fear driving him. He waited a few heartbeats, then knocked again, every muscle tense.

He had no idea what he was going to say, but their conversation wasn't over, not by a long shot. No way was she making this decision for both of them.

He was raising his hand to knock a third time when the door opened. Robyn stood there, her face very pale.

"Joe," she said.

"I need to see her."

Robyn shook her head. "I'm sorry, but she doesn't want to see you."

"I don't care. There are some things she needs to hear."

He stepped forward but Robyn didn't budge.

"I need to see her," he said again.

"You're shocked and upset."

"No shit."

Robyn eyed him steadily. "Have you ever dealt with a very sick person before, Joe? I have. My mother died from bowel cancer. Took her nearly two years to fade away to nothing."

"I'm sorry, that must have been tough. But that's not going to happen to Hannah."

"I hope not. God, I hope not. But it might. And even if it doesn't, things are going to get pretty scary. She's going to be up and down, weak and strong, high and low."

"I don't care."

Robyn nodded. "Good. Now come back tomorrow and say the same thing."

He swore under his breath. "I want to talk to her now."

"She won't talk to you. She wants to protect you."

"That's my freaking decision, not hers."

Robyn's gaze was searching. "What about your children?"

"They love her."

"And what if they lose her?"

"Hannah is not going to die."

"There aren't many times in a parent's life when you get the chance to stop your children from experiencing pain." Robyn's face was grave, her voice quiet. "Mostly it happens and you have to watch and wish you could take it away or feel it for them. But Hannah's giving you the choice, Joe. She's thought long and hard about this, and she's doing what she thinks is the right thing for your kids. The least you can do is offer her the same consideration before you make your decision."

He closed his eyes and swore again.

His gut reaction to Hannah's news was to want to wrap her in his arms and tell her the world was going to be right and move mountains to make it so. But Robyn was right—there were no guarantees, and he had more than himself to think about.

He had children. He was their sole guide in life, their everything. No matter what he wanted to do, what his gut was telling him, he had to put his children first.

He leveled a finger at Hannah's mother. "I'll be back tomorrow."

"Good."

She closed the door between them. Joe stared at it for a few seconds before turning on his heel. Head down, he made the short walk to his house. He went straight to the cupboard in the living room where he kept his stash of whiskey and poured himself a glass. Then he took the bottle with him and went through to the kitchen. He sat down at the table, the bottle on one side, the glass on the other.

He took a mouthful of whisky and thought about Hannah. Her laugh. Her stubbornness and spirit. The way she pressed against him when he kissed her. The way she watched him sometimes when she thought he wasn't looking. How honest she was. How bold, yet at the same time so very vulnerable. The way she touched his children, the tenderness in her eyes.

He took another mouthful and thought about Ben. The guilt and grief that had come out in counseling. The heavy weight his son had been carrying. The sadness that was still inside him.

Then he thought about Ruby, with her infinite trust and craving for connection. She'd forged a bond with Hannah right from the start. How was this going to hit her? How would she cope with knowing that someone else she loved might leave her?

The glass was empty. He reached for the bottle and poured.

And then he thought about Hannah. And he thought about Ben. And he thought about Ruby.

Hannah sniffed loudly. Her mother passed her another handful of tissues, her third since Joe had marched away from their front door.

"This is the right thing," she said for the tenth time.

As always, her mother remained silent. Hannah blew her nose.

"He sounded angry. I knew he'd be angry, but once he thinks about it he'll know I'm right," Hannah said.

Her mother shifted on the bed beside her. "He was very angry. Scared, too, I think."

"Once he calms down and goes over it all in his head, he'll realize I'm right. This is the best thing for everybody," Hannah said.

"Is it the best thing for you?"

"I want them to be happy."

"And what if being with you makes them happy?"

"For how long?"

Her mother had no answer to that. Hannah took her hand and gave it a squeeze.

"Thank you for answering the door. I appreciate it."

"He said he'd be back tomorrow."

"Fine. I'll tell him the same thing."

"He loves you."

Hannah stared at the scrunched tissues in her lap. "He'll get over it. There are plenty of women out there who would jump at the chance to be with a great guy like him." She could barely get the words out. The mere thought of Joe with another woman made her want to punch something. So much for her self-sacrificing streak.

"You always were stubborn. It's what's going to get you through this, you know. Nobody this stubborn dies from cancer."

"I hope you're right. Bloody hell, I hope you're right," Hannah said. She took a deep breath. "Mom, I'm so scared."

Her mom put her arms around her and pulled Hannah against her chest. She soothed a hand over Hannah's hair and pressed a kiss to her brow.

"Of course you're scared. Cancer is scary. But people beat it all the time, Hannah. And you're going to be one of them."

There was so much certainty, so much determination in her voice that Hannah couldn't help but take heart.

"If you say so."

"I do. Now, we need to make a list of questions we want to ask the surgeon on Monday. All the magazines say you have to be your own medical advocate when you have a serious illness. You have to be informed."

Her mother let Hannah go and started searching in Hannah's bedside table for a pad and pen. Hannah watched her for a moment, touched by her stern earnestness.

"Thank you, Mom."

Her mother looked up, surprised. "What for?"

"Not falling apart."

In truth, Hannah had expected her mother to crumble when she heard the news, but she'd simply stared at Hannah for a long moment before reaching out and taking both her hands. *You'll beat this* had been her first words, something Hannah would be eternally grateful for.

"Oh, there's plenty of time to fall apart later, sweetheart. Right now we've got a fight on our hands."

They talked until the small hours, until they'd both run out of things to say. Finally Hannah let her mother tuck her into bed.

She rolled onto her side and stared into the darkness. She had no tears left, nothing but emptiness. Tomorrow she would wake up and face the first day of her new reality.

She'd expected to toss and turn, but she slept like a log. The events of the past forty-eight hours had left her so drained, so exhausted, she didn't even have the energy for dreams. She woke feeling puffy-eyed and heavy. A flutter of dread raced through her as memory descended.

She had cancer. And Joe and his children were no longer a part of her life.

She stared at the wall and took a deep breath. If ever there was a day to stay in bed and hide from the world, it was today. She flung back the covers. Hiding from the world wasn't going to get her anywhere, and she had things to do, plans to make.

She thought about Ben and Ruby as she showered. She'd do her best to hide her illness from them, but it was inevitable that they would find out. They lived next door, after all. But hopefully by then Hannah would have had the time to create some distance between them. She'd tell Ruby she was too busy at work to finish their latest restoration project, a '56 Harley they'd bought from the scrap yard. That would keep any contact to a minimum. No more visits to The Watering Hole. No more watching the kids while Joe worked late or taking Ben to cricket practice. The kids would think she and Joe had simply broken up. They'd be hurt for a while, but a little hurt now was preferable to a lot of hurt later.

And Joe… Joe would move on, too. He might be angry with her for a while, and sad, but she knew he would eventually understand she'd done the best thing for him and his children.

She'd never thought she could love anyone so much that she would be able to let them go when everything in her screamed for her to cling fast. But she wasn't free to love them. She had nothing to offer. It was as simple and as painful as that.

She looked in the mirror as she dried off after her shower, her gaze dropping to her breasts. Slowly she cupped them in her hands, feeling the weight of them, the shape of them, trying to imagine what it would be like to have a scar instead of rounded flesh, to be lop-sided and bare.

It was impossible, but she figured the reality would come soon enough. She let her hands drop. If she was ever in a position to be worried about her vanity again, she figured she'd be one of the luckiest women in the world.

She dressed in jeans and a T-shirt and wandered out to the kitchen. Her mother was busy juicing oranges.

"Lots of fresh fruit from now on," she said. "There's a cookbook I've seen, too, about positive eating."

"That sounds good," Hannah said.

"How are you feeling?"

Hannah shrugged. "Like it's the calm before the storm."

"I can imagine."

There was a knock at the door. Hannah glanced at her mother.

"Would you mind? In case it's Joe."

"It probably is. He said he'd be back this morning."

Her mother simply looked at her. Hannah sighed. She'd always known it would take more than one conversation to convince a man as loyal and loving as Joe to protect himself.

"Okay, I'll get it," she said.

She took a deep breath, then went to open the door.

She retreated a step when she saw he wasn't alone. He was standing hand in hand with his children, Ben on his left, Ruby on his right. Ruby's eyes were puffy from tears and Ben looked as though he'd been crying, too. Joe held her gaze steadily when she looked at him.

"I've come to give you our answer," he said. He was pale but his gaze was very direct.

"I didn't ask you for one."

"That was your first mistake."

"Joe, don't," she said. "Please. This isn't fair."

"I don't care," he said. There was a hardness to his face, a fierceness that she'd never seen there before.

"The kids and I have been talking. I told them your news," he said. Ruby sniffed and wiped her nose with the back of her hand. Hannah looked at her small, pinched face, her heart aching.

"You shouldn't have."

"They deserve to know. They love you."

Ben's eyes didn't waver from her face. Despite the fact that she'd cried buckets last night, she felt tears welling again.

"Joe, please—"

"The least you can do is hear them out," he said.

Ruby stepped forward.

Oh, God.

She couldn't believe he was putting her through this. Didn't he understand she was walking away because she loved him?

"I haven't said it to you before because I was too shy, but I want you to know that I love you," Ruby said. "And I want you to get better and I'll do whatever I can to help you. Keep my room clean and help with the cooking and go to bed on time without being asked. Anything you need."

Hannah blinked rapidly. This was too much. She glared at Joe but he stared back at her, implacable.

It was Ben's turn. He took a step forward, his hands clutched together in front of him.

"I know I was mean at the start, but I think you're ace and I really want you to come to Queensland with us because it would be cool to go on the big waterslides with you," he said, his speech so rapid the words almost ran together. He stepped back by his father's side.

She cleared her throat and opened her mouth to speak.

"Wait," Ben said suddenly. "I didn't finish properly." He blushed deeply. "I love you, too. And I don't care if you're sick."

He ducked his head bashfully. Hannah closed her eyes, but the tears spilled out anyway. She heard Joe murmur something, and when she opened her eyes again it was just him standing there. She stared at him, her chest aching with sadness.

"It doesn't change anything," she said.

"Don't you get it, Hannah? You think you can protect us but it's too late. We already love you. We're committed. You're a part of our family now, and family doesn't walk away when the going gets tough."

"I don't want to hurt you," she said, her voice barely a whisper. "Can't you understand that?"

Joe closed the distance between them. He wiped away her tears with his thumbs.

"I know, and it's one of the many reasons I love you. But you're not doing this without us, Hannah. No way. That's our choice, and we've made it freely, and we'll camp out on your doorstep if that's what it takes to make you see sense."

To her utter astonishment, Joe dropped down to one knee.

"But I'm kind of hoping it won't come to that," he said.

"No," she said, trying to pull him back to his feet. "You don't have to do this."

"I think I do. I don't want you getting any stupid ideas like this again."

He reached out and took one of her cold, trembling hands in his.

"Hannah Louise Napier, will you marry me?"

"You know my middle name," she said stupidly.

"Yes. I know a lot more than that, too. I know I love you, even though I never thought I'd feel this way or even want to feel this way again. I know I want to fight over the remote control with you and make pizzas with you and ride that Thunderbird of yours one day. I know I want to make love to you and wake up with you in my bed each and every day. I know I want to stand by your side while you fight this battle so we can grow old together."

"What if I lose?"

He didn't break eye contact for a second. "Then I'll be with you till the end. I'll take whatever chance I can get, Hannah. If the past two years have taught me anything, it's that happiness and love are too bloody precious to walk away from, no matter how fleeting they might be."

She stared into his face, taking in the clearness of his blue gaze, the proudness of his nose, the strength of his jaw.

"I love you," she said.

"I know. Say yes."

"It's crazy. We should wait until we know more."

"Until when? I love you now. I want you to be my wife now."

He was too strong. Too sure. Too compelling. And it was too close to what her heart craved. "God, I can't believe I'm even considering this."

"Is that a yes?"

"Joe…"

"Just say yes."

The word seemed to form itself on her lips all on its own.

"Yes."

Joe leaned forward from his kneeling position and wrapped his arms around her waist, his head coming to rest against her belly.

"Don't ever do that to me again," he said fiercely.

She couldn't believe how brave he was, how determined. And how brave his kids were, how generous. She remembered the way they'd stepped up and said their piece and her heart swelled in her chest.

After a long moment Joe pushed himself to his feet.

"Let's go tell the kids you've come to your senses.

Then we need to go buy you a ring. Ruby offered her Barbie ring, but I figured you might like to choose your own."

"You told the kids you were going to propose to me?"

"Of course. It's their family, too, you know. They have minds of their own, in case you hadn't noticed."

"I noticed."

"Thought you might have."

He slid his hand along her jaw and into her hair. "I love you, Hannah. We're going to get through this."

"I hope so."

He kissed her. "I know so."

Then he led her out into the street to find the children.

Epilogue

Two years later, Hannah hovered in the wings with Ruby as she waited for their cue to hit the catwalk. This was their third appearance in the annual mother-daughter fashion parade fund-raiser. Last year, Ruby had insisted on shaving her hair because Hannah's chemo had left her with nothing but baby fuzz. They'd worn matching punk outfits and received a prize for being best dressed. This year they'd opted for a more conservative look, both sporting shoulder-length haircuts and strappy floral dresses.

Hannah had been lucky. The surgeon had recommended a lumpectomy to treat her tumor and performed a partial reconstruction at the same time. She had scars, and the radiation therapy had left her breast tissue sore and red for months, but she still had a breast.

The chemo had been harder in many ways, sapping

her energy, sending her lurching to the bathroom morning, noon and night, making her hair fall out in handfuls. But she'd gotten through it.

Joe had rubbed her back and bought her scarves and hats to keep her head warm through winter. Ruby and Ben had played board games with her and educated her in the ways of *Spore* and *The Sims*. Her mother had come up with a million different ways to tempt her with food, even when she had next to no appetite at all. Joe's mother had made sure the house ran smoothly so Hannah and Joe could concentrate their energies where they were needed. And her sister had taken her for regular massages and brought her new niece to visit.

They'd started talking soon after Hannah's surgery, in time for her sister to attend her wedding. Hannah had decided that if she was only going to be around for a short time, she wanted her days to be as positive and full of happiness as possible. That meant forgiving and moving on and being a part of the new life her sister had brought into the world.

But it was looking more and more likely that she was going to be around for a long time. She'd seen her doctor for her regular six-month follow-up last week. Her scans were clear and she was officially in remission. She'd been tested and did not carry the breast cancer gene, which was another point in her favor.

If her luck held, she would pass the five-year mark and be officially classed as a survivor.

She was going to get there. She knew it. She already felt like a survivor.

The music changed and the stage manager pointed at Hannah and Ruby. They smiled at each other and caught each other's hands. Heads high, they started down the catwalk, strutting their stuff.

She still got nervous before doing things like this. She still hated fussing over her hair and makeup and much preferred jeans to skirts and dresses. But she enjoyed the sheer fun of it so much more now, the being alive-ness of it. Especially when she looked into the audience at the end of the runway and saw Joe standing there, arms crossed over his chest, a small, satisfied smile on his face as he watched his wife and daughter.

Their gazes locked for a long moment and Hannah imagined how the evening might unfold, how they'd go home after the fund-raiser and pore over the photographs Ben was taking and tease Ruby about her growing vanity. How Joe and Hannah might wait till the kids were in bed before having a glass of wine then turning in themselves. How Joe might undress her slowly and kiss each newly exposed swath of skin. How they'd make love with tenderness and patience, or passion and urgent need. And how they might then lie in each other's arms and make plans for the future.

She smiled, and Joe smiled back, his face full of love and heat and more than a little lust.

Another good day together, with another to come tomorrow, and another after that.

It was all anyone could ask for.

* * * * *

REQUEST YOUR
FREE BOOKS!

2 FREE NOVELS
FROM THE ROMANCE COLLECTION
PLUS 2 FREE GIFTS!

YES! Please send me 2 FREE novels from the Romance Collection and my 2 FREE gifts (gifts are worth about $10). After receiving them, if I don't wish to receive any more books, I can return the shipping statement marked "cancel." If I don't cancel, I will receive 4 brand-new novels every month and be billed just $5.99 per book in the U.S. or $6.49 per book in Canada. That's a savings of at least 25% off the cover price. It's quite a bargain! Shipping and handling is just 50¢ per book in the U.S. and 75¢ per book in Canada.* I understand that accepting the 2 free books and gifts places me under no obligation to buy anything. I can always return a shipment and cancel at any time. Even if I never buy another book, the two free books and gifts are mine to keep forever.

194/394 MDN FVU7

Name	(PLEASE PRINT)	

Address		Apt. #

City	State/Prov.	Zip/Postal Code

Signature (if under 18, a parent or guardian must sign)

Mail to the **Harlequin®** Reader Service:
IN U.S.A.: P.O. Box 1867, Buffalo, NY 14240-1867
IN CANADA: P.O. Box 609, Fort Erie, Ontario L2A 5X3

Want to try two free books from another line?
Call 1-800-873-8635 or visit www.ReaderService.com.

* Terms and prices subject to change without notice. Prices do not include applicable taxes. Sales tax applicable in N.Y. Canadian residents will be charged applicable taxes. Offer not valid in Quebec. This offer is limited to one order per household. Not valid for current subscribers to the Romance Collection or the Romance/Suspense Collection. All orders subject to credit approval. Credit or debit balances in a customer's account(s) may be offset by any other outstanding balance owed by or to the customer. Please allow 4 to 6 weeks for delivery. Offer available while quantities last.

Your Privacy—The Harlequin® Reader Service is committed to protecting your privacy. Our Privacy Policy is available online at www.ReaderService.com or upon request from the Harlequin Reader Service.

We make a portion of our mailing list available to reputable third parties that offer products we believe may interest you. If you prefer that we not exchange your name with third parties, or if you wish to clarify or modify your communication preferences, please visit us at www.ReaderService.com/consumerschoice or write to us at Harlequin Reader Service Preference Service, P.O. Box 9062, Buffalo, NY 14269. Include your complete name and address.

ROM13

We hope you enjoyed reading

QUINN'S WOMAN by *New York Times*

bestselling author SUSAN MALLERY and

HOME FOR THE HOLIDAYS

by acclaimed author SARAH MAYBERRY.

Both were originally
Harlequin® series stories!

Discover more compelling tales of family, friendship
and love from the Harlequin® Superromance® series.
Featuring contemporary themes and relatable,
true-to-life characters, Harlequin Superromance
stories are filled with powerful relationships that
deliver a strong emotional punch and a guaranteed
happily-ever-after.

Wild for the Sheriff

by Kathleen O'Brien

On sale February 5

Dallas Garwood had always known that sooner or later he'd open a door, turn a corner or look up from his desk and see Rowena Wright standing there.

It wasn't logical. It was simply an unshakable certainty that she wasn't gone for good, that one day she would return.

Not to see him, of course. He didn't kid himself that their brief interlude had been important to her. But she'd be back for Bell River—the ranch that was part of her.

Still, he hadn't thought today would be the day he'd face her across the threshold of her former home.

Or that she would look so gaunt. Her beauty was still there, but buried beneath some kind of haggard exhaustion. Her wild green eyes were circled with shadows, and her white shirt and jeans hung on her.

Something twisted in his chest, stealing his words. He'd never expected to feel pity for Rowena Wright.

She still knew how to look sardonic. She took him in, and he saw himself as she did, from the white-lightning scar dividing his right eyebrow to the shiny gold star pinned at his breast.

Three-tenths of a second. That was all it took to make him feel boring and overdressed, as if his uniform were as much a costume as his son Alec's cowboy hat.

"*Sheriff* Dallas Garwood." The crooked smile on her red lips was cryptic. "I should have known. Truly, I should have known."

"I didn't realize you'd come home," he said, wishing he didn't sound so stiff.

"Come *back*," she corrected him. "After all these years, it might be a bit of a stretch to call Bell River *home*."

"I see." He didn't really, but so what? He'd been her lover once, but never her friend.

The funny thing was, right now he'd give almost anything to change that and resurrect that long-ago connection.

Will Dallas and Rowena reconnect? Or will she skip town again with everything left unsaid? Find out in *Wild for the Sheriff* by Kathleen O'Brien, available February 2013 from Harlequin® Superromance®.

HARLEQUIN

super romance®

More Story…More Romance

Save $1.00 on the purchase of

WILD FOR THE SHERIFF

by Kathleen O'Brien

(available February 5, 2013)

or on any other Harlequin Superromance® book.

Available wherever books are sold, including most bookstores,
supermarkets, drugstores and discount stores.

- ✂

Save
$1.00

**on the purchase of
WILD FOR THE SHERIFF
by Kathleen O'Brien**
(available February 5, 2013)
or on any other Harlequin Superromance® book.

Coupon valid until May 6, 2013. Redeemable at participating retail outlets
in the U.S. and Canada only. Limit one coupon per customer.

5 26106 57

Canadian Retailers: Harlequin Enterprises Limited will pay the face value
of this coupon plus 10.25¢ if submitted by customer for this product only. Any
other use constitutes fraud. Coupon is nonassignable. Void if taxed, prohibited
or restricted by law. Consumer must pay any government taxes. Void if copied.
Nielsen Clearing House ("NCH") customers submit coupons and proof of sales to
Harlequin Enterprises Limited, P.O. Box 3000, Saint John, NB E2L 4L3, Canada.
Non-NCH retailer—for reimbursement submit coupons and proof of sales directly
to Harlequin Enterprises Limited, Retail Marketing Department, 225 Duncan Mill
Road., Don Mills, ON M3B 3K9, Canada.

65373 00076 2   (8100)0 11827

U.S. Retailers: Harlequin Enterprises
Limited will pay the face value of this coupon
plus 8¢ if submitted by customer for this
product only. Any other use constitutes fraud.
Coupon is nonassignable. Void if taxed,
prohibited or restricted by law. Consumer must
pay any government taxes. Void if copied. For
reimbursement submit coupons and proof of
sales directly to Harlequin Enterprises Limited,
P.O. Box 880478, El Paso, TX 88588-0478,
U.S.A. Cash value 1/100 cents.